THE LAST COLLECTION OF FICTION AND NON-
FICTION OF JAMES TIPTREE, JR., ONE OF THE
CLASSIC FIGURES OF TWENTIETH-CENTURY SF

By James Tiptree, Jr., from Tom Doherty Associates

Brightness Falls from the Air
The Color of Neanderthal Eyes
Crown of Stars
The Girl Who Was Plugged In
Houston, Houston, Do You Read?
Meet Me at Infinity
The Starry Rift

MEET · ME · AT INFINITY

JAMES TIPTREE, JR.

A TOM DOHERTY ASSOCIATES BOOK

NEW YORK

MEET ME AT INFINITY

Copyright © 2000 by Jeffrey D. Smith

All rights reserved, including the right to reproduce this book, or portions thereof, in any form.

This book is printed on acid-free paper.

Edited by David G. Hartwell

An Orb Edition
Published by Tom Doherty Associates, LLC
175 Fifth Avenue
New York, NY 10010

www.tor.com

Book design by Lisa Pifher

The poem on page 284 is from "The Affinity," in *The Contemplative Quarry* by Anna Wickham, copyright © 1915 by James and George Hepburn.

Library of Congress Cataloging-in-Publication Data

Tiptree, James.
    Meet me at infinity / James Tiptree, Jr.
        p.   cm.
    "A Tom Doherty Associates book."
    Contents: Meet me at infinity: uncollected fiction—Letters from Yucatan and other points of the soul: uncollected nonfiction.
    ISBN 0-312-85874-4 (hc)
    ISBN 0-312-86938-X (pbk)
    I. Title.
  PS3570.I66 A6 2000
  813'.54—dc21   99-058425
                                                      CIP

First Tor Hardcover Edition: April 2000
First Orb Edition: June 2001

Printed in the United States of America

0 9 8 7 6 5 4 3 2 1

CONTENTS

MEET · ME · AT
INFINITY

INTRODUCTION

Meet Me at Infinity is, inevitably, a book *about* James Tiptree, Jr., more than it is a book *by* James Tiptree, Jr. All of the other Tiptree books consist of a lot of excellent science fiction, with maybe a brief note by the author or an introduction by a friend or admirer. The lack of frills was deliberate, the purity of the stories maintained. There were to be no explications of concepts, no chatty reminiscences of the sources of inspiration.

And yet, Tiptree *was* chatty. Tip loved to tell you things, things about the stories, about other writers' stories, about culture and nature, about people, and art, and life.

So this time we'll do it differently. This time we'll pay more attention to the storyteller than to the story. It's okay; we aren't going against the author's wishes and we won't betray any confidences. This book was largely compiled by Tiptree for publication years ago, and is finally being realized now.

Alice Bradley Sheldon was born in 1915. Her autobiography appears later in this book, and is packed with interesting stories itself. What's important to us, and what she felt was one of the most important things she ever did herself, is that in 1967 she wrote four short stories and sent them off to science fiction magazines. Unwilling to be published in SF magazines under her own name, she used a pseudonym. And under that pseudonym, for a period of time, she became one of the best science fiction writers in the world.

"James Tiptree" had a lot of friends in the science fiction field, but he couldn't meet any of them. He could and did carry on voluminous correspondences with dozens of people, but he couldn't talk to any of them on the telephone. His reclusiveness made him an object of curiosity, but his secret was too big for him to give away gracefully.

Eventually, his cover was blown, and Alice Sheldon stood in his place. Alli still wrote letters (she loved letters; notice how many characters write letters in her stories), but she could talk to people as well. She could even meet them, though she preferred not to. She could still write science fiction, still write *good* science fiction, but it was different. In the first phase of her SF career, when Tiptree was "alive," she wrote the stories as if she were James Tiptree. Later, she wrote them without that filter. For one thing, she told me, she had tried to scrub out all traces of her natural sentimentality out of Tiptree's fiction, but didn't feel the need to after the secret was out. (For continuity's sake she still used the Tiptree name.)

How much the disclosure itself affected her writing is impossible to say. Tiptree's stories were changing, possibly due to their increasing length, even before his traumatic unmasking. In one of the letters used for "Everything but the Signature Is Me," her first public statement to the SF field as Alice Sheldon, she wrote, "As to who or what will be writing next . . . I dunno. It may be that Tiptree is written out for a while. With each story I dug deeper and deeper into more emotional stuff, and some of it started to hurt pretty bad." She said that if she could see her first novel, *Up the Walls of the World* (Berkley Putnam 1978), through publication and "let Tiptree rest a while, he may do that." And about "Slow Music," the story she was working on at the time (in *Out of the Everywhere*, Del Rey 1981): "It reads like a musical fade-out or coda to Tiptree's group of work." She even kills Tiptree off as a character in that story, an event which may or may not have been in the first draft.

The Tiptree persona existed for ten years, from 1967 to 1976. Alli Sheldon wrote for about another ten, from 1977 until her death in 1987. The Tiptree years were more productive, but not by a great degree. The first half of her career, though, was certainly the one for which she is best known. Her later essays in this collection mention her disappointment that the mysterious male writer was more highly regarded than the "ordinary" female one. Still, she wasn't ignored. She had stories nominated for Hugo Awards ("Time-Sharing Angel," "The Boy Who Waterskied to Forever," "The Only Neat Thing to Do") and for Nebula Awards ("Lirios: A Tale of the Quintana Roo" and "The Only Neat Thing to Do"). She won the World Fantasy Award for *Tales of the Quintana Roo*, but that was bestowed posthumously.

Alice Sheldon's life ended May 19th, 1987, by her own hand. She had long been under a doctor's care for depression, and had a history of suicidal threats stretching back to adolescence. She was married, though, and her feelings for her husband, and the difficult time he would have if she killed herself, kept her from pulling the trigger. When his health deteriorated to the point where she felt that there was no quality left to it, she shot him and then herself. She left several notes, mostly instructions to their lawyers, but also a suicide note—dated September 13, 1979, and kept until needed.

This collection spans Alice Sheldon's writing career, from her first published story in 1946 to her first science fiction story in 1955 to her last long novella in 1986, and includes the letters and informal essays she wrote for publication. The fiction section contains mostly minor work, stories she passed over for her other collections but which are interesting in the context of her life and the development of her ideas; they seem more relevant to this book than they would have in others. The nonfiction section started coming together in April 1976, when Tiptree was still Tiptree, and a small press asked about the possibility of collecting her essays on the Mayas. (These essays had been appearing in my amateur magazines, which had print runs of three hundred or less, and we wanted to see them circulated more widely. My friendship with Tip grew out of my publishing these letters and essays, and developed to the point where she named me the literary trustee of her estate.) The project migrated from publisher to publisher, with Jeffrey Levin of Pendragon Press and Donald G. Keller and Jerry Kaufman of Serconia Press making contributions to its focus, before ending up at Tor Books under the stewardship of David G. Hartwell. By Alli's death it looked a lot like it does here. She had given it the *Letters from Yucatan and Other Points of the Soul* title, and had even decided to include some of the short stories that ended up in the front section here. ("Press Until the Bleeding Stops" and "A Day Like Any Other" were in her version of the manuscript.) She had also made some slight revisions to some of the letters. She had intended to revise them more heavily closer to publication, and perhaps add some bridging material. Fortunately, they're fine without it.

Here, then, is the James Tiptree who peeked out from behind Post Office Box 315 in McLean, Virginia, to say hello, and the Alli Sheldon who could actually present herself in public—as she wanted herself presented.

—Jeffrey D. Smith

— · | · —

MEET ME AT INFINITY: UNCOLLECTED FICTION

Happiness Is a Warm Spaceship

The rainbow floods were doused. The station band had left. Empty of her load of cadets, the F.S.S. *Adastra* floated quietly against the stars. The display of First Assignments in the station rotunda was deserted. The crowd had moved to the dome lounge, from which echoed the fluting of girls, the braying and cooing of fathers, mothers, uncles, and aunts, punctuated by the self-conscious baritones of the 99th Space Command class.

Down below, where the Base Central offices functioned as usual, a solitary figure in dress whites leaned rigidly over the counter of Personnel.

"You're absolutely certain there's no mistake?"

"No, it's all in order, Lieutenant Quent." The girl who was coding his status tabs smiled. "First officer, P. B. *Ethel P. Rosenkrantz,* dock eight-two, departs seventeen thirty—that's three hours from now. You have to clear Immunization first, you know."

Lieutenant Quent opened his mouth, closed it, breathed audibly. He picked up the tabs.

"Thank you."

As he strode away a tubby man wearing a *Gal News* badge trotted up to the counter.

"That lad is Admiral Quent's son. What'd he get, Goldie?"

"I shouldn't tell you—a peebee."

"A what? No!"

She nodded, bright-eyed.

"Sweetheart, I'll name you in my will!" He trotted off.

In the medical office Quent was protesting, "But I've had all my standard shots a dozen times!"

The M.O. studied a data display which stated, among other things, that Quent was a Terra-norm Human male, height 1.92 m., skin Cauctan, hair Br., eyes Br., distinguishing marks, None. The data did not mention a big homely jaw and two eyebrows which tended to meet in a straight line.

"What's your ship? Ah, the *Rosenkrantz*. Take off your blouse."

"What do I need shots for?" persisted Quent.

"Two fungus, one feline mutate, basic allergens," said the M.O., briskly cracking ampoules.

"Feline what?"

"Other arm, please. Haven't you met your fellow officers?"

"I just got this rancid assignment twenty minutes ago."

"Oh. Well, you'll see. Flex that arm a couple of times. It may swell a bit."

"What about my fellow officers?" Quent demanded darkly.

The M.O. cracked another ampoule and cocked an eye at the display.

"Aren't you the son of Admiral Rathborne Whiting Quent?"

"What's that got to do with my being assigned to a clobbing peebee?"

"Who knows, Lieutenant? Politics are ever with us. I daresay you expected something like the *Sirian*, eh?"

"Well, men considerably below me on the ratings did draw the *Sirian*," Quent said stiffly.

"Clench and unclench that fist a couple of times. No, unclench it too. Tell me, do you share your father's, ah, sentiments about the integration of the Federal Space Force?"

Quent froze. "What the—"

"You've been in space a year, Lieutenant. Surely you've heard of the Pan Galactic Equality Covenant? Well, it's being implemented, starting with a pilot integration program in the peebees. Three of your future fellow officers were in here yesterday for their pan-Human shots."

Quent uttered a wordless sound.

"You can put on your blouse now," said the M.O. He leaned back. "Life's going to be a bit lumpy for you if you share your father's prejudices."

Quent picked up his blouse.

"Is it prejudice to think that everyone should have his own—"

" 'Do you want your boy's life to depend on an octopus?' " recited the M.O. wryly.

"Oh, well, there he went too far. I told him so." Quent wrenched his way into his dress blouse. "*I'm* not prejudiced. Why, some of my—"

"I see," said the M.O.

"I welcome the opportunity," said Quent. He started for the door. "What?"

"Your hat," said the M.O.

"Oh, thanks."

"By the by," the M.O. called after him, "*Gal News* will probably be on your trail."

Quent stopped in midstride and flung up his head like a startled moose. A small figure was trotting toward him down the corridor. His jaw clenched. He took off down a side corridor, doubled through a restricted zone and galloped into the rear of the freight depot, shoving his tabs at a gaping cargoman.

"My dittybox, quick."

Box in arms, he clambered into a cargo duct, ignoring the chorus of yells. He made his way down the treads until he came to an exit in the perimeter docks. He climbed out into the spacious service area of the *Adastra* from which he had debarked two hours before.

The inlet guard grinned. "Coming back aboard, Lieutenant?"

Quent mumbled and started off around the docking ring, lugging his box. He passed the immaculate berths of the *Crux, Enterprise, Sirian,* passed the gleaming courier docks, plodded on into sections crowded with the umbilical tubes of freighters and small craft and criss-crossed with cables and service rigging. He stumbled and was grazed by a mobile conveyor belt whose driver yelled at him. Finally he came to an inlet scrawled in chalk "P B ROSEKZ". It was a narrow, grimy tube. Nobody was in sight.

He set down his box and started in, trying not to rub his white shoulders against the flex. The tube ended in an open lock which gave directly into a small wardroom cluttered with parcels and used drinking bulbs.

Quent coughed. Nothing happened.

He called out.

A confused sound erupted from the shaftway opposite. It was followed by a massive rear end clad in shorts and a shaggy gray parka. The newcomer turned ponderously. Quent looked up at an ursine muzzle set in bristly jowls, a large prune of a nose.

"Who you?" demanded the ursinoid in thick Galactic.

"Lieutenant Quent, First Officer, reporting," said Quent.

"Good," rumbled the other. He surveyed Quent from small bright eyes and scratched the hair on his belly. Quent had erred about the parka.

"You know refrigerate for storage?"

"Refrigerant?"

"Come. Maybe you make some sense."

Quent followed him back into the shaftway and down a dark ladder. Presently they came to a light above an open hatch. The ursinoid pointed to a tangle of dripping tubes.

"What's it for?" Quent asked.

"Make cold," growled the other. "New model. Should not slobber so, *vernt?*"

"I mean, what's it refrigerating?"

"Ants. Here, you take. Maybe better luck."

He thrust a crumpled folder into Quent's hand and shouldered past him up the ladder, leaving a marked aroma of wet bear rug.

The leaflet was titled: *Temperature-Controlled Personnel System Mark X5 Series D, Mod., Appvl. Pdg.* Quent peered into the hatch. Beyond the pipes was a dim honeycomb of hexagonal cubicles, each containing a dark bulge the size of a coconut. He heard a faint, chittering sound. Quent began to examine the dialed panel beside the hatch. It did not seem to match the leaflet diagram. Somewhere above him the ladder clanked.

"Futile," hissed a voice overhead. Quent looked up. A thin gray arm snaked down and plucked the folder from his grasp. Quent had a glimpse of bulging, membranous eyes set in a long skull, and then the head retracted and its owner clambered down. It, or he, was a lizardlike biped taller than Quent, wearing a complicated vest.

"You are Quent—our new first officer," the creature clacked. Quent could see its tongue flicker inside the beaked jaws. "I am Svensk. Welcome aboard. You will now go away while I adjust this apparatus before the captain buggers it completely."

"The captain?"

"Captain Imray. Hopeless with mechanisms. Do you intend to remain here chattering until these ridiculous ants decongeal?"

Quent climbed back to the wardroom, where somebody was trying to sing. The performer turned out to be a short, furry individual in officer's whites with his hat on the back of his head and a bulb of greenish liquor in one brown fist.

"*Il pleut dans mon coeur comme il pleut dans la ville,*" caroled the stranger.

He broke off to pop round yellow eyes at Quent.

"Ah, our new first officer, is it not? Permit me." Incisors flashed as he grabbed Quent by the shoulders and raked sharp vibrissae across Quent's cheeks. "Sylvestre Sylla, at your service."

Quent exposed his own square teeth.

"Quent."

"Quent?" Sylla repeated. "Not Rathborne Whiting Quent, *Junior*?" he asked in a different tone, touching a black tongue to his incisors.

Quent nodded, coughing. The wardroom seemed to reek of musk.

"Welcome aboard, First Officer Quent. Welcome to the *Ethel P. Rosenkrantz*, patrol boat. Not, of course, the *Sirian*," Sylla said unctuously, "but a worthy ship, *voyons*. I trust you are not disappointed in your first assignment, First Officer Quent?"

Quent's jaw set.

"No."

"Permit me to show you to your quarters, First Officer."

Sylla waved Quent to the upper ladderway, which opened from the wardroom ceiling. Above the wardroom was a section of cubicles for the crew, each accessible by a flexible sphincter port. Beyond these the shaftway ended in the bridge.

"Here you are, First Officer," Sylla pointed. "And your luggage, sir?"

"I left it outside," said Quent.

"Doubtless it is still there," replied Sylla and dived gracefully through another sphincter.

Quent climbed down and exited from the tube in time to rescue his dittybox from a grapple. As he wrestled it up the shaftway he could hear Sylla promising to defeather Alouette.

The cubicle proved to be slightly smaller than his cadet quarters on the *Adastra*. Quent sighed, sat down on his hammock gimbal, took off his hat and ran a hand through his hair. He put his hat back on and took out his pocket recorder. The recorder had a played message tab in place. Quent flicked the rerun and held it to his ear.

Ping-ping-ping, went the official channels signal. He heard a sonorous throat-clearing.

"Congratulations on your Academy record, Lieutenant. Your mother would have been, um, proud. Well done. And now, good luck on your first mission. One that will, I trust, profoundly enlighten you."

The recorder pinged again and cut off. Quent's frown deepened. He shook his head slowly. Then he took a deep breath, opened his dittybox and rooted through a bundle of manuals. Selecting one, he pushed out through the sphincter and climbed up to the bridge.

In the command chair the ursine Captain Imray was flipping fuel selectors and grunting into the engineroom speaker. Quent looked around the small bridge. The navigator's console and the computer station were empty. A little old man in a flowered shirt sat in the commo cubby. He glanced around and batted one baggy eye at Quent, without ceasing to whisper into his set. He had a gray goatee and yellow buck teeth.

The first officer's chair was beside the shaft ladder. Quent removed a parcel from the seat, sat down and opened his manual. When the captain ceased grunting Quent cleared his throat.

"Shall I take over the check, sir? I gather you are going through phase twenty-six."

The ursinoid's eyes widened.

"Some help I get," he boomed. "Sure, sure, you take."

Quent activated his console.

"Gyro lateral thrust, on," he said, manipulating the auxiliary. There was no reply from Engines.

"Gyro lateral thrust, on," Quent repeated, thumbing the engineroom channel.

"Morgan don't say much," remarked Captain Imray.

"The engineering officer?" asked Quent. "But—but you mean he would respond if the function were negative, sir?"

"Sure, sure," said Imray.

"Gyro torque amplifiers, on," said Quent. Silence. "Primary impellor circuit, live," he continued grimly and worked on down the check. At: "Pod eject compensator—" a brief moan came from Engines.

"What?"

"Morgan says don't bother him, he done all that," Imray translated. Quent opened his mouth. The main voder suddenly began barking.

"Control to peebee *Rosy!* Pee bee *Rosy,* prepare to clear dock at this time. Repeat, peebee *Rosy* to station north, go! Peebee *Kip* four-ten, repeat, four-ten. Control to peebee *Kip*, dock eight-two now clearing. Repeat, peebee *Kip* green for dock eight-two."

"Morgan, you hear?" boomed Imray. "We green for go, Morgan?"

A faint squeal from Engines.

"But Captain, we're only at check-phase thirty," said Quent and ducked as Lieutenant Sylla hurtled out of the shaft to land in the navigation console with a rattle of claws. Sylla slapped the screens to life with one hand while punching course settings with the other. Imray and the commo gnome were yanking at their webs. From below came the clang and hiss of the disengaging lock, and the next instant the station gravity went off.

As Quent pawed for his own web he heard Imray bellowing something. The auxiliaries let in and the *Ethel P. Rosenkrantz* leaped to station north.

Quent hauled himself down to his chair, trying to orient the wheeling constellations on the screens.

"How's she look, Morgan?" Imray was asking. "Green we go out?"

Another hoot came from Engines. Sylla was smacking course settings with one furry fist.

"Svensk! Appleby! You set?" Imray bawled.

"But Captain—" Quent protested.

Sylla kicked the fix pedal, twiddled his calibrator and dropped the fist.

"*Gesprüch!*" roared Imray and slammed home the main drive.

Quent's head cleared. He was crosswise in his seat.

"With no web is risky, son," said Imray, shaking his jowls.

"We weren't due to go for forty-five minutes!" expostulated Quent. He righted himself as acceleration faded. "The check is incomplete, sir. Control had no right—"

"Apparently the first officer did not hear the four-ten," said Sylla silkily.

"Four-ten?"

"Four-ten is ship in bad trouble, must dock quick," Imray told him.

"But that should be three-three-delta-ex-four-one-otto point with the vessel's designation."

"Doubtless in the star class vessels First Officer Quent is used to," said Sylla. "Here he will find life less formal."

"What was the four-ten, Pom?" called a clear, sweet voice.

Quent twisted. Looking up from beside his elbow was a dazzling girl-face framed in copper curls. Quent craned further. The rest of her appeared to meet the wildest demands of a man who had spent the last year on a training ship.

"Huh?" he asked involuntarily.

"Hi," said the apparition, waving her hand irritably in front of Quent's nose and continuing to gaze at the commo officer.

"The *Kip*," said the little man over his shoulder. "That's the pee-bee *Kipsuga Chomo*, sir," he waggled his goatee at Quent. "Three hundred hours with some contaminant gas. They sealed up in the bridge but Ikky had to bring 'em in by himself. Not much air in these here peebees."

He turned back to his board.

Quent glanced around. Three hundred hours was over two weeks. He shuddered.

"But why didn't—"

"Why did not someone come to their rescue?" Sylla cut in. "The first officer forgets. Patrol boats are the ones that go to the rescue. Who comes to aid a patrol boat? Only another patrol boat—in this case ourselves, who were sitting at Central awaiting our new first officer. *Tant pis*, they were only a gaggle of Non-Humans—"

Imray swatted the air crossly.

"Now, now, Syll."

"Soup's hot," said the girl. "Ooh! My jam."

She reached a slim white arm around Quent's ankles. Quent tracking closely, saw that the parcel he had displaced had collided with the gimbals—together with his hat—and was exuding a rosy goo.

"Tchah!" She snatched it up and departed down the shaft.

Quent picked up his hat and shook it. Jam drops drifted onto his leg.

Captain Imray was clambering into the shaftway.

"The first officer will take the first watch, is that not correct?"

Without waiting for an answer Sylla sailed past the captain and vanished. Only the commo officer remained absorbed in his inaudible dialog.

Quent collected the floating jam in his handkerchief and wedged the cloth under his seat. Then he kicked off on a tour of the cramped bridge. The screens were, he saw, inoperative under drive. He pulled up to the library computer and signaled for their course data display. Instead of the requested data the voder came on.

> I must go down to the seas again, for the call of the running tide
> Is a wild call and a clear call—

Quent reached for the erase.

"Don't do that, sir," the commo man said.

"Why not? I want some data."

"Yes, sir. But that's Lieutenant Sylla's setup, sir. Very fond of water poetry, he is. Just leave it, sir, Lieutenant Svensk will get whatever you want."

Quent glared at the computer, which was now reciting:

> Degged with dew, dappled with dew,
> Are the groins of the braes—

He switched it off.

"Perhaps you would be so good as to inform me of our course and of the parameters of our patrol sector?" he asked icily. "I am Lieutenant Quent, First Officer."

"Yessir, Lieutenant." The little man's face split in a grin that sent his goatee pointing at his buck teeth. "Pomeroy here, sir. Lester Pomeroy, Ensign. Sure is good to see a fellow Human aboard, sir, if you don't mind my saying so."

"Not at all, Ensign," said Quent.

"I guess maybe you feel a bit put out, sir," Pomeroy went on in a confidential tone. "Them en-aitches prob'ly never even introduced themselves—right, sir?"

"Well, I haven't had time to look over the roster yet."

"What roster?" Pomeroy chuckled. "Anything you want to know, sir, just ask Pomeroy. You want to know the gen? Well, there's Captain Imray, he's from Deneb way. Navigator, Lieutenant Sylla—I don't know exactly where he's from. He's what they call a lutroid. Puts out terrible strong when he's wrought up. And Lieutenant Svensk, he's Science when he's set low of course, and conversely he's Guns when the need arises. His vest, see? And then there's me for Commo and Morgan for Engines—he don't say much. Wait till you meet Morgan. And there's our combat team—but they don't count."

"Why not?" asked Quent dazedly.

"They're froze, that's why. And froze they'll stay. Nobody wants to get them boys out." Pomeroy gave a nervous giggle.

"But I know the one you're itching to meet, Lieutenant, sir. Miss Mellicent Appleby, Logistical supply. Ain't she a treat? Cooks up a storm, too. But there's one thing she don't supply, I better warn you, sir." His grin faded. "She don't supply no Appleby. So far, anyhow."

Pomeroy paused, waited. Quent said nothing.

"Now, you ask about our patrol beat—no, sir," he broke off as Quent moved to the display tank. "No use to try that, sir. Svensk has it stressed up as a psoodospace—some crazy snake game. But it's simple. We're Sector Twelve, like a big piece of cake, see?" He gestured. "Here we are at the point. That's Base Central. First stop is right close in— that's Strugglehome. If they're all green we go on to Davon Two. If they're not hurting we swing over to Turlavon and Ed. And if nothing comes up we dock in at Midbase. If they haven't any grief we hang around and check Route Leo—service the beacons and so forth—and then we hit the Chung Complex. That's a mess. When we're through there we make the long hop out to Farbase—and if they're all quiet we start on around through Goldmine and Tunney and Sopwith and so on, back home to Central. Eighteen mail colonies, one route and two bases. Takes about a hundred and twenty days, provided nothing comes up."

"What sort of thing is apt to come up, Mr. Pomeroy?"

"Distress calls, wrecks, jitney duty for some royal groundhog going from here to there, wonky beacons, exploding mail, field freeze-ups, ghost signals, flying wombats—you name it, we get it sooner or later." His poached eyes rolled mournfully. "We're the boys that do the dirty, sir, you know. If it's too clobby to mess with, lay it on the poor old pee-bees. Take our last tour. Everything was tight till we hit the Chung Complex. They got a crustal instability on a little water planet and both their big ships blowed out on the other side of the system. So *we* have to ferry the bleeders off—and *they* won't go without their livestock. Thirty-three days hauling octopuses, that's what."

Quent frowned. "In a Space Force vessel?"

"Ah, them en-aitches don't care," Pomeroy grimaced.

Quent kicked back to his chair in silence.

"Never you mind, Lieutenant sir," the little man commiserated and hoisted an amber bulb, his wrinkled neck working.

He wiped the bulb with his shirttail. "Have some Leo Lightning, sir?"

Quent jerked upright. "Drinking on the bridge?"

Pomeroy winked broadly.

"Captain Imray don't care."

"Mr. Pomeroy," said Quent firmly. "I appreciate your intentions—but there will be no drinking on this bridge while I am O.C. Kindly stow that bulb."

Pomeroy stared blankly.

"Yes, sir," he said at last and turned to his board.

The bulb remained in plain sight.

Quent opened his mouth, closed it. Muscles flickered in his square unhandsome countenance. A clamor was rising from the wardroom below: Svensk's clack, Sylla's waspish tenor, mingled with the captain's boom. The words could not be distinguished, but his fellow officers were clearly not a harmonious team. Presently they subsided, and the ladder clanked as they retired to rest.

Quent sighed through his teeth and picked up the jam-spattered manual. The *Ethel P. Rosenkrantz,* of which he was first officer, was in full star drive with twenty-three essential operational procedures, all his responsibility, unchecked.

*   *   *

Five hours later the ladder clanked again and the hulk of Captain Imray heaved up to the bridge. He was followed by Lieutenant Sylla in free glide. The lutroid landed in his console with a passing flick that made Pomeroy jump for his bulb.

"Twenty-twenty hours, First Officer Quent relieved by Captain Imray," said Quent formally to the log.

"Sure, sure, I take her, son," chuckled Imray, settling himself.

"You go look Appleby, *vernt?*"

"I am going to make a preliminary inspection of the ship, Captain."

"Good." Imray beamed. "See how conscience the humans, Syll? From them example you could learn."

"Sans doute," snarled Sylla. "It is also possible that our first officer feels a need to familiarize himself with the humble patrol boat, which perhaps did not engage his attention during his training as a future star-class admiral."

"Now, Syll," growled Imray.

"Come on, Lieutenant, sir," Pomeroy pulled Quent's sleeve.

Quent's right fist unballed slowly. He followed the little man into the shaft.

In the wardroom Pomeroy helped himself from a net of wrapped sandwiches and settled down with his bulb at the gimbaled table. Quent surveyed the room. It was a cylinder with walls composed of lockers in which, according to his manual, were stored suits, tools, repair and grappling rigs, fuse panels, and the oxy supply. These could be checked later. On his left was the lock and a slave screen, now blank. Across from the lock was a pantry cubby and the shaftway down which he had first followed Imray.

Quent kicked over to the shaft and started aft. The next section contained the main food stores, a small galley-cum-infirmary, waste intakes and the fore quadrant of the regeneration system which ran through several sections of the hull. He glanced through its hatch panel at a lighted mass of culture trays and continued crab-wise along the dim shaft, vaguely aware that his feet were encountering a filmy substance. He was now passing more sphincters which gave access to cubicles for transient passengers and package mail.

"Must you trample on my laundry, Lieutenant?" inquired a soprano voice in his ear.

Miss Appleby's head protruded from a port behind him. Her gaze was directed toward his leg, which seemed to be wrapped in turquoise silk.

"Oh. Sorry." He disentangled, trying not to kick. "I'm doing a tour of the ship."

"Well, do your touring someplace else, please," she said. "These are my quarters."

"All these?" He gestured.

"When we haven't any transients, I don't see why not."

He parted a port at random and looked in. The cubicle was draped in fluffy stuff and the hull wall sparkled with holograms. Quent had the impression of an offensively healthy character in ceaseless action. He moved to another cubicle—it proved to be full of bundles tied with bows. Not mail. He tried another, Miss Appleby's head revolving as she watched him. This one held what appeared to be a private kitchen and it smelled of fudge.

"These wires," he called back to the head. "Are they authorized?"

"Captain Imray never objected. Please get on with it. I'm trying to take a bath."

Quent peered. There were indeed rainbow droplets in the curls around her delicate ears. He licked his lips.

"Yes, ma'am," he said absently, drifting toward her.

"By the way, Lieutenant," said the charming head. "Did you notice those holos in there?"

"Very nice." He drifted faster, smiling hopefully.

"Didn't you recognize them?"

"Should I?" he beamed.

"Yes, I think so," she said calmly. "That's my fiancé, Bob Coatesworth. Vice Admiral Robert B. Coatesworth. Think it through, Lieutenant."

With a soft sucking sound her head vanished back into the cubicle.

Quent halted. He pounded his fist slowly against his head—several times. Then he resumed his journey aft.

Beyond the bulkhead he found emergency pod inlets, which would require a careful check, and the refrigerant storage quadrant he had met before. He peered through the view panel. The drip seemed to have stopped.

The regeneration chamber ended here, giving room for the landleg stabilizers and the *Rosenkrantz*'s small-weapons turrets, all of which he would have to go over in detail later on. This ship was old. The manual referred to it as a heavy-duty, primitive type, equipped for planetside landings. Was the system still operational? Pomeroy had told him that their mail exchange was normally conducted from orbit.

Through the next bulkhead the shaft opened into the echoing gloom of the main cargo hold. This felt dank, perhaps in memory of the octopi. He made his way along the hull past the airsled and the cradles filled with mail pods. He gave the main cargo hatch a brief check and turned to the engineroom hatchway.

The hatch refused to open.

"First Officer to Engineer," he said to the speaker. "Open up."

The engineroom was silent.

"The first officer speaking," he said more loudly. "Open the hatch."

The speaker gave a squeal that sounded like "Blow."

"What's wrong?" Quent shouted. "Open up."

"Blo-oo-oo-ow," moaned the speaker.

"I'm inspecting the ship. Engineer, undog this hatch."

No reply.

Quent pounded on the grille.

"First Officer Quent," said Sylla's voice from the hold voder. "The captain requests that you cease annoying the engineer."

"I'm not annoying the engineer. He won't let me in."

"Better you try some other time, son," said Imray's rumble.

"But—yes, sir," Quent gritted.

He pounded his head again, less gently. Then he started back through the hold, pursued by the dim sound of bagpipes from Engines. The shaft was now empty of Miss Appleby and her laundry. Pomeroy was still in the wardroom, nursing his bulb.

"Morgan throw you out, sir? Them en-aitches got no respect."

Quent silently helped himself to some sandwiches and a tea bulb and rummaged through the cassette locker until he recognized some Sector Twelve names—Strugglehome, Turlavon, the Chung Complex. He carried the lot to his cubicle, carefully stowed away his stained dress whites and slung his hammock cocoon. The sandwiches turned out to be delicious. Before he had heard through the data on Turlavon his eyelids closed.

"Wake up, Lieutenant."

Quent came half out of his cubicle and with Pomeroy hanging onto his arm.

"You was having nightmares, sir."

The little man's left eye seemed to be swelling shut. Across the way Svensk's bony head poked out. Imray and Sylla were peering down from the bridge. They were all grinning.

"Uh—sorry."

Quent disengaged himself and pulled back into his cabin.

"Orbit in an hour, sir," Pomeroy called. "Strugglehome."

In the twenty ship days to Midbase, Quent acquired considerable enlightenment. At Strugglehome he asked Sylla to show him the mail-pod exchange routine. Here he learned that the slow man on a pod grapple can get a set of mashed fingers. The lutroid apologized effusively. By Davon Two Quent's hand was in shape to help Svensk prepare a shipment from the culture chamber. The big saurian became animated in the fetid warmth and treated Quent to a harangue on phytogenetics. Quent finally told him to go away. He then learned, too late, that the chamber hatch controls were defective on the inside. Three hours later, when Miss Appleby decided to investigate the pounding noises, Quent was purple from breathing CO_2 and she had to help him out.

"Wha's girl doing on this thing anyway?" he gasped.

"Oh, a lot of us log officers take en-aitch tours," she dimpled. "It's so restful."

Quent shuddered and clamped his big jaw.

About Appleby herself he learned that she spent all her time in her cubicles fixing up her trousseau and her hoard of stuff for her future home. The amount of loot she had astonished him. But she seemed to have been equally effective in loading up the *Rosenkrantz*'s T.E.—the ship bulged with stores. She also emerged on the dot with excellent meals, which seemed to be Captain Imray's chief interest in life.

During the hop to Turlavon Quent made two more efforts to get into Morgan's domain, and was again rebuffed. He settled down to learning the ship bolt by bolt, manual in hand.

Turlavon passed without incident, but at Ed they had to wait for the planet station crew to finish harvesting. For three whole watches Quent struggled with unstable orbits, until he learned that Ed had enormous masscons and that someone had disassembled the ship's grav-mass analyzer. He bore it all stoically, but his jaw was corded with knots which seemed to have been there before. He had, after all, been an admiral's son for a long time.

At Midbase they lay into the main cargo umbilical to offload a flywheel for the station gyros. The delay at Ed had thrown them out of synch with Base time and the station dark-period caught them early. Quent used the chance to check over the ship's exterior valve seals. He had worked back to the main lock when his hand light picked up a small gray creature flitting past the aft fins. It was about a meter tall and roughly humanoid.

Quent called out. The figure accelerated and vanished among the dock belts.

Quent frowned after it and went into the wardroom. Captain Imray was grunting over his greenbook tabs. The others were on the bridge, listening to the station newscast.

"Morgan," said Quent. "Would he be about so high—and gray?"

Imray leaned back and rubbed his prune nose.

"That's him. He go now listen is them gyros all right. Like a mother for gyros is Morgan."

"He must have left by the engineroom crash hatch." Quent pointed to the panel. "Why isn't the telltale light on?"

"The first officer's appetite for the minutest details of our humble craft is truly admirable," yawned Sylla, lounging in. "If it were not so tedious."

"Mr. Sylla, if that hatch lock—"

"Sure, sure," said Imray. "But Morgan never leave nothing open. Not Morgan. He like to come, go, private, *vernt?*"

"Do you mean that you've allowed Morgan to kill the telltale circuits, Captain?"

"The mammalian insecurity syndrome," remarked Svensk, unfolding himself out of the shaft. He was playing with a small wire toroid which changed shape disturbingly. "The leaky-womb phobia," he creaked.

"I give you the panic of the omelet," Sylla snapped.

"Captain Imray," said Quent, "by regulation it's my responsibility to oversee the engineroom. With your permission, this would seem to be the time for me to take a look."

Imray squinted at him.

"Morgan very sensitive being, son, very sensitive." He wiggled his big black-nailed hands to show Morgan's sensitivity. Quent nodded and started aft.

"Nothing touch, son," Imray called after him. "Morgan—"

The engineroom personnel hatch was still dogged. Quent went to the hull and unbolted a pod cradle, revealing a duct panel designed to service the life-support conduit to Engines. He unscrewed the panel and tugged. It did not move. He displaced another cradle and found a magnetic contraption with no discoverable leads. He summoned Svensk, who arrived unhurriedly and gave it a brief inspection.

"Can you open this?"

"Yes," said Svensk, and started back through the hold.

"Mr. Svensk, come back. I want you to open this lock."

"The semantic confusions you homotherms get into are beyond belief," croaked Svensk. "Are you not aware that Morgan desires this to remain closed?"

"As first officer of this ship I am ordering you to open it."

"When I said I could open it—I meant with the proper tools."

"What are the proper tools?"

"Linear force must be applied in the presence of a certain set of alternating pressures in a gaseous medium."

He arched his long neck. Quent scowled at him.

"Pressures? Mr. Svensk, are you deliberately—" Quent suddenly stabbed his wrench at the saurian. "It's a sonic lock, isn't it? Set for . . . Mr. Pomeroy, bring that recorder in the wardroom locker back here. I want you to imitate Morgan's voice."

Reluctantly, Pomeroy tooted while Quent tugged, and the panel slid open. Instead of the shining banks and alleyways of a normal engineroom they were looking into a pitch-dark tangle.

"What in the name of space—?" Quent reached into the filaments.

"Sir, I wouldn't do that," warned Pomeroy.

"Fascinating!" Svensk's skullhead came over Quent's shoulder.

"What is that mess?"

"I fancy it is part of the sensor system by which Morgan maintains contact with the stress structure of his mechanisms. I had no idea he had achieved anything so extensive."

"Just close it up, please sir," Pomeroy begged.

Quent stared into the web.

"I'm going in," he gritted.

From behind them came a piercing wail. Quent spun and a gray wraith flew at his face, spitting sparks. He reeled back, his arms over his eyes. The hatch clashed shut.

"Oh sir, that's done it!" cried Pomeroy.

The lights went out. The hold voder broke into a skirling, howling din. Quent heard Svensk pounding away from them, and stumbled after the sound. The wardroom voder began to roar. Quent found his hand light and rushed to the bridge. The deck was a bedlam of noise and every console was flashing. Svensk and Sylla were yanking out computer cables. Quent slammed down the circuit breakers. There was no effect. The hideous din yammered on.

"Nothing to do but get out till he calms down," Pomeroy yelled in Quent's ear. "Thank the Lord we aren't in space."

The others had left. As Quent went out Miss Appleby flew past in a whirl of turquoise silk.

"You idiot," she raged. "Look what you've done."

Imray stood glowering on the deck. Svensk towered at full height, his eyes veiled in membranes. Sylla paced with ears laid back and there was a decided pungency in the air.

Quent slammed the lock but the uproar reverberating through the *Rosenkrantz* was clearly audible.

"He's got an override on those circuits," Quent fumed. "I'm going in there and cut off his air."

"Asinine," grated Svensk. "We are in air."

"His water, then."

"To do so would render the refrigerant exchange inoperative."

"There must be something—what does he eat?"

"Special concentrates," snapped Miss Appleby. "I stocked him with a year's supply at Central."

Quent kicked a freight belt.

"In other words, Morgan runs this ship."

Imray shrugged angrily.

"He run it—we run it—we go," he growled.

"When Space Force Monitor hears about this it'll be Morgan who goes," Quent told them darkly.

Sylla spat.

"The first officer had forgotten the *Kipsuga Chomo.* Or perhaps he recalls the four-ten which inconvenienced him?"

"What?" Quent turned on the lutroid. "I have forgotten nothing, Mr. Sylla. What has the *Kip* to do with Morgan?"

Imray shook his jowls.

"No, Syll, no!"

Svensk coughed.

"Look, sir," said Pomeroy. "Morgan's fixing to make a night of it. He don't quit. How's for you and me to go by the office and see about a place to sleep?"

Miss Appleby sniffed. "That would be useful."

The din continued unabated. Reluctantly, Quent went off with Pomeroy to the Midbase station offices, where they found one billet for a female only. Midbase was bulging with colonists awaiting transfer on Route Leo. In the end the male complement of the *Rosenkrantz* settled down to doze uncomfortably on a textile shipment and to endure the jibes of the cargomen when the lights came on.

Horrible sounds came from the *Rosenkrantz* all morning. After noon mess Morgan appeared to tire. The officers went warily back on board.

"Have to give him time to cool down," said Pomeroy. As if on cue the voders erupted briefly. A few minutes later they did it again. The others went to their hammocks, leaving Quent in the wardroom to brood.

He was still there when Miss Appleby came in.

"I'm afraid I was rude to you, Lieutenant Quent."

He looked up dully. She seemed to be all aglow.

"Actually what you did was ever so lucky for me."

She smiled, setting down a parcel. She served herself tea and a cookie. Instead of taking them to her quarters she came back and sat down at the table with an excited wiggle.

Quent's eyes opened. He sat up.

"That Mrs. Lee," she confided happily. "You know, the colonist? She's got twenty meters of Gregarin passamenterie. It took me all day to talk her into swapping me one meter for a petite suit liner and a case of bottlehots. I'd never have got it if we hadn't been held up, thanks to you."

She glowed at him over her tea bulb.

"Well, I—"

"It'll make *the* vest of all time for Bob," she sighed. "Bob loves vests—off duty, of course."

Quent put his head back on his fists. He had been raised with two older sisters.

"That's—great."

"You're depressed," she observed.

Quent heaved a sigh and shook his head. Against his better judgment he found himself looking into her large green eyes.

"Miss Appleby," he blurted. "When I came on this ship I was completely unprejudiced against Non-Humans. Completely. I welcomed the chance to show my father that other beings were just as fit to serve in space as—" His voice faded. "Now I just don't know. This mess—that insufferable Morgan—"

"Yours is a strange reaction, Lieutenant. We girls always say it's much safer on a ship with one of Morgan's people. They'll do anything for the ship. Like the *Kip,* you know."

"What do you know about the *Kipsuga?*"

"Why, just that their engineer saved them. He got them back to Central. Ikka somebody. Pom says he died."

Quent frowned.

"Funny they didn't tell me about him."

"Probably your father is the reason they keep things from you, don't you think, Lieutenant?" She stood up, hugging her parcel. "They're fine people," she told him earnestly. "You just have to understand their ways. That's what Bob says. He says a lot of Space Force officers are prejudiced without knowing it."

Quent looked up at her. She radiated Galactic amity.

"Could be," he said slowly. "Miss Appleby, maybe I haven't—"

"Try a little harder," she encouraged him. "That Mrs. Lee said a newsman was asking about you."

"It is time to eat."

The harsh croak cut her off. Svensk unfolded himself from the ladder.

"Right away."

Appleby vanished. Svensk turned a suspicious eye on Quent.

"Serpent," jeered Sylla, bouncing down, "You reptiles did not understand that time existed before until we provided you with thermal vests. At home we have still the taboo against eating lizards because of their unfortunate tendency to putrefy while torpid."

"Activity fails to correlate with intelligence," Svensk clacked haughtily.

"On the other hand," Sylla licked his vibrissae, "our primates are regarded as quite palatable. Braised, naturally, with just a *rien* of celery. Amusing, is it not, First Officer Quent?"

Quent exhaled carefully.

"If you feel so, Mr. Sylla." He stretched his mouth sideways in a lifelike smile. "Excuse me, I believe I'll lie down."

The silence behind him lasted so long he almost wondered about it.

The next fortnight was spent laboriously servicing beacons along Route Leo. The beacons were elderly M20s, which Quent had cursed while navigating from the *Adastra*. Now he found their trouble lay in the bulky shielding which attracted dust, thus building up electrostatic imbalances that distorted the beacon's spectrum and eventually its orbit. They had to be periodically cleaned and neutralized. The job required long hours and close cooperation among crewmen. By the fourth and last beacon Quent's jaw had developed a permanent ache.

"Have you not yet finished, First Officer?"

Quent was clinging awkwardly to the far end of the slippery kinetic bleeder. Above him Sylla wriggled through the beacon grids with the agility of his otter forbears, warping his vacuum line expertly as he went.

"It is clear that the Academy does not contemplate its graduates shall endure the indignity of labor," Sylla jibed.

"I admit I'm inexperienced in this and not as fast as you are," Quent said mildly. "Mr. Svensk. Where are you casting that sweep line?"

"As per your request, down," said Svensk from the far side. "Although it seems senseless."

"I meant down here—toward me." Quent took a deep breath. "Not toward the center of gravity of the beacon-ship system. A loose way of speaking, I'm afraid."

"Lieutenant Quent, sir," said Pomeroy's voice from the ship.

"If you wouldn't mind sir, could you turn your volume down a bit? There seems to be some sort of grinding sound in your speaker and the *Greenhill* signal is awful weak, sir."

Greenhill, a colony ship out of Midbase, was running a check on the beacon calibrations as it went by.

Quent swore and snapped off his helmet speaker. A moment later he felt a jerk on his lines and found himself revolving in space two meters from the end of the bleeder. His line had no tension. When he stopped his tumble he saw that Svensk had fouled him with the sweep and was departing over the limb of the beacon. Sylla was nowhere in sight.

"Do you want your life to depend on an octopus?" Quent muttered under his breath. He reached for the speaker switch, then paused. His orbit was decaying. He straightened out and began to breathe measuredly.

The others had gone inboard and unsuited when Quent finally finished clearing the bleeder shaft. In the wardroom he stumbled into Miss Appleby taking a server of food to Imray's cubicle.

"I want you to know I'm trying," he told her wearily.

"That's the spirit, Lieutenant."

She would make a super admiral's wife, Quent realized.

The *Greenhill* confirmed the beacon calibrations and the *Rosenkrantz* headed out to the Chung Complex. When they came out of drive their screens lit up in glory. The Chung was a cluster of colored suns, warm and inviting after the bleakness of Route Leo.

"Don't you believe it, sir." Pomeroy broke the thread of his crochet work against his stained frontals. "I dread this place, I do." His eyes rolled as he reached for his bulb. "All en-aitches here. Under water, too, most of 'em, the slimy things. Even Mr. Sylla hates them."

Despite Pomeroy's forebodings the first calls passed off with only routine problems of mail and message exchange. The little man continued to follow Quent about, mumbling gloomily. He was also dosing himself with increasing quantities of Leo Lightning whenever he could sneak off the bridge.

"Let Pomeroy tell you, sir," he grumbled in the night watches, "They're devils down there. We oughtn't have any dealings with things like them. Pomeroy knows. Pomeroy's seen sights no Humans had ought to bear. Worms. Worms is the least of it." His goatee bobbed over his scrawny adam's apple. "Worms and worse."

The Chung orbits continued without troubles other than those provided by Svensk and Sylla—and even these two appeared to be letting up. Quent's only view of the "worms and worse" was on the ship's screens. Most of the alien commo officers were aquatic. A few did appear wormlike and two had tentacles. There was one truly repellent squid affair with unidentifiable organs floating around its eye stalks. There was also a rather genial dolphinoid to whom Pomeroy was vitriolic. They were the ones who had required transport for the octopi.

"I'm a broadminded man, sir," Pomeroy told Quent that night. "Tolerant, Pomeroy is. I put up with 'em." He hiccuped. "No choice. Pomeroy's sunk low. I don't deny it. But them things down there—" He shuddered and hitched closer confidentially. "They think they're as good as Humans, sir. Just as good as you, or better. What'll happen when them things decides they wants to come in the Force, sir? Expect a Human to take orders from a worm?" His bloodshot eyes bored anxiously into Quent's.

"Mr. Pomeroy. In case you are under the impression that I share my father's views on Non-Humans in the Space Force, you are mistaken."

"That's right, sir, you're a tolerant man too, sir. But a person can't help wondering—"

"Kindly wonder to yourself in the future, Mr. Pomeroy," Quent said coldly. "For your information, I am fully in favor of the integration program. If a being is a competent spacer, I don't see that his personal appearance enters in."

Pomeroy closed his mouth and turned back to his board in offended silence. Presently he paid a prolonged visit to the wardroom and returned, wiping his mouth. For several watches he spoke only when Quent addressed him.

At the last Chung stop they picked up a short-range freight shuttle whose jockey needed a lift to Farbase. The jockey was a smaller version of Svensk. They got his shuttle stowed without mishap and the *Rosenkrantz* went into drive for the long run out to Farbase. Quent's eyebrows began to unknot.

The run was made in comparative peace, for Quent. Svensk and the freighter pilot bankrupted each other at some exotic topological game, while Sylla occupied himself with trying to key a poetry-scanning function into the computer. Imray grew increasingly taciturn and spent long hours in his cubicle. Sometimes Quent would hear him in a rumbling argument with one of the others. Quent devoted himself to a discreet inspection of the ship's wiring and managed not to upset Morgan. Things seemed to be settling down.

This impression strengthened when they got to Farbase. They exchanged the mail and off-loaded the freight shuttle with surprising dispatch. Pomeroy actually changed his shirt. He and the others set off to call on another peebee, the *Jasper Banks*, which was there en route to a long distance job. Miss Appleby went after the depot officer who had promised her a set of Chung pearl glasses for herself and a case of fish-eggs for the mess. The small, bleak station offered Quent no diversion. He decided to go out and check over the exterior antennae.

He was suiting up when he heard the others coming back onboard. He climbed to the bridge to find them preparing to take off.

"Call Appleby," Imray grunted curtly. "We go now."

The next leg was to the sector rim colonies of Goldmine, Tunney, and Sopwith. The ship lifted off with scarcely another word exchanged by its officers. And as soon as they were in drive Imray left the bridge.

The short run to Goldmine was made in thickening silence. Imray stayed in his cubicle. The others seemed on edge. Only Pomeroy had anything to say—he kept pestering Appleby for reports on Imray's health.

"He says his heart bothers him but he won't let me use the medical analyzer," she informed them. "His appetite's good, though."

"He's due to retire soon, sir." Pomeroy shook his head.

Imray did not appear on the bridge at Goldmine. When they were on course for Tunney he called Quent to his cabin.

"Is no good," he said hoarsely as soon as Quent's head came through the sphincter. The ursinoid's muzzle looked haggard and his fur was staring.

"You take over, son." He gestured feebly, dislodging an empty server.

"Sir, I think you should let Miss Appleby bring the medikit."

Imray groaned.

"For old age, medicals can nothing do. Little pills I try. No good."

"We'll turn back to Farbase hospital."

"What they do? Torture me only. I know. With my people—goes quick. You captain. I tell Morgan mind you."

"You're ordering me to take over as acting captain, sir?"

Imray nodded, his little eyes roving feverishly.

"But—"

"No but. You captain."

Imray's eyes closed and his breathing became noisy.

Quent studied him, scowling.

"Yes, sir," he said slowly. "I'll have Pomeroy patch you into the record log."

One of Imray's eyes glinted briefly and closed again.

Quent withdrew into the shaft of the *Rosenkrantz*. His first command. All the knots which had been smoothing from his face came back, tighter than before.

The others accepted the situation without comment, beyond Sylla's sarcastic use of his new title. Morgan, too, proved as good as Imray's word. He continued silent but during the maneuvers at Tunney the energics were flawless. Quent's frown deepened.

He took to roaming the ship at odd hours, sleeping little and poorly. They were now at the farthest leg of their patrol, running along the sector rim to Sopwith. On their starboard the Galaxy was unpatrolled and largely unknown. Quent spent hours at the scanners. He had seen wild space before from the bridge of the mighty and virtually invulnerable *Adastra*. From a peebee with four small rockets and only meteor shielding it looked decidedly wilder. Quent dreamed of nucleonic storms and got up to check over the sensors again.

> Toujours j'entends la mer qui fait du bruit,
> Triste comme l'oiseau seule . . .

Quent groaned and pulled the cocoon flaps over his ears to shut out the mechanical drone from the bridge. Sylla was making the computer translate poetry into his native Ter-French. Presently the droning was replaced by incomprehensible wrangling.

Quent sighed and jackknifed out of his cocoon. It was nearly his shift and they would be coming into Sopwith soon.

In the shaft he found Pomeroy backing out of Imray's cubicle, bulb in hand.

"How is he, Mr. Pomeroy?"

The little man wagged his head, bleary eyed, but said nothing.

In the wardroom Miss Appleby was setting out fresh smoked ham she had wangled at Tunney.

"Just coffee, thank you," Quent told her.

She smiled sympathetically at the standing furrow in his brow and vanished back to her storerooms.

Quent took his coffee up to the bridge, relieving Svensk and Sylla, and settled wearily to hear a data tape. Pomeroy straggled into his cubby and began to doze. In the wardroom the other two continued to argue fitfully.

Suddenly Pomeroy sat up.

"Sopwith, sir. Seems to be a bit of trouble."

"What type of trouble, Mr. Pomeroy?"

"Too early to tell yet, sir. Mostly noise."

Sopwith was a Non-Human affiliated planet whose native name was Szolphuildhe. The native race was described as small, timid, pinkish in color, bipedal, and probably bisexual, with a fibers-and-ceramics technology. It was Human habitable but no Humans lived there.

"Sounds like they been attacked by a band of marauding monsters," Pomeroy reported presently. "Says they came in a sky-boat—wait a minute, sir." He squinted, listening. "About them monsters, sir. Appears like they're Humans."

"Humans?"

"That's how the kinks describe 'em, sir. Like us."

"What are they doing to the ki—to the Sopwithians?"

"Seems they're eating 'em, sir."

"Eating them, Mr. Pomeroy?"

Pomeroy nodded. Quent leaned over the shaft and called Svensk. When the saurian's big head appeared, Quent asked, "What Human spacers could have landed here and attacked the natives or—ah—exploited them as food?"

Svensk's raised his eye membranes reflectively.

"Possibly you refer to Drakes?"

"What are Drakes?"

"The Drakes, as they call themselves, are a band of Humans, strength unknown, base unknown, possessing not less than five spaceships, who maintain themselves by sporadic raids upon shipping and colonies," Svensk creaked. "Until recently reported only in Sector Ten, they—"

"One of our little sector problems." Sylla grinned. He bounded to his console and began to polish his claws. "Quite beneath the notice of the Academy."

"Navigator, a sensor orbit, please. Mr. Svensk, let's pick up the location of that vessel as soon as possible. Mr. Pomeroy, ask them where that sky-boat is, how big it is, how many attackers, and what weapons."

The Sopwith commo officer believed that the ship had come down somewhere northeast of the port city. It was bigger and brighter than the sun, carrying at least five hands of monsters. They spouted burning flames which made no noise.

"That's thirty of 'em," said Pomeroy. "As to their weapons, Drakes would have lasers, flame-throwers, grenades, and maybe a rocket-launcher or two, groundside. Them kinks don't know ships or weapons, sir. Flinging stones is about it, with them."

They still had not located the alien ship when the Sopwith city area went into night. The Sopwith commo officer on the ground was growing balky.

"He says the monsters are coming in again," Pomeroy reported. "Listen."

The voder gabbled wildly, gave out a string of shrieks and cut off.

"That's it, sir. He's taken off. Well, there'll be no business here. We'd better log up the report and get on."

"Mr. Svensk, what's that field like?" asked Quent thoughtfully.

The lizard was absorbed in his sensor adjustments.

"Mr. Svensk. Is that field usable?"

Svensk reared up. "Very primitive." He shrugged.

"Navigator," Quent said icily. "Landing trajectory to field, please."

Three pairs of eyes rounded on him.

"Landing?" Sylla licked his chops. "The acting captain is perhaps unaware that patrol boats do not—"

"I've inspected our system, Mr. Sylla. It's fully operational. In case you're concerned, my training has included the landing of comparable craft."

"But sir," protested Pomeroy, "What about Morgan? He don't like going planetside, sir."

Quent glanced at the voders and cleared his throat.

"Mr. Morgan, there is an emergency on this planet and we must land. I count on your cooperation. Mr. Sylla, is that course ready?"

"Set," snapped Sylla through his teeth.

Quent engaged the auxiliaries and started to code in the autopilot. As he touched it the familiar din cut loose from the voder.

"Mr. Morgan." Quent rapped the speaker. "Stop that racket. We must land, do you understand? I'm taking us down!"

To the din was added a crackling sputter and the lights jumped. Svensk dived for his computer leads.

"Stop that, Morgan. Stop it. I'm going to land or I'll crash the ship. Hear that—you'll crash us."

"In the name of the Path," Imray roared from the shaft. "What?"

"It's our duty to land, sir," Quent said. "Emergency on the planet."

Imray burst onto the bridge, paws over his ears. He stared at Quent.

"I'm committing us."

Quent slammed the manual override.

Imray grabbed up his speaker.

"Morgan—Morgan, boy, it's me." Imray's voice sank to a huge croon. "Be good boy, Morgan—down we must go. I swear you, for little minute only—ship it will not hurt. Morgan! You hear, Morgan? Morgan boy, listen Imray—ten meters superconductors I get you. Beautiful."

The uproar dwindled to a mewling in Imray's speaker.

"You let us go down nice, Morgan, *vernt?*"

Silence. Imray clapped his fist to his chest and his head slumped.

"Is too much, son," he wheezed and retreated down the shaft.

"Counting to autopilot," said Sylla. Quent coded feverishly as deceleration grabbed them. On the screens the arid, undistinguished planet whirled closer.

The autopilot took hold unceremoniously and spiraled them in, shaken but right side up. When the roil cleared they looked across a moonlit field to a cluster of sheds around the antennae rig. There were no lights.

"They've all sloped off, sir," said Pomeroy. "Nothing we can do here till morning."

"Mr. Pomeroy, you speak the native language," said Quent. "I will meet you at the cargo lock. Have the sled ready."

"But sir—"

"Mr. Svensk, am I correct that we need no special masks or suiting on this planet?"

Svensk gave a sighing exhalation.

"No need," he croaked.

They followed Quent in silence while he broke out two field kits and two ballistic hand lasers. At the cargo lock he opened both ports and ordered Pomeroy into the sled.

"Lieutenant Sylla, you will take over the ship. One of you will be on the bridge at all times. If we're not back by sunrise, make what investigation you can without endangering the ship. If you can't help us without hazard to the ship, lift off at once and signal the facts to Farbase. Understood?"

Sylla's eyes were popping.

"Understood, Acting Captain!" He sketched a salute.

Svensk watched in silence, his bony head folded to his shoulders in the gravity.

Quent launched the sled out into the moonlight. The country below was flat scrubland gashed by a few dark arroyos, now dry. The "city" was a huddle of hivelike buildings with a central plaza. Quent hovered by a torch-lit structure, a shrine. Nothing moved.

"No damage visible so far. We'll go down and talk to the chief."

"Be careful, sir," Pomeroy warned uneasily.

In the plaza they pounded and shouted at the door of the largest hive-house. It was finally opened by a small squat Sopwithian entirely draped in a softly gleaming robe.

"Tell him we're friends. Where's the chief?"

The doorkeeper scuttled off on his knuckles, robes jingling. The inside of the adobe hive was a labyrinth of basket-work passages, every surface bossed with bits of metal and colored tassels. The native returned, beckoning, and they scrambled up a wicker corridor to a chamber where an even broader Sopwithian in a shinier robe sat impassive in a lanterned alcove. The ceiling was so low even Pomeroy had to squat.

He gurgled at the chief, who replied briefly, now and then flapping his long robed forelimbs with a sharp jangle. The raiders, Pomeroy reported, had burned several farms northeast of town and carried off the families. Herdsmen had spied them roasting and eating the captives beside their ship.

"All right," said Quent. He ducked his head to the chief and they scrambled out to their sled.

He took off in a howling rush northeast. Beyond the town the pasture scrub stretched barren to a line of mesa, all brightly lit by the big moon. Here and there were small beehive farms set in irrigated gardens.

"Where are those burned farms?" Quent peered. "Where's that ship?"

"Take care, sir," Pomeroy pleaded. "Them Drakes'll come on us like devils—"

Quent began to fly a low search pattern. As he circled a farm heads popped out.

"They're scared to death, sir. Think we're Drakes. Pitiful."

"Frightened." Quent frowned around the moonlit horizon. "Ah, what's that?"

Pomeroy writhed nervously.

"That's a burnt one, all right. No need to look farther."

Quent circled the blackened shell. Suddenly he skidded the sled into the farmyard and jumped out, kicking ashes. In a moment he was back and flung the sled airborne. He seized the speaker.

"Quent to *Rosenkrantz.* I've found that ship."

The speaker crackled. Quent fended off Pomeroy's arm, deftly appropriating the little man's laser.

"Do you read, *Rosenkrantz?*"

"The ship is where, Acting Captain?" asked Sylla's voice.

"About fifty kiloms northeast of field, in a canyon," Quent told him. "There is also a raiding party in sight, headed this way. They are armed. They have sighted me. Now hear this: You will signal Farbase at once and prepare to lift ship. I'm going after these raiders. Repeat, signal Farbase and secure ship. I am now being fired on. Out."

Knocking Pomeroy into the corner, Quent yanked out the speaker leads and slammed the sled at top speed back toward the field.

"Sir—Lieutenant Quent, sir, don't—"

Quent ignored him. Presently he cut power and glided around the end of the field at bush level. They whispered out to the ship, dodged behind a landleg, and came upon Svensk and Sylla in the open port.

Quent vaulted out, weapon in hand.

"Have you signaled as ordered, Mr. Sylla?"

The lutroid shrugged.

"But what was one to report, Acting Captain?"

"Precisely," snapped Quent and started for the bridge with both lasers in his belt. They followed.

Imray hulked in the command chair. He eyed Quent in silence, arms folded over his massive chest.

"Feeling better, sir?" Quent snarled. He wheeled and thrust his jaw into Sylla's muzzle. "I'll tell you why you failed to signal Farbase. And why you two were hanging out in the open lock when I ordered you to secure ship. Because you know damn well there are no raiders here."

He had his back against the screens now and a laser drawn.

"No ship! No Drakes. It's all one big farce and all of you are in it. You, you clown Pomeroy—you, *Captain* Imray! What are you trying to hide? Smuggling? Extortion? Or do I have to pound it out of you?"

He heard a rustle, saw Svensk's hand at his vest controls.

"No, no, Svenka," Imray growled. "Battles we don't need." He shook his head heavily. "We been *gesprüchtet*. I tell you boys, Drake business no good."

"Agh, your Drakes, the whole thing stank from the start. Let me tell you something, gentlemen." Quent shook the laser at Sylla, "You jeer about my training, but there's a thing you don't know about Academy life, my furry friend. In the years I've been a cadet I've been hazed and hoaxed and put on by experts. Experts!" His voice rose. "Caristo, what I've put up with. And you, gentlemen, are a clobbing bunch of amateurs. Tri-di gigs."

He snorted, glaring contemptuously at them. No one spoke.

"You didn't think I caught on when you handed me the ship? Cooking up some way to gash my record. Here in Sopwith—I was supposed to pass it up, wasn't I? Oh, yes. And you—" He stabbed the laser at Pomeroy. "You were going to bugger the log so you could show I refused to aid aliens against Humans, right? Then bring charges? But why? I'll be rotated out soon enough—why did you have to ruin me, too?" He scowled, "My father. Blackmail. You've got something going here. I'm going to take this ship apart, right here on the ground. It's on record that you're unfit for duty, Captain. You didn't think of that when you got so clobbing elaborate!"

They gaped at him. Sylla's pupils swelled, contracted.

"I tell you, smart boy," Imray grunted. He scratched his chest. "Son, you mistake—"

A shrill mew from Engines split the air. Imray jerked around. He yanked at his webs.

"I got you, boy."

"Hold it," shouted Quent. "Don't try—"

Sylla and Pomeroy dived for their consoles. Svensk was vanishing down the shaft.

"I said 'hold it.' " Quent grabbed the override lever. "You're staying right here."

"Sit, son, sit," Imray rumbled. "Is danger, I swear by the Path. If don't go up, lose ship."

"That's straight, sir. We'll be killed if you don't let us up."

Sylla was coding frantically, his crest fur ridged. The cargo lock changed.

"If this is another—" Quent rasped. He released the lever and began to web up one-handedly, laser ready.

Imray's hand smacked down and several invisible mountains fell on them as the *Rosenkrantz* careened off-planet.

"Back side moon, Syll," Imray wheezed.

"All right. What goes?"

"Drakes," said Pomeroy.

"You trying to go *on* with this?"

Svensk was scrambling out of the shaft, headed for his console. He brushed against Quent's laser. On the screens the moon was ballooning up. They rushed across the terminator into darkness.

"Drakes is real, son," Imray told him. "Catch ship on dirt—we finish. Is maybe judgment on us. Boys, they smell us?"

"I rather think they may not." Svensk's clack seemed to have been replaced by a cultivated Gal Fed accent. "Morgan sensed them just below the horizon and our emissions should have decayed by the time they get around."

Frowning, Quent watched Imray braking to stability over the dark craters of the moon whose lighted side had guided his ground search.

"They're coming around," said Pomeroy. "Listen."

A confused cawing filled the bridge. Quent made out the word *kavrot* in coarse Galactic. A kavrot was a repulsive small flying reptile that infested dirty freighters.

"Talking about us," Pomeroy grinned. His goatee no longer waggled. "Kavrots, that's us. Doesn't sound like they know we're here, though." He cut the voder.

"Braking emissions," said Svensk. "It appears they're going down."

Quent pushed up and moved in behind the lizard, laser in hand. Svensk did not look up,

"If this is another gig—" He studied the displays. Nobody paid attention.

"Captain?" Sylla's fist was up.

Imray grunted and the *Rosenkrantz* began to glide silently on her docking impellors down toward the sunlit peaks at the moon's eastern horizon. Sylla's paw beckoned Imray left, pushed right, dipping, banking as the mountains rose around them. His fist chopped down, Imray cut the power and they floated under a peak outlined in crystal fires. They were just shielded from the field on the planet below.

"Last pass coming up," said Svensk. "Splendid. They've blown up the field antennae. That eliminates our trace. Sitting down, now."

"From which one deduces?" asked Sylla.

"From which one deduces that they either do not know we are here or do not care or have some other plan. Possibly a trap?"

"First one best," said Imray.

"They're going to send out a party." Pomeroy patched in and they heard the harsh voices now augmented by clangings.

Quent stowed the lasers by his console. "Are they Human?"

Imray nodded gloomily. "Is a judgment, boys. They going to mess up."

"Eating the natives?"

"Maybe better so," Imray growled. "No—we don't know exact what they do. They come here once only, burn two farms, go quick. Why they come back?"

"You will recall my hypothesis at the time," said Svensk.

"Heheh!" Sylla made a frying sound.

"Yes. Crude but effective." Svensk nodded. "The adobe shells should make excellent hearths and the heat developed would be adequate to refine out most of the metals."

Pomeroy caught Quent's look.

"You saw the metal in their houses? All woven in, even on their clothes. Every house is loaded, accumulation of centuries. Haven't a cat's use for it—purely religious. They pick it up on ritual collecting trips. Spicules, nuggets, it's all scattered around in grains in alluvial rubble. You couldn't mine it. Point is, there's tantalite, osmiridium, maybe some palladium. Big price around here. When we found those farms burned, Svensk noticed they'd been at the ashes. Metal was gone. He figured they'd come back for more, burn the town out. And the damnfool Sops run *in* when they're scared." He grimaced, not comically.

"Why wouldn't they make the natives bring it to them?"

"Never get it. Sops are difficult. Much simpler this way. Also hairier, Drake style."

"If this is true, it's our clear duty to stop it," said Quent.

"*À la* tri-di?" Sylla laughed shortly.

"Son," said Imray, "Space Force is long way away. We here, only. What they got down there, Svenka?"

"Sector Ten was quite correct," said Svensk. "Unmistakable. They have succeeded in repairing that A.E.V. The shield was on for a minute just now."

Quent whistled.

"Do you mean they've got an Armed Escort Vessel? That shield will be a phased englobement—they can sense and fire right through it."

"Drake damn good spacer," Imray told him. "Always watch. We try sneak in, we get fireball in nose. We stuck, looks like."

"*Je me demande,*" said Sylla, "How do they propose to conflagrate the city?"

"A good point." Svensk stretched. "The farms, of course, were fired with portable flamers. This seems a slow method. Possibly irksome as well. I fancy they may intend to use the ship as a mobile torch."

"If they hover that low," Quent said thoughtfully, "they could only use the top half of their shield. An A.E. shield forms in two hemispheres. Same for the sensor field, too. They can't fully englobe much below a thousand meters."

"Ahe!" exclaimed Sylla. "One could thus attack them under the belly, *non?* But—we cannot get our ship from here to there undetected. And the sled, it functions only in the air . . . If only we possessed a space-to-air attack pod!"

"You do," said Quent.

They stared at him.

"The aft rocket turret. Look at your manual."

"Manual," said Imray blankly.

"In a few early peebees, the aft rocket cell is demountable and converts to a module capable of limited in-atmosphere function," Quent recited. "The empennage is sealed flush to the hull. You unbolt a stabilizer fin and swivel it around for the delta. I checked it over—it's there. Didn't you ever notice the shielding and lock on that thing?"

"Fantastic," said Svensk. "Now you mention—but how is it powered?"

"You couple on an emergency booster and impellor unit from the ship's drive after the thing is set up and the pilot is inside. Preferably a spare, if you have one—you'll recall that my inspections terminated at the engineroom bulkhead," he said bitterly.

"You sure manual say all that, son?" Imray demanded. "This thing work?"

"Certainly it says it," Quent snapped. "How do I know if it works?"

Sylla licked his chops.

"Thus, one could employ the thrust while concealed by this moon, and descend without power, avoiding detection because of the small size, and brake after one is below their horizon. One then approaches silently at ground level, on impellors—and when the enemy elevates himself, boom." He sprang to the shaft. "Let us view this marvel!"

In the hold Quent showed them the old demount levers, long since obstructed by mail-pod racks.

"One wonders how orthagonal a trajectory this thing would endure," said Svensk.

"Thermallium." Quent shrugged. "If the delta didn't come off."

"Somebody going to get killed bad." Imray peered suspiciously into the turret. "For engine I must talk Morgan. Pfoo!"

"You talked him into harassing me easily enough," said Quent.

"No, that natural," grunted Imray, hauling over to the speaker.

"Someday that spook will meet a Drake and find out who his enemies are," said Pomeroy's voice from the bridge. "They have a party in the city now. Looting. Gives us some time."

"*Allons,* the suits," called Sylla from the ladder.

In an hour's sweating hullwork they had uncoupled the turret and dogged it to the fin. The old sealant was vitrified but the assembly went in with surprising ease.

"That stuff will burn off," said Quent. "What a contraption!"

"The aerodynamics of a rock," Svensk murmured. "Podchutes, perhaps, could be attached to these holes? I suggest as many as possible."

"The engine arrives!" Sylla popped out of the turret as the massive shape of Imray appeared around the *Rosenkrantz's* stern, propelling a drive unit bundled in a working shield.

"Two gross nanocircuits must I get," he grumbled as they all wrestled the inertia of the big unit. They brought it into line with the turret lock. Imray glanced in.

"You check how it steers, Syll?"

"That rather mystifying secondary panel on the rocket console," said Svensk. "Perfectly obvious, once the power leads were exposed. I shall have no trouble."

His long figure contorted as he groped for the leads to his thermal vest.

"*Fou-t'en!*" Sylla slid between him and the turret. "Is this a swamp for overheated serpents to combat themselves in? Desist—you will be worse than the ants. It is I who go, of course."

"So." Imray turned on Quent, who was moving in on the other side. "You want go, too?"

Quent grabbed the lock. "I'm the obvious choice."

"Good," said Imray. "Look here."

He tapped Quent on the shoulder with one oversized gauntlet and suddenly straightened his arm. Quent sailed backward into Sylla and Svensk. When the three sorted themselves out they saw that Imray had clambered into the turret, which he filled compactly.

"Close up engines, boys," he blared jovially into their helmets. "Watch tight, is hot. Syll, you set me good course, *vernt?*"

The three lieutenants glumly coupled the drive unit, bolted and thermofoamed the extra chutes, and piled back up to the bridge.

"Foxed you, didn't he?" grinned Pomeroy. He sobered. "They're still tearing up the chief's house. We may have them figured all wrong."

The screens showed Imray's vehicle lurching past on a climbing course above the dark moonscape.

"Svensk, explain to him the navigation." Sylla crouched over his console. "He must modify to azimuth thirty heading two eighteen or he will burst into their faces at once. Now I devise the settings for his burndown."

"Sure, sure," said Imray's voice. They saw his rocket module yaw to a new course. "Svenka, what I do with pink button?"

"Captain," Svensk sighed, "if you will first observe the right-hand indicators—"

"At least the impellors work," said Quent.

Pomeroy fretted: "This is all guesswork."

Svensk was now relaying the burn configuration, which the ursinoid repeated docilely enough.

"At one-one-five on your dial, check visual to make sure you are well below their horizon. Do not use energy of any sort until you are two units past horizon. Captain, that is vital. After that you are on manual. Brake as hard as you can, observing the parameter limit display and—"

"After that I know," interrupted Imray. "You take care ship. Now I go, *vernt?*"

"You are now go," said Sylla, motioning to Pomeroy.

"Gespro-oo—" trumpeted the voder before Pomeroy cut it.

"What does that mean?" asked Quent.

"I've never known," said Svensk. "Some obscure mammalian ritual."

"Our captain was formerly a torch gunner," Sylla told Quent. "But perhaps you—"

"I've heard of them," said Quent. "But I thought—"

"That's right," said Pomeroy. "Ninety-nine percent casualties. Flying bombs, that's all. He can run that thing, once he gets down."

"He will be out of the moon's shadow and into their sensor field in fifteen seconds," said Svensk. "One trusts he remembers to deactivate *everything.*"

Pomeroy switched up. They heard Imray humming as he tore planetward at full burner. Sylla began chopping futile cut-power signals. The humming rumbled on. Pomeroy squeezed his eyes, Sylla chopped harder. Svensk sat motionless.

The rumble cut off.

"No more emissions. His course appears adequate," said Svensk. "I suggest we retire to a maximally shielded position and signal Farbase."

"Impellors, Mr. Morgan," said Quent.

When Sylla put up his fist Quent followed it until they reached a deep crater which would block the scatter of their star-to-star caller.

"If we're in luck," said Pomeroy, "Farbase can get their tea kettle here in three days, plus or minus a week. All they have is a ferry for picking up pieces. Bound to be pieces—of somebody." He sighed. "Let's get back where we can hear 'em."

They tiptoed back to the horizon. The Drakes below them gave no sign of detecting the approach of Imray's meteor. Neither did they reveal any intent to use their ship to fire on the town. As the moon on which the *Rosenkrantz* was riding sank below the horizon of the field they were obliged to leave it and maneuver into full sun-blast. Quent's eyes burned; he was becoming aware that he had scarcely slept for a week.

"If only we could give one little burn planetward," Sylla chafed. "How soon, my scientific serpent?"

"With their drive off—well—they would be able to read ship-sized burst from our present orbit for at least another hundred degrees of planetary rotation," said Svensk. "Don't you agree, Quent?"

Quent nodded wearily. "And that A.E.V. has about double our acceleration and six times our rocket range and can turn inside us. We wouldn't have a prayer." He had said it twice before.

The lutroid spat dryly and put his elbows on his console. Pomeroy sat, hands cupped over his earphones, motionless.

"Emission," said Svensk suddenly. "Imray is down and braking."

"That damn ship hasn't even budged," Pomeroy said. "I can still hear them yakking to the shore party. We're all wrong."

"Still braking. It just occurs to me, there was space for two more chutes."

"He requires rather two more gravity webs," said Sylla. "He is mad."

"Torchers," said Pomeroy.

"There is some distortion for which I cannot compensate," Svensk complained. "He is very close to their horizon—ah—I believe he has managed to deflect."

"That ship isn't going anywhere," Pomeroy fumed.

"If I could suppress this wretched bias," said Svensk. "He is on impellors now, I think. But moving very erratically."

"He finds perhaps a ravine." Sylla was kneading his console.

"Toward the field again," said Svensk. "Much too near. One fears that he is omitting to wait for them to lift."

"The old maniac will sail right onto their screens," Pomeroy groaned.

"While we sit here," Sylla muttered.

"If he's in that canyon in back of the field," said Quent, "he might sneak under their shield. Provided they weren't looking. It's a fairly broad target. Can he—"

Sylla's head had snapped around.

"He understands to shoot," he told Quent.

"Can I rely on that, Mr. Sylla?" Quent met the lutroid's yellow stare.

"Accelerating on the same line," Svensk announced. "Dismal."

"Got it!" Pomeroy shouted. "Secure locks—but there isn't time. Up, you bastards! Up!"

"How long before he cuts their line of sight, Mr. Svensk?"

"This detestable—at ground level, maximum two minutes. Much too close. They're bound to spot him."

"Over to me on manual, Mr. Sylla," said Quent. "If you can get to the wrecking lasers it'll help the display. Ready, Mr. Morgan?"

The lutroid shot over him and down the shaft.

"Stay braced and warn Appleby!" Quent yelled after him, coding for drive. "If Imray can hit what he shoots at, this'll distract them. If not—"

He rammed home the lever and they pitched in their webs. As the screens faded out the planet bloomed up and swirled crazily.

"We're in their sensors now," gasped Svensk. "I believe—"

"They're lifting." Pomeroy was plastered on his board. "They see us."

Quent bent the *Rosenkrantz* into an atmosphere-grazing turn. Pomeroy was struggling to move a switch. The bridge filled with Drake voices, reverberating lashback. A siren honked.

The voder cut off. For a flash Quent thought his eardrums had gone but as acceleration topped out he heard the others fill their lungs.

"Their shield does appear to have collapsed," said Svensk. "I can't be positive in this—"

"He got 'em" Pomeroy yelled. "Power's gone! Wait—they're coming back on emergency. Listen to 'em cry!"

Noises blared from the Drake ship.

"Where's Imray?" Quent threw in the retros and they pitched again. Sylla came scrambling out of the shaft, hanging onto Imray's chair.

"Where is he?"

"I can't at the moment," Svensk protested. "The resultants—"

"Listen." Pomeroy tuned the uproar to ululating wails. "The Denebian national anthem." He flopped back in his seat, grinning. "Might as well go get him—that ship's dead in the dirt. He cracked one up their landleg socket while they were gawking at us. Must have been bloody under 'em!"

Quent jolted to a thump on his back. Sylla climbed down, grinning. Svensk arched his neck—his bony beak was not adapted for expression.

"Is he all right?" called Appleby's voice. "I fixed some hot jam truffles."

"So that was the anomaly," said Svensk. "Incredible. The nutritive drive of the Human female."

"Bloody good, too," said Pomeroy. He jerked to his board. "Holy Space—"

"What is it?"

"The *Jasper* just hailed us," he told them. "She's coming by. Five minutes earlier and we'd all been up the pipe."

He sagged again and reached for his bulb.

"By the Path!" Imray howled on the voder. "You pick me up or I *sprücher* you too."

Quent was clumsy with exhaustion by the time they got the rocket module stowed and the hot drive unit back to Morgan. He gave a perfunctory glance at the wrecker ports and then followed the others to the bridge, where Pomeroy was watching the grounded Drakes.

"I take over, son." Imray sprawled in his command chair, rolling his hide luxuriously. "Watch tight. Bad mess they get loose before Farbase come." He chomped a jam tart.

"Are you all ready for the bad news?" Pomeroy wheeled around to face them. "Remember that *Gal News* man we ducked at Farbase? He's on the shuttle. Coming here."

Imray choked.

"Wants to interview you." Pomeroy pointed at Quent. "And Appleby, too."

Quent shut his eyes. "He can—why won't they let me alone?" Absently he fingered the laser by his console.

"Admiral Quent's son in battle with Drake pirates," Pomeroy grinned sourly, "while Admiral Coatesworth's fiancée cheers? His board's all lit up."

"This rather cooks it," said Svensk. Sylla was drumming his claws. They all looked at Quent.

"What you tell him, son?"

"Tell 'em," Quent muttered exhaustedly. "Why, I'll tell 'em the ship stinks and your computer is full of mush—and the engineroom is a fugnest—" his voice rose—"infested by a spook who has you so terrorized you have to bribe him to move the ship. And my fellow officers are a set of primitive jokers captained by a maniac who has to resort to physical force—and the only Humans who can stand the ship are an unshaven alcoholic and a madwoman who buggers the sensors with fudge machines and underwear, and—Heysu Caristo!" He rubbed his neck. "My first ship. Look, I'm going to sack out, alright?" He pushed off for the ladder.

"You tell them that?" Imray demanded, beaming. "Flying fugnest?"

"Hell no, why should I? It's not true."

He pulled to the shaft and rammed into Imray's hard paw.

"Son, you got to."

"*Huh?*"

"Tell them can't stand. Want new job. Must!" Imray was shaking them both for emphasis.

"Wait—one—minute." Quent disengaged himself. "That's exactly what you were putting me on to think, wasn't it? But why?" He frowned around at them. "Why? I mean, hell, I'm *for* integration."

"Precisely the problem," said Svensk.

Imray whacked his thigh exasperatedly.

"Who you think build this boat?"

"Well, it's a Human design—"

"Human fix up. Is build by Svenka people, original. Was part their navy. Space Force say, indefinite loan. Little boats, you never hear. Space Force come along, make treaty. Suck up little boats. Even ants they got some type space boat, *vernt*, Svenka?"

"More of a pod, I believe." Svensk crossed his long legs.

"Something, anyway. Son, you think like your father say, all en-aitch people want integrate with Space Force?"

"Well, uh," said Quent. "The Gal Equality party."

"Sure, sure." Imray nodded. "Some en-aitch people want be officer big starship, is fact. Also fact, en-aitch people want have say in Gal Council. But is different here."

He leaned back, folded his arms.

"Here is original en-aitch space force, us little boats. We been on these boats long time. Long, long time. We been patrol since was no sector, eh Syll? When Humans come with us, is only individual Humans. One here, one there. Pom know. But we not integrated with you. *You* is integrated with *us*."

"Bravo!" cried Sylla.

"Hear, hear," said Svensk gravely.

"But, what—" said Quent.

"The captain means," Pomeroy told him, "that *he*'s not about to get integrated with the Space Force. None of us are. We do our job. They can stow their sociological programs. Their directives. Channels. Personnel fitness profiles. Rotation and uptraining tours. Pisgah! If this integration trail business goes green, we've had it. And—" he poked his finger at Quent—"you are a prime test case, Lieutenant."

"Even Morgan they try steal," Imray rumbled angrily.

Quent opened his mouth, closed it.

"We were so confident," said Svensk. "It did seem ideal, when you turned out to be Admiral Quent's son. We felt it would be simple to impress you as being, as it were, quite unintegrable." He sighed. "I may say that your determined optimism has been a positive nightmare."

"Let me get this straight." Quent scowled. "You wanted me to yell so hard for reassignment that the program would be shelved?"

"Correct." Sylla slapped his console. The others nodded.

"What about this flimflam here in Sopwith?"

"Too fancy," grunted Imray.

"We were getting desperate," said Pomeroy. "You just wouldn't discourage. So we thought maybe we could work it the other way, build up a case that would convince the Gal Eq crowd that Humans weren't ready to, ah—" He looked away. "Well, you figured it."

"I knew you were out to clobber me," Quent said grimly. "Only I thought it was my father."

"It was in no way personal, Quent," Sylla assured him heartily. "Believe me, we would do the same for anyone, *non?*"

"But this is insane!" Quent protested. "How can you? I mean, do you realize my father got me assigned here? He's sure I'll come around to his way of thinking and furnish him with political ammunition to use against integration."

"That rather optimises things, doesn't it?" Svensk rattled his neckplates. "Increased familial solidarity is a plus value for primates."

Quent snorted.

"What were you supposed to be, Mr. Spock? I knew damn well you're a Gal Tech graduate. You should have taken the course on oedipal conflicts. Also the one on ethics," he added acidly. "Some primates set quite a value on truth."

"But you've got to help us, Lieutenant," Pomeroy said urgently.

Quent was preoccupied. "How many languages *do* you speak, anyway? There was a Pomeroy who wrote some text—"

"Lieutenant! Look, we'll all help fix up a tale of woe you can give them—"

"Are you serious?" He looked at them, appalled. "You expect me to falsify my official duty report? Lie about you and the ship?"

"What one little lie?" Imray's voice sank to the crooning tone he used on Morgan. "Son, you good spacer. Save ship, *vernt?* You say this integration nonsense okay, we finish. You not let Space Force mess up old *Rosy*, son."

"But goddammit," Quent exploded. "It's not just one lie. It'd go on and on—investigations, appeals—my father smirking around with the Humanity Firsters trumpeting every word I said on one side—and the Gal Eq people reaming me from the other. I'd never be free of it. Never. How could I function as a space officer?" He rubbed his head wearily,

"I'm sorry. I'll say as little as possible, believe me. But I will not put on any act." He turned to go below.

"So stubborn, the Humans," Sylla snarled. Quent continued down the ladder.

"Wait, Quent," said Svensk. "This publicity you dread can't be escaped, you know. Suppose you say nothing. The facts speak for themselves. Gal Eq will be delirious: *Arch-racist's Son Leads Non-Human Attack on Human Pirates*, for starters. Prolonged cheers. All-Gal network showing the hero and his en-aitch pals. I daresay they'll nominate you for the next Amity award. Really, you're just as well off doing it our way."

Quent stared at him in horror.

"Oh, no. No." He began to pound his forehead on the ladder. "It's not fair." His voice cracked. "I thought when I got to space they'd forget me. It's been bad enough being Rathborne Quent Junior, but this—spending the rest of my life as a—a ventriloquist's dummy for Integration politics. Everywhere I go! Every post, my whole career. How can I be a spacer?"

Imray was shaking his head. "You natural victim social situation, son, looks like. Too bad." He exhaled noisily, and licked a piece of jam off his fist. "So, is settled. You going help us, *vernt?*"

Quent lifted his head. His jaw set.

"No, I told you. That's out," he said bleakly. "I didn't come into the service to play games." His voice trailed off. "Call me next watch, right? We're all pretty weary."

"Sure, sure," said Imray. "Syll, Svenka, you boys go. We got time think something."

"Forget it," Quent told him. "There's no way out of this one. Caristo!" He sighed, hauling down the shaft. "I wish I could just disappear."

He stopped dead and looked up thoughtfully.

"Ah-ah," he said.

He climbed back up and retrieved the lasers. The last thing he remembered was leaning back on his hammock fully dressed with a laser in his hand.

Gal newsmen yelled at him, crowds jostled him. The bridge of the *Adastra* swarmed with kavrots. Quent came groggily awake, sure that he had heard a lock open. But the ship seemed to be normal. He sank back and dreamed that he was wearing a clangorous glass uniform. When the cocoon grabbed at him Quent struggled to consciousness. The *Rosenkrantz* was going into full star drive.

He plunged into the shaft and found himself nose to nose with an unknown girl.

"Gah!"

"Hello, Lieutenant," she said. "Want some breakfast?"

She was a dark girl in silver coveralls.

"Who—who're you?"

"I'm Campbell, your new log off." She smiled.

"Drakes." He hurled himself headlong for the bridge. "Where are they? What's happened?"

"Hi, there," said Pomeroy. The others looked up from their consoles. They seemed to be drinking coffee.

"Where are we headed? Where did she come from?"

"Sit, son," said Imray genially.

The dark girl bobbed up to place a bulb of coffee on his console.

"Is she a Drake?"

"Good heavens, no," she laughed. Quent blinked; the conformation under the coverall was interesting.

"I'm a duck." She vanished.

Dazedly Quent gulped some coffee.

"How long was I asleep? Farbase—they've come and gone, right?"

"Not likely." Pomeroy snorted. "They won't get to Sopwith for thirty hours yet."

"But who's watching the Drakes?"

"The *Rosenkrantz,* who else?" said Sylla, deadpan.

"What? Captain Imray, what is going on?"

Imray waved his paw.

"Problem finish, son." He belched comfortably. "We fix, eh, boys?"

"Oh, God." Quent squinted at them. He gulped some more coffee. "Mr. Pomeroy, you will explain yourself."

"Well, you can forget about that newsman and all that," Pomeroy told him. "When he gets to Sopwith he'll find the *Rosenkrantz* and he'll find Miss Appleby all right—but he won't find you. Nobody'll find you."

"Why not?" Quent glared around nervously.

"Because you are no longer on the *Rosenkrantz,"* said Svensk.

"Brilliant, really, your notion of disappearing. Since we could scarcely remove you from the *Rosenkrantz,* we simply removed the *Rosenkrantz* from you." He stretched pleasurably. "Solves everything."

"What have you done now?"

"Observe!" Sylla pointed to the sealed log certificates.

Quent pulled himself over, eyes wary.

"P-B 640T J-B," he read. "But's that's wrong. That's not—"

"Peebee *Jasper Banks,* that is." Pomeroy chuckled. "We're the *Jasper Banks* now, see?"

"What?" Quent pawed at the case. "Those are official seals. You—"

"Not to worry, it's just temporary. *Jasper* owed us a couple of favors. They were glad to oblige. Fact, they wanted to head back to Central anyway. So we just traded registry and log officers and gave them our mail. They took over the Drakes, see?"

"But that's—"

"Beautiful." Pomeroy nodded. "*Gal News* can pull the *Jasper* apart, they never heard of you. No one ever actually saw you on *Rosy,* did they? He'll figure it's some garble. Has to—there's Appleby, all as advertised. And the Drakes. He'll have to be satisfied with that."

Quent took some more coffee. He felt like a man trying to shake off a bad dream.

"And the beauty part," Pomeroy went on, "*Jasper's* an all-Human peebee. That'll really befuddle them."

"No integration aspect left," said Svensk. "Gal Eq will be dashed."

"It can't work. It's—what about Appleby?"

"I hope this one so good cook," muttered Imray.

"Appleby's fine—she never heard of you," Pomeroy assured him. "Morgan let her have these crystals she's always wanted, see?"

"Uh. But—they're going back to Central as us? What happens there? Personnel. My father," Quent yelped.

"Personnel," Pomeroy scoffed. "They're dingled up half the time. They won't get their circuits flushed till we've swapped back."

"But my father—when do we trade back?"

"When we intersect, *bien sure,*" said Sylla.

"When's that? Hold it. Wasn't the *Jasper* headed on some job way out?"

"That's right," said Pomeroy. "The wild sector. Thirteen-zed, they call it. Wasn't due to start patrol there for a while but they got this emergency call. So they sent out the *Jasper*. That's us, now."

"Quite remote and unexplored, really," said Svensk, stretching. "Challenging."

"New patrol good job," Imray grunted. "You want be spacer, son, *vernt*? Nobody mess your career out there." He scratched his broad chest contentedly. "Integration program? Pfoo! Never catch."

"You mean we start patrolling out there? And they take our old one. When do we trade back with *Jasper*?"

"Assuming our circuit is, say, twice the length of theirs," Svensk ruminated, "and assuming they keep near schedule, the perinode should precess around—"

"Spare me."

Quent's big jaw began to grind and he breathed forcefully. The reaction pushed him slowly out of his console. He hooked one leg around his seat back and hung over them scowling.

"My career," he said tensely. "Your unspeakable solicitude . . . Sixty days on my first duty, I find myself involved in an actionable conspiracy. First officer of a vessel under fraudulent certification, on an illegal course in defiance of orders—without one clobbing prayer of ever getting back into anything resembling legal status. My career. Who'd believe me? What happens when—gentlemen, did it never cross your conniving minds that this is a general courts offense?" He reached out and laid his hand on the emergency starcall cradled between him and Imray. "My only sane course is to bring this to a halt right now—regardless."

He yanked the caller from its cradle.

They gaped at him. Sylla's ears folded back.

"Lieutenant, no," said Pomeroy.

Quent fingered the starcall. His solemn face was corded.

"What's the nature of this emergency, Mr. Pomeroy?"

"Some en-aitch trouble." Pomeroy spread his hands. "Signal split before they got much. They gave the *Jasper* some stuff—"

"Three argon cylinders, one case of mudbinds, one pan-venom kit," said Miss Campbell from the shaftway. "And an incubator."

She placed a breakfast server on Quent's console and departed.

"You figure it, sir," Pomeroy chuckled hopefully.

Quent's face did not soften. He tapped a square nail on the starcall, slowly, desperately. Nobody moved. Sylla's leg muscles bunched; Quent's free hand drifted to the laser. There was a faint slithering sound. Quent's jaw jerked around to Svensk.

The big saurian's fingers came away from his vest and he stretched ostentatiously, jogging the computer.

> Roll on, thou deep and dark blue ocean, roll!
> Ten thousand fleets—

Quent slapped it silent with the laser. He lifted the starcall.

"No, son, no," Imray protested.

Quent drew a deep breath. For a moment the *Jasper Banks* née *Rosenkrantz* fled on through the abyss in humming silence. The aroma of bacon drifted through her bridge. Quent's strained face began to work convulsively.

"*Kavrots,*" he muttered.

He let out an inarticulate howl.

Sylla's reflexes carried him into the bow grips and Pomeroy dived under his board. They goggled at Quent. He was making a wild whooping noise which they could not at first identify.

Then Pomeroy crawled out, grinning, and Imray's shoulders started to quake.

Quent roared on. His face was astounded, like a man who hasn't heard himself guffawing wholeheartedly in years. Invisible around him, ghosts of the *Adastra, Crux, Sirian* shriveled and whirled away.

"All right," he gasped, sobering. He pushed the starcall and the laser back in place and reached for his breakfast.

"Kavrots. So be it. Who's on watch in this fugnest?"

One night in 1967 or 1968, during the second season of *Star Trek*, Alice Sheldon happened to see an episode. She quickly became a fan and supporter of the show, writing letters to NBC and the sponsors thanking them for its existence (and later, taking them to task for its cancellation). As Tiptree, she wrote to Gene Roddenberry and Leonard Nimoy (praising Nimoy for his depiction of an alien, "the first *real* alien ever").

Tiptree even decided to try and write for *Star Trek*, and sent a story entitled "The Nowhere People" to Roddenberry on August 28, 1968. It was returned unread on September 20, with a letter stating that the studio could not "read or consider unsolicited literary material." Tiptree wrote to Fred Pohl, Harry Harrison, and David Gerrold asking for advice on getting the story on the show.

She eventually gave up on the idea of writing for the series, and it was canceled, anyway. "The Nowhere People," after a couple title changes, was published as "Meet Me at Infinity" in the *Star Trek* fanzine *Eridani Triad* in 1972.

Ideas for several other *Star Trek* stories went undeveloped, but while still trying to sell "The Nowhere People" to the show she created her own starship and crew, and plotted out four storylines for them ("two adventures, two deeper types"). Before writing them, though, she went back to do a story introducing the crew. This was submitted to John W. Campbell, Jr., at *Analog* on November 18, 1968, as "Happiness Is a Warm Spaceship" (the alternate titles " 'Two—Four—Six—Eight! Don't Want To—' " and "The Shakedown Artists" were offered). Campbell rejected it as "too discursive," and on December 9, 1968, it went to Fred Pohl, who was then editing *Galaxy* and *If*. Pohl returned it as too long, but he said he'd look at a revised version, which went to him on February 8, 1969, "totally rewritten and shorter." Pohl accepted it, complaining that "I like it, but . . . it still dawdles," and said he would only be interested in further stories in the series "if they are tighter and preferably shorter."

"Happiness Is a Warm Spaceship" was published in the November 1969 issue of *If*, by then under new ownership and with a new editor, Ejler Jakobsson. Tiptree wrote to Jakobsson on June 16, 1969, asking if he would be interested in the series; there is no response in her files. No other complete stories were written, although two versions of a book proposal and some brief fragments were. One plot shows up as both a *Rosenkrantz* story and a *Star Trek* one.

This story was included in the original manuscript for the first Tiptree collection, *Ten Thousand Light-Years from Home* (Ace 1973), and indeed her proposed title for the collection was *Happiness Is a Warm Spaceship*, but she eventually decided to remove that story from the book.

(Alternate titles for the first collection included:

News from a Warm Spaceship
Making It Through the Night in a Warm Spaceship

Tiptree Is a Warm Spaceship
Fragments of Angry Candy
If We Go to the Stars This Morning Where Will We Sleep Tonight?
I See People in Spacesuits They Are Making Love
Up the Main Sequence
Starproof Earwarmers
Some People Like These Stories
Comfort Me with Comets)

Alli grew disenchanted with this story. She mentions it disparagingly several times in the nonfiction portion of this collection and wrote this to me in August 1972: "Someday I might use part for a series—it started as a spoof on *Star Trek*, but then I thought of a couple good weird episodes—but it has to be reworked out of that 'Dear Diary' style. Anyway, the story as is—isn't."

The two versions of the book proposal, written in 1969, had slightly different lists of projected stories. I have blended the two manuscripts into one document:

This series, tales of the adventures of the integrated crew of the Patrol Boat *Ethel P. Rosenkrantz*, was intended in part as a loving spoof of *Star Trek* and would appeal to the same or more mature audiences. The heroes operate an old space tub some centuries after the *Enterprise*, giving scope for some 1969-type problems. ("Space: a finished frontier. These are the voyages of the *Ethel P. Rosenkrantz*, her mission to go where every Tom, Dick, and Bemmy has been before, and clean up the mess!"—as one of them says.) But of course there is some wildness left.

The adventures are of two types. Some are stories about the whole crew; then there are stories from the standpoint of various officers. The introduction and the last are from the Human Quent's point of view.

1. The first story of the series has appeared in the November 1969 *If* under the above title. Introduces the "hero," a shiny new lieutenant burdened by a big brass pa. He is and isn't a dope; he's a good officer who is "liberal" despite Pa's violent anti-alien politics. Assigned to an alien-run patrol boat, he is astounded to discover

the crew doesn't want to be integrated. He gets involved with them and the story leaves him headed for extended duty with them, happily oblivious to hints that the lower echelons of space duty are sloppily run and full of obscure hanky-panky. (The cop on the beat.)

2. They are called in to police a planetary mob scene caused by a sensory-religious revival movement analogous to Woodstock or Altamont. They have a combat crew of mercenaries, and the story revolves around their efforts both to control the mob and control their own blindly aggressive ant mercenaries.

3. They are provided with a batch of super-scientific remote-control gadgets for exploring new planets, which do *not* work—the turtle-like robot is taken as a love object by hostile aliens, the implanted voice transponders fail to turn off, etc. etc. General comedy with the point that there are still situations in which a living body and brain are the best miracle gimmick.

4. A sex-crisis story. Patrol boats have one female supply officer, on short assignment, often Human but sometimes alien. The Human hero, Quent, assumes that the Human girl is his prerogative, discovers that patrol boat custom dictates that she gives to none or to all who want her. The other officer interested is a furry lutroid, Lieutenant Sylla. There is interaction with an odd sex setup on a humanoid alien planet. Natives recognize two sexes, men and mothers, mothers the bosses. (Also too nonsexes, very young and very old.) Sex impersonation is a crime. The supply officer is arrested for impersonating a mother. Quent, temporarily caring for some kids in transit, is arrested for impersonating a man.

5. The bearlike captain, Imray, is aging and vitiated by space life and feeling impinged on by humans. And his sexual urges are tied to planetary rhythms, so he is a shadow-male. The *Rosenkrantz* is rebuffed in attempting to aid a luscious ursinoid princess who has been converted to mysticism and is a hermit with a Human guru. Captain Imray finally goes berserk, defies orders, and goes down single-handed to rescue her, in the process renewing his youth and having an A-1 time.

6. The lizardlike science officer, Svensk, has a coldly superior facade but complicated inferiority feelings about being a nonho-

motherm. He should have a slightly eerie plot where he makes it in some shuddery situation. There may also be a subplot for him where he lays an egg.

7. The furry, sexy otter, Lieutenant Sylla, is a fairly simple soul and should have an action plot, but I haven't got quite the right thing for him yet. He loves water and has a poetic streak, maybe also a mean carnivorous streak, something really feral . . . ?

8. The only other Human in the crew is a runty old communications officer, Ensign Pomeroy, once probably a professional linguist, who has dropped out to the foreign legion life and a plentiful supply of Leo Lightning. He seems like a great guy, but he has a furtive side which never quite comes clean, and he does some smuggling. For a while this seems like good clean fun, but the *Rosenkrantz* gradually gets infected with too much corruption. I haven't got the plot clear, but the idea is that somewhere along the borderline between harmless illegality and real crime one can slip too far and make a real mistake. The crunch probably comes when the crew finds that a bunch of baddies known as Drakes actually has a hold over them. A morality tale; Pomeroy or Imray may get killed.

9. The finale story, told from Quent's view. Again not yet plotted, but the idea is a big jolt of strangeness. After we've been all through a nice cozy series, and the *Rosenkrantz* is like Quent's home, something happens which casts a doubt on the fabric of this reality. In some turbulent way Quent's fellow officers suddenly come to seem, for a moment, profoundly alien. He wonders if perhaps they are not quite other than they have appeared to him. The universe is bigger and stranger than he had supposed. The moment passes, and they set off once more with everything quite normal, but with a small cold place in Quent's liver which will never go away. Coziness and familiarity are only glosses on the reality of an Otherness which is itself, and maybe what is most familiar is most alien of all . . . i.e., not Svensk's scaly blue face, but Pomeroy's goatee, or Quent himself.

As can be seen, these stories are not conventional hardware-adventure tales, but chew around on the kind of problems we all deal with in everyday life. And with some (hopefully) humor. Hence the title. But they are not intended as rosy-goo optimism. The author's view is that the warmth of the spaceship is real, but it is an isolated and precarious warmth in a large, chilly, dark, and dubiously benevolent universe.

It might be of peripheral interest that part of the writer's youth was spent as a member of a small expeditionary group in foreign parts, where the main problems always turned out to be, not the hostile environment, but the in-tent relationships.

A final note: These stories will get written, but *slowly*. I am a spare-time writer, a heavy reviser, and type agonizingly slow.

Please Don't Play with the Time Machine, or, I Screwed 15,924 Back Issues of *Astounding* for the F.B.I.

Four thousand Ångström glimmered on the pile at the left side of the table. In the pile were scripts, scrolls, shards, spools, cassettes, a large leaf. On the right side of the table was a funnel of luminous wire. Beside it was a spider holding two pieces of pumice. The owner of the table sat before a scanning lens and read:

—relief quirked Captain Herring's thin, bronzed lips as the quantameter lights steadied on the control spectra. The blurry outlines of the cabin came back to sharpness. Safe in Ur-time! Captain Herring straightened his thin, bronzed shoulders. There was a faint *plop!* as they passed Planck's constant. *Ocarina III*, intergalactic space tramp, had made it again.

Smiling under his thin, bronzed mustache Herring reached down for the lever to release himself from the antigrav cabinet. Nothing now to do for weeks but paste up his collection of recipes, he thought, his thin, bronzed ears twitching in anticipation. Then he froze. The antigrav lever felt odd. It felt like an ankle.

Space-torque, he thought. Better take it easy, old boy. He wobbled the lever. It still felt like an ankle. He fumbled for the fail-safe. That felt like an ankle too. Gathering them in his thin, bronzed fingers Herring reached down. Another ankle! He yanked it up.

"By Arcturus, it *is* an ankle!" Herring grated. "And that dainty chain looks like an unknown high-tensile molybdenum alloy!" Gingerly, Herring bent to read the inscription on the locket attached to the slim, warm joint. He had just made out the words, *if you can read this you're too damn*—when something jabbed him in the inguineum.

Instantly the ice-hot reflexes which had carried him through many a rhubarb with the radioactive Khurds of Wey sent him five meters into the control panel.

"Come out of that, you!" he rasped, gammator at the ready.

Nothing happened. He tried it again in Lower Martian and was working up to Glottic when the owner of the ankles hoisted itself over the rim of the grav cabinet.

"*Do* stop spluttering," it said. "I thought you'd *never* get up. What kind of heap is this anyway? Ten gees to get off a filling platform and you sitting on my eyelashes." Gurgling irritably it began to preen itself.

Captain Herring looked the thing up and—more or less—down, in Ur-time it was difficult to tell. He who had faced a thousand alien forms of life from the musical brain slugs of Ech to the flaming crystal cannibals of Utr Nadr was unnerved. This is the worst yet, he thought, choking.

"By the laws of intergalactic navigation," he ground out, narrowing his thin, bronzed eyelids, "you—whatever you call yourself—are a stowaway. You are, I trust, familiar with the regulations governing the disposal of stowaways?"

"Ah, stow it, Buttons," said the Thing composedly, picking at its toenails. Herring shuddered; they were an icky pink. "The way you flow this pig you need some ballast. What do you use for fuel, Saniflush?"

"Kerosene," Herring blurted. "I mean, Hexadinitrobetameta-dioyla—"

"Hiccups, eh?" said the Thing. It uncoiled itself from the cabinet. "We'll soon fix that."

"Now look here!" Herring barked. "Ignorance is no excuse. You've got to go. Courtesy of the spaceways and all that, but there's only room for one on the *Ocarina*. When I count to three I'll pull the trigger. One!"

The Thing paused in its undulant advance.

"What are you going to pull?" it asked interestedly.

"The trigger," Herring grunted, his thin, bronzed lips set in a lethal line. "Two!"

"What trigger?"

"If you have a god, pray! Thurr—"

"You do realize that's a box of penuche you're holding," the Thing murmured.

"*eee!*" shouted Herring and pulled. Then he glared incredulously at his hand. It was indeed the box of penuche he had tucked behind the control panel to munch in the long space night. He dashed it furiously at the floor which happened just then to be the ceiling. Mass being constant in free fall, the box sailed into the fuse clips with a solid bonk and the lights went out.

"Oh dear," cooed the Thing in the darkness, "it looked so good. Dense, though. Who made 'em?"

"I did," muttered Herring, groping for the fuses. In the darkness he could hear the Thing groping too.

"Oh, here's one!" it trilled and began chewing loud and wet. "What's your name, Tiger? You make smashing penuche."

Suddenly it was snuffling on his neck. And elsewhere.

"Red," he gulped, wildly clutching at his thin, bronzed flight shorts.

"Reddy, baby," the Thing was mumbling sloopily through the penuche, "don't you really know what I am, Reddy dear?"

"Wha—what are you?" Herring squealed, his thin, bronzed toes curling and uncurling as he struggled in the dark. To die like this, he thought, trapped in my own control room by a Thing from the abyss—

"Why, Reddy-Beddy," it tongued in his ear. "You poor deprived engineer! I'm a w——n!!!"

"Great Lorenz!" Captain Herring gibbered faintly. "The old t-tales are t-t-true!" Then he passed out.

On *Ocarina*'s control panel the quantameter was clicking. Googol minus eight, googol minus seven . . . googol minus six . . .

Under the violet lamp the reader lifted one mandible and let it sag. He laid down the page, picked up one of the pumice stones, and bit into it. Savoring the rich cadmium creme filling, he selected a small one-time tape and reversed its polarity to stick it on the manuscript.

"Dear Being: Thank you for permitting us to inhale your emanations. We regret they are non-isomorphic with our needs. Due to the large input received it is not possible for us to comment live but we suggest that further study of the style and content of our send, say for about three cycles, would help you. We enclose a convenient species-null subscription form."

He placed the manuscript in the illuminated funnel where it dematerialized while he plucked out the leaf at random from his pile and centered it under his lens. At that moment his lamp winked three times. He laid down his work and stretched hugely. Then, unfolding three meters of thorax from his Formi-balm Komfort Kase, the editor twitched out his light and flew away.

Although Alli generally claimed to have done little writing before the first Tiptree stories in 1967, what she meant was that before Tiptree she hadn't prepared much for publication. She wrote throughout her life: stories, essays, poems, novels. Most of these were unfinished or in early drafts.

This story dates from the 1950s. Two early fragments survive. The earliest is the rejection letter at the end, a much longer piece than the one used in the final story. The second is the complete story except for the rejection letter. This is probably from the 1960s, because it is typed in the blue typewriter ribbon that Tiptree bedeviled editors with—but it's single-spaced, so not prepared for submission. Neither fragment is titled, but the next one, under Tiptree's name, is: "Please Do Not Play with the Time Machine or, I Screwed 15,924 Back Issues of *Analog* for the F.B.I." This has a revised version of the story from the single-spaced manuscript, and the new rejection letter (and opening paragraph).

She first sent the story out to Fred Pohl on June 5, 1968. It didn't sell until May 1971, to an amateur publisher for an anthology project that never got off the ground. In a letter to me in April 1971, Tiptree said of this story:

> Written while experimenting with a mixture touted as Wild Mares' Milk which is basically yoghurt & vodka. Subtitle explanatory . . . also always wanted to type Å. Privately circulated to people like Harry H/arrison/ and Fred Pohl for chuckles, then sent in tentative seriousness to Harlan E/llison/. . . . His comment: "A sad little old cliche gag." He was right . . . but the stupid thing still makes me chuckle.
>
> PS Not to worry about the Thing having 3 ankles.

Somewhere along the way the "Do Not" in the title contracted to "Don't," and of the subtitle, Tiptree said to me in a letter on May 20, 1971: ". . . maybe it should be changed from *Analog* to *Astounding*, which actually is truer anyway.

That was, it so happens, the first SF thing I ever wrote, in a letter to a friend in Vietnam in . . . 1958, for crissake." (The letter in the original manuscript is dated 1955, so that may be the story's true date of composition.)

Here is the original rejection letter:

ASTRONAUGHT
"For the Truly Modern Man"

3 May 1955

Dear Sir or Madam, as the case may be:

Your manuscript entitled "Herring and the Thin Bronzed Line" was received and reviewed by the staff of our Sex in Space Department with ennui. We regret to inform you that it has been rejected as amateurish.

Initially, we wish to point out that our reader audience is sufficiently familiar with space travel to recognize instantly the error in describing the sound in passing Planck's Constant as a "faint plop." It is more accurately a distinct "ftoop," similar to the withdrawing of a cork from a bottle, a sound with which, in fact, it has frequently been confused as the seasoned astronaut normally accompanies the passing of P/C with some small libation especially when traveling alone. Such descriptive errors, if printed, would undoubtedly cause *Astronaught*'s reputation for accuracy of onomatopoeia to suffer. This is a reputation which we treasure above all things except, of course, profits.

A more important consideration in rejecting this manuscript is the fact, which, we are sure, will, when called to your attention, be immediately apparent to you, that, given the degravitized condition of the average space tramp, and given the constancy of mass in free fall, the Act to Which Your Story Was Leading Up (To) is utterly impossible of accomplishment without special equipment and would therefore tax the credulity of our esteemed readers. This has been carefully tested by a volunteer from our staff with the full cooperation of a volunteer from *Mademoiselle* in a specially constructed chamber simulating actual space tramp conditions. A cinematic recording was made of this daring experiment and is available on a rental basis to Teen Age groups who, we feel, may well profit by our experiment.

Soundtrack is by Professor Lehrer of Boston. It may be mailed under plain wrapper.

We nevertheless wish to extend our thanks, dear Sir or Madam a.t.c.m.b, for the submission of this manuscript, and to suggest further study of our magazine over a period of, let us say, three years, will better acquaint you with our editorial standards, which we hardly consider astronomical. A subscription order blank is enclosed. No stamps, *please*.

Spaciously yours,
The Editor.

Virginia Kidd, Tiptree's second agent (following Robert P. Mills), read this for the first time in the manuscript for this collection and offered it to *Amazing Stories*, which published it in the Fall 1998 issue.

A Day Like Any Other

Man is a product, like so much else, of the play of natural garble

He decided to be a man today. He dressed in his executive doublestripe carefully with medallion: Gloves not to match boots. Masterfully in Sphinx to offisolarium, put in creative morning on landline option. Lunch conference multimedia potential Ontario: Note. After noon was payoff matinee with partner's new secretary. She had gas pains but extra-dedicated. Appreciatively he put her name in the Fruit-of-the-Month file when he got

> Ill fares the land, to hastening ills a prey,
> Where *garble* accumulates and men de

During the night he was a hamster. He ran 15,924 revolutions of his 45 cm. exercise wheel. About 24 miles; too much for a male hamster. Tired, he debated the anomaly, finally let it

> Your hooves have stamped at the black *garble* of the wood,
> Even where horrible green parrots call and swing.
> My works are all stamped down into that *garble* mud.
> I knew that horseplay, knew it for a murderous th

He awoke in the morning as a premenopausal housewife. He loved up the house all day, Windex on the windows, Soilex on the floors, Ovenex on the oven. In the evening he used Husbandex on the husband. His husband went to sleep

> Whose was the *garble* that slanted back this brow?
> Whose breath blew out the light within this brain?
> Is this the *garble* the Lord God made

He went out in the night as a child laughing, zap-whirling Hey Hey Hey Holy spring leg of Lamb ecstasy-strobe FREEZE! Electric joke cascade! Cool vomiting angel ho ho ho he killed everybody & threw the world away

So long, Mom! I'm off to *garble* the Bomb!
So don't wait up for me

Only in the morning buttoning his aqua lab coat he forgot he had thrown the world away until just. Too. Late. When he perceived this down the gleaming corridors he knew something terrible had happened, he had lost his last chance. No help in the frost-free cryostats, lost in the fume-hoods he cried and cried, cried or

Bequeath us to no earthly shore until
Is answered in the *garble* of our grave
The seal's wide spindrift gaze toward Paradi

This miniature was originally submitted to Harry Harrison for his anthology series *Nova* on September 22, 1968. Neither Harrison, Harlan Ellison, nor Michael Moorcock could use it.

When George Hay of the British academic SF magazine *Foundation* expressed an interest in reprinting some of Tiptree's nonfiction, Tiptree also sent him a copy of "A Day Like Any Other." *Foundation* never published the nonfiction, but they ran the short story in their third issue, March 1973.

Here are the comments on the story that Tiptree sent to me in April 1971:

A sober comment on the real world. Twenty-four hours. (Can you look me in the eye and say no?) Harlan said in part, "Quite a different can of worms. It has something. What, I have no idea." And called it, correctly, "a pastiche." The missing glue is undoubtedly in part the fact that the interpolated quotes are, I guess, not very old friends to all readers. Private faces in public places. . . .

By the way, Harlan is a first-rate editor sound of nose and workmanlike-sympatico about all the mechanics . . . as of course he should be.

The quotes are in order from: Sherrington, "The Destiny of Man"; A. Pope, "Essay on Man"; Yeats' "Portrait of a Black Centaur by Edmund Dulac" (oh, that "murderous horseplay"!); Edwin Markham, "The Man with the Hoe" (should have been required reading not only in Dixie for the last fifty years); Tom Lehrer, "Song for World War III"; and Hart Crane's "Voyages II." Do your life a favor, read a couple of these. Out loud.

Press Until the Bleeding Stops

When the man who loved the wooded valley awoke and saw the young men carrying gaily painted stakes, he listened. And with some difficulty, because of great horror, he understood. He looked around then and saw that things had gone further than he had realized; this was in fact the last valley. And he went in haste to the people who lived on the slopes of the valley, to tell them.

They are going to drive a huge highway through the valley, he said, and the chain saws are going to fell the trees that give us air and the bull-dozers are going to tear the earth and destroy her life and her waters that we drink. And the beauty and the quiet will be replaced by a horri-ble and unceasing din of machines spewing foul gases into the barren wind and the lovely soul of the earth that is here in this last valley will be gone forever.

And the first of the people who lived beside the valley replied, Well this is terrible and grievous, thank God you told us, because our son needs to go to medical school and now we can sell our land and send him. And the next people said, That is indeed shocking news and we couldn't approve more of what you're doing but it's no use our signing anything because we are leaving for an overseas assignment; here is ten dollars. And the next man said, This is a brutal outrage and I'm so glad you called it to my attention because my wife loves nature and she is in such frail health that the sight of this hideous destruction would finish her; I must get her away quickly and I wish you all the luck in the world. And a woman said, Yes it's just awful and I'd love to sign your paper if only my husband wasn't in the concrete business. And another man said, It's a damn shame to spoil the woods but as they say, if you can't lick 'em, join 'em, and my brother-in-law wants me to go in with him on a fried chicken franchise. And another woman said, Yes it's so sad about the trees and all the little animals, but think how happy all the people will be to drive through here and which is more important, a tree or a person? And the two girls who lived at the end of the valley said, That's all middle-class shit, don't you know there are babies burning?

The man saw that the people were going to be no help at all. And then he remembered the great horn made from a mammoth's tooth that had been buried in the secret heart of the woods. It was green by age and nature and he knew it had only been blown once before in a legendary emergency. So he dug it up and blew three long solemn blasts, like glaciers creaking. And when he put it down all the animals and every living thing in the woods was looking at him.

Life of the earth, he cried, listen to me! Rabbits, stop munching the green leaves! Foxes, stop preying on the rabbits and the birds! Hawks, stop seeking out the voles and squirrels, and all you little birds stop eating the insects! And insects, stop sucking the juices of the plants, and you trees and ferns and creepers, still your feeding roots in the germy loam and listen to me! And you, stag of the forest, and you, raccoons fishing frogs in the stream, and all you frogs and newts and crickets and spiders and moles and mice in your burrows, listen to me and attend!

My brothers the men, he told them, are now planning to blast a road through here! Their giant machines will rip away the living soil and grind up the field mice's nests and the bob-white's babies and knock down and crush the tall trees with all your homes and young ones and even the bees in their hives and ram you all broken into a great pile of death. And they will seal the flayed earth under a plain of concrete and the sweet rain will run off into a foul channel and the mold and mulm that was the life of the earth will pour into the far ocean where it will kill the fish. And no water will sink into the earth to refresh it, and even those trees which they will leave torn and crippled will die and the last of you animals and birds with them. And they will sow the clay with coarse wire-grass and spray poisons, and the stink of their burning fuels will fill the air with death. And the people who ride a stream of roaring machines will throw trash and crap unceasing to bring more kinds of death when your young ones eat it. And even you butterflies and winged creatures will end up as squashes on their hurtling metal. Join me and we will fight this thing!

When the creatures heard this they looked at each other and at the man, and they understood, because the horn of legendary emergency had been blown. And the old badger of the cave whom nobody had ever seen before, advanced and spoke for them all, saying, Oh Man, we hear and understand! This is truly a time when we must stand together in battle for our lives. And we will! Moreover, it will be a sight never before seen, because behind us will arise the dread might and majesty of our Mother, the Earth, who is also the Mother of you men, though I have never understood why. She will strengthen us to invincible power. Even the soft wings of the mayflies and the very softest moles will take on the fury of our offended Mother. When your killing machines come they will be met by a terror never before seen and the men will know fear at last and flee!

To which the man said, So be it. I will stand with you.

And so one morning when the great yellow earth-gutting machines roared over the horizon into the little valley, there stood ready for them all the creatures of the forest. In the forefront the air was filled with moths and butterflies and every flying insect in waves and clouds, and underfoot the mice and the frogs and turtles in ranks, and all around them even the smallest blades of grass and leaves of the trees were drawn up and hard as spears. And behind them were the armies of woodchucks and squirrels and foxes unsmiling, right down to the rac-coon babies unnaturally grim. And in their midst stood the proud stag of the forest with the sun gleaming on his antlers, and the man standing beside him. And every single one of them felt the power of their Mother the Earth surging through them, invincible at last, a thing which had never been known before. And swooping from the sky came the birds large and small in squadrons dazzling to the eye, and all this took place in perfect silence, which is the voice of Earth.

When the first bulldozer driver saw them he yelled through his transceiver, Hey, look at the birds! And the second driver bellowed back, kee-rist there's a hell of a lot of animals in there! And the third driver shouted, Look out, maybe they're rabid or something, I can't see any-thing; my glass is covered with bugs. And they all lurched to a stop.

But the foreman came tearing up in his Jeep, yelling Gimme that shotgun, there's a buck! By God, I haven't shot a rack like that since I was a kid! And the support crew ran up after him and started shooting streams of chemical fog into the sky.

The first bulldozer driver said, I feel sick. If you're sick go home, the foreman shouted, by Jesus I'm going to get that buck.

At that moment the man walked out of the woods and stood before them with his arms lifted, saying *Stop!* I command you in the name of our dread Mother, the Earth. This valley is under her protection forever. Turn and go!

The second bulldozer driver asked, What is that gray thing? Do you hear some kind of squeaking?

The foreman, sighting down his barrels told him, Nothing but a shadow, goddammit, you seeing ghosts?

When the man heard those words he felt draftiness and faintness. He looked down at his body and saw that the air was mingling through him; he was in fact only a gray shadow. And he groaned and said, Yes, it is true. I am only a ghost. I am dead. Now I remember.

And the foreman let off both barrels crash, blam, straight into the throat of the stag of the forest, and the great horns fell and gored the ground.

The first bulldozer driver jumped out and said, Screw you, I'm going home. But the foreman went and dragged the stag and he heaved him onto the Jeep and climbed in the bulldozer cab himself, howling Hit it! And the line of earth killers moved forward.

The foxes and raccoons and chipmunks and all the animals bared their teeth and called on the deep power of the Earth, standing their ground bravely around the ghost of the man, and the old badger dipped his heavy claws in the blood of the slain stag and charged. And the birds dived screaming and the baby quail and mice rushed into the treads to jam them and the butterflies and bees rained into the cabs, all calling on their Mother the Earth.

But the terrible machines ground forward uncaring and the fearful knives tore into the roots of the trees and tumbled them and the earth and the bones and bodies of the animals, into huge windrows, and other machines roared behind, shoveling everything together, oriole nests and badger teeth and mouse eyes and flowers and rocks and the milk of the squirrels all ground into a great heap of death down the center of the valley.

Next came the gravel trucks and the bluestone grinders and graders and the reinforcing rod layers, and they churned to and fro, flattening and mangling everything by day and by night, and the rains carried blood and mulm in a torrent to the sea. And presently a perfectly graded ribbon of concrete was spewed over the whole length of the murdered valley. And when it was all done the foreman said, Boys, it's a great job, and I'm going to Florida this winter and sit in the sun and drink beer. Man, you should see how nice those horns turned out, I mounted them myself on walnut veneer.

After the valley was concrete from end to end the landscape crew sowed wire bunch-grass on the dead soil with tar mulch, and the contractor himself came out and said, Now that's what I call pretty.

So the road was opened at last and all the people who had been impatiently awaiting the day started fiercely driving over it, exulting in their tremendous horsepower and noise and the speed with which they arrived at the next traffic jam, all the happy people in campers and hard-tops and Minis and Caddies and muscle-hogs and beetles and panels and cycles and ranch-wagons, and all air-conditioned too. They only open their windows to cast out paper and plastic and tin and broken glass, which nestles in the wire-grass roots to form burning lenses in the smoky sun, and when the rain falls it is carried off in cleverly engineered sluiceways so that the water dries up in the flesh of the earth and the sea is fouled. And the shining cars rush on smoothly night and day burning the black secret blood of the mother and sending its smoke upon the lifeless air.

The people are happy in their thrumming cars, on their fine new road. Only sometimes, as they zoom through the place where the valley was, their faces become strained and bleak and they have an absurd momentary fear that perhaps they cannot ever stop their engines or get out of their metal shells, but must roar on forever. But they know this is nonsense. Nothing will interfere with them. They will get where they are going.

And when they indeed and finally get where they are going some among them may have time to ask, Why did we come here?

Alli Sheldon's *second* science-fiction-writing pseudonym, Raccoona Sheldon, first appeared August 25, 1972, when she submitted "Angel Fix" (included in *Out of the Everywhere,* Del Rey 1981) to *Fantasy & Science Fiction.* The story was rejected, as were most of Raccoona's. This frustrated Alli, because editors were begging Tiptree for stories but not interested in stories that they didn't know were by the same writer. She had, however, deliberately given Raccoona minor stories that would seem to logically come from a beginning writer. And she had apparently forgotten that even "Tiptree," whom she had considered an instant success, had sold only ten of thirty-three stories on initial submission.

The letter from Raccoona accompanying "Angel Fix" included this "autobiographical note":

> I used to sell feature reporting and travel type pieces. I guess my status peak was the *New Yorker.* Then I got locked into teaching and research, which shows in this story. But SF is my true love. Please be warned, I'm going to learn to write it, *ruat coelum*!

Ed Ferman at *F&SF* returned it October 6, saying, "Sorry that this one did not appeal to me quite enough to take. I did like the writing, though, and I'd be glad to see others." By then she had already sent him "The Trouble Is Not in Your Set" (on August 28) and "Press Until the Bleeding Stops" (on August 31), the latter with the short note: "This one is just bare-faced pain." Ferman rejected that on October 31, and she sent it to Ted White at *Amazing* on November 22. When he rejected it, she retired the story.

In a letter to me on November 23, 1973, Tiptree wrote:

> Hey, I'll tell you a secret. Being an incurable weirdo, I decided to send out a couple stories under an assumed name—sorry, I mean a nom de plume. So far neither have sold—the same editors who are ragging me for stuff bounced 'em out of the slush-pile! Instructive, eh? . . . I'm just stubborn enough to keep on with it.
>
> I'll let you know if one sells. Private entre nous, right?

Earlier, in an undated letter to me (circa Sep. '72), Tiptree told me of:

> . . . an old pal of mine who does drawings. She goes by the name of Raccoona, her own name having been, she feels, used up by a high-voltage media star so it no longer belongs to her. I enclose a sheet of doodles I extracted from her pad. . . . I think she may try

writing again, she did once. Doesn't take herself seriously.

In my reply I said, "Perhaps some time the two of you might be able to work up some words and pictures collaboration. Some of her drawings look a lot like some of your writing."

A year later, in the same November 23, 1973, letter:

> Oh, listen, before I end this—talk about the surprises of people, remember my asking you about drawing because of this Wisconsin friend, "Raccoona" Sheldon? Well, she never sent any drawings but she did send me, I mean, gave me when I was there, a couple very short pieces of writing. One I don't understand too well, but the other is quite moving. A sort of ecology fantasy, only—pause for scrabbling in my cartoons—6½ pages of real big type. Want me to send it along? Even if you have no use for it, she'd be delighted to hear any comments. As I think I mentioned, she's a shy type. Retreated up there after god knows what. But cheerful. (All my *old* friends are cheerful. We have to be.) I dunno why no drawings, maybe she's secretly into writing. She has a lot of nuisance family to take care of—what the world puts on people . . .

The story was sent to me in January 1974. As usual, there were hand-corrections on it, and at the last minute Alli, afraid that I would recognize them as Tiptree's, rolled the letter back into the typewriter and typed this out-of-alignment P.S.: "Looking it over I see my hash-tracks and recall I fixed it up a trifle. With her consent, I'm like you persnicky about other people's mss. Maybe you like her version better."

I accepted it a couple weeks later: "It's really nice. Weird. I'll keep it and run it in *Kyben* someday soon. I'll drop her a line and tell her so. Thanks for passing it on." I ended up publishing it in the first issue of a new fanzine, *Khatru*, in February 1975.

Go from Me, I Am One of Those Who Pall
(A Parody of My Style)

Scene: A deserted slaughterhouse, early Sunday morning

Heroine, stark naked except for a pair of thumbscrews, staggers out of a badly tousled bed. A large box of ten-penny nails falls to the floor. Bed bursts into flames.

Heroine: "Oh my God, the milkman!"

Struggles into a hair shirt, opens door.

Heroine, standing on doorstep: "The air! To breathe the diamond elixir of the great world! Oh, my electric nerves! Where is the milk?"

Snatches up scrap of lavender johnny paper.

Heroine, writing furiously: "I must have more milk! The smoldering fires in my bones must be quenched. My blind hunger must be assuaged. What do they call that stuff with the vitamin B in it? Oh, this struggle to communicate!"

Milkman is heard approaching. Heroine tears off hair shirt.

Milkman: "All right, Miss, what'll it be?"

Heroine: "So! You too are committed!"

Flings herself around Milkman's midriff.

Milkman: "Hey!"

Heroine, choking: "My love, my love! Mine! Loneliness is finished for us two! Your great eyes gaze at my flesh . . . Come, love!"

Milkman, bursting into flames: "Uggrrgrrg!" Rushes from scene.

Heroine, dejectedly picking up bottle of milk: "Oh, fool that I am! Now I'll have to switch to Borden's. My heart is a stone, a little black stone. A chip off the rock of death. There must be something wrong with my style. Where the hell is *The New York Times*?"

Wanders over to a fresh grave in the front yard.

Heroine, drinking milk: "Ah yes, now I remember . . . That delivery boy.

Utter peace . . . My very hair stands on end, remembering the quivering intensity of his naked foot nakedly in the small of my back . . . Death, sweet friend, keep him safe for me . . . No! I am sentimental! It was my fault, my damned fault! Responsibility—that is the great word. I accept—Human responsibility. I stare at the facts. Expiation! . . . I will order the *Herald Tribune.*"

Places empty milk bottle on grave, returns to house and commences to clean the floor, very humbly, with a blowtorch. Sings to herself.

Heroine: "I'm going to buy a paper dolly I can call my own . . ." Bursting out: "Me! Me! Me! That's all I hear! What's the use of being a schizoid if I can't get away from myself? Hate and fear, fear and hate, miserable, puking, sniveling, groveling, ignominious snotfaced limpet that I am! What will I do when the papers give out, read the *Christian Science Monitor?* What's the use of using six adjectives if I don't express what I mean—the incommunicable quintessence of me? The stammering question of my blood, that's what I mean, if I may say so, call it what you will, but those who know it, knowing naught else beside—what am I saying? I need light, although it will not improve matters much, it's honest."

Sets house on fire.

Heroine, reflectively: "Men—I hate men. Ugh, the brutality of them! Women are good. Why haven't I some great women friends? I love women—I will find women! Christ, it's hot in here. Water! Water for my fevered fetid flushed frenzied . . ."

Walks out, muttering. House burns to ashes, leaving heroine sleeping peacefully on grave.

Ghost of Ernest Dowson, reading a copy of *Gone with the Wind,* wanders in and sits down beside her. Several puking, snot-faced, etc., limpets emerge from grave and stare reproachfully at Heroine.

Heroine rolls over in sleep, clutches gravestone. Ghost of newsboy breaks from grave at a fast canter and dashes from scene.

This could go on forever. CURTAIN

Among her papers after her death, we found a group of poems (published as *Clean Sheets,* Tachyon 1996), which were written in the late 1940s and early

1950s, and included the one she would mention in "If You Can't Laugh at It, What Good Is It?", which actually begins,

> Sitting on a crate before the sunrise,
> I am eating a speckled banana in the public park

With the poems was this playlet, which was also first published in *Clean Sheets*. It may be an early parody of Sheldon's style rather than Tiptree's, but it helps demonstrate the continuity between Alice Bradley, Alice Davey, Alice Sheldon, James Tiptree, and Raccoona Sheldon.

THE TROUBLE IS NOT IN YOUR SET

—live from our studio in beautiful Porcupine Crossing, the voice of the Near North Woodlands. And folks, to those of you who have been saying we can't find fabulous fascinating interviews in upper Bluegill County especially this late at night, I say, Wow! Do you have a surprise coming! Wait till you meet our guests tonight, brought to you by Uncle Carl's Candlelight Supper-Club on Route 101, blacktop all the way to the bridge. Remember, Uncle Carl says come as you are, folks, sophisticated fun for the whole family. Oh, man, those beef patties. And now I want you to meet our first guest, Mrs. Charlene Tumpak of Wabago Falls. Mrs. Tumpak, you're looking terrific. Why don't you call me Dick? Now tell us, Mrs. Tumpak, how does it happen that you're suing the township for thirty-two new stop signs?

Sure, Dick, ha-ha. Well, I like stop signs. Don't we all?

How about that, folks? Didn't I say we have some terrific personalities? Tell me, Mrs. Tumpak, why do you like stop signs? When did it start? May I call you Charlene?

Sure, go ahead, my husband's deaf. Oh, it started with the yellow, I guess.

You mean you, uh, dig yellow, Charlene?

No, first there's that *green* light, Dick, it's so awful cold. Like it just wants you to go on. Go on, keep moving—that's what the green says. We don't want you here. No love *at all*. And then it goes yellow, you know? Warmer. Like it changed its mind.

Well, that certainly is an intriguing idea, isn't it, folks?

Yes. And then it goes *red*. Real warm! Like stay awhile. Look around, enjoy yourself, the red says to me. And I do, doesn't everybody? Always something to see and all the other cars, it's like a party. I *love* parties.

Say, that's some kind of philosophy you have there, Charlene.

Yes. So when I see the yellow I always go real slow. Because it's going to get *red*, you know. And when I see that old green I slow down too because the yellow might come, see? And all the little stop signs, the ones with no lights, you can just stop as long as you want and look all around. You know what I saw yesterday, by the arterial sign? Two gophers. I shouldn't tell what they were doing, ha-ha. We should have more stop signs so people can enjoy themselves.

Well, I must say that's a fascinating viewpoint, Charlene. You mentioned that everybody loves stoplights. Do you know for a fact that other people really enjoy them the way you do?

Oh sure, Dick. Why they always wave at me. And honk. Oh boy, do they honk.

Well, that certainly was great, Charlene. I'm sure we all wish you luck in your campaign for more stop signs. Don't we, folks? Whee! And now it's time for our next fabulous upper Bluegill County personality, brought to you by Bill and Betty's Bait and Booze Shoppe at Square Corners. Folks, whatever you need for that big one, Betty has it. And listen to their special this week—two dozen night crawlers with every single fifth of Wilkins Family, the whiskey you can't forget. Wow, save one for me, Betty. And now our very special guest, Mr. Elwin Eggars. Mr. Eggars moved here from London, England, folks. I guess he knows you can't beat the Near North Woodland for all-year fun. Tell us, Mr. Eggars, is it true that there was something unusual about your birth?

Well, yes, you might say so. I was born fully formed. But much smaller, naturally.

Oh golly, you mean you were a fully formed man at birth, Mr. Eggars? But small?

Oh, yes. Luckily my parents practiced natural childbirth. Otherwise I'd have been done for, you know.

Why was that, Mr. Eggars?

The doctor, you know. The obstetrical chap. Actually it wasn't the main man himself, it was an intern who got hold of me. First thing I knew he had me upside down, pommeling away. I was choking, of course. All that slime. But I could *feel* the hate coming at me. Had my Dad not been there they would have done away with me at once.

Oh, what a Human-interest story, folks. How did your father happen to be there, Mr. Eggars?

That's the natural practice, you know, with the husband—my dad, that was—standing by. Really a piece of luck. You see they had discussed the whole thing, many times over in complete detail. So I knew just what to expect. Birth is a terrifying business, I couldn't get my arms up at all.

I'm sure the folks would like to know all about this tremendous experience, Mr. Eggars. Can you tell us, what did your father do?

Well, I knew he was there, you see, although I couldn't spot him right then what with being upside down and the pounding and the glue. But just as quick as I could I shouted out, "Dad! Dad! Help!" As loud as possible. I picked on him, you see, because I realized Mother would be in an uncertain state.

How did you know English? I mean, so soon?

Oh, that came quite readily. The rudiments rather, I should say. I began to catch on about the fifth month, I should guess. I shan't tell you what I learned first. Ha-ha.

Oh, why not, Mr. Eggars? I bet everybody out there is just as thrilled as I am to be hearing this. We want to hear all about it, don't we, folks? What did you learn first, Mr. Eggars?

Oh, no, really, I shouldn't. Ha-ha.

Come on, you can't stop now, Mr. Eggars. All the kids are in bed.

Well, ha-ha. Perhaps I can put it this way. The infant picks up language by association, you know. He sees a dog and hears someone say maiow, or whatever.

Bow-wow—don't let me stop you.

Right. Well, of course I wasn't seeing anything but I could *feel* quite a lot, you realize. As well as hear them speaking. And considering my position in those early months, you will readily understand that I had many, shall we say, striking experiences associated with certain words?

Fantastic, just fantastic, ha-ha-ha.

I must say it made me intensely curious, you know. I couldn't discover what on earth the simplest things were. Of course various gurgles and so on could be identified as *food*, and the jiggling was the *auto*, et cetera. But imagine trying to decipher *shirt*, for instance? Or—well, I'd best not.

Hey, aren't you just crazy about the way he talks, folks? Mr. Eggars, what did your pop do when you called him?

He made the intern let go of me, naturally, and I managed to stand up. I didn't realize at the time that I was leaning on part of Mother. But I said, "Hello, Dad," and we shook hands.

You shook hands, really?

Yes, I'd planned on that, you know. I felt rather proud of myself for working it out, what *hands* were and all. I was keen on doing the right thing. To show him I was a son he could be proud of. A chap feels very strongly about the right sort of Dad, you know. Which mine was.

Say, that's a very moving attribute. How about your mom?

Oh, I was eager to meet her. But of course it was a bit confusing, seeing everything for the first time, and I was in a bloody great mess, sorry. I said to Dad, "If I could just wash up first?" He understood. One of the nurses washed me with a cloth. Clumsy idiot. The intern I believe had run off, and there was somebody on the floor. When I was freshened up Dad took me on his arm around to Mother—to her head end, you know.

How about that, folks? What did she say?

Oh, well, it was rather emotional, you realize. I thanked her, of course; I had thought for some time of what I would say. I felt I knew her already, you see. I recall I kissed her. On the cheek.

I bet she loved that.

She wasn't feeling too talkative, poor dear. But she did admire my hands. "So small and yet perfectly formed," she said. You know how mothers are.

You better believe it. Leona, that's my wife, she just goes ape if there's a baby carriage around. So you didn't have any serious problems?

Oh, the usual adjustments, I expect. The only slight difficulty was the feeding, you know.

How do you mean?

Well, in view of their attitude toward natural method, of course they had planned on breast feeding.

I don't follow you there, Mr. Eggars. What went wrong?

Oh, nothing, really. Just the embarrassment, you know. And the size. Imagine one's feelings when they poke a nipple a foot wide at one! A bit awkward. But we got sorted out in no time when I told her how much I'd been looking forward to trying some of the dishes I'd been hearing about. Particularly bubble-and-squeak, I recall. Of course she was an absolutely superb cook, my mother. Pity.

Bubble-and-squeak, I'll have to try that some time. Well, I do thank you very much, Mr. Eggars, on behalf of the folks out there, for sharing this great Human experience with us. Wasn't that educational, folks? And we're proud to welcome you to wonderful Bluegill County, vacationland in the woods. And now our next guest, who is brought to you courtesy of Rudy's Wrecker and Rescue Service, that's Mud Lake 205 three short. Rudy wants you to know he's put in brand new upholstery in the ambulance. And he's solved that little problem about hunting season, folks. His wife's mother is going to be staying with them, and she'll be right by the phone. Remember, if you or your loved ones need help, call Mud Lake 205 three short, and good luck. Now I want you to welcome our next guest, Mr. Al Rappiola of Timberton. Great to meet you, Al. I understand you have some kind of problem with the time?

Well, it's not me, Dick, it's my wife. She's from Oshkosh.

Oshkosh, hey? I guess they haven't all got the word down there, ha-ha. No offense, Al. What seems to be her trouble?

Well, I noticed it as soon as we got married. I mean, the following day, ha-ha. We went to Thousand Lakes, that's a great spot for a honeymoon. Anyway, the very next morning. I woke up and there she was all packed up, walking out of the cabin. So I said, "Hey, Marie, where're you off to?"

That certainly is a natural question, Al.

Yeah. I thought I'd done something, see. But then it turned out she wasn't mad at all, she was just leaving. Like it was the thing to do. So I said, "Marie, hon, we're married!" But she said, "That was *yesterday*, Al. You mean you still want to be married *today*?" Well, I said, "What's the matter with you, hon? Sure I do." Thinking it was a joke. So she stayed and everything was a-okay. Just great. But then next morning she pulled the same thing again. And the next day after that, and so on. Every morning.

Wow, that is weird, isn't it folks? How'd you handle it?

Well, I tell you, I had a time. It was like she couldn't believe that anything that happened the day before carried over into next day, see. Like everything all got washed out every night. *Everything.* I had to keep convincing her she was still married to me. She was real nice about it, I'll say that. I could see she was glad to stay. To tell the truth I thought it was an act, until we had the anniversary.

Was that your first anniversary?

Yeah, we invited our folks and a lot of the older crowd for a big dinner. I mean, I was pretty busy with my job all year, we'd kind of postponed the celebrations. So this was a big event. And then the day of the party I got home from work and there she was in her jeans, cleaning the oil-burner. And no food, *nothing.*

Golly, Al, that's really frightening.

> Yeah. Oh, we had a real go-round, I tell you. I recall she said, "You mean all those people are getting into cars and buses and traveling from all over to come here *tonight*—just because of what we said *three weeks ago*? I don't believe it!" She was so sincere, man, I started wondering. Well, that party was pretty crazy. When they all showed up that really began to shake her, you know? Like she was seeing ghosts. But I could see she was glad to see them, after she got over the shock.

Say, didn't you fear for her mental health, Al?

> Oh no, she's just as sane as I am except for this one little quirk. Marie's fine. Well, after the party she was kind of dazed for a while. She got me to write her down a list, every day. All the things she should remember, especially doctor appointments, stuff like that. She carries it clipped to our marriage certificate, ha-ha. Anything I put on that list she does. Of course now she's expecting, I really have to watch it. She more or less blames me for that.

You mean for the baby, Al, ha-ha?

> You better believe it. No, what I mean is she blames me for things carrying over from one day to the next. She claims up until she got married everything—I mean the whole world, like you and me and all except her—it would just flush out at midnight. Every day started fresh, she says. So she thinks it's my fault. I guess she's still expecting it to wear off. I catch her trying little tricks.

Can you tell the folks about those little tricks, Al? I know they're finding this tremendously interesting.

> Oh, you know, kid stuff. Sticking leaves in her shoes, foolishness like that. I don't want to give you the wrong impression,

Dick. We all have our little quirks. Outside of that you couldn't ask for a better wife. I mean, Marie is tops, she really is. Hi, hon! I'm a lucky guy.

Beautiful, Al, did you catch that, folks? Oh, oh. Speaking of midnight, I see we have only a couple seconds to go. So from our studio in beautiful Porcupine Crossing, here's the voice of the Near North Woodlands saying goo—

Alli didn't try real hard to sell this Raccoona Sheldon story. She sent it to Ed Ferman on August 28, 1972, with the note: "By the way, what's herein is scarcely fantasy. Florence County was settled by refugees from a skink famine on Arcturus. They only vote for Nixon because they think he's one of them."

The story was rejected without comment, and retired. This is its first publication.

TREY OF HEARTS

"Dear Bolingbroke, dear Loomis," she says to the letter-writer. "Do you remember the Terran woman you met at Centaurus Junction, while you were waiting for the shuttle?"

No, that won't do. By this time they might have trouble recalling where Terra is, or what "woman" means. And she should relax her throat, let her voice be more alluring.

She reverses and starts over, putting "Human female" instead. Humans are known all over the galaxy.

"Well," she goes on, "she remembers you. Poignantly. And this is just to say—" Here she halts the writer to think. What exactly *does* she want to say to them, after all these years? Really, just what she's already said—that she remembers, indeed can't forget, can't forget at all. Though her life is certainly rich and varied enough to let her forget most anything in the way of casual sex. Why not forget these two, this Loomis and Bolingbroke? Why not? It's something about the whole thing, about what they did to her and she to them, about what they tried to do *through* her.

She sighs luxuriously, letting it all come back; while outside the windows of her beautiful office the lights of Luna City are coming on, far below . . .

It had started as the most ordinary of encounters, in this age of star travel and shape-changing. She can see herself back then as if it were today, standing in Centaurus Junction in her best white travel-jumper, a mantilla on her long black hair, and her best jeweled belt and slippers— a typical high-class junior sales rep.

She has come to Centaurus Junction on the shuttle from Terra; as usual, it took longer to get to the Deep Space jump-port than it'll take her to get to the Deneb system, where she will try to sell the ruling life-form a lot of the new macrocelluar devices her company makes.

She finds she has twenty-six standard hours to wait.

After seeing that her precious sample cases are stowed in the Deneb destination-chute, she wanders out to take a stim-drink under the huge wall of clocks that show the local times all over known space. Might as well get used to Deneb time—although of course she will travel in cold-sleep, which will reset all her physiological cycles.

As she looks for Deneb she becomes aware of a pleasant tightness in her crotch, the tingle and tickle of arousal. She's been too busy lately to think of sex—and cold-sleep won't cure *that*. Yes, and this is about her last chance to be among many Humans. She can put the wait to good use, if she can spot a suitable partner.

Forgetting Deneb, she glances around, but the tables and bar display no other Humans who interest her. There are a few nice aliens whom she knows are keen on Human sex, but these all seem to be in groups with young—family parties on vacation, no doubt. The few lone aliens she can see are strange to her; she wouldn't chance a sexual encounter with any except as a last resort. And of course there is the usual Ovidian or so, who are always about, and whose sex habits don't interest anybody. Well, maybe someone will turn up.

She goes back to studying the clock wall, and has just found that it's midnight on Deneb IV, when someone bumps her drink-holding arm.

"Excuse me," the stranger says. He's a Human. She blinks and looks again—he's outrageously handsome, a tall tanned youth with curly red hair, usually a disastrous combination, but on him, great. And nicely dressed.

"Excuse me," he says again in quite a strange accent. And repeats it. "Excuse me, please."

"Oh, it's nothing." She smiles. She has just noticed that he has an unmistakable erection pushing up the corner of his sports tabard, which he is making no effort to conceal. And another young man is with him, a dark-haired type who would have been attractive in his own right had he not been eclipsed by the spectacular redhead. And he too has a highly visible tent-shaped bulge in his well-cut panters.

"Excuse me," the redhead says for the fourth time. She's about to become irritated, when she realises he's having trouble with Galactic, trying to say something further.

"Excuse me, I may ask a personal question? Yes?"

"Why, yes."

"You are naturally in this form? And of Terra, right?"

"That's right. I'm naturally a Human female, a woman of Terra. Do I guess correctly that you've just recently shape-changed?"

"Ah! Yes! You understand well!" He throws a gratified glance at his companion, and they both accept her gestured invitation to sit down. "It was all done in a great hurry, you see, the appointment to take the diplomatic post on Terra just opened. We had to take whatever was available, with almost no information. We are by profession diplomats of Thumnor, but we have not been Human before. We seem to be having trouble with the biology"—he points to his lap—"and the instruction manual was stupidly packed in our check-through bags. Even the most rudimentary formals we don't know."

"I see. Well! Well, first, my expression is a smile, indicating good will." Both the strangers immediately grin winningly. "And on meeting, it is customary to exchange names—not necessarily your full name, just something to be called by. For example, I am Sheila. And often we shake hands as we do that. Your right hand, please. Oh! My goodness, you're *hot*! Is that normal, or do you feel ill?"

"Oh, no," he says as she gingerly regrasps his hand and demonstrates shaking. "It must be that some of our natural metabolism comes through. The changemaster said it would not injure the bodies. But is it unpleasing?"

"No, just impressive. And in strict politeness I shouldn't have mentioned it—but perhaps you might make a little joke to warn people. And your names?" As she speaks, she's wondering if his whole body is hot like that. Interesting . . .

"I am Bolingbroke," he tells her. "And my colleague superior is Loomis."

"*Really*? Like old-fashioned Terran names?"

"Are they unsuitable? It is as close as we could come, in what Terran literature we have. At home in Thumnor I am Bol——" He utters a tangled skein of syllables. "And he is Low——" Another unpronounceability.

"No, quite suitable. And picturesque. And very sensible—Terrans would have had trouble with those. Now, you mentioned biology. On Terra you will find it customary to make an effort to suppress or conceal such obvious sexual reactions." Discreetly, she points at the bulge, which quivers. "Or perhaps you didn't know that's what it is?"

"Oh!" He looks down and slaps at the offending member, jumping a little. "The changemaster said that the bodies were extra young and vigorous, and that part might inflate if we became in reproductive mode. But we didn't expect—is it offensive to you?"

The dark lad he called Loomis, his "superior colleague," speaks up suddenly. "Boley, it is something about her proximity. Our proximity to you." His voice is soft and low and pleasing. Smiling intently, he asks, "May we draw the conclusion that you too are in reproductive mode?"

Sheila laughs. "Well, it's not a safe general rule because such young bodies as yours may, ah, inflate spontaneously. But yes, as it happens, I was thinking about some such way of passing the waiting time."

"How splendid!" exclaims Bolingbroke. "When we learned that we must wait here for so long, twenty-four standards, we determined to experience some major Terran activity. So we decided on sex. Would you say it *is* a major Terran activity?"

She laughs again. "I certainly would say so, yes. But tell me, are matters on our two planets roughly similar? I mean, do you have different sex types or genders who must couple to reproduce? And who also do it when they don't intend to make young, but just for the pleasure? And the pleasure of Contact culminates in a sort of spasm, or body sneeze, which is most pleasing of all?"

"Yes, indeed. That describes it well, and the changemaster told us these male bodies emit fluid. But with us, so many people are incomplete. Is it not so with you? We were assured these bodies are complete. But are you?"

"Yes. In fact, on Terra, except for a few medical oddities, everyone is sexually complete."

"But," says Loomis in his soft voice, "how in the stars do you keep from making young whenever you meet and having frightful overpopulation?"

"Oh, we did have trouble for a time. Then we invented good chemical preventions."

"Ah, the famous Terran technical ingenuity!" laughs Bolingbroke. "So, then, there is no impediment. But as I said, our manual is unavailable. Would you care to assist us in doing sex? Judging from our reactions—" He pauses to look down and cuff the obstinately upright organ, then winces. "Ow! This is more tender than I thought!"

"Yes, Myr Bolingbroke, you must be more careful. I'm told that a blow in the male genital region can be very painful."

"Yes. Well, as I was saying, it appears from our reactions that you are very compatible to us. Right, Loomis? But are we compatible to you, Myr Sheila? I can see no signs." They are both looking her over anxiously.

"No, nothing at all," agrees Loomis. "Except perhaps a faint reddening around your ears?"

Sheila is almost overcome by laughter. The idea of instructing these two Thumnorians appears quite delightful. There is a little danger, of course, because those male bodies are a lot stronger than hers, and if the Thumnorians' sex habits turn out to be unpleasant she would regret it. But surely *diplomats* can be expected to be safe? Meanwhile she is saying:

"Myr Loomis is very perceptive. Any blushing or reddening in the female is a favorable sign—unless it comes from anger. No, Myr Bolingbroke, with women the signs are far less obvious. You see, our sexually responsive tissue is mostly hidden between our legs. So you simply have to judge as you go along. In fact, sometimes the woman's reaction isn't clear until you actually initiate contact."

"Confusing," mutters the redhead. "But maybe the manual will help. Now, what do we do first?"

They both look at her expectantly.

"Well, there are a few preliminaries. And I should warn you that in general the female is slower to arrive at complete arousal. Of course, it is physically possible to have sex with an unready or even unwilling female, but I believe most males agree that in the best experience both partners are highly aroused."

"Both partners," murmurs Loomis, apparently puzzled; "Ah, you mean the woman-female like you, and the male-mans such as we are? No more?"

Puzzled herself, Sheila can only laugh and say, "That's all it takes, yes. But now there is the question of where the sex is to be done. It is very noncustomary to engage in it in public, or even to be too obvious about intending to. It has a disruptive effect on others, you see. For example, shall I go and book my room, and then drop back here, as if saying good-bye, while slipping my key to you?"

"Oh, we thought of that!" says Bolingbroke proudly. "Even without the manual! I believe it's a nice room. Will that influence your arousal?"

"Yes, a secure, comfortable, private environment is very favorable, Now, it is a pleasant gesture, though not necessary, for you to settle any small account I have here. I'll tell you about feeding symbolism later," she adds to Loomis, as the redhead summons the robot and inserts his credit chip.

When they go out, the aliens guide her into corridors she knows as high-credit territory. Their diplomatic service must do better by them than poor old Terra's, she thinks, as they pass a luxurious floral hydroponics display.

Despite a slight difficulty in walking, Bolingbroke strides ahead to fling open a door.

"Stars! What did you do, book a Human royal suite?" She advances into an extravaganza of pale furs and satins, alabaster and mirrors—mirrors everywhere, all centered on a huge, ornate bed. As she catches her own image she is ridiculously pleased to see herself looking quite in place; she knows she's a very good-looking woman. Of course these Thumnorians wouldn't know if she looked like a baggage-basher, but it will do them good to set a high standard.

"Oh, nice! See the little feast they've laid out for us for later on. And, oh! Real flowers!" She buries her nose in the rare fragrances.

"This is suitable?" Loomis inquires. "Do you feel yourself becoming aroused?"

Sheila's answer is cut short by Bolingbroke, who goes straight to the bed and plumps down on it. "This is where we do it, right?"

"Exactly . . . I hope it isn't *too* soft."

"Why? How can I tell?"

"That will be self-evident later," she chuckles.

"Always later! Why don't you approach me? Come on, Loomis."

"I think she has more preliminaries," says Loomis, who has been quietly watching her. "Remember she said there were."

"That's just right. We women vary a great deal, but I am one of those who prefer to become more relaxed before leaping into bed—unless time is very short, which I gather it's not. For instance, you haven't properly locked the door."

"Oof!" Bolingbroke jumps up and beats Loomis to the door.

"Now, Myr Bolingbroke, when you close or lock the door, you might look at your female in a way signifying that you are locking the world out. You see the idea, make everything contribute to arousal."

"I'm not sure I need any more arousal," he says.

But Loomis tells him, "Boley, listen to her. You won't get such guidance again. I have an idea she's very good. Aren't you?" he asks her.

"I've been told so, but of course people are polite," Sheila laughs. "Now, another preliminary is undressing—which is customary unless, again, you're in a fearful hurry." Enjoying her school-mistress role, she throws back her mantilla and is kicking off her slippers when her attention is distracted by the sight of a magnificent cluster of Martian pi-fruits.

"Myr Loomis, these fruits are an extraordinary delicacy to Humans. On such an occasion it would be customary, and a good intimacy factor, to offer them to your woman. In fact, they would be a good pretext for inviting a female to your suite to share them. If she assents, it is her implicit acceptance of sex activities later. Does all this sound too complicated?"

She helps herself to a handful of the tantalizing pi-fruits.

"Well, yes," sighs Bolingbroke, struggling out of his panters.

Loomis, following her lead, is taking off his boots. "You said you would tell us about feeding symbolism," he says in his soft voice.

"Oh, yes. Well, a classic form of male sexual attention to a female is to give her something to eat. It is physical and intimate, and we share it with many simple Terran animals, especially the birds. You will see a female bird flutter and crouch like a nestling, while her male places berries in her beak. So you can see it's a symbolism that runs deep. He offers her something to take into herself, right? And women may serve pleasing food to men, but that's a different symbolic story."

She seats herself on one of the little love-couches to investigate the wine.

"What if I do this?" asks Loomis. "Here, wait—"

He picks up a particularly tempting pi-fruit and holds it before her mouth. As she reaches for it, he pushes it gently between her lips, then withdraws it again and again inserts it. The smooth sliding Contact makes her gasp.

"Your breathing has changed!" he exclaims delightedly.

"What are you doing, Loom? Where did you learn that?" demands Bolingbroke, while Sheila leans back, smiling in a new way at Loomis.

"I just thought of it," beams Loomis modestly. "It was right, Myr Sheila?"

"Myr Loomis, I don't think you need any instructions," says Sheila a trifle thickly. "Your natural impulses are enough. Oh, Myr Bolingbroke! Oh, dear—" She breaks into helpless laughter.

"What's the matter? What's wrong?"

"Oh, nothing's really *wrong*. It's just customary to undress in a different order. Because, to Human womens' eyes a man looks ridiculous wearing only boots and tabard but no panters. And in your condition—" Sheila emits muffled giggles while Bolingbroke tears at his boots.

"Top first, then bottom, then panters?" asks Loomis. "Right?"

"Perfect." Sheila rises and keys open her jumper bodice. "And of course, hats off first of all if you have them. Same for a woman, except"—she gracefully divests herself of the jumper, revealing a lacy teddy—"except a woman may leave a headdress or mantilla for last, as an ornament. But I know Myr Bolingbroke is eager to get to the essentials, so I'll skip everything except one important point which affects the quality of the experience: These lights are much too bright. Soft light lets the woman relax more easily, and is flattering to everyone. Yes." Loomis has found the dimmer and brings the chamber to a shadowy glow. "You'll find your Human eyes adapt amazingly. And now—oh, dear, look what I've done to poor Myr Boley!"

Bolingbroke is sitting naked on the bedside, contemplating his limp penis with dismay. He looks at her reproachfully. "It deflated. When you—"

"Yes, I know. When I laughed. But that would be serious only if you had a much older body. With yours it doesn't matter at all. You'll see." Sheila steps out of her last lacy covering and stretches happily, making a slow twirl so the aliens can see all of her. "Myr Loomis, under the circumstances I'll attend to your colleague first, may I?"

He waves assent and seats himself on the love-couch by the bed, his erection apparently durable as rock. "Go ahead. I feel that watching will please me."

Sheila, naked now except for the gauzy flutter of the mantilla, advances on the dejected red-haired alien and smiles mysteriously.

"Myr Bolingbroke, we will now play an informal sex game called Discover the Sleeper. You are the Sleeper. You must lie back comfortably on your back with your head resting on your hands." She raises her arms and crosses her wrists behind her head, catching her nipples in the filmy mantilla. "That's right. Some prefer to close their eyes. Now the object of the game is for you to try to remain still and passive as long as possible. You must *not* on any account *try* to, ah, inflate. And I am the Discoverer. I can do whatever I like. I'll start by kneeling at your other side"—she steps around the huge bed—"so Myr Loomis can see. And by the way, this game can be played with the sexes reversed, it works beautifully."

As she speaks she has climbed onto the downy coverlet, and is kneeling by Boley's supine body.

She allows herself a moment to admire his really elegant Human form. Long, cleanly molded limbs, with a little curl of red hair in each armpit matching the wiry copper mat around his genitals—that will feel satisfying on her clitoris. His torso is perhaps a little thin, but well muscled—and she can feel his superhuman warmth rising to her. She lays her hands on him—his flesh *is* hot, but not uncomfortably so—and caresses him in long gentle strokes, just flicking his nipples to see his belly jump. "Still, you must lie still . . ." she murmurs, lightly brushes his already half-erect penis. "Lie *still*, relax . . . be asleep . . ."

As she bends down to sniff and taste his skin, her long raven hair trails on him, making his flesh quiver visibly. She pauses to fling it back, and sees Loomis watching intently. In a low voice, she tells him, "He will climax or come, as we call it, much too soon for me. That's because of his body's youth. If this were our only chance, as Discoverer I could now stimulate myself." She rises on her parted knees, and fingers her swollen clitoris to show him. Boley too, she sees, is peeking. "But your bodies will come twice or more, so I shall wait."

She sinks down again and gives him one more long smooth caress, then joins her palms together and pushes her hands between his thighs.

He gasps, breathing hard. "Lie *still* . . . be asleep . . ." she whispers. She can feel her own moisture now wetting her labia; good, just in time. She cups his testes in her palms and fondles them a moment, smiling at the stiffly distended penis standing upright from his curls. A milky drop appears on the tip of his glans. It's time.

She rises on one knee and slides the other leg across him, straddling his groin. The heat of his body is pleasant on her whole crotch; that penis will be hot! Holding her labia open with one hand, she guides herself halfway down on his erection—oh, it's delicious!—and then goes nearly up again before letting herself sink down fully onto him.

As her clitoris crushes his wiry curls he can bear it no longer. Uttering an inarticulate cry, he whips his arms down and pins her hips to him. She lets her body collapse onto his as he convulses and bucks in his first Human orgasm.

Her wiggles against his hot sex excite her more, but she restrains herself so as not to get too close to coming and spoil it. Seeing Loomis's face quite close to hers, she tells him, "Boley's ejaculating. That's it, what we call coming or spending . . . and a dozen other things." Loomis nods, bright-eyed.

"Was that what it was?" Bolingbroke asks thickly. "I thought I was a rocket."

"And you?" Loomis asks her.

"Not yet. Young males are very fast."

"Then I wish to try that. But in reverse. You will be the Sleeper. I find I want to examine your body."

The quality of his voice suddenly reminds her that Boley had called Loomis his superior. Yes, he has a senior authority, although they are evidently warm friends.

As Boley's grip loosens, Sheila lifts herself off his penis, which is already beginning to stir again—what youth!—and sees she's forgotten to have a towel handy. But Loomis has already seen the need and tosses one to her.

"Oh, thanks. I failed in my instructor's duties." She laughs, mopping up semen and juices. "Some men would like a shower and a bite of refreshments now."

"Refreshments yes, shower no," he tells her, grinning, "I find I like the after-effects, it—it reminds me of home." He and Loomis exchange a surprisingly warm look that makes her wonder how much she knows of these Thumnorians.

While Boley applies himself to the snacks, Sheila sets aside her mantilla and stretches out in the bed, supine, arms crossed behind her head. Loomis takes his place kneeling beside her.

At first he copies what she did, looking her over carefully, and then bending to sniff and touch his tongue to her flesh.

"I find your body really very appealing, though strange. It is as if my Human body knows, while my Thumnor mind is just discovering it," he tells her softly. She smiles and closes her eyes, and feels herself beginning to shiver with pleasure as his hot hands examine her, carefully, gently, thoroughly. He inspects her from top to toe, her face and ears, her armpits, and when he comes to her breasts, says, "These are how you feed your young?"

"Yes," she says sleepily. "Do you want to play infant?"

"Like this?" He starts to bend to her, but his erection makes him awkward until he goes on one knee. Then she quakes as those overly hot lips close on her nipples.

"Y-yes," she manages to say. "Good . . ."

"I too find it pleasant. I will remember." He leaves her breasts to continue his examination. First he passes down her sides to her legs and feet, and spends a moment with her toes, then he gently forces her legs apart and continues up the insides of her thighs. Her glimpses of his face through her lashes show him as intent as an artist. Or a surgeon. She trembles harder.

As his fingers reach the fur around her vulva he pauses to bend low by her ear. "You are becoming aroused," he says in his low voice. "I can see it. So am I."

"So am I," speaks up Bolingbroke from somewhere by her knees. "I don't know why."

Loomis chuckles. "Sshshsh," he admonishes his friend, "This is a spell, don't break it." His searching fingers gently probe behind, find out her anus. "Your other aperture," he whispers. She can only nod tremulously. With exquisite care he pushes, enters the opening. "So small, so tight." She nods again, manages to say, "It expands. But not l-lubricated."

"Ah." She has the impression he has turned momentarily to speak to Boley. But then his hand moves purposefully into her dark curls, and with slow pressure he forces her legs farther apart so he can see. He seems to know by instinct the exact rhythm of advance and retreat, pressure and relaxment; she cannot restrain a little moan of pleasure as he parts her outer and inner labia and looks down.

"This . . ." His heated fingers press the stem of her clitoris, her head rolls in her arms, and she moans again as his touch comes on her most sensitive point. "So distended," he murmurs. "Ah, I see, I see. This part corresponds to the tip of mine." He strokes it slowly. "Doesn't it, little Human? Doesn't it?"

"Y-yes . . . oh, oh—" His touch leaves the fire point, and comes again below it. "This, for urination, yes?"

She manages to nod. And then his hot touch comes thrillingly to her vagina. Carefully he pulls the lips apart, and she can feel his eyes on her flesh like a physical pressure; he is watching the opening contract, open, and contract again. She feels moisture gush and senses his puzzlement.

"Are you ejaculating?" he whispers, close to her ear.

She gulps for air, and finally whispers back, "N-no . . . that is lub-bri-cant." The next instant the burning fingers slide into her, withdraw, slide again in deeper, and her muscles convulse around him. This evidently is too much for his enforced calm. His grip on her tightens. "Now I must insert—I—I must—how?"

"You—between my legs—" She draws up her spread knees, inviting him in, and brings a hand down to guide him. But he has already understood; she feels the hot blunt head of his large penis pushing just right. Her fingers reach her clitoris as he pulls slightly out, then thrusts in all the way—and they are in orgasm together.

Distantly she hears Boley give a kind of suppressed wail.

What should be the last tremors subside, but they are not the last. She realises that her long-deprived body has gone into its multiorgasmic state. Inside her, Loomis too is stiffening again. He starts to withdraw, then experimentally thrusts back in, and his thick pubic hair crushes against her pulsing clitoris, sending her off again. Her arms tighten around him, he gives a deep sound in his throat and thrusts in hard, seeming to appreciate her superexcited state. But a moment later he is unsure.

"Am I harming you? Do you need to finish?"

"No—no. I can do more . . . you have excited me . . . so I may come several times—"

"Good," he says, with what seems like real tenderness. "But now I wish you to be on top. Can you?"

"Yes," Sheila answers. "Roll." She clamps him between her knees and twists, and he with surprising strength pulls them both over so that she lies on him with bottom upturned, feeling luxuriously impaled, half coming.

Suddenly a touch makes her conscious that Boley has climbed into the bed behind her and is cautiously feeling between the cheeks of her rump. The long, hot fingers find her anus, and Boley's head comes down beside hers.

"That's your second aperture? The changemaster said—"

She regains her senses enough to say urgently, "Yes, but there's no natural lubrication! Stop, or you'll hurt me! Cream or oil is needed—"

"Stop," says Loomis authoritatively. "Go in the bathroom, there's some stuff beside the pink mirror. I warned you. Go."

"Yes." She has a moment of absurd giggles, hearing an unspoken "Sir."

In a moment he's back, and she feels cool cream being pushed attentively deep into her anal opening. "On yourself, too," she tries to say, but he has already done so, and his now trembling erection pushes slowly through her sphincter, already tightened by the presence of Loomis. It has been some time since she's enjoyed two men at once, she's almost forgotten the indescribable visceral sensations. Relax. Still half coming, she makes her body relax, while the almost painfully delicious pleasure builds.

"It so tight," Boley complains. And then, "Oh! Great! Ahhh-hh."

"Are you all right?" Loomis whispers worriedly into her ear. "This is suitable?"

"Yes . . . yes . . . suitable, but . . . rare." Her blurry eyes find his face, she smiles. "Stop if I cry out."

"We will," he assures her. "Boley, be careful. I sense she is very vulnerable."

"Right," says Boley thickly, and plunges himself home.

There ensues a time which afterward she cannot remember coherently, only as a smoldering montage, punctuated by the brilliances of orgasm. Pressures that are delectable pain, long-drawn suspensions over delight, quivering hot explorations of ecstasy, hot limbs, mouths, fingers, hair, everywhere around her body, weights that alternately squeeze her and release her, synchronous tender battering that becomes counterpointed, langourous wrestlings to utter urgency triply fulfilled . . .

She has never felt her body so totally sexualized. All of them . . .

There must, of course, be intervals—but of these she can only remember one, because of what is said. The air is pervaded with a warmth and tenderness which is far more than merely the spectacular physical fires. An awareness has been with her so strongly that she voices it, dreamily.

"You love each other."

Boley looks up; his tongue has been meeting with Loomis's through her fingers. "Oh, yes. We're married, too. But we're not supposed to say so on Terra."

"Well, men can have good sex with each other, I'm sure."

"We tried that, the changemaster told us."

"It's no good," Loomis agrees. "We miss our third too much."

"Third?" Languidly, she puzzles.

"Yes, on Thumnor it takes three."

"He means we have three sexes," Loomis explains. "We're not really the same sex, you see. But there aren't names for them."

"Ohhh . . . so I am like your third?"

"Almost," Loomis tells her. "Really almost, at moments. But these bodies . . ."

"Oh, I'm sorry. I really am."

"Don't be, my dear. We knew what we were in for. This has been wonderful."

"Yes, it *is*," says Boley. "The changemaster told us it was physically possible, but that females like you are rare. We're godlost lucky." He hugs her.

"So am I." She strokes them both. "I know you'll find more, if that helps."

"Oh, it does. And meanwhile we have you, our first, you darling little alien!"

And they were off again.

The deep sleep of blissful satiation finally claims them. But Sheila awakens early to one more experience which still lives in her mind today.

The other two are locked in the unshakable slumber of their boys' bodies. She thinks it would be nice to leave them some time together, so she slips out from among their intertwined limbs, over the foot of the bed. That luxury tub-room holds all she needs to dress, she need only open her handbag for a fresh disposable teddy—and her notepad.

She is standing, dressed, at a little ornamental shelf, to write affectionate good-byes, when an unframed holograph catches her eye—evidently propped up there to remind them of home. Curious to see the real forms of her alien lovers, she picks it up.

She is really surprised. Most aliens are fairly ordinary, after all. But the forms looking out at her from a volcanic landscape that must be Thumnor present such a distraction of what?—golden horns, metallic blue-green scales, great membranous wings, vivid crests, huge eyes and nostrils—from which unmistakable tiny plumes of smoke or stream are rising—fierce fanged jaws, talons, monstrous, glittering, armored bodies, with heavy tails—why, she has been in bodily union with dragons! No wonder their diplomatic service rents other bodies.

The creatures are so fantastic that for an instant she wonders if it can be a holo of their favorite pets? But no, looking closer, she can see Boley's bright green eyes, made huge, and Loomis's dark gaze. The third has eyes of a celestial blue; that must be their missing partner. To her Human eyes, no genders are apparent, outside of slightly different scarlet-edged drapings of scaled skin. But she knows that aliens find it hard to distinguish men and women. And in the foreground, evidently caught in motion, are two much smaller dragons—their kids. She's looking at a pleasant family party, perhaps a backyard picnic, in what to her is an ashy blasted wilderness.

On impulse, she brushes the image lightly with a kiss before setting it back. She must finish her note and scoot out, not forgetting to leave a desk call for them so they won't miss the shuttle.

She does so, and books a simple sleeper in which she can finish her wait and have a meal in bed, and is soon herself asleep again. It is not until she wakes for good, and realizes that Boley and Loomis are long gone, that she begins to feel a trifle thoughtful.

She has just had what may well be the peak erotic experience of her young life. Will sex from now on be a bit . . . anticlimactic? There is no hope of repeating it; meetings and partings on the starways, over such immense time distances, are likely to be once in a lifetime. In fact, she won't even know their full names, nor they hers. Even if she calls their embassy, on her return, it will be far too late.

She sighs, smiles tremulously to cheer herself. Perhaps, back on Terra, they will have left their mark, maybe she can found a club. Dragon-Lovers Anonymous.

Well, she had gone and returned successful, and all these things had proved true—except of course the joke club. And now so many years later, she has by chance come on an address for them in the Hyades Complex, and is writing them a little note. Is it folly?

You can never step twice in the same river.

She knows that. But would it hurt to wave?

"Dear Bolingbroke, dear Loomis," she tells the letter-writer, and notes, from the corner of her eye, the colors of the rising Earth in Luna's black sky. "Perhaps you remember the Human female you met at Centaurus Junction so long ago. This is just to tell you that she remembers you, and wishes you most warmly well. With love,

Sheila."

And adds, like a lost mariner sending a note in a bottle,
"Of 209 Silver Terrace, Luna City, Sol."

In May of 1983, Lonnie Barbach offered Tiptree a spot in her anthology *Pleasures: Women Write Erotica,* a book of vignettes based on personal experience. Alli was unable to contribute at that time, but in 1985 was invited to write for *Pleasures II,* this one a collection of erotic short stories by women. "Trey of Hearts" (one of many titles considered, along with "Junction at Centaurus," "The Star-Traveling Saleswoman," "The Star-Traveling Saleswoman and the Love-Sick Dragons," and "Discovery of the Sleeper") was completed in May 1985 and sent to Barbach. It was longer than the editor could use, and she returned it with extensive, line-by-line suggestions for shortening. Unwilling to make that many changes Alli politely withdrew from the project. Virginia Kidd felt that this specialized a story wouldn't suit the SF market, and Alli agreed to retire the piece. This is its first publication.

THE COLOR OF NEANDERTHAL EYES

It's my fault, all of it and Kamir is dead.

But something must be done.

Now it is afterwards and I am recording this on shipboard so that you will understand. Much of this belongs in a Second Contact Report. Much more does not. But I am too torn up and tired to make a formal report. I am simply talking out what happened so you will see that something must be done.

It started while I was lazily cruising along just outside an island coral reef, on the beautiful sea-world unimaginatively christened "Wet." I see it now: turquoise sea and creamy small breakers, and across the green bay the snowy expanse of sand, backed by the feathery plumes of that papyruslike plant I learned to call *cenya*. The sun has started down, so I start my motor and go along the reef, looking for a pass. I find one, and cautiously zigzag through; my little new-rubber dinghy is too precious to risk hitting that sharp coral. Once through, I stop and turn, watching. Something has been following me all afternoon. I don't want to spend the night alone on a strange beach without checking out the creature.

Will it follow me in here?

I am, so far as I know, alone on Wet. And I'm tired. I'd been on a very strenuous year-long tour as Sensitive on an Extended Contact party six lights away. It's hard work, building up an FVV—First Verbal Vocabulary—and the aliens I was dealing with had complicated, irritable, niggling minds. The niggling made for an accurate vocabulary, but it was tiring for the lone telepath on the team. And it was a high-gee planet, which made for more fatigue. I had earned my post-tour leave. When we passed near Wet, I opted to be put down in a lander for weeks of restful solitude.

Wet has been visited only once before, by a loner named Pforzheimer, who stayed only long enough to claim a First Contact. His notes in the Ephemeris say that there are humanoid natives, confined to the one small continent, or large island, on the other side of the planet from me. Besides that, what land there is consists of zillions of small islands and islets, mostly atolls, long looping chains of them everywhere, archipelagos forming necklaces around friendly seas.

Wet seems to be in an interglacial period with the ocean at maximum height, and only a tiny ice cap on the south pole. And its sun is yellow, like Sol but smaller, so that even here near the equator the noon heat is merely pleasant. A tropical paradise in this season. There is even a magnetic field; my compass works. I left the lander at my base camp due south, and have come exploring this pretty chain of islets.

Ah!

In the pass I am watching there bobs up a round head, rather like a seal's, but glinting a fiery pink in the sunlight. The creature is following me into the bay.

What to do? Is it a predator? If so, it has had plenty of chances to make for me while I was diving, but did nothing. More important, is it a marine animal or an amphibian? Much of Wet's wildlife seems to be amphibious, their lives and bodies undecided between sea and land—a natural development here. If my follower stays in the sea, well and good; but if it comes ashore, I won't have a reposeful night.

As I look, the head swivels, apparently spots me, and submerges again. A ripple in the water shows it coming on in. I float quietly, undecided. Perhaps it is merely curious. That might imply high intelligence. But what persistence! It has been around me, now near, now farther off, since noon. What should I do?

Then something happens! A swirl in the water behind the creature, and a glimpse of something white. I have a notion what it is—one of the giant white crabs I have seen (and avoided) on the reefs. Our passage must have attracted it.

At this moment the creature accelerates to a very respectable speed and heads straight toward me. The swirl of the crab accelerates, too. I receive a mental flash of excitement, mixed with a trace of fear. Clearly the creature is racing to get away from the crab; but why toward me? Does it feel I am somehow a refuge?

I check my impulse to start my motor and take myself out of the path; I feel responsible for my follower's plight.

I shilly-shally until there is a commotion in the water alongside. The alien creature has arrived right by me. Then two pale green arms shoot out of the water and grasp the dinghy, and, so suddenly I have no time to react, the creature boosts itself up and tumbles into the bow of the boat—with a startlingly Human laugh!

Can it be Human? No—a humanoid, I see as I get a better look at its waving feet. Long membranous flippers are folding themselves around its toes, and the fingers are webbed. But the form is Human— quite beautifully so, I notice. And the creature is sending out a wave of excited pleasure.

I have evidently encountered the hominid inhabitants of Wet.

My first reaction is—damn it all. I'm in no condition to exercise my special talents, to do a Contact routine. But somehow the laugh beguiles me. I don't need to do more than a minimal scan to grasp that my visitor is in no way hostile.

But there's no time for more—a big white pincer-crab claw has lashed across the boat and is coming at the alien. I fumble for my harpoon.

Before I can find it, the situation is solved. Still laughing, the alien expertly grasps the claw and whips out a shell knife from its belt—yes, it is wearing a belt and loincloth—and runs the knife down the claw, severing its "thumb," or lower pincer. The thumb drops to the bottom of the boat, the now-harmless claw batters about a bit, and a second, smaller claw comes aboard. The process of dethumbing is repeated. For a moment both ex-pincers are battering and waving, and then the great crab, seeming to grasp its trouble, gives up and slides back into the sea.

The alien, grinning, bends and retrieves the thumbs, shaking its flaming red hair back from its face. With its knife, it scoops the meat out of their shells and leans aft. It is offering one claw meat to me! I take it, puzzled. It is like a big white banana.

The alien pops the other piece into its mouth and bites, nodding and smiling at me. Good! Cautiously, I taste it without swallowing. It is delicious—but alien food like this can contain an infinity of hazards. The crab's flesh could be laced with something lethal to me—as simple as arsenic—to which the locals are immune.

Regretfully, I lay the luscious white meat down on a thwart and gear my mind up to communicate the thought, "Thank you. It is very good. But we are very different. I come from another world."

To my inexpressible surprise and relief the alien, its deep blue eyes fixed on mine, sends back, "I know, I know." So they are natural telepaths! How rare, how wonderful!

And more is coming: "Other one came from sky a long time past." A foggy picture of what must have been Pforzheimer forms in my head, evidently a passed-on image. "Are you like that?"

Mind-questions are hard to ask. The alien does it by superimposing a figure I see is me, and flashing back and forth fast to the Pforzheimer image with an eager feel. "Yes," I send. "We come from the same world."

The alien eats more crabmeat, considering this.

Then comes another, more complex question I don't get. Foggy flashing images of Pforzheimer opening and shutting his mouth, blurry pictures of what might be planets of different sizes and colors . . . "many worlds . . ." I am roused to make the effort to probe for the alien's verbal speech, and try a guess.

"You say, the other-one-like-me said there are many worlds, many peoples?"

Enthusiastic assent. I've hit it.

And from then on, we converse in an irreproducible mix of verbal and transmitted speech, unmatched for fluency and ease. I report it here as close as purely spoken speech can come.

"Yes, that's true," I tell the alien. "There are many races. Some stay on their worlds, others travel much—like me."

The alien smiles broadly, the blue eyes in what I realize is a very beautiful face bright with pleasure. He snuggles down into a comfortable position in the bow, reaching for my rejected crab claw.

"Show me! Show me all!"

He is evidently prepared for a long session of entertainment. But the sunset is casting great golden rays across the sky, tinting the flocks of little island-born cumuli and generating lavender shadows on the blue-green sea. I must prepare for the night.

"Too many to show all. Too many to know all. I will show you one, others later. The night comes."

"Yes, I know how you do in the night. You take this"—he slaps the boat with the knife—"onto land, and sleep. I have watched you two days." There is a smile of mischief in his blue eyes.

What? But I only spotted him this noon. However, I recall some vague impressions of sentience nearby that had caused me momentary disquiet. So that's what they were—emanations of my new acquaintance, watching!

"Good. Here is one other world." I send a nice detailed view of the fiery planet of the Comenor, with a few of its highly intelligent natives hopping about or resting alertly, tripedal, on their large, kangaroolike tails. The Comenor had been one of the races I trained on.

"Ah! And they think, they speak? Do they make music?" The alien raises its voice in a provocative little chant.

"Yes . . . yes . . . let me remember—" I try to render one of the Comenor's pastoral airs.

"Hmm . . ."

As he sits there reflecting, with the golden light playing on his flaming hair, I realize I may be mistaken. I have been calling him "he" because of his breastless body, flat belly, and slim hips, and perhaps also because he is apparently alone in the open sea. But that face could belong to a beautiful woman. And he is *not* Human; there is a strange fold running down the throat, and the pupils of his eyes are hourglass-shaped. Nor is he even mammalian; no nipples mar the pale green curves of his pectoral muscles, although he has a small navel. Perhaps "he" is female, or epicene, perhaps it is the custom of his race for females to wander far alone. Whatever, my new friend is enchanting to look at; even his accoutrements of knife, belt, and loincloth are charmingly carved and decorated.

"Wonderful," he says at length. "And you have seen this and more?"

"Yes."

"I would like to do so."

"It might be possible, someday. Maybe. But now I must go ashore." I send him an image of himself getting out of the boat so I can drive the bow up the beach.

"Yes, I know." Again the hint of mischief in the smile. He pops the remains of the crab claw in his belt, and in one graceful flash is overboard. As he sails past I glimpse that strange fold on his neck opening to show a feathery purple lining. Gills! So he is truly aquatic. No wonder I didn't see him until he decided to show.

I start the motor and examine the beach. As often here, a small stream meanders to the bay in its center, marked by clumps of the tall, plumy papyruslike plants. I'll have fresh water to top off my canteens.

I choose the larger expanse of beach and head for its center, where I'll have maximum warning if anything approaches. I've searched inland on several atolls, and so far found no sign of any predators—indeed, of anything larger than a kind of hopping mouse and a wealth of attractive semi-birds. But I'd prefer not to have even hop-mice investigate me in the night.

I rush the dinghy up a smooth place, jump out, and drag it beyond the tideline. There are low, frequent tides in this part of Wet, generated by a trio of little moons that sail across the sky three times a night, revolving around each other. Like everything else here, they are attractive—one is sulfur-yellow, another rusty pink, the third a blue-white.

The alien offers to help me with the boat. I warn him about punctures and letting the air out. He steps back, warily.

"Thank you."

When I detach the motor and batteries, he comes to examine them.

"More wonders. How does this work?"

"Later, later." I am puffing with exertion as I take out all my gear and turn the boat over to make a bed, hopefully out of reach of the little nocturnal crabs and lizards on these beaches. The alien watches everything closely, nodding to himself. When I have dried the dinghy's bottom and laid out my sleep shelter, he sits down on the sand alongside.

"Now you will—" Quick images of me relieving myself among the papyrus and returning to sit on the boat and eat.

I laugh; the pictures are deft cartoons, emphasizing our mutual differences and also the—I fear—growing plumpness around my belt.

"Yes. And I fill my canteens. The beach last night had no fresh water."

"Good. I, too, will eat." He opens his belt pouch and extracts the crabmeat, together with two neatly cleaned little reef fish. Raw fish must be a staple here.

When I return, he is still delicately eating. I offer him water but it is refused. "You don't need fresh water after such a long time in the salt sea?"

"Oh, no." I reflect that their bodies must have solved the problem of osmosis, which dehydrates seagoing Humans. Perhaps that beautiful pale greenish, velvety-looking skin is in fact some sort of osmotic organ.

I settle down with my food bars, enjoying the unmistakable sense of companionship that emanates from the alien. We are both examining each other between bites, and I find that his smile is contagious; I am grinning, too. Extraordinary! Especially after my last aliens.

Now I can see more signs of his—or her—aquatic origins. A rudimentary, charmingly tinted dorsal fin shows at the back of his neck, running down his spine to surface again just above its end. There is a frilly little fin on the outside of each wrist. All these fishlike trappings fold away neatly when not in use. The flipper-fins on his feet fold over the toes so as to appear as merely decorations. And his hair isn't true hair, I see, but more like the very thin tendrils of a rosy anemone; a sensory organ, perhaps. Am I seeing a member of a race that has evolved directly from fishes? I think so; these appendages look more like evolutionary remnants than new developments to my untrained eye. He is on his way out of, rather than back to, the sea. But could he be cold-blooded? No; when our bodies had brushed together, I had felt solid warmth under the thick, cool integument.

But perhaps he is not "on his way" at all; on this world, his adaptations seem perfect. There is every reason to retain his aquatic features, and none at all to lose them. I think I am seeing a culminant form, which will not change much, at least from natural pressures.

He for his part is looking me over with care.

"You do not swim well," he concludes, extending one foot and flicking the flippers open.

"No, but we have these." I reach under the dinghy and pull out my swim fins to show him. He laughs appreciatively, and I reflect that my race, like seals, *is* returning to the sea—by prosthesis.

"My world has much dry land," I explain. "My race grew up from land animals who never went to sea." What am I doing, assuming a grasp of evolution theory on the part of one whose mind may not be much more than a fish's? Yet he seems to understand.

"Wonders." He smiles.

Next he is fascinated by my teeth. I show him all I can, and he in turn displays the ridges of hard white cartilage I had taken for teeth.

And so we pass the evening, chatting like amiable strangers, while the golden sun turns red and sinks, silhouetting the fronds of the papyrus. We exchange names late, as is customary with telepaths. His is Kamir. He has a little trouble with mine, Tom Jared. His people, he tells me, are three days' travel away, to the east. Why is he alone? That one is difficult; I can only guess that he means he is exploring for pleasure. "It is the custom."

Somehow I cannot bring myself to take up the question of sex, even though I know he is curious, too; once or twice I catch a tendril of his thought lingering around my swim trunks.

But through all our talk, I am amazed by what can only be called its courtesy. Its civility. Never do I strike a hostile or "primitive" reaction. It is a little like being questioned by a bright, well-brought-up child. Innocence, curiosity, those are neotenic—childlike—traits. Neotenia has been a feature of Human development. Kamir's race is neotenic, too. But beyond that, he is indefinably but unmistakably *civilized*. Whatever may turn out to be his technological level, I am communing with a civilized mind.

It grows darker, and a myriad of unknown stars come out. I grow sleepy, despite the interest of the occasion. Kamir notices it.

"Now you desire sleep."

"Yes."

"Good. We sleep." And he pulls up the back flap of his loincloth to make a pad for his head and simply lies back peacefully. I wriggle round in my sleep shelter and do the same.

"Good night, sleep well, Kamir."

"Sleep well, 'Om Jhared." Then suddenly he adds a question I sense as deadly serious: "Will more like you come?"

I am glad to be able to reassure him. "No, unless you ask. Oh, maybe once a small party to record your world, if you do not object."

"Why should we?"

And so we both relax, the alien on his warm white sand, me on my galactic dinghy, and the little crabs and lizards and other creatures of the night come out and sing or fiddle or chirrup their immemorial chorus. I remember thinking as I drift off that they are a good warning system; only when all is still do they sing.

When I waken in full sunlight, all is calm and still. Too still; the sea is like glass. I check my barometer. Yes, it has started downward.

Kamir is nowhere in sight. I feel a sense of loss. What, has he abandoned interest in me to return to his watery world? I hope not.

And—good!—in a moment or two there's a splash out on the reef. Kamir surfaces. He comes quickly back to shore, towing something. When I go to meet him, I see that it is a silky purse-net, full of flapping fish.

Too preoccupied to greet me, he hurries up the beach and kneels over his catch, his beautiful face tense. He begins quickly decapitating them, finishing the last one before cleaning any. Then he sits back, sighing relievedly.

"Their pain and confusion are hard to bear," he tells me. Then, smiling, "Morning greetings, 'Om Jhared!"

"Greetings." I know what he means. I once made the error of going too near a meat-killing place; it had taken me a fortnight to recover.

"I wish we could eat some other way. We all do," Kamir tells me, working on the fish. "But plants are not enough."

I agree, looking over his net. An elegant little artifact, clearly handmade. His is not a machine culture. "I think there is a storm coming."

"Oh yes." He touches his shining hair. "My head is full of it."

"When?"

"This evening for sure." He looks me over again, curiously. "What will you do in the storm, 'Om Jhared?"

"Take my stuff farther up on land and wait it out. What will you do?"

"Well, of course, we go down into the deep water where all is calm and wait it out, as you say. Very boring . . . But today I think I will stay with you. I haven't seen a storm on top since I was a child. Would you like me to be with you? I can help carry your things." His head cocks to the side as he looks up, shy, coy, absolutely charming. I can no longer stand this convention of "he."

"Kamir—"

"Yes?"

"Kamir, in my race there are two types of people, because of our way of reproduction—" I begin a clumsy exposition of gender and sex. What's the matter with me? I never have trouble with this part of Contact, never thought about it before.

I am halfway through when Kamir bursts out laughing. "Yes . . . yes . . . We also have two. And . . . ?" Another of those killing smiles.

"And which are you?"

"Do you ask?"

"Yes."

"I thought it was plain. Perhaps because I am so ugly it is not."

"Ugly? But you are very beautiful, Kamir."

The lovely face turns on me, the incredible deep blue eyes wide. "Do you *mean* that, 'Om Jhared?" A hand comes timidly to clasp my forearm.

"I mean it. *Yes*."

Very softly Kamir says, "I thought never to hear those words." Then whispering, "I am an egg-bearer. What you call a female."

And her—her!—red head goes down on my forearm, hiding her face.

I can only stammer, "Ah, Kamir, I wish we were not of different races!"

"I too," she breathes.

It is incredible, whether a chance match of pheromones across the light-years, whatever, I am trembling. I look down her graceful back, with its lacy frill proclaiming her alienness, and it does not seem alien at all. My mermaiden.

But I am in mortal danger, I must straighten up and fly right.

"Kamir, I do not think you should stay with me through the storm."

"Why not?"

"It—there might be dangers—" It is impossible to lie to a telepath.

"If you can endure them, so can I! Ah, why do we speak nonsense? For some reason you are afraid of my nearness."

"Yes," I say miserably. What can I tell her convincingly? Of the iron Rule Number One in ET contacts? Of the follies that Humans, men and women alike, succumb to? Of the fact which I have just realized, that I have been a very lonely man? Why else, I ask myself, should I be so smitten by a purely chance resemblance to Human beauty?

"Look," she says, lifting her head to the sky. "The storm is coming much faster . . . I don't think I will have time to swim to a really safe place. If my presence disturbs you, I will stay far, very far away. When we have moved your things."

Little mischief, is she lying? My senses tell me so. But when I, too, look up, I see that the sky has taken on a curiously yellowish tint, though no clouds show yet. The sea is so flat it looks oily, and the air is ominously still and hot. She is right, whatever is coming is moving fast. And these seas *are* shallow, it may be a long way to a deep place. In any event, it is time to secure my possessions.

"Very well," I say with profound unwisdom. "Then if you want to help me, we will move my boat and the rest up into the dunes behind the beach."

She smiles radiantly, and we go to it.

But it is a slow process; she exclaims with interest and curiosity over all my things, wet suit, waterproof recorder, pump, repair kit, camera, lights, charging device, scuba gear, first-aid kit, my lighter—I find she knows fire, which her people accomplish by twirling hardwood sticks—and all, down to the binoculars, which charm her, and the harpoons, which turn her very sober.

"You kill much."

"Only for food, like you. Or to save my life."

"But this is so big."

"Well, I might be attacked by something big, like the crab. You killed it, you know. Without claws it will die of starvation."

"Oh, no! It will eat algae. And the claws will grow again. We use them like that to pull building supplies." Image of a big crab with a harness hooked on its carapace, hauling a laden travois. "When they get dangerous, we chase them back to sea."

"Ah."

Some perverse honesty compels me to show her my waterproof laser, which I carry in my swim trunks.

"This is for use if I am attacked on land." I demonstrate on a nearby shell. She runs to examine the burn.

"It would do this to flesh?"

"Yes."

"Why, when I came in your boat, you might have done this to me?"

Blue, blue eyes gaze at me, horrified.

"Not unless you attacked me so viciously that my life was in danger."

"Oh, but could you not *feel* the warmth?" She flutters her hand from herself to me and back. I think. Yes—from the first moment, I could. Damn it.

"Well! You are strange." Shaking her head, she resumes lugging a battery up the dune. She is very strong, I notice.

We have found a splendid hollow in the high dunes in which to ride out the storm. Somehow nothing more is said about her staying far, far away.

Finally, we stake my big tarpaulin over the heap of belongings and bring up the boat. I rope it upside down to three stout plant roots. The scrub "trees" growing here resemble giant beach gorse and have great hold-fast roots.

By now, the air is so humid and strange that our voices seem to reverberate on the still beach. And we can see a level line of white cloud rising up at us from the horizon, growing against the upper wind. Under it is a tinge of darkness, the first sight of the squall line. And in the far distance beyond towers pale cumulus. It looks like a whole frontal system coming on us. Will the weather change?

"You may grow cold here, Kamir."

"Oh, I am used to that."

"You could put on my wet suit." (What, and leave me naked? I am mad.)

"No, when we cover our skins, we grow too thirsty."

Aha, I was right about the osmotic protection in the skin. Perfect adaptation.

"Well, if it turns cold, we can always make a fire. Let's gather some of these heavy stalks and stems."

When all is ready, we sit on the dune top, swinging our legs and eating our respective provisions, watching the squall line rise until it divides the visible world. On our side all is still and sunny and hot; we are caught in an eerie stasis. A kind of water animal I haven't seen before paddles about in the bay, followed by a line of small ones.

"Jurros," Kamir observes. "They are very tame. Only the big fish bother them."

I wonder about those "big fish." Are they sharklike? But in response to my query Kamir only laughs.

"Oh, you pop them on the nose. They run away."

Well, I have heard people say that about white sharks. I resolve to watch out for any "big fish."

The storm is closer and closer, but still nothing stirs around us. Half the sky is shuttered with black roiling clouds, yet here it is impossibly bright and calm. The barometer must be falling through the deck, it is suddenly a little hard to breathe. I check it; yes, it's at the lowest point I've seen it. This is going to be ferocious.

We watch quietly, gripped by the drama of the scene. The water animal has now disappeared.

Just as it seems that nothing will ever happen, a shudder runs through the world. Still in total calm, the sea wrinkles itself like the skin of a great beast. A tiny puff of cool wind lifts our hair. And a few big drops of rain, or perhaps hailstones, plop into the surface of the water and onto the beach.

And then, with a rush and a bellow, the storm hits.

In a moment the flat water has reared itself into a thousand billows two meters high, running unbroken from shore to shore. The breeze becomes a blast of wind against us. In the last rays of sunlight, a million specks of diamond flash from the waves into darkness. And then the sun is eclipsed by cloud, the world is twilight-dark.

Eerily, the papyrus plants all bend over with a whipping sound before we feel the wind that bent them. And then it hits, and the boat bangs up and down as if it will tear from the earth.

We scramble back from the dune-top and get under cover of the boat, holding it down over our heads. Then the sky opens, and tons of water dump on us, drumming intolerably on the boat. I am sure it is hail that will tear the boat, but when I stick out a hand, it is not. The world is in uproar around us.

Kamir is going excitedly "Whoo! Whee!" I can barely hear her over the storm, but I can see her eyes flashing blue fire and her little back fin standing straight up.

"This is not boring?" I yell.

"No!" Laughing, grinning with excitement.

"But—" I begin and am drowned out by a *crack!* of lightning, and

thunder like a gigantic bolt of tearing silk. Then the cracks and flashes
and roars and rumbles are all about us. The strikes seem to be hitting
the beach and the dunes. I see Kamir's fin suddenly clamp itself into her
back, and her laughter changes to a squeal. I realize she hasn't seen, or
has forgotten, the lightning part of a storm. She hangs on to my arm,
quaking as each bolt hits. And then, somehow, she is in my arm, her face
pressed against my chest, while I hang on to the boat for dear life with
the other arm.

"It won't hit us, the boat will stop it," I howl at her.

Water is coursing down the sides of the hollow we are in. Down
below, the beach has disappeared under a wilderness of sinister yellow-
gray breakers that are striking and tearing against the dunes, and throwing spray to mingle with the rain on us.

But by degrees, the wind changes from a wild whirl to a steady
blow, driving the rain across us, and I am able to release my aching arm
and rope the boat more securely.

That was, I think, my last chance to escape.

But I do not take it. That arm joins the other around the slender
quivering Kamir, and she clamps her whole body against me. For
warmth.

Her back is cold. I rub it to warm her, cannot resist fingering the
pretty little fin, which makes her giggle. I rub, stroke, but the coolness
seems to be in her skin. It feels thick, a pale green velour over soft
curves. I try to concentrate on its interest, its prevention of dehydration.
Yes, I see there are tiny pores, but how they function is beyond me. I am
stroking rhythmically now, unable to keep from enjoying the exquisite
forms of her back and flanks.

And oh! Warmth comes, but not the warmth I wanted. Her shivers
have turned into unmistakable, sinuous wiggles under my hand. She is
whispering something, her free hand feeling for my swim trunks. And,
gods! Her silken loincloth seems to have come undone. . . . Tom Jared,
what are you doing? Stop now, you fool. This is no girl, but a grown
alien—a god-lost *fish!*

There is no stopping. I have only time to glimpse what seems to be
an organ on the front of her lower belly, a solid mounded track running
up to her navel, like a newly healed scar. My body has taken me over,
relieved me of the cold swim trunks, and is longing to press into her.

Only, where? Her crotch is as smooth as an armpit. I can only lay myself alongside the "scar" and squeeze our bodies together. "Yes," she says, "Oh yes." There is a feeling of clasping.

From there on I don't know exactly what happens. It isn't Human, but exciting beyond words, and finally, somehow, fulfilling. And at its height, a tremendous lightning bolt hits the beach. . . .

Much later, I come back to consciousness. The rain is still drumming on our shelter, but the wind has abated somewhat, and the waves aren't quite so fierce. More water has drained into our hollow; we are lying in a puddle.

Kamir is asprawl, half under me and wholly wet. For a moment I fear I have hurt her. But she is only deeply asleep.

And I—I have broken Rule One, and the sky will fall on me. And I do not care.

"Kamir? Kamir?"

Answering smile, long, slow, and beautiful. Lazily the big eyes open their sea-blue pools.

"Are you all right, my dear?"

"Umm . . ." Sleepy, obviously as fulfilled as I. Her lips move.

"What?"

"Never . . ."

"Never what?"

"I thought—never would I know—Oh, you have been sent from the skies to rescue me."

Wild bells of warning—new ones—ring in my head. Does she assume I will stay here with her? Oh gods—I bitterly reproach my offending body, my weakness. But looking at her lying there, the mere thought of leaving gives me a pang. Can it be that I truly love this little alien? Oh gods! How wise are the Federation regs!

"Let me get you out of this water."

"Why? It's comfortable. . . ." As if daring greatly, she puts her hands up to my cheeks, the dainty wrist frills quivering.

"Tell me, 'Om Jhared: Do I still seem beautiful to you?"

"Yes . . . oh, yes! But why do you ask? Don't you know you are beautiful?"

"But I am ugly, everybody knows that. My people say I am so ugly it is good when I leave!"

"No!" I protest. "But to me, and to the eyes of all my people, you would be considered wonderfully lovely."

"Ahhh . . ." She gives me an adoring look and a smile and the next moment is fast asleep again, like a child. My mermaid.

There seems nothing better to do. I follow suit.

We wake in darkness. The wind has died, and the three little moons are rising, showing a sky of racing cloud fragments.

"Hungry!" exclaims Kamir, grinning.

"I too."

And we rise from our puddle and go up to sit on the dune top, now scoured almost flat by the gale. Below us the beach is emerging from the waves. It is chilly; a fire seems good, so I bring up the dry stuff we had collected and soon have a comfortable little blaze.

She is fascinated by my lighter. Soon she has satisfied herself that it uses the principle of friction, too, like her people—but what is it *made* of? What is this stuff, "metal"? Rock, coral, and shell are the hardest substances she knows.

So the evening starts, unexpectedly, with a lecture on metallurgy. Oh, if I could only find deposits of something, iron, copper, silver, tin! I rack my memory, can only remember something about manganese globules on the seafloor—or is it magnesium? There must be some metal available to these people, if only I could tell them what to look for. I dream of precipitating them into an Iron Age before—before I go. I wince.

As to my plastic gear, I can only describe to her a gross oversimplification of petrochemicals and polymers. She shakes her head worriedly.

"So much! You have so much. . . . But do you have music?"

I fish in my recorder pack and come up with a lovely piece by Borgnini.

"Listen. This reminds me of you." Which it does, especially the flute solos.

She cocks her head at the first notes. Then, seeing me lie back, she flops down with her head on my stomach to listen. I am diverted by the shining red silk of her pseudohair.

"Oh!" she exclaims once or twice. "Ah!" I think she likes it.

When the piece has drawn to its ravishing finale, she turns to me with glowing eyes. "Oh, you have beautiful music! I never—we never heard such sounds. But no voices?"

"Not in this one. They are what we call musical instruments."

"We must make some," she says determinedly. "You will show us how. Now, more!" She leans back again.

"I haven't much in this little box. But here is another from my homeland." I give her Brahms's *Quintet for Clarinet in E.*

And so the evening passes. . . . I am impossibly happy.

Before retiring, we drag the boat up to the top to sleep on, and spread out her loincloth to dry. It's more complex than it looks, with four small pockets. The fishnet goes in one. I concentrate on this to avoid looking at her body.

"You shall wear this now," she says shyly, patting the cloth.

"Me? Oh no."

"Yes. It is right."

"Why, what does the loincloth mean?"

"Well, first they mean that we are ripe. All my age-group are wearing cloths now. When all are ready, they go out to sea, to explore and to meet each other. When"—I think she says—"when a couple forms, they exchange clothes and return so, to let everybody know they are together. Of course I went out alone, this way where nobody will come, because I knew nobody would want me. I expected nothing. And I found you! Oh—"

In an exuberance of love, she pounces on me, and before I can protest, rolls me off the boat and around in the sand, nuzzling and kissing me. Strong little mermaid!

I catch her and roll her back and we play like puppies.

When we are both gasping with laughter, naked and sandy, we fall into each other's arms and let nature have her will. Blissfully, there are no insects here. We fall asleep once more, enmeshed in love.

Only, just as I am drifting off, I catch her whisper.

" 'Om Jhared?"

"Yes?"

"You will, won't you?"

"Will what?"

"Care for them. You will?"

"Them? What?" I force myself awake.

"Our babies."

Oh, gods.

"Kamir," I say gently, "I hope this will not make you sad, but there won't be any babies. Our physical beings, our bodies are too different."

She frowns. "You don't think there will be babies?"

"No. I'm sorry."

"Well," she says, with a return of her old mischief, "I think differently!" And she lays one hand on her abdomen, smiling, and lies back.

So do I, but not restfully. It has occurred to me that some Terran mammals, like rabbits, will give birth parthenogenetically if stimulated by saline water. What if, gods, what if she is right, and some monster is born?

" 'Om Jhared?"

"Yes?"

"Even if there are no babies, as you say, you will at least stay until I die?"

Oh, no—does she mean, spend my life with her? Gods, what have I done? "Oh my dear, do not talk of dying. Not now."

"Yes," she says musingly, "maybe you are right. But I think of it."

And I can feel a dark shadow on her mind.

"But why think of it? Please don't, my dear."

"Why? Because it comes so soon. Do you not know? This is my last season in the world now."

"Oh, Kamir. What's wrong? What's wrong?" I am bending over her, afraid of I know not what. "Tell me!"

"Why, because we love. Because I love with you. It is not so with you?"

"Kamir, I don't know what you're saying. What is wrong?"

"Nothing is wrong. When you love, you die. The woman dies. The man lives, to feed the babies. Is it not so?"

"No! No! In my race, the females live long, whether or not they love. Longer than the men, often. Do you mean you expect to die because we made love?"

"Why, yes. We all do. Only I feared I would live forever, alone."

"Good gods . . . But I am sure you won't have a baby, Kamir. We are too different. Like a—a crab and a fish, they can't have young together."

"And you are the crab?" She laughs playfully. "But no, perhaps you are right. We won't think of it. This is our happy time."

She snuggles down closer in the hammocky boat. "Sleep well, dear 'Om Jhared. Sleep well."

"Sleep well, my darling."

I lie sleepless, incredulous.

What horrible wrong have I committed in my selfish lust? Even if I call it "love," it led me terribly astray.

The little beach-life is tuning up its night song, but I am in no mood to appreciate it. A million unanswered questions are revolving in my head like rolls of barbed wire. What is this murderous process she believes will kill her? There must be a way to stop it. It can't be biological, the species wouldn't survive. Perhaps the people in the village make some lethal potion or charm they give the women. I could stop her taking it. Maybe they acquiesce in their deaths, by stopping eating, or something of that sort. I could stop that, too. There must be a way—I *must* stop it.

Eventually fatigue takes me and I lose consciousness, to dream of a terrifying great crab taking Kamir.

The morning is washed clean and clear, the barometer is high. Kamir gets up and announces she will go to the reef for fresh fish. I get out my scuba gear and prepare to go with her; I don't want us to be parted.

She is still nude, and as she stands, stretching luxuriously in the morning sun, I make myself inspect her.

She is a radiant figure, palest of green-whites in the golden sun, with that mop of fiery "hair." A faint flush suffuses her cheeks and lips and touches her body here and there. There is no other hairlike stuff on her; she is as smooth as a marble statue. Only, on her lower abdomen, there is this vertical thick welt I had glimpsed, like an old cicatrice. I see it is composed of two long lips, tightly appressed. Evidently their opening discloses the softness I had found. Closed, it is only a keloidlike ridge.

I find I, too, am being inspected. After a moment she comes close and touches me. Involuntarily I react, and she draws back, laughing and shaking her head.

"So different!" she says. Then, "Show me a picture of your women."

But I find I can barely summon up an adequate image of a Human female, so much has this little mermaid obsessed me. When I do, it seems, well, messy and strange.

"Hmm," she says. "So all are ugly, like me!"

"What is this 'ugly'?" I am becoming exasperated. "What about you is supposed to be ugly?"

"Why, I am so thin and bony, all over." She puffs out her cheeks and with her hands sketches over herself the outlines of a very fat woman. "I should be like this! Then you live long enough to help. Oh, but I see you don't want me to say that. Let's go to the sea."

So we run down the dunes and splash out until I have to stop to put on my gear. It all amuses her vastly. When I submerge, she circles me, swift as a fish, with her flared-out gills. I have trouble making her take my needs seriously; she tries to slip my mask off for a kiss, and I have to surface and explain that if she wishes to keep her lover, she must allow him to breathe. She sobers quickly, catching my serious feeling-tone, and after that we have no more trouble.

It is enchanting, down below, watching her herd little reef fish into her net. And I, too, sorrow when we come out and have to kill them.

I have an idea.

"Kamir, have you ever looked at yourself?"

"Oh yes. Mavru keeps a polished shell. And sometimes in very still water."

"Look." And I root out my little mirror. "Now you will see beauty."

She loves it, turning it to catch me, too. But she cannot resist trying to make a "fat" face.

I try to convince her, tracing my fingers over her delicate features. But she only hugs me.

"I may keep this? No one has seen anything like it."

"Certainly."

That reminds me. While she is tucking away the mirror, I try to ask her what her people call themselves. It's the same old situation, they are only "the people," or "us." Her particular settlement is "the Souls of Ema," after some legendary father, and a neighboring group is the "Souls of Aeyor," for a woman who made an extraordinary trip.

"But we must have a name for you. You don't want to let outsiders name you something like 'Homo Wettensis'?" (Or, gods forbid, Homo Pforzheimerana.)

"Homo Wettensis?" she mimics, giggling. "Why?"

So I have to explain about her world being called "Wet." That sends her off into paroxysms of laughter. But then she sobers. "Mnerrin."

"What?"

"An old word that means 'wet,' or 'the wet ones.' Would that not do?"

"Why yes, if your people agree. *Mnerrin* is quite fine."

"Oh, they won't mind. Very well; your Mnerrin asks, what shall we do today?"

"Well, would you like to explore inland? Or shall we look for some islands you haven't visited? I thought we might go in my boat, it will just take two."

She clasps her hands like a delighted child. "I'd love that! Yes, there are islands there"—she points north—"that haven't been seen for lifetimes."

"Let's go see!"

So we launch and repack the boat, and set off. She is much pleased with our speed, only once or twice she puts her hands over her ears as if the motor's hum bothers her.

"How fast does it go?"

I show her, but she soon covers her ears and cries, "Slow, slower, please—I can't see anything!" I realize that she has been mostly peering down into the water, while my eyes are on the sea and sky.

"Look, there is a big fish."

I see a moving shadow of enormous size, perhaps three meters. And before I can protest, Kamir throws a last morsel of fish overboard. The shadow surfaces—a big tan shape with round eyes. As it spots the fish, a long beaked bill breaks the water and clamps down. I get a glimpse of big, sharp cartilaginous ridges inside.

"That thing could take your arm off!"

"Well, if you let it, maybe. But look!"

To my horror, she rolls overboard. I see a flurry and a swirl and the thing hurriedly departs.

Kamir jumps and flips back in, laughing. "See? I just popped it on the nose, I told you."

"Don't ever do that again, my crazy little darling. It frightens me for you."

She rolls over and cuddles between my legs, still laughing. "Well, your driving this boat frightens me for you! But there is our first island."

The new island turns out spectacular, an old volcanic cone with strange tunnels running into the sea, from former lava tubes. So Kamir must be shown my instant camera, and exclaims over the tininess of the images. She wants to sleep there, but I detect enough signs of possible activity to make me discourage this, and toward evening we push on.

The next island proves to be full of the birdlike creatures. I pick one up—they are perfectly tame—and fancy I can trace signs of its evolutionary course from fish, too.

The next day there are two islands covered with a multitude of flowers, and the day after that, one whose river and bay teem with bright-colored, harmless sea snakes. And some days later comes a highlight; some river fish are clambering out of water and up in the undergrowth in pursuit of butterflies: And the next day an oddly barren island; and the next day, and the next . . .

I am guiltily aware that I should be making a record of all this. But when I get out my recorder and start, Kamir is so amused at my solemn tone of voice that we get little work done. My only concession to practicality is to keep a route map of our travel; so far it has been due north, so that my little base camp and the lander—about which I refuse to think—are still straight south.

We junket on and on over the turquoise sea, sometimes stopping to dive at barely-submerged coral reefs that would tear the bottom of a larger boat. And when the spirit moves us, we make love, sometimes in a fit of passion, sometimes gentle as children.

It is the happiest time of my life.

Only, one day I notice that where Kamir's stomach had been elegantly flat, it now seems to have taken on a womanly curve. I put it down to the extraordinary number of little butterfish she eats, and forget it . . . or try to. The weather is halcyon beautiful. A few times we see storms in the distance, but they do not come near.

One very clear night we are camped on a beach like the one on which we met, with a small estuary and its group of papyrus-cenya in the center. Kamir finishes the handsome wristband she has been making for me from the tail of her loincloth, using a splinter sliced from a cenya stem for a needle. (Regretfully, she has had to admit that we couldn't comfortably exchange clothes.) In lieu of my trunks I give her my identity bracelet; it won't do on her wrist because of the fin, but it goes nicely on her slim ankle.

When she sees the lettering, and I spell out my name, she frowns.

"I think this is something for Maoul," she says.

"Who is Maoul?"

"An old man, very wise. He made some of those land pictures you call 'maps.' These are something like that."

"Yes," I say, surprised. Bright little mermaid!

"And now"—she stretches out with her head on my lap, and hands me the binoculars—"you will tell me more, please, about those stars."

It is a topic we have just broached. I lament my star charts, left back in the lander; it is a perfect night for viewing, the moons are down for the hour, and the heavens are a riotous sight. I do the best I can; she is very keen and remembers well. Later we drift off to sleep, entangled in the binocular strap, with images of dark nebulae floating in our heads. . . .

—And then I am suddenly awake. What's happening? All is still; too still, that's what waked me. All the night creatures are silent.

Something is on the beach.

I listen hard and catch a faint splashing. Correction, something is coming out of the sea, over by the river outlet where papyrus-cenya hide the view. The moons are just rising. I sense Kamir is awake and listening, too.

Can it be a giant crab?

But as I form the thought, the last thing I expected in this world happens—a light shines out.

It's not a torch, but a bright greenish glow. Then it begins to blink, rhythmically. Signals?

"Ahhh," says Kamir. "Wait one moment, my love. I go."

"Kamir, wait—"

But she is up and racing down the beach, toward the cenyas.

I wait tensely, straining my ears. Aha—a faint colloquy; of course, I remember, I'll hear little, these people are telepaths. Anger rises; who or what dares to intrude on us? Who can it be? I realize I know so little about Kamir; could this be a father? A lover? A pang of raw jealousy grips me, the thought that it might be another woman never enters my besotted mind. And I've forgotten, or never believed, Kamir's story of being unmarriageable. Can this be a *husband*, hunting her?

And then abruptly, without my hearing footsteps, they are beside me, two forms blocking out the moonrise. The stranger is taller and much stouter than Kamir.

" 'Om Jhared? This is Agna, my egg-mate."

What is she telling me? I get the image of a large object, which crumbles or splits to reveal—no, not objects: babies. An image of a woman holding two of them.

"Your *brother?*"

"Yes, yes!"

Vast relief for me. I remember my manners.

"Greetings, Agna." But wait—has he come to charge me with violating his sister? Gods! No, he returns my greeting cordially, adding, "For three days I track Kamir. Now I find her here with you."

"Yes," says Kamir. "Agna, great happiness has come to me. 'Om Jhared is my mate."

"No!" says Agna, looking at me in astonishment. "But Kamir is so—so—"

I get an image of the unsaid word and push it away. So Kamir was being truthful about her "ugliness."

"In my eyes," I say firmly, "and in the eyes of my people if they could see her, Kamir is a very beautiful woman. Her appearance is so lovely that I was attracted to her at once. I only hope that I am not too ugly, as you call it, in your eyes."

"Never!" exclaims Kamir loyally, and adds with more realism, "He is so strange altogether that 'ugly' has no meaning. Oh, Agna, couldn't you tell? You followed a trail of happiness."

"Yes." Agna nods. "I was puzzled. Well, little sister, the sun of the seas seems to have smiled on you. Just when we gave up hope that you would develop, a mate comes from the skies!" He chuckles. "But I have come to bring you home. And 'Om Jhared, too, of course, if he will. The season of storms seems to have come unusually early this year. We should make the Long Swim now. And one has come from the Souls of Aeyor with very bad news."

"What news? What has happened? Aeyor is the campment near us," she reminds me.

"Later, later. You will have many questions, and I was not there when he came. Right now I need a bit of rest, and tomorrow early we will start."

"Oh, you are a tease, my solemn brother!" Kamir chides.

I am rather relieved that some Mnerrin are "solemn"; my little mermaid's unfailing merriment in the face of danger doesn't strike me as a survival trait. And I notice again what I had felt with Kamir, the sense of this person's profound civility. And he must be very tired; he apparently has been swimming for three days straight.

"You have eaten?" I inquire.

"Oh yes."

"Then let us go back to sleep, night traveler!" Kamir laughs, flopping down on our boat bed.

"Right."

Agna's preparations are as simple as Kamir's were; he untucks the tail of his finely decorated loincloth, sits down, and spreads it on the sand to protect his face and, saying, "Sleep well, little sister. Sleep well, 'Om Jhared," he lies back, face to the skies.

"Sleep well, Agna," we say.

I close my eyes against the bright, tricolored moonlight, and hold her close in silence. So our halcyon time has abruptly come to an end. I sigh, sad beyond measure. And what is this Long Swim Agna spoke of? It must be the seasonal migration Kamir had told me of; apparently the Mnerrin spend the stormy months at another island far to the south. I will, of course, go with them, somehow. Tomorrow I must calculate my batteries; perhaps I will have to return to the lander for recharge on the way . . .

My last thought, as sleep takes me, is the inflexible value they seem to place on what they call personal beauty. It is almost tangible to them—yet Agna was willing to accept my relative viewpoint. Civilized!

The nightly chorus is tuning up again, the three little moons ride high. What will the morrow bring? No—the day after; Agna estimated we were about two days' travel away in a straight line. . . . Out of the darkness comes a sleepy chuckle: Agna is laughing in his sleep. Kamir answers with an unconscious grunt, and I go to sleep.

The trip is dreamlike. Again I am struck by Mnerrin simplicity: next morning, after a quick breakfast and a pause to help me set a compass heading, Agna simply wades into the water and starts swimming. Through the pass, he turns due east, while Kamir and I pack up my gear and launch the boat.

It takes us a surprisingly long time to catch up to him—those pale flashing arms really cover the distance, and he swims in a knife-straight line. Kamir has shown me how her red "hair" works as a direction-finder in the sea. Still it seems strange to find a lone swimmer heading so confidently with no land in sight. I wish I could take him on board, but the dinghy only holds two.

We match our pace to his and settle down, sleepy in the balmy air. Kamir, too, is saddened by the end of our happy days. But presently she is restless.

" 'Om Jhared?"

"What is it, darling?"

"If you would not be too alone, I want to swim for a time with Agna. I need exercise, and I'd like to see more in the sea."

"I'll miss you, my darling. But if you want to, go."

So she tumbles overboard, and after that we go through regular exchanges, with Agna taking a rest now and then. As we follow Kamir, I think of how my little mermaid must have been before we met—a small person swimming alone in the wide seas. She had seen the fires of the lander's retro-rockets, she'd told me, and come to investigate. Fearless little mermaid!

Agna proves to be pleasant company, with an inquiring and thoughtful mind. Like his sister, he has red "hair" and blue eyes, though his crest is darker and his eyes lighter than hers. His features would have been handsome had they not been so larded with fat.

Following my theory of the ultimately utilitarian base for standards of beauty, I ask him if the plumpness they value so has any purpose.

"Does it serve to warm you in cold water?"

"Oh, perhaps. But certainly it means long life."

"Long life? How do you mean?"

"For the female, after bearing young. And for the male, too. It helps with the feeding time. See me; I have just finished feeding five young, so I am thin. But I could not have fed my babies so well, had I been this thin at the start."

Complexities. I realize I have spent my time enjoying myself with Kamir instead of collecting data. Yet somehow I am unwilling to pursue the matter now, and am grateful when he says, reflectively: "Yes, I see what you mean. We have never thought of it like that—interesting! And thus you must have a different system, in which fat plays no part?"

"Yes, we do, although I'm not sure of the details of yours. But we regard fat as unhealthy. For us, *fat* seems to threaten short life."

His eyes sparkle with interest.

"So! How fascinating. Yes, a good theory! But look, there is our dinner. Kamir!"

Without pausing, she shouts back over her shoulder, "I see it! Do you think I am asleep?"

"A reef, thick with *emalu*," Agna explains to me. "A pity we cannot bring some back for the people, it is delicious."

"We could pile it in the boat," I suggest; hoping that "emalu" is not, say, a stinging jellyfish.

"No; it wouldn't keep," Agna says regretfully, and dives overboard.

Kamir, too, has submerged.

They come up with handfuls of a golden, anemonelike fuzz, which they devour like Human children into cotton candy. Emalu is, it seems, a fabulous treat. I get out my food bars.

And it is fabulous, dining there on the sea with a pair of merpeople. At the moment, no land at all is yet in sight. I somehow hadn't realized, when Agna spoke of a two-day journey, that he meant two days and a night of simply swimming and sleeping on the open sea. Well, I'll be comfortable in the boat, and the weather seems settled. How will they do? I'm aware that there are a million questions I should be asking. But somehow it is difficult, conversing with two heads bobbing about on the ocean. The truth is, I'm unwilling to break the spell.

Their dinner over, Agna starts off again, and they swim till darkness. Agna calls for a conference and pulls out his light, which proves to be a small bundle of a lichenlike plant.

"Fish come to this," he explains to me. "I have to keep it in a dark pocket or I'd get no sleep! Tell me, little sister, do you wish to continue? I could lead with this light. But we have made good distance; I can feel home strongly. And there is a reef just ahead where we could have fresh breakfast."

"I feel it, too," says Kamir, who has been swimming with him. "I think we should stay here. I didn't get enough sleep last night, thanks to you." She laughs.

"Very well." Agna repockets his light and swims to a tactful distance. "Good night, little sister. Good night, 'Om Jhared."

"Good night," we call as Kamir climbs on board to join me.

We stretch out in the little boat and let the wavelets rock us to love and sleep.

But toward morning, Kamir nudges me awake. It's bright moonlight.

"Dear 'Om Jhared—I want to go in the sea now. To have a last sleep in the sea. Do you mind?"

"Yes, I mind. But go ahead, darling. Only don't go too far away."

"I won't. Oh, my sweet darling, my mate-from-the-stars!" And with a hug and a kiss she has gone into the deep water. I shudder with unknown fear. But she simply says good night again and turns over, gills open, to sleep in the sea. I see Agna's dark head floating, only a few yards away. Evidently there is no current here. I relax and try for sleep but it does not come. The image of my little mermaid slipping away from me into darkness haunts my mind. I watch her until the moons go down and I can no longer see.

Next morning we awaken still together, and the Mnerrin dive for their morning meal. Studying the horizon, I see, straight ahead, the kind of long, low cloud that means land. But the Mnerrin are scarcely interested; their senses had long told them it was there.

We set off as before. It is again dreamlike, but hour by hour the cloud grows higher, closer, until my binoculars show the island beneath, where the dream must end. Or change. But what a wonderful way to travel, I reflect, watching the two pairs of arms flash rhythmically. Living, sleeping, eating, *at home* in the sea. For all their Humanness, they are also aquatic animals. . . .

And I catch them mind-speaking each other as they go.

"See, Agna—new fish over there. Yellow, red, black tail . . . Will you remember it? I have at least twenty new ones to report."

"Yes . . . there must be a reef ahead," comes Agna's thought.

I am almost in a trance state when suddenly the unmistakable sound of voices singing comes across the water. We are arriving. I turn to my glasses and make out that we are coming to a large river estuary, surrounded by a low green swamp of delta, through which thread numerous streamlets. Behind the delta is the shore proper, a low bank running up to a plateau on which I can glimpse land vegetation, trees. And beyond that in turn rises a central mountain, green to its summit. A large island.

As we come closer I see that the swampy delta is full of small huts. And a column of smoke is rising from before a larger hut in the center. Most of the small ones appear in need of repairs, I see, as if no longer in use.

But most important, I see the people.

They are all on the beach, it seems, strolling or chatting in groups. One sizable group is lying down. And children are playing around them, seemingly all of one age. Babies, too, lie about doing Human-baby things, or are held in arms. All eyes are focused upon us; even through the glasses I can catch the gleams of blue. And I feel the feathery touch of mind-search.

I decide Kamir should arrive in style, so I bring her in the boat and put her up front with a paddle. As soon as we get closer I will hoist the motor and paddle her in.

The bay in front of the delta is quite narrow. Agna arrives at the reef and waves me to follow him through one of the many passes. Kamir is waving her paddle excitedly.

The mind-search and mind-greetings have become overwhelming. My mind-speech has much improved, so I send a formal greeting to the people, who respond in a babble. Evidently they have no formal spokesman.

"Whom shall I speak to, Kamir?"

"Oh, call to Maoul. That tall old man, there."

Agna is already wading ashore in Maoul's direction; we follow him in. And from there on, the afternoon is a genteel pandemonium.

Maoul greets us cordially, having received Agna's news. But everyone on the beach must receive it, too, and share it with others, and everyone must meet me and congratulate Kamir—with varying degrees of incredulity—and Agna disappears to go to his mate, who is one of the invalids lying down.

Finally he returns to direct us to his hut, and I make a fool of myself splashing through the swamp carrying my stuff, until someone points out that one walks in the little hard-bottomed rivulets, one of which, I now see, runs by every hut. By the time we get the boat and the gear up to Agna's terrain, after demonstrating everything to the crowd, dark is falling. And Maoul, it appears, has laid out a feast of celebration. They have caught a large fish to roast in cenya leaves, with various delectable fruits.

"Whoee!" Kamir laughs, plumping down on the boat after our last load. "That was fierce! Oh, 'Om Jhared, how I wish we were back alone with our islands!"

For me, too, the afternoon has been a melee of pale plump genial gentlemen in loincloths, eager children, ethereal invalids opening huge blue eyes at my strangenesses, and endless repetition by mind and speech.

"Me too." I hug her. "But what is the bad news Maoul started to explain? I got carried off to be shown to the ladies. What's the matter with the women, by the way? They're so thin. Emaciated. Have you had an epidemic?"

"Oh, no!" Kamir laughs. "It's just the birthings. Well, Maoul said that one came, wounded, from the Souls of Aeyor, the next encampment, to say that they had been set upon by terrible gold-skinned people, who tried to kill—yes, actually *murder*—all of them. Some have escaped by going in the sea—the gold-skinned ones do not swim, it seems—but the rest were killed. Isn't that terrible? What could such people be, how can it *happen?*"

I am shocked into sobriety. Oh gods, my paradise planet isn't all paradise, it contains others who are killers. Homo Ferox. Unless by chance this is an invasion of Black Worlders or other moral barbarians with high technology, out to conquer an attractive world?

But no, Kamir tells me. They are people of this world, only with strange tools to hurt and kill. And they have only the crudest mind-speech, and do not go in the water, as she'd said. The man who swam here—two days, with a bad spear cut in his side—said they had come from somewhere far, far to the west. "Where legends say we also came from," Kamir adds.

That would be the small continent Pforzheimer had seen, I figure. Perhaps it is still spawning out new races of Homo Wettensis, as a part of Old Terra once did. A dreadful parallel jumps to my mind; I push it aside resolutely.

"Kamir, I have seen such things on other worlds. I must talk with Maoul tonight. If this is what I think, you are in danger here. These gold-skins will not stop with one encampment."

"Oh, no . . . Yes, you must speak with Maoul. And why don't you talk with Elia?"

"Who's Elia?"

"The man who swam here. He is lying in the big hut, ill with his wound. Maybe you can help him. Oh, 'Om Jhared, I showed your beautiful bracelet"—she points to her ankle—"to Maoul. He said they were pictures of sounds, and we should learn them and make one for everybody. *And* make a picture of important things, too. I didn't understand it all but he was very excited."

Fantastic. So I will end by having these people transcribe their speech into Galactic! I must see more of Maoul. Is he a lone genius, or is this the level of their intellects? Meanwhile, it's a good idea to talk with this Elia.

I do talk to Elia, and am not made happy. These goldskins appear to be journeying from island to island, attacking everything they meet. They cross the sea by large, ugly war canoes. And they have lost their flock, or herd of some kind of land animal, so that they're hungry.

"How did you learn all this?" I ask Elia.

"I hid two days, watching and listening, until I was able to travel," he answers. "Man-from-the-skies, I thank you for your medicines. The people here have been very kind, they even made a song in my honor. But the relief from pain is better still!"

"And I think that will end the infection," I tell him, putting away the universal antibiotic the spacers give us.

The feast that night is held in front of the hut in which Elia lies, where I had seen the cookfire; it is the only bit of hard ground in the swampy delta. All this is very informal—we simply sit about on tussocks of grass, and the children pass us succulent-looking morsels of fish, beside which my food-bars seem very bleak. The invalid women, at whom I will not look closely, are helped to small portions of a soup made by their mates from the fish drippings. And I get my first good look at Mnerrin teenagers, who, like the children, seem to be all nearly the same age. Aside from the overweight, they are charming, most with rufous crests, plus a few blondes and brunettes, and all with the blue, blue eyes. As I sit there, the majority of the people are looking curiously at me between bites, and the impression made by those eyes is very striking. From dark to pale, from aquamarine to lapis lazuli to sapphire to crystal blue, all, all are as blue as if they carried a bit of the shining sea within their heads—as perhaps they do.

I think of a race whose eye color we will never know, and it motivates me to tackle Maoul. But first I must settle one question.

"Maoul, how does it happen that you are eating this large fish? Kamir gave me the idea that you do not kill, except the brainless little butterfish, and even those reluctantly?"

He becomes grave. "It was perhaps very wrong of us, 'Om Jhared," he admits. "But this fellow here was also eating our butterfish. And he began tearing our nets. All over the reef. He harassed us until Pamir hit him too hard on the snout. We call him *omnar*—and legend has it that omnars are very good to eat. And so it's proving!" He laughs—that universal Mnerrin laugh that seems to express the purest of happiness.

"Well, that makes my task easier. For I must explain that you have encountered another omnar—a land omnar, who will not stop with your nets, but will kill and perhaps eat everything, including you."

"You mean . . . the goldskins?" he asks dubiously.

"Yes, I do. The point is this. You and your people are very different from the great majority of races. In my life of traveling and learning of travels, I have never encountered a race who so hated killing. You have not even the words for what is the daily occupation of many peoples— war, aggression, fighting, invasion, attack. Here, let me show you." And I sent out horrible images, to him and the other men who were leaning to hear. I saw their faces change.

"How unspeakable!" Maoul exclaims with loathing. The others joined him. "Why do you show us such things?"

"Because you are in danger. I, too, hate what I have just shown, and so do most of my race. I thought I had come to the happiest world in the Galaxy when I found you. But now we must face the fact that you are not alone, that there is another people here, cruel and aggressive, who have found you. And they won't stop until they have attacked you and taken over your nesting site here."

"But there is plenty of room in the world. Why should they come here?"

"Yes. But people like that do not see it so. They want *all*. And maybe they want slaves—people to carry their burdens when they travel on land, or to paddle their canoes in the sea. Or they may want you who go in the sea to catch fish for them."

Maoul laughs. "If they make us go in the sea, we will leave."

"Not if they hold your children. Oh, they have terrible ways of forcing you to do their will."

"Hmm . . . You seem to know much about this." Maoul eyes me with a trace of dubiety.

"Yes, unfortunately. I told you, you are the only people I have met in a lifetime of traveling who are free of aggression."

Maoul ponders. "Well, it seems we must leave here and find another nesting place. But our women still live, yet are too weak to travel."

"Would you just give up your home to these intruders?"

"What else can we do?"

"You can fight. I can show you how. It means changing your way of life for a time, but that has been changed anyway. Wherever you flee to, these predatory goldskins will find you again."

"How can we—what did you call it—fight?"

"What did they attack with? Spears—which are long sharp staves— or perhaps arrows shot from a bow? Like this?" I mimic shooting.

He shakes his head. "The, ah, spears, I think. And—" He lowers his eyes as if to shut out some vision too sickening to look at. "They came also with *fire*, Elia says." Maoul's voice drops to a whisper. "They burned huts—some with babies still in them."

"Oh gods. My friend, I am so sorry this evil thing has come to you. I believed I had found a world of peace, the most beautiful thing in the universe."

"What is *peace*?"

"What you have. How you live. No fighting. No killing. Harmony . . . When I leave, I'm going to petition the Federation to save you, to exterminate these gold-skinned aggressors."

"Oh no. That would be evil. This is their world, too."

"But they are destroying this world. . . . Maoul, when these gold-skins come, you people will be like helpless infants before them. And they will come before you depart—they might be on us tonight, and you don't even have watchers out. Will you let me train the men in some self-defense so they may at least protect their women and children? And will you let me organize a watch? We have a word for such a leader and trainer of armed men: a 'general.' Will you let me be your general for this purpose alone?"

Maoul's blue eyes bore into mine, I can feel his mind searching me. And tendrils of mind-search come from the other men. I open to them, show them all I am. They must be right about this, sure of their choice.

"Very well, 'Om Jhared," Maoul says after a busy silence. "You have convinced me that we do face some trouble." The others nod. "We will call a council and you will show them such images as you showed me, and be our general."

"Gladly," I say, wondering at the same time what I have let myself in for. To transform a profoundly pacific people into a defense force in a few days? Obviously it can't be done. But anything would be better than their present helplessness. I must try.

Maoul is pointing to my wrist. "Now there is another matter." He smiles. "Kamir."

She has been beside us, listening intently.

"We see you have, against all hope, found a mate," Maoul continues. "Our congratulations." He puts an arm around her, kisses her cheek. She smiles radiantly—my little mermaid bride.

"And you, 'Om Jhared, strangely are the father; father-from-the-skies. But Agna says you know nothing of caring for young babies."

"I did not think there could be young. We are so different—"

Maoul is laughing wholeheartedly. He places both hands along Kamir's belly so I can see. And I can no longer delude myself—it is the belly of a pregnant woman.

"Oh gods! Have I done something evil?"

"I helped you," says Kamir smugly.

"No," says Maoul, suddenly grave. "How can babies be evil? They are the consummation we all long for. But how will you care for them? What will you *do?* I fear Kamir will not be much help."

Agna speaks up from where he had been sitting beside an invalid woman. "I have been thinking of this, Maoul. They can of course have my hut and birthing-place—I will replace its roof, tomorrow. And I will help him feed them until we start on the Long Swim. Then maybe Donnia here—" He turns to a plump young Mnerrin who has been standing by us, his attention divided between Agna and me. "Donnia is also our egg-fellow," he tells me, meaning, brother to himself and Kamir.

"Yes," says Donnia. "Brother and sister, I will help. My mate"—he bows his head briefly—"has already gone. And you can see that I am far from drained."

"His babies did not live," Kamir whispers to me.

"Your sorrow is my sorrow," I say formally. "I—we thank you deeply for your help. As I said, I had not believed that two such different people could have young. And I don't know what may come; the results may be bad. But surely we need your help."

"Good, then it is settled," says Maoul. "Tell us, 'Om Jhared, why did you come to our world?"

"To rest," I tell them. "I was very tired after a long task, and your world looked so beautiful."

"And now you have another task," the old man smiled.

"Two tasks," I remind him. "Tomorrow I start teaching you how to defend yourselves against these goldskins. For tonight I will just say this: Remember, the eruption of these people is going to change all your lives, for a time at least. And you are going to have to prepare yourselves to hurt, to harm, to kill, other Human beings, who seek to kill you. Think on that."

Looking and searching about, I see that my speech evoked mainly puzzlement. Gods, what have I undertaken? I must plan. . . .

At Maoul's council the next day, I see that the children and many of the teenagers are absent. Maoul says that he thought such plans were not for children.

"To the contrary, it is important that they learn. They will have parts to play, and this problem may be with them all their lives." So they are brought, down to the smallest, who stare at me with huge blue eyes, so much like plump little Human kids, despite their straight-up small fins.

I start by repeating what I had told Maoul, and showing them images of war and of the goldskin's probable attack. They respond, as I'd expected, with horror and the suggestion that they at once go someplace else. I try to convince them that mere flight is useless, that the goldskins will pursue them, and that they may well attack before they are prepared to move.

"You would be simply laying this upon your children, and upon your children's children, if you fail to solve it now."

The mention of children turns their minds. These people are amazingly tied to their young—all of them, even the young boys, place great value upon babies, I find. Perhaps because, I have noticed, they have relatively few compared with the other hominid races I know. I make a mental note to find out if the goldskin people are faster breeders.

I then outline my plan.

"When the goldskins attack us here, they will have learned from their last attack that you will seek to escape to the sea. So they will make sure to seize the beaches quickly, maybe even sending a separate party around the shore. If you attempt to flee that way, they will catch you easily. But tell me, that river"—I point to the line of papyrus plants marking the main stream to the estuary—"does it have a deep channel in the center all the way to the sea? Yes? Good. Then instead of going to the beach, you will make for the river. The problem is to defend yourselves and the women and children until you can all get there. One way is for the men to form a circle, with shields and spears on the outside, in which the children and weak ones can shelter. The goldskins will think you are making a final stand, and indeed, you can hold them off until all are assembled. But then you head for the river here, all in a group. That way you will fare much better than if you break and run individually; those who try that would be easily run down and killed." I show them an image.

The idea appeals to them, perhaps because of its symmetry.

"But the circle is no good unless we have shields and spears, and also warning of the goldskins' approach. So the first things we must do are make weapons, and set out a guard. The seasoned wood in these unused huts will do for spears. Every man shall make his own—I will show you how—and his shield. I have a spear-proof cloth, my tarpaulin, which we can cut up for shield covers. For the watch, I need volunteers among the boys with the best mind-hearing, four for the shore and four for the beach. And an older boy who will supervise them."

So I proceed to organize a watch, and a weapons sergeant. When I ask for something that would make a tremendous noise, they produce conch shells for the watchers to blow. And then I ask for a volunteer or two to go down the coast and keep watch on the goldskins' encampment at the lost village of the Souls of Aeyor.

A man named Falca speaks up. "It is my misfortune that I cannot mind-speak well. But I hear well. So I will go and watch and listen. And maybe my young friend Kimra, who swims so fast, will come with me to bring word back if need be?"

Kimra, a relatively slender lad, jumps up with shining eyes.

"Oh yes, Falca! Let us start now!"

I see that my message has been far more keenly received by the younger Mnerrin. So their pacifism is not some innate predisposition, but a matter of culture, of training. What carefully wrought beauty I am destroying!

But I push the thought aside and proceed to set out our first watch shift, telling their sergeant to be sure to check on them at random, unpredictable times. And then I tear out suitable wood from a storm-wrecked hut, and give a demonstration of spear-making. Strong knives are the bottleneck; their shell knives are too frail. I ransack my gear for extra knives and end by using my laser to prepare a supply of rough staves. As the first spears shape up in the hands of my future "warriors," I find another problem: I must dissuade them from weakening the spears by making handsome slim places for hand-holds, and wasting time on ornament and polish.

"I see that being a general is complicated," Maoul observes with a smile.

"Oh, it's an old, sad story. . . . But I have never met a people who were so far from war. I greatly fear for you."

That night about third moon I waken in Kamir's embrace and go as stealthily as I can to surprise our lookouts. I find, as I expected, two of them fast asleep. I rouse them roughly and give them a lecture on the sacredness of guard duty. The younger boy is nearly crying, but I ignore it—with difficulty. His eyes are so much like Kamir's. During the early morning I get the sergeant of the watch to repeat the same trick on the next shift.

* * *

The next day I vary the menu by arranging a drill. I get all the boys and girls to impersonate goldskins, and have them come down the coast onto the lookouts, who respond enthusiastically with horrific conch-blasts. The men come out of their huts and uncertainly form a loose circle near the riverside, into which the women, carrying babies, feebly come, and the smaller children. I see that some of my least-promising "warriors" will have to be spared to help the women take shelter, and sort them out.

My remaining corps of potential fighters, while overweight, looks more promising. Like many fat men, they are light on their feet and supple, and like all Mnerrin, very strong. I explain how we will use the shields, held alternately high and low, and briefly impersonate a goldskin—whom I have as yet never seen—in coming at them. They tremble and make way, and I harangue them like a drill sergeant on the need to hold their places and protect the children behind. After I have harassed them into tightening to a respectable defense, we practice moving all together to the river and forming a corridor to protect the women and children going in the water. The idea of *protection* is, I find, the best spur.

Then we turn to shield-making; a wicker frame covered with a piece of my best tarp held on with spacer's glue makes a pretty spear-proof defense, even if—which I can't find out—the goldskins have metal spear points. Against mere firehardened wood it is impressive, and gives my warriors confidence. They are not cowardly, but merely totally unused to the idea of war itself, of hurting and being hurt.

This becomes clear when we go on to practice actual combat. I sacrifice one of my two canvas ditty bags, stuff it with sand and moss, and hang it up to give them a target to thrust at. It is very hard to get them even to pierce the "skin." When I tell them to hit me, to make me fall down, their blows are mere taps. In desperation I pretend to fall; my assailant looks horrified, though I jump up and congratulate him.

But then comes assistance of a dreadful kind.

Young Kimra, who had been spying on the goldskins with Falca, comes swimming in one afternoon, broadcasting for attention. We gather round him as he wades ashore.

"The goldmen are definitely preparing for something," he tells us. "They have been holding conferences. Falca told me to tell you that. And—" he pauses. "We have seen several of the men they took prisoner.

The golds have cut off their crests. Shaved them bald." He sends us the images.

"Now they can never escape," Maoul groans. But that did not seem to be all; Kimra is looking at the ground and biting his lip.

"What more?" I ask.

"And—I cannot say it. The children . . ."

"Yes, what about the children? What have they done to them?"

"They—they are *eating* them!"

"Oh, no!"

"Yes." The boy's lips tremble. "Yes . . . One night we swam in close—and saw. A child's body was hung up by their fire, hung up like, like *meat!*"

Maoul looks at me. "Is this possible?"

"I fear it is. You see, they do not regard you as people. And they lost their flock of some kind of animals."

"This must be stopped!"

Around us I can hear the report being whispered from man to man.

"We must go there!" Maoul declares.

"No," I tell him. "You could not equal them in fighting. You would only be killed. And then they would come here for your children."

"Can you stop it, 'Om Jhared?"

I have been thinking hard. "I can try. Tell me, is there an island nearby which is on the route of your Long Swim?"

"Yes. The Island of the Green Coral. It is small, but with good food."

"Then here is what we can do: there is one time when their camp will be little defended. That is when they start to come here. Find me a good swimmer, a boy too light to fight well. I will take him in my boat at top speed down to their camp. When the men leave to come here, I will go ashore with my fire-weapon and free the children and any other captives they have, including the mutilated men. Your boy can lead them all to the Island of Green Coral to wait for you. I will return here at speed and be with you when they attack."

"Can that be done? Let us question Elia closely on the distances by water and land."

"Spoken like a general."

As we go up to Elia's hut, I see a man attacking the canvas dummy with his spear. He runs it right through. The horrible news has wrought a change.

Elia tells us that the plan is feasible. To get here by land, the gold-skins must go around a range of foothills; it might take them as much as two days.

As we come away, the sergeant of the watch comes to tell us that his boys have sensed minds nearby in the dawn. But the trace faded soon.

"That will be their spies," I tell Maoul. "They will go back and report on this village, how many we are, and the lay of the land. Thank fate they didn't see our weapons; they will think we are just like the village they crushed."

So I must wait at least two days before trying my rescue raid. Young Kimra goes back to watch with Falca.

We spend the days improving our drill and solving last-minute problems. Such as, what if the goldskins attack the circle with fire? Torches? I set out big containers of water, with a delegate to keep them filled. But the prospect of torches is too daunting. In desperation, I give the fire-control sergeant my can of extinguisher and explain its use. But in future they will have to depend on water alone.

And I confer with Mavru, their quasi-official Healer, to set up the way to treat spear wounds—packing them with the water-moss, which seems, like a similar Terra sphagnum, able to suppress infection. We set up a first-aid station by the river.

Strangely enough, in those last hours of peace, I get to know the Mnerrin better than ever before. I stroll the beach, watching their recreations. Among the more expected sights—boys and girls playing ball—I find a man surrounded by onlookers. He is drawing circles and triangles in the sand and, with a knotted string, explaining what he calls "Relations." This seems to be their art of geometry and mathematics. I am startled to find diagrams that imply knowledge of the Pythagorean theorems. So these people are not just simple Polynesianlike paradise-dwellers! No, this beach is more like the Athenian agora, where men in simple lengths of cloth discussed the eternal verities.

"We plan to make a permanent structure of stone at storm-season home," one man told me. "And we are going to use Relations to make it beautiful."

I find that one of their carefully preserved possessions is a big shell straightedge, marked off in equidistant intervals. They have a standard of measure! The man who carries it across his back has found a friend who has promised to take it over in case he is wounded in the coming fighting with the goldskins.

Nor has Maoul forgotten his discovery of the Galactic alphabet on Kamir's bracelet. He has been talking it over with others. They get me to teach them the whole alphabet and begin discussing whether more letters are needed to "picture" Mnerrin phonemes. The agora, indeed!

For my part, I take time to teach the Relations enthusiasts about our system of written numbers. Typically, they grasp it at once, and start transcribing them onto their shell measure. They are especially interested in the concept of zero.

"With this, we can do many things!" exclaims Kerana, the Relations explainer. I wonder by how many centuries—or decades—I have speeded their mental evolution. I wonder about their minds; this is no case of an isolated genius, but of a group with high, though unexploited, mental capability. And they seem not to be in danger of the fallacy that brought Plato and Aristotle's deductive logic low, the fallacy of refusing experiment. No; they test out every step of their Relational logic.

I tell them the story of Aristotle's deduction that women must have fewer teeth than men, while refusing to count his wife's teeth. They laugh. I sigh, and wonder if I should expose them to Bacon's scientific method. I try.

But time is growing short. I have scoured the land that lies behind the beach, and on the last day discover a flintlike rock. I bring it to two men who have been doing shell knives.

"Look. I think you can chip this into blades which will be stronger than shell. Let me show you." Inexpertly, I flake out an edge. They assent with pleasure to trying.

Maoul has produced a youth named Manya to accompany me on the rescue party. On the last night I pack a few rations and emergency supplies into the boat, and we leave it secured to the beach, to start at dawn.

That last night with Kamir she is untypically thoughtful. I think that the reality of all this has just come through to her, preoccupied as she is with her monstrously growing pregnancy. She has been lying lazily on the beach by day, sunning her vast belly, and smiling to herself, only distantly interested in my warlike activities. She is still enchantingly beautiful in a different way; my little mermaid has turned into a nature goddess.

"Darling, take this." I extract from my gear my last resort, a tiny close-action personal laser. "Defend yourself with it if I do not return in time. But remember, sweetheart, you must wait until your attacker is very close, almost within arm's length."

"I will kill for our babies," she says calmly. "And you are right to go to save those children. We Mnerrin, as you call us, do not have many. All are precious." she hugs me again, then pushes me away.

It is very hard to leave her.

But Manya and I get into the dinghy, and shortly the little craft is leaping through the green waters at its great top speed. In a couple of hours we are within sight of the other settlement's bay, a journey which had cost the wounded Elia two painful days. The birthing huts here are different, somewhat larger, and supported by a center pole. Falca and Kimra are still on the reef, invisible until we catch their mind-call.

We stop out of sight, where we will wait for the goldskins to leave, and hold conference.

Falca says he expects them to leave very soon. "And see, they are loading three canoes. I think it is as you said, they are sending a party by sea to cut off escape on the beaches."

"How many are there in all?"

"About ninety, counting thirty-six in the canoes."

"It is bad odds for our people. But I have a very powerful weapon which will kill many. I shall be busy!"

"Kimra told you about the children?"

"Yes. That is why I'm here." I tell him my plan. Falca sighs.

"That is a great relief. Last night . . . they killed another. It was all we could do not to rush ashore and assail them. Stranger, you are a good man. Kimra and I were going to try alone, but we had no place to send them. The mutilated men cannot guide."

"Manya here will take care of that. Meanwhile, you and Kimra are no longer needed here. You might as well start swimming home. But be wary that those canoes do not overtake you in the water."

"Good. I go. The children are in that large hut with two entrances, and so are the other captives. They are tied with ropes."

"I can take care of that." I show him my shark knife. "Fair travel, friend." He nods, and without more ado he and Kimra take off in long, flat dives.

And then we wait. It becomes clear that the goldskins' start will not be made till next morning; they are preparing for a feast. I make the mistake of giving my binoculars to Manya, and he sees the fresh-killed body of a child hung up by the fire. He chokes with fury, then weeps quietly. I take the glasses and try to soothe him as best as I can.

"Oh, if only I had those long-range weapons you told us about! No—I would go to them, I will kill them with my bare hands. I would *kill!* I will kill! . . . We will return in time, won't we?"

"Yes, but you won't be with me, Manya. You will be leading the children and the mutilated men to safety on that island."

He heaves a sigh. "Yes, I forgot. But if there is a goldskin left ashore, I will kill him with my bare hands."

"Don't be rash, Manya. Those men are practiced fighters. One of them could destroy you. I will attend to the killing."

"Then I will kill their children!"

He seems to hear himself then, and looks shocked. But he continues in a grim voice, "Their children will grow into such as they. They have devoured our babies. Yes, I will kill them."

I, too, am shocked. What have I created ? Or no, it was not me, but the circumstances, the irruption of the goldskins. The sight of one's children being butchered like animals is not to be reacted to in a civilized way. He is not to be blamed.

But what about me? I contemplate cold-blooded genocide. No, not cold-blooded; these Mnerrin are in a sense my children. My ideal of Human life . . . Grimly, I realize that I have fallen into every psychic trap that spacers are warned of. I love these people.

So be it. When I return, I will pull every lever, press every button known to me to obtain official intervention, to save this planet for the Mnerrin. It's just possible, especially if one or two of my friends are still in their offices. . . .

Twilight has come. We eat and settle for the night, thinking our different thoughts. This is, in fact, one of the few times I have had pause from my duties to reflect. Manya's slight form beside me in the boat reminds me of Kamir. What of her? What of my babies, if incredibly they are born whole and viable? Can I stay here with them? Could I endure this tranquil life, as a non–sea animal? I don't know. . . .

In any event, the need to get off-planet and do something for the Mnerrin will dominate my life for a while. After that, we'll see.

The fact is that my conviction that our mating would be infertile has been so strong that I still do not believe I am about to father little half-aliens, if all goes well. I have never fathered others. What is this recurrent question, How will you feed them. How *are* they fed, without mother's milk, by non-mammals? I had vaguely supposed that they would eat fish, like the adults. Evidently there is something that I, helped by Agna and Donnia, am going to have to do. And Kamir—I shudder away from the mounting evidence that somehow this birthing will mean her death. Surely those were older women, there in the village. Not my bright, vital little mermaiden! No . . . no . . . These concerns are for after the coming battle. . . .

Finally I sleep, and the balmy night goes by.

We rouse to dawnlight, at once aware that the camp is in motion. I check the glasses. Yes, goldskins are loading the canoes, preparing to cast off. We had better conceal ourselves.

We paddle in among some rocks that have tumbled to the sea, forming one arm of the bay shore. There we eat and watch.

This settlement is similar to the one I know in that it is in a delta around an estuary. Evidently these marshy places are proper sites for birthing and rearing the newborn. And there must be a limited number of them. By driving the Mnerrin from them, the goldskins could make it impossible for the Mnerrin to breed. Idly, I wonder why the deltas are so favorable. Perhaps tiny babies are taught to swim in the little streamlets, before their gills are strong enough for the open sea? And I am still not clear as to what role fresh water versus salt plays in their lives. Really, it is shameful how I have simply *lived*, without collecting any respectable body of data!

At this moment Manya nudges me, and we hear the *chunk, chunk* sound of paddles. A long low dark canoe, gaudily bedizened, comes in sight. Six paddlers to a side. We crouch low.

It passes by, about fifty meters away, followed by another, and another. And then no more. Cautiously, we nose out of the rocks to where we can see the camp.

It is so still that we can hear voices. After we have waited about two hours, we hear a different sound, a kind of chanting. It takes on a marching tempo. And then we see a band of about fifty men tramping up out of the swampland, chanting and blowing on pipes. They gain solid ground and set off down the coast. My heart has sunk—fifty and thirty-six, more than two to one against the Mnerrin. My laser will have to do good work.

But now we have other work in hand.

We still avoid starting the motor, but paddle in to their beach. We beach the dingy and start at a crouching run toward the big hut Falca had pointed out. Women must be all about us in the camp, but we see none—until suddenly we come on a party of them right outside the hut. They have knives in their hands.

I notice only that they are brightly gilt, their hides like goldfish, and could be called handsome if your taste runs to eighty-kilo bodies.

Manya behind me is making an extraordinary noise through his clenched teeth.

I make a sweeping pass with the laser, and they go down like ten-pins without making a sound, their throats burned through. Behind them the door to the hut is ajar. Had they been going in to murder another child?

Mind-cries are coming from the hut. I send strongly, "Friends come!" and Manya joins me. We step over the golden corpses and go in to a pitiful sight.

The hut is full of rails and posts, and everywhere are tied children, ranging from toddlers to teenagers. Some grown men, shaved bald, are tied up at one end. The hut stinks.

"Cut them loose, quickly." I have brought a spare knife for Manya.

"Hungry, hungry," comes the mind-cry, especially from the smaller ones, as we free them.

"You will have food soon," we send. But how? I shudder to think what meat we will find beside the cookfires. Still, surely they have already fed on it. And would their dead friends object to giving their flesh to save the living?

A spear clatters in at the other door, a woman dives back.

"You finish freeing them, I'll attend to the village," I tell Manya. "Can you guard the outer door?" I ask a bald man, who is rubbing his limbs.

"Yes."

I go out and start through the village like a dervish, burning everything that moves. From one hut I am greeted by a spear. Inside, a man obviously sick or wounded is clinging to the center post. Beyond him crouch two women and children. Mercy is not in me that day; when I leave the hut, nothing lives behind me.

At intervals I check back to the big hut, where Manya is leading the children out. They stare at the goldskin corpses. The mutilated men look nervously about. Their heads are covered with pink fuzz.

I have found a pot of meat stew simmering at a hearth, and basket bowls. I put it before the kids without looking too closely.

"Can you catch reef-fish, after what they have done to you?" I ask the men.

"Oh, yes, if we can find our nets."

As luck would have it, a pile of their filmy nets, loincloths, and other belongings has been thrown beside another hut.

"Good. Now, when you have eaten enough, you and the children will follow Manya here to an island—I think you know it—beside the path of the Long Swim. The people from my settlement will pick you up as they go by."

"They haven't left yet?"

"No." And then I have to respond to the overwhelming mind-question coming at me from everyone, even as they begin to gulp food: "Who are you?"

"A friend from the skies, Tom Jared. I have been living with your people since I met a girl named Kamir and mated with her. Now, these goldskins are going to attack our village. I must return quickly and help them fight. I can carry only one. Is there a man here who can strike and kill? Kill goldskins? Our people need defenders." I send an image of a goldskin leaping at a Mnerrin.

To my surprise, amid the blank looks I had expected from most of the men, a younger one steps smartly forward. "I think I can do what you call fight, O friend from the skies. I have thought much during our captivity. Now I can kill. But I need things to strike with. Here!"

He bends down to the row of corpses and takes a strong-looking knife from a dead woman's hand.

"And now a long one—"

"We call those spears. Maybe we will find some in this big hut."

And indeed we find a cache of spears. But they are mostly slim, decorated things for rituals and dancing. Again to my surprise, my new recruit sorts out some that are sturdy and useful. This lad is an untypical mutation, in theory, maybe, a dangerous one. Right now I wish I had a hundred of him.

"Good. Now we go. I have fish in the boat, you can eat on the way. And you others had best be on your way with Manya, lest some goldskins catch you again."

I bid good-bye to them as they eagerly follow Manya to the water's edge. The men have found some rope, and start tying the smaller children on towlines to their belts. Always this care for the young! I cut short their curiosity about my boat.

"Later. No time, now."

The warlike lad's name is Sintana. His eyes shine as I direct him to help me tow the dinghy to deep water and hop in. When I start the motor and start skimming along the reef, he is visibly ecstatic.

"Now, I don't know whether we will overtake the canoes before they reach my village or not. So we must proceed with care whenever we cannot see a long way ahead. I want you to watch and listen with all your power for those canoes. I will have much watching to do to avoid hitting coral heads this close to shore. If you see or suspect a canoe, raise your arm like this and be ready for a quick stop, right? If you are *sure* that all is clear ahead, go like this."

Enthusiastic assent from Sintana. I gun up the motor to full speed, and we rip along at top speed toward my village. I want to keep close to the reef to avoid being sighted by the canoes ahead, but the danger from isolated coral rocks strings my nerves tight. Luckily, there is enough wave action to show where most of them lie. Avoiding one at the last minute, I nearly spill us. Sintana looks round questioningly, and after that I see him hang on.

He is radiating pleasurable excitement like a child, but looking him over, I see he has plenty of muscle to go with his combative spirit. A gods-sent ally.

It's getting dark. Each time as we round a shallow point, Sintana waves me on. Those canoes have really covered ground. I'm not afraid of their hearing my motor over their paddling splash—and even if they did, they would not know what it was. But where are they?

We approach the last point before our bay. Suddenly Sintana's hand goes up and we jolt to a stop.

"I think I hear minds from around the point. Maybe quite close."

"They could be holed up, waiting for the men on land to arrive. No more talking now."

At lowest speed we nose around the point. Presently we can see most of the bay, but no canoes.

"They're hiding right on the other side of these rocks," Sintana whispers. I listen, and fancy I can catch a crude mind-murmur.

"Can you paddle quietly?"

"I think so."

"Fine. Let's try to get a look."

We paddle the dinghy silently forward, about an arm's length from the rocks. Sintana's hand shoots up and I stop. Eyes glowing with excitement, he whispers, "I can see the bows of two canoes, in a cove in the rocks. I don't know where the third is."

"Sintana, get down low in the boat. I am going around fast and fire my weapon at them. But we will be within spear-throw. Make sure they do not hit you. And *do not throw your spear*, you will need it later," I add, knowing what the excitement could do to such a boy.

"And your part is to keep watch for that third canoe. Got it?"

"Yes." He is reluctantly crouching down.

"Get farther down. The air will be full of spears, and I must fire over you. Can you *stay* down?"

"Yes."

"All right. Hang on, here we go!"

I slam the lever to high, and we round the point in a great rooster-tail of spray. In the cove behind the point are two canoes full of gold-skins—good, I had feared some might have gone ashore. I fire as soon as I'm in range, zigzagging as I come at them. Screams, barely audible over the motor and spray. I roar in as close as I dare, and then twist the dinghy into a hair-raising U-turn, firing all the time. Spray splashes over the canoes, but I can see goldmen struggling up, lifting their spears. I turn again and make another pass, managing to laser every standing man.

But Sintana is in my way.

"Get down!"

"The third canoe! Look out, look out!" he yells.

I glance back and see the third canoe, come out of nowhere, rushing straight at me. I turn and fire. Luckily, from dead ahead, the spearmen are blocking each other. But they are also shielding each other from my fire. I whip around fast and slice in close to the gunwale, doing slaughter—and then I'm out of the little cove, heading for the reef. Luckily, moons are up.

But that's as far as we go. The feel of the dinghy warns me—I see two spear shafts sticking from the pontoons. Oh gods. I turn toward the beach, weaving between the rocks at the start of the reef, and just make shallow water as our craft collapses around us. No one is in pursuit.

Sintana and I jump out. I wrestle the motor from the sagging folds and hand it to him while I rescue the batteries. Thus laden, we struggle ashore, towing the half-submerged dinghy. Sintana, I'm glad to see, still has his spear. A cool boy.

At that moment a fearful hooting hits our ears from the delta beyond. The watchers have sighted goldskins and are blowing their conches.

I hate to leave my wrecked dinghy to the attentions of any survivors from the canoes—it is my only link to the lander—but there's no time to do more than throw a couple of armfuls of brush over it. We start for the village at a run.

As we near it, I see splashing in the shallows. A Mnerrin family has forgotten the drill and is heading straight for the sea. Ahead of me two goldskins, shining in the moonlight, race after them, spears lifted. They throw before I can get the range; the man of the fleeing groups goes down into the water. The children stop, trying to pull him up, but the goldmen are upon them; I manage to pick one off, but the other is too close to the children.

He whips out something silvery—it's a rope, he is tying them up. He starts out of the surf, dragging them behind him, screaming.

We pound after him, Sintana in the lead. I see his spear flash, and the goldman goes down. By the gods, my Mnerrin has killed! We cut the children loose and tell them to follow us.

"No, Father Pavo is out there!"

"He'll be all right. Come." I know that if Pavo has survived the spear, he will be safer under water than on shore.

We run on.

Most of the goldskins are still coming down the bank onto the delta. I can see the main hut now, see that my Mnerrin have actually formed a protective circle. Women and children are still being thrust in.

I identify us by mind-call.

"Quick, there is time to start for the river *now*!"

"But Pavo's family are not here."

"He ran to the sea and got caught. I have his children. Here," I tell them, "get in behind these men."

The leading goldskins are upon us. I fire, pick them off. Others are circling, trying to get between us and the sea.

"They are after the children! Quick, to the river! All together, go!"

The circle starts off at a wobbly trot, the men in the rear having a hard time shepherding the children and fending off goldskins, who are now arriving in force. I fire, fire till no more are in range, wishing that I were within the circle firing out—too many times I have had to hold fire to avoid hitting Mnerrin. And then another shining rank of goldmen is upon us.

The next hour is collapsed in my mind into a montage of firing, running, firing, running. The goldskins catch up with the Mnerrin circle before they reach the river, and there is wild spear-jabbing, hand-to-hand combat. Children's skrieks fill the air.

At last they reach the river and form a corridor as I had taught them. Children rush down it, women hobble after, babies in arms, and fling themselves into the deep channel, followed by the men. Goldskins rove the banks, searching futilely for some shallow place where they can get at their prey. I lurk behind, picking them off as I can. I do not think many of them are clearly aware of me. Finally when they pause at the beach, I have a clear shot at a mass of them, and wreak scorching havoc. Sintana is busy chasing stragglers.

There is a moment's lull. I stand up to look—and am jolted by a blow. A spear shaft in my shoulder. But moments later I am aware that Sintana is by me, having dispatched my attacker.

"Pull this out of me, Sintana."

He does so, surprisingly gentle. I watch the ripples that mean Mnerrin are reaching the sea, gritting my teeth.

"Is there much blood?"

"Some."

"Pack that moss in the hole." I cut off a length of rope and make a sling for my arm. Fortunately the spear doesn't seem to have hit anything vital.

"Where are the rest of the goldmen?"

"I don't think there are any more standing," he says with quiet pride. I can see in the moonlight that he is bloodied all over and has a different spear.

"You have been busy. Are you wounded?"

"In the leg. A little."

We go through the moss-packing routine. He has a fat shaft broken off in the big muscle of his thigh.

"That will hurt worse later. How do you like war?"

He grins and sighs together. "I think—too much!"

"Yes, it is like that. . . . Now, if you can walk, we must find my light and check all the wounded goldskins."

"And kill them?" He makes an eager motion with his spear.

"Yes. All except two whom we will tie up for questioning."

Then I feel free to do what I'd been desperately longing for. I send out a focused mind-call to the Mnerrin hiding in the water.

"Can you hear me?"

"Yes." A head surfaces just inshore of the reef.

"I think it is all safe now. But wait until dawn to come ashore. And—*is Kamir safe?*"

What must be her head surfaces, too, and I receive a sending of such love and longing that I can scarcely resist going to her. "Till daybreak, darling. Now I have work to do."

"Always work!" Her laugh, my mermaid's laugh, rings out over the water, piercing me with sweet memories. I sigh, and turn back to the job.

Sintana and I go first to the pile of goldskins I created on the beach, and then start searching systematically through the marsh for gleams of gold. Their shining skins are a great liability.

"In the future we will not be able to assume all is over so soon. They will learn to take us more seriously, and arrange a second wave of attackers to come in just as the Mnerrin think all is safe."

We also come upon three Mnerrin dead and two wounded, men whom I don't know well, and three children who have been stabbed. To my amazement, a dark figure is there, bending over a child. I hold my fire just in time, as the mind-signal comes.

"Mavru! What are you doing here?"

"I swam upriver and waited," he replies. "I thought I might be more needed here."

"And you are. Wonderful. Mavru, meet my young friend from the lost village. He has worked hard in your defense."

The two Mnerrin greet warmly. I go in search of my medical supplies to help Mavru, and we resume our search of the marsh.

Long before we are through, Sintana is weary of killing the wounded. His battle fever has ebbed; only when a "corpse" surprises him by striking at him does it return briefly. This, I think, is a good lesson for him.

We save out two captives who seem in fairly good shape, and tie them up far apart so they can't communicate. As I'd been told, they seem to have no mind-speech except a sort of alarm call, and a threat-sending, hostile blare.

When the moons go down we rest and eat. Mavru joins us.

"Their bodies are different from ours," he says. "I think I will cut up one or two and find where the vital centers are. Do you think that's a good plan, 'Om Jhared?"

I agree, and warn him about the dangers of handling cadavers. "You must wash your hands scrupulously. I, too, would like to see."

Sintana meanwhile has been questioning the nearest prisoner. He has picked up a few words of their tongue, which sounds barbarous in contrast to the Mnerrin's.

"I asked him why they ate children," he reports. "He only shrugged and said, because they were hungry. So I asked him why they did not catch fish. He seems not to understand. I think anything connected with water is entirely strange to them. I remember there was a great fuss about who was going to go in the canoes."

"And that reminds me," I tell him. "We must go and try to salvage those canoes and fix up my boat."

"Why do we want those ugly canoes?"

"First, to keep them out of the hands of any more goldskins who come here. And, most important, I think our people can use them on the Long Swim. They could transport the wounded; some will take a long time to heal. And babies could go in them, too."

"Oh, good idea. Hey, it's like you said, my leg hurts more."

"I'm sorry. But we have a job to do."

We check the other prisoner, who glares at us mutely, and hike down the beach to where the dinghy lies. It's untouched, thank the gods, and the repair kit, like all my supplies, is fastened inside. The spacer's gooey stuff really works well, but will take an hour to dry.

We leave it and climb over the headland to where two canoes float aimlessly in the little cove. A moon is rising again; I can see the glitter of bodies inside. The third canoe is only a prow sticking up. Its former contents are floating about.

"We have to go through the check again," I tell Sintana. "And then we have to fish those corpses out so they won't foul the sea. We can put them on the rocks up here, maybe the crabs will eat them."

Sintana shudders. "Parts, anyway . . . I didn't know, when I volunteered to fight, that it included cleaning up the battlefield!"

"It includes whatever it includes," I tell him grimly. But I am suddenly dead tired, and my shoulder is on fire. I have been running on pure adrenaline. Do we really have to do this task? And my boat will take strength to pump up . . . The first pink light of dawn is in the sky.

"I have a better plan," Sintana says. "Your people here have been idling in the sea all night." He goes back up on the headland, and I hear him send out a mind-call.

To my astonishment, three heads pop out of the water below us almost at once.

"No need to shout," comes a young voice. "We followed to see what you were up to. Hello, 'Om Jhared, I'm Pelya! What do you need?"

We tell them, and soon, to my great pleasure, three sets of strong young arms are hauling dead goldskins ashore and up the rocks. The goldmen are short and compact, heavy-boned.

"How many of you in the sea are wounded?" I ask Pelya.

"Three. And Pavo's mate got a spear through her arm. She was very weak, you know. She died soon after we got to the bar."

"Oh, I am sorry."

"Yes . . . But you did so much. We boys have been thinking. We will have to train ourselves to do this thing, to do fighting. War. Some of the older men think it is all over, but we don't agree. . . . But 'Om Jhared, just *why* do the goldskins attack us?"

"I don't really know, except that it is their nature."

But later, when we have pumped up the dinghy and are leading the procession of canoes back to the village, I tell them what I fear.

"I'm afraid that what I have seen on other worlds may be happening here. Somewhere far to the west there may be a great many goldskins, so that beaches and food are in short supply. They would be fighting over them, and the losers may pack up and come east, looking for new homes. If that's true, it means there will be more coming, and more after that, without end. I think they have more babies than you, so the pressure will go on and on. I hope to the gods this isn't true, that this was just a wandering band, but as I said, I have seen this thing before. That is why I am going to appeal to the power of the Federation to help you. But that will take a long time. Meanwhile, you are wise to try to help yourselves. We can question the prisoners, and it might be good to send a couple of scouts back along their trail to see what we can find out."

"I see," says Pelya, and the other boys agree. For once they do not laugh.

Nor do I. In the growing light I can see the Mnerrin coming ashore. There is old Maoul, there is Agna, and Donnia, helping Kamir. I can already sense tendrils of Contact, carrying gratitude to me. I hope there are not to be speeches, I am dead. And all too keenly I realize that I have now broken all the Federation's Rules of Contact. I have interfered massively with the Mnerrin's life-ways, and I have taken a decisive part in a war. . . . So be it.

"Wake up, 'Om Jhared! Kamir is giving birth!"

It is Agna's voice. I come to, groggily.

We are in Agna's birthing hut. Kamir is lying beside me on the crude bed, which is covered with moss and hay. She is on her side, curled around her vast belly, her hands pushing at it as though trying to push it away from her. Agna is beside her, doing something. I hear Kamir whimper.

Gently, Agna takes her hands and pats them.

"Here," he says to me. "Hold."

I take the hands. Kamir's eyes open and meet mine. With effort, she smiles. "Don't be afraid, darling. This is normal."

Normal? I am looking for some sort of opening, some birth canal through which the babies will emerge. There is no sign of anything like that. Instead, Agna's hands seem to be working on the "scar" or line I had seen, running around her abdomen. He is kneading it, carefully pulling it apart. I see that the scarlike line is starting to separate, like long, threadlike lips.

"In a moment now," he tells Kamir. "You can push."

Kamir puts her hands with mine up on her great belly. It is hot, hot. Then she pushes at it again.

Suddenly, with a dreadful caving-in feeling, her whole belly, containing the fetuses, starts to *separate* from the rest of her body! It tips forward, away from her, as the scarlike "lips" open. Agna is furiously working at this line, pushing his hands under her. She whimpers again. I see that the lips are actually a deep separation line, circling her whole belly, from ribs to pelvis. Oh gods, what is happening here?

Slowly, deliberately, yet too fast for me to follow, the fetal mass tips forward farther, revealing a deep cleavage. It tips, separates farther yet, and then rolls over, away from her, onto what had been the outside of her belly. Agna steadies it. Kamir gives a series of loud sighs, and then rolls away from it, onto her back.

"Whew! That feels better."

But I have a horrifying look at the shell of her body left after the fetal mass tore loose. From diaphragm to hips it is *empty*, covered by a rapidly thickening gel membrane. Through it I can see, under her ribs, a dark mass pulsing: her heart. Below that, by her spine, I can see the great cords of nerve and blood vessel running along her backbone, inside her empty flanks, to her hips and pelvis. Nothing more.

Agna is looking, too, as the membrane becomes opaque.

"See? Almost no fat at all. My poor little sister will not live long."

"Why?" But the answer is before me. Stomach, intestines, digestive organs, all are gone, taken away with the fetus-bearing mass of her belly. She has no means of taking in food. A fast-sealing tube end that must be her esophagus is visible near her heart. I can only hope that her kidneys are left, so she won't die of thirst.

I am squeezing her hands so tightly I must be hurting her. I relax them and make myself kiss her face, despite the ghastly display of her body. She strokes my hair with trembling hands.

"I'm fine. See to the babies."

The babies? Dimly I am realizing that this is no catastrophe, but a natural process of parturition. Or rather, it is a catastrophic process, deadly to the mother. But the babies are alive, the fetuses; through the gel of the torn-away side I can glimpse aqueous forms moving vaguely. Clearly they are too young for independent life. A great placenta lies on them, with coils running to each fetus—there are three. And there must be some sort of secondary heart with them, there is the throb of circulation.

Indeed, this mass that has torn itself loose from Kamir is almost a primitive animal in its own right, with organs it has stolen from Kamir.

To me it is a monster, which has mutilated and killed my mermaiden, my girl.

But Kamir is gazing at it with fond eyes. Her babies.

I make myself look at it. It is a globular mass about half a meter in diameter, lying on what had been the outside of Kamir's abdomen. All the part that had been inside Kamir is covered with this gel membrane, now fast thickening to opacity. Agna is bent over it, inspecting and feeling it all with tender hands. He points out a circular ring, or tube, set in the "top."

"That is where we feed the babies."

Oh gods; it is the remains of Kamir's esophagus, leading to her stolen stomach. I begin to shake with delayed horror, scarcely noticing that Donnia has come in, and is offering to me, of all things, a great bowl of butterfish, cut in pieces. When I see it, I am revolted at his apparent callousness.

"Fathers first," says Agna. He and Donnia each take some and begin to chew.

Then I am even more revolted by the understanding of what they are doing. They are taking food for the fetuses, substituting for their mother's missing mouth. Preparing it for digestion by her stomach, somewhere inside that monstrous package. Grimly I force myself to take some and begin to chew. A vaguely consoling thought comes to me: many Terran birds feed their new-hatched chicks like this.

Weakly, Kamir demands some, too. Now that her huge pregnancy has gone, I can see how thin the rest of her has become. Her limbs are no longer slender, but bone-thin, and her beautiful face has been fined to where it seems all great dark blue eyes. But how short a time ago it was that we played and tussled with each other on our magic isles! What a terrible thing I have wrought on my little mermaid, what evil I have done! Yet she seems strangely content, her eyes are luminous with joy when she gazes on the dreadful lump that contains our babies. Mysterious are the ways of instinct! Something in her makes her accept happily the shortness of her life for its irrational reward.

Agna is speaking to me. "Empty your mouth into this, new father." He grasps the tube opening on the monster and pulls it free. I realize, for Kamir's sake, I must.

It would have been appalling were it not that the fetus-monster has an oddly attractive smell. Organic, but very sweet and clean. A lure to feed it, I think. Well, it works.

After I have fed it in this strange fashion, Agna and Donnia follow suit, and last, Kamir. "Are there three?" she asks.

"Yes," says Agna. "Lucky you did not make more. It will be a job to feed these, they also have no fat."

"I wonder what they will look like," Kamir says dreamily. She is sinking into sleep. Yet she turns to me and hugs me, with a momentary return of her old strength.

"Oh, my darling strange one, I am so happy! Never did I think I would have babies to watch over. Never! And you came from the skies and gave them to me." She kisses me again.

"But—" As I look at her exquisite young face, my heart feels as though it will burst then and there. How can she be so truly happy? Wait; is it conceivable she doesn't know her fate?

"I hope I will live to see them. I must. I *will*." She sinks back, blue eyes brave with resolve.

She knows, all right.

Agonized, I watch her drift smiling into sleep. Donnia is nudging me, holding out the bowl of fish. I turn to my detested duty. I am very tired.

I wake to morning light.

Kamir is beside me. The monstrous baby-package is still there.

"Hello, my darling. How you slept! Do you know you fell asleep in the middle of feeding our babies? Fighting must be very tiring."

"Yes."

"I did some!" she tells me. "A goldskin came at me, and I burned him with the little weapon you gave me! But he was so strong. And falling down, he kicked me where the babies were. I was afraid he'd injured them. Then Agna came and helped me run away, to the men. And oh, I was so glad when you came back."

"I was too."

"Agna and Donnia have gone for more fish. See how the babies are stirring? That means they're hungry."

I see signs of movement within the fetus-package. Gods, what appetites!

"Tell me, darling. How long will they stay like that?"

"Oh, twenty, thirty, forty days, it varies. I think ours will come out sooner, because they were with me so long. That's why I think I can live to see them."

Twenty days? Is that the span of our time?

"Don't talk about dying. If you die, the sun of my life will go out."

"Oh, don't *you* say that, although it is beautiful. If things were the other way round, it's how I would feel, too. When you were so long in coming, I feared the sun of my life had gone out."

And we have more private things to say, until Kamir pushes me away, with "Friends come! I think it is that fierce boy, what's his name— Sintana. And old Maoul."

There is a knock on the hut wall. Even I can pick up Sintana's mind.

"Greetings, all."

They come in and sit on Agna's log. I see that Maoul is actually carrying a spear.

I congratulate him again on having got the Mnerrin to form their circle.

"It *was* a task," he admits. "I only wish Pavo had heeded."

"People panic and forget. He thought the way looked clear—he forgot that goldskins can run faster than a man with children."

"Listen, 'Om Jhared," Sintana interrupts. "We have got some news out of our captives. They say there are no more goldskins on this island, or nearby, but there are many, many more very far to the west. That sounds like your theory."

"Yes. I was never more sorry to be right. Did you ask why they eat your children?"

"Yes. They say they had a group of somethings, and they ate them. But they died, from drowning I think. Animals about so high." He put a hand about a meter from the ground. "And I think they have come on others like us and taken their children, too."

"A flock or herd of meat animals . . . This is common on other worlds. It seems clear they don't regard you as people, but as a sort of food animal. They might get the idea of taking a group of you captive and eating the young."

Maoul's face is a mask of fury, but he says nothing.

"We're not people because we don't fight, is that it?" Sintana asks.

"Something like that. Did you ask about their own children?"

"No, but he saw one of our women die and seemed to understand. He said their women do not die like that."

"Hmm . . . a real mutation. That fits, too. A higher birthrate."

"Mutation?" asks Maoul.

"A word we use when some of a group of beings become quite different. It usually starts with one or a very few, and the new form spreads because their offspring survive better."

"This sounds interesting," Maoul says. "I wish we had time to talk of it now."

I laugh. "You are learning bad ways, friend. In the old days you would have gone ahead and discussed some topic no matter what practical matters called you."

He laughs, too, somewhat sadly. "I feel I have aged ten years since the day before yesterday. But what must we do with these goldskins now? Kill them, as Sintana says?"

I'm glad he's said it. "Yes, I'm afraid so. You can't take them on the Long Swim, and if you let them go, they will certainly make their way back to the main goldskin group and lead others here. That way they gain chieftaincy. . . . If you are revolted by killing them, would you rather I did it?"

"No," says Sintana.

"I am revolted," says Maoul. "But I will do it. It is right."

"Then will you let me give you one last lecture about this?"

"Speak on. Your last lectures saved our lives."

"I'm very glad. You know I feel one with you. Your pain is mine, too. Listen: *It is very hard to kill helpless men—or women—in cold blood.* And they will be talking, pleading, promising anything, to save their lives. They will promise not to bring others, to stay and wait for you, to work for you. They may claim they are not like the other goldskins, but that the others made them attack you. They may claim they can guide you to somewhere, that they have secret weapons. They may fall down and clutch your ankles and beg for mercy. They may tell you that they have young children to care for—anything! They may swear they never ate of the children's meat. Remember, to them; a promise made to an enemy need not be kept, lies told to an enemy or an inferior do not count. They will be talking and acting solely to save their worthless lives. What you must keep in front of your minds is that they have eaten your children and got caught trying to kill more. Then strike! Close your ears completely, and strike! And beforehand, send away any softhearted one who might be fooled."

The two men think this over for a moment.

"It seems very difficult," says Maoul. "What if we took them by surprise, while they are sleeping?"

"No, that is not the best way. And *you* would be surprised at how quickly they woke up and read your intent—because this is what they themselves would do. No; you should be brave and tell them, and ask them if they have some supernatural entity they pray to. Tell them to do so now."

"I have heard of such a thing," says Maoul.

"If you need more, remember that it is as necessary to kill them as to stamp out sparks of fire nearing your hut. Do you think your resolve will hold?"

Maoul sighs, straightens up; Sintana takes a deep breath.

"Thank you for warning us, 'Om Jhared. I think we can do this thing."

"Good. It will be harder for you, Maoul. Sintana has already had a taste of it. But to you, maybe this saying from my land will help. We have had wars and fighting, too much, as I told you. And one of our wise men said, 'They who live by the sword must die by the sword.' You have met Homo Ferox, who lives by the spear. That was their choice. Now they must die by it."

"Yes." Maoul nods gravely. "I see."

Kamir has been listening wide-eyed. "How many evil things you know, dear 'Om Jhared." she says. "Oh, Agna and Donnia come."

Then Maoul shakes his head, as if to chase out dreadful thoughts, and says in his normal tones, "But I have also come to tell you that we must leave soon for the Long Swim. Only two of the women yet live, and the star we call the Wind Bringer has appeared. The season of storms will be on us if we don't go soon. So we will be leaving you, man from the skies. What will you do? Will you come with us?"

"I was expecting this," I tell him. "I know you are late. I don't dare come with you, the call from my ship may come at any time now. When it does, I must go with all speed back to the island where I left my camp and the little sky-ship that will take me up to them. I can take Kamir and the babies. But someone will have to come with me to take over the babies when I leave. Of course, I will give him the boat and anything else I have that would be useful to you."

Agna and Donnia, who have come in with baskets of butterfish, join us in time to hear all this. Conscientious fathers, they are already chewing. Donnia speaks up.

"I can go with him, Maoul."

"And I," says Sintana unexpectedly. "Every day I am with him I learn. But I can't make a swim alone, like this." He taps his still nearly bald head.

"I wish I could stay with you, 'Om Jhared and little sister," says Agna. "But I must go to relieve the friends who are caring for my five little ones."

"I shall be delighted at your company, companion-of-battles."

"Well then, that is settled," says Maoul, rising. "You will await your signal, while we leave, I think, on the second morning."

"Are you taking the canoes?" I ask as they leave.

"We're thinking about that. Right now I have this evil job to do," says Maoul, and they depart.

We go back to feeding the baby-monster. Just as I have contributed my mouthful to the sweet-smelling sac, Agna pushes past me.

"Hold a moment, let me look."

Gently he rocks the baby-sac until he can see beneath. I notice a bluish-black discoloration at the bottom, where the membrane joins with what had been Kamir's skin.

"How long has this color been here?" he demands.

No one knows. Kamir has struggled up to look. "What is it, Agna? What's wrong?"

"Trouble." He tips the big bundle up so we can all see the bottom on which it has been resting. The evil-looking purplish color is heavy there, with yellowed streaks in it. "I think that is about where the gold-skin struck you."

"Yes," says Kamir. "Oh, I feared he had harmed them! We must get Mavru."

"I go!" says Donnia, and ducks outside. We can hear him break into a splashing trot in the stream.

When Mavru comes and sees, he looks grave.

"One of the babies is, I fear, dead. I must cut it away lest the trouble spread to others. 'Om Jhared, I need the sharpest possible knife. May I borrow yours?"

"Yes. And I'll clean it as thoroughly as I can first." My shark knife takes a keen edge and will stand heat.

Mavru calls for an armful of moss and washes his hands thoroughly in the stream outside. Then he produces a packet of long, slender thorns. "I have dipped these in your cleaning solution," he tells me. "They are for sewing."

He turns to the fetal package and carefully turns it over to show the discolored side. This had been the outside of Kamir's belly; it looks eerie to see her navel there. Mavru is studying the stains, figuring where to make his cuts, as carefully as any surgeon of a technological culture. There are no magical passes, no shamanism.

When he is ready, he slices into the mass with delicacy and boldness, beyond the farthest stain of blue, and continues around to the side, folding back the skin. The characteristic sweet odor of the babies fills the hut, but it is mixed with the sickening smell of infection.

Kamir winces in sympathy as he cuts, but says nothing.

The exposed mass of flesh and organs looks a healthy pink. I can see a tiny pink foot through the membrane enclosing it. Mavru gropes deep into the sac with both hands now. I find myself feeling queasy, and quickly turn my head away. When I look back, Mavru has pulled out a nasty-looking length of stained purple and yellow gut. He drops it into the waste moss and reaches in again. Exposed now is a discolored fetal sac. He palps it carefully, and mutters, "Dead." He sighs, and with one quick gesture pulls and flips the fetus out and onto the moss, its umbilical cord tight.

Mavru pays no more attention to it, but goes into the wound with his knife, cutting the cord far in, and cutting away all infected tissue. Very little of the dark purple blood flows. I notice he is careful not to contaminate the knife by cutting into infection. He seems to know the anatomy of the fetal sac well.

When he has finished, the hollow he has made where the dead baby was is clean-looking, with only the ends of a few thorn-sewn vessels sticking out. Mavru inspects it with care, then bends down and sniffs thoroughly. Satisfied, he asks me, "A dusting of your wonderful powder now?"

"I think so, yes."

He takes the antibiotic flask out of his loincloth and dusts sparingly. Then he takes up clean moss and carefully packs the wound, pulling the skin back as far as it will go and fixing it with thorns.

No advanced surgeon could have done better with the tools at hand.

At last he turns away from his completed task and, with the point of his knife, slits the discolored membrane off the discarded dead fetus.

I gasp.

Lying there on the moss is what appears to be a Human baby boy, an infant almost ready to be born. There can be no doubt that I have fathered this child; it is no parthenogenetic alien, but Human in every way that I can see. My son. My almost-son . . . What about the other two?

Kamir is staring, too. "Oh, what that goldskin did," she mutters through clenched teeth. "Oh, my little stranger baby! How beautiful! He is—was—just like you, dear 'Om Jhared. What about the others? Are they all right?"

"I believe so," says Mavru. "I think we caught this in time. And they are like us, by the way; Mnerrin, if that is to be our name. I had a good look at both their feet and they have our fins, as this poor little lad had not." He touches the dead baby's Human toes.

"Are they to be girls or men?" Kamir asks.

"Oh, I couldn't tell. But one is decidedly larger."

I have pulled myself together. "Healer Mavru, all our thanks. Now tell me: on most worlds, it is customary to pay healers, or give them a present. What may we do for you? Of course I will send you my good knife when I go, but there must be something else."

He starts to wave me away, but checks. "Well, if you are serious, would it be improper to ask that you give me this dead baby to study? I want to compare it with our own. And it might help me if ever I have to deal with more Humans."

"Gladly," I say. "And you will, of course, bury him with a little marker or whatever is appropriate?"

"Yes. With a marker saying it is the first Human child born of Mnerrin."

"But—" says Kamir. "Oh, but . . ." Then she seems to reconsider. "I guess it's all right, Father Mavru. Only . . ."

"I know," says Mavru compassionately. "I know. I thank you very much. And this will solve what might be a problem for you."

It would indeed. I had been thinking that.

When he goes out, taking the baby, Agna and Donnia hurry in to resume the feeding. I hold Kamir quietly for a while to comfort her—and myself.

That evening Agna and I take a few minutes off to go down and join the conclave on the beach. The Mnerrin habitually gather here to watch the sunset and chat. Agna leads me around to the five men and their children who have been caring for his young. The babies are all appealing plump little Mnerrin, three girls and two boys, one of whom can already swim strongly, as Agna demonstrates.

Old Maoul is here, too, earnestly debating something with several men.

"They are deciding whether to take the canoes," Agna tells me. "I think we will. Normally the babies swim, fastened to their father; but that of course slows us down. If they were in a canoe, we could travel faster. The two wounded men and Elia could go in them, too. But some of the older men are afraid that this will change our way of life too much."

"I can understand that. . . . Hello, Sintana. How goes it?"

The young man has a worried look. " 'Om Jhared, do you know any way to keep those canoes from tipping so easily? That is one of the objections to taking them. I thought that if they had a down-thrusting wood piece below, it would stabilize them, but I don't see how to do that."

Inventive boy. "That's what we call a keel. It would indeed stabilize the canoes, but it would also hit rocks, if it was long enough to do good. But there is another way, which we call outriggers." I smooth off a spot of sand and draw him a picture.

"I see. But there isn't time to build these, 'Om Jhared."

"Well, can you produce two long logs each and some rope? I'll show you a quick and dirty version." I make another sketch, showing a canoe with a log loosely lashed on each side. "The idea is that the logs must be loose enough to float when the canoe is loaded. It will slow down the paddling a bit, but you will be surprised at how hard it is to tip. Want to try it?"

"Absolutely! I knew I could count on you, 'Om Jhared!"

I reflect that it is best I leave before my meager store of information runs out. Meanwhile Agna is looking wistfully at a group still deep in their study of Relations.

"I used to love that," he says. "But now I am so rusty."

"My case too," I tell him. "Tell me, what are those men playing at? It looks like a game I know."

"Oh, it's an old game we all love. Legend has it that the other man who came from the skies taught it to our forefathers. Do you really recognize it?"

"Yes, I think it is a game called 'chess,' only the pieces are carved a little differently."

"Yes, 'chess,' you say? We call it 'Shez'! It must be the same. So some legends are true!"

But I have something else on my mind.

"Agna, Donnia says that you know the straight-line direction to the island where I left my sky-ship. Can you show me? Then I can set my instrument here. It would be much quicker than retracing my steps."

"Yes, I do. Don't you recall, when we first started home with Kamir, you showed me where you'd come from? Let us go in the water, I'll give you the line."

We swim out, and Agna submerges for a few minutes. When he comes up, he has one arm pointed west-southwest. I set my compass pointer.

"You must have thrown something in the sea there," says Agna disapprovingly. "I could sense alien stuff in the current."

"Yes, I fear my ship must have sprayed exhaust when I landed. And it will again when I take off. I'm sorry—I hope it will dissipate soon."

"Oh, it's almost gone," Agna concedes.

"The island is such a small, flat one, Agna. Do you think this line will really carry me to it? At least, near enough to see it?"

"Yes," he says firmly. "If I were swimming, I'd say, seven days."

"Good enough." Then something inside me lurches, as if a curtain were rent. "No, *bad!*" I blurt. *"Agna, I don't want to leave!"*

He looks at me with affection. "I know. I, too, will miss you. But speak to Maoul of this. I am not sure you know your own mind."

"Yes. I will," I say, near to weeping.

When we get ashore, I confide my feelings to Maoul.

"I know, I know," he tells me. "You are sending sadness all about. But tell me: if you go, you *can* return, can't you?"

"Yes."

"While if you stay here, if you refuse this sky-ship, no other may come for you, right?"

"True."

"And if you go, you may be able to help us against the goldskins? And in other ways, Mavru says?"

"I can try. I can always do something, even if only to send you weapons and supplies."

"You could not do that if you stay here."

"No . . . Oh, I see what you mean. If I truly love you and want to help you, I should go. . . . And I should take the course which is not irrevocable, which again means I should go."

"That is my thought."

I sigh deeply. "Then it is my thought, too. Thank you, Father Maoul. . . . But oh, I shall miss this world so."

He too sighs. "It has been for you a happy time, out of your real life, which we cannot imagine. But for us this is real life, with all its good and evil."

I see what he means, and bow my head. To me, this is still a dream-world, though the people are real. I have not been truly into life here, as I would have to be if I stayed. As I would have to be if I come back to stay. Dreams must end.

"You are wise."

He shrugs this off. I see Agna looking at me anxiously. It is time to go back and feed.

And just then, in the midst of everything, I hear a loud, familiar sound from the hut. Everyone looks up.

"What is that?"

"A beep from my transponder. That is, a signal that the ship which will carry me away has come into your sun's system. I now have only a few days to get back to that island. If they have to wait, they will charge me money, and I can only pay for two days."

"Pay?" asks Maoul.

"A system of portable value we use for returning the favors of people we may never meet again."

"Legend says," Maoul tells me, "that the one who came here before tried to explain something of this. To us it sounded unharmonious."

"Unharmonious" is a term they use for, roughly, *uncivilized* and perhaps inhumane. It amuses me to hear our great economic system so brusquely—if perhaps justly—dismissed.

I bid Maoul good night and return with Agna to the hut.

That night Kamir faints for the first time.

The last day passes quietly. I cannot bring myself to start until the Mnerrin leave.

I watch them making up seaproof packets of their scant possessions and, one by one, placing them in the canoes. They consist primarily of a few small looms and supplies of thread, a musical instrument someone has been working on, some pots, several large pieces of cloth. I reflect on how little of their rich life would remain for archaeology if anything happens to the Mnerrin themselves.

When it comes to the spears and shields, the canoe-paddlers object. "There will be no room left for the babies and the wounded men." In the end a few are taken.

I watch a burial party taking the body of the last woman up into the hills. In the past I have avoided looking at such scenes, though I knew they went on. But now I wonder how soon I may have to undertake such a grim trip myself.

Kamir is all over her fainting fit and says she is looking forward to traveling again. I marvel at how she can do with no food except the clear broths we make for her. She drinks more water than before; perhaps it has some richness in it. I would give an arm for an intravenous feeding rig. There will be one on that big ship. I have wasted hours trying to figure how I could get it to her.

The last night there is much singing. Kamir asks to be taken to the beach. I pick her up, almost weeping to find how light she is. She who only weeks ago had been my strong little mermaid, rolling me in the sand. . . . Now she scarcely weighs as much as the canteens I bring with us.

On the beach I pack moss around her poor knobby knees and hips, and prop her up where she can greet all. The Mnerrin are kind to her, particularly Sintana and his friends, who rally her about "fighting like a man."

The singing rises around us, sweet and true. Kamir joins in, surprisingly strongly. I hold my face up to the moons and wish I could howl like a hound. Dreamworld or not, I love these people, love Kamir. Even love my dead son, and the other two . . . Of that last night I shall say no more.

The next morning there is a surprise—one of the rare fogs has closed in. It makes no difference to the Mnerrin's plans. The canoes are loaded; I see the fathers of toddlers tying them to the thwarts. The first shift of paddlers is in place.

And then they simply walk into the sea. Many turn to wave at us and for the last time I get the impact of so many blue, blue eyes. Then they are gone under sea and into the fog, leaving only the dark shapes of the canoes.

The paddlers dig in rhythmically, and the canoes, too, fade and vanish into the white wall.

It is very lonely on the beach.

But it is time for us to go, too. Donnia and Sintana carry the boat to the beach and return for the sac of babies. I am astonished to see how they have grown in the last days; the skin now seems almost too small for the full-size infants within. I carry Kamir down and arrange her in the stern beside me. The babies, and a big pot of fish, go in front, where she can touch them. It has been arranged to stop every hour for feeding, since I can do little while driving the boat, and Kamir is so weak.

Then the two Mnerrin wade out into the bay. I follow, expecting them to want Agna's heading once they are past the reef. Instead, they simply submerge briefly and start off, straight on target. Wonderful instrument, those guide-hairs! Even Sintana's fuzz seems long enough to give him some help.

Then we set off behind them, much as we had arrived, except that different arms are flashing ahead. And Kamir lies dying at my side. We settle into the dreamlike trance of travel over the blue sea, and the mists gradually clear.

And that's about it.

On the third day there is a tear in the babies' envelope and the whole skin looks dry and different. Kamir is excited; her eyes glow, she seems to be keeping herself alive on sheer will. But she can't speak. "I will see them!" she whispers to me.

On the fourth morning it is difficult to feed. Donnia says that the babies must come out. He grasps the edges of the torn skin and pushes it down. It peels away; a shriveled placenta comes with it. As we tear it loose, the two babies roll out on the moss. One is exposed, I see it breathing, but the other is still in its fetal covering. I cut it free quickly, and the baby takes a great gulp of air and begins to cry—the immemorial infant squall. It is a Mnerrin baby, and so is the other, a girl and a boy.

Kamir tries to crawl toward them, her eyes burning hungrily. "Wait; darling," I tell her. We swab the babies off, and put them in her arms.

"They're perfect," Donnia says.

But after a moment her head falls to one side. She has fainted, I hope, and I take her in my arms. She breathes for a minute or two; that is all. She is dead in my arms, with the babies in hers.

Gently we take them from her and feed them. To me they seem sturdy little things, but Donnia says they are thin. "We have work to do."

There is an island nearby, a pretty one with a mountain. We take Kamir's body there, up above the dunes, with a headstone on which I inscribe words too emotion-laden to repeat here.

And we continue. . . .

After a time it becomes clear that my batteries will more than hold out, so I suggest that both men get in the boat. Thus burdened, our progress becomes something of a wallow, but still much faster than swimming. On the way, I teach Donnia and Sintana to drive it.

And so we arrive, on the morning of the seventh day, at the small island I had left a lifetime ago. The little space-lander is just as I left it, my camp is untouched. As though on signal, my transponder beeps again that evening, signifying that the ship is taking up an orbit above us. I signal her and arrange a rendezvous at dawn my time.

Then I busy myself with a quick check and turn to giving away everything I can possibly spare. The lander's big batteries will recharge the boat and the laser; I estimate their battery lives at years with a little care. My best knife I send to Mavru via Donnia, along with the big medikit. The laser is for Sintana and the little one for Maoul. Everything else—blankets, lenses, a small microscope, emergency cook pans, and all—I heap on them.

"Use your judgment. Something nice for Agna—and this waterproof drawing pad and stylus for the older man who does Relations. God, I wish there were more."

"It is ample," says Sintana. His eyes are on the lander, I sense that both are anxious to see it go up.

But there isn't room for them to stay on the island, with the exhaust. So I bid them farewell and send them out in the boat. They seem reluctant to have me leave. As they motor out I catch a last gleam of blue.

Waiting to lift, I allow myself to think of what has haunted me, ever since the goldskins' coming:

On ancient Terra there was once another race of Humans. They were big-brained and, some think, unaesthetically formed. They flourished for a time, leaving few signs in the stone records except their bones and a grave lined with flowers. We call them Neanderthals.

And then came Cro-Magnon, our direct ancestors, and after that Neanderthal was seen no more.

What happened no one knows, whether some interbred, or whether they were wiped out in one of our first acts of genocide. (We left no living close relatives.) What thoughts Neanderthal thought, what intellectual discoveries he made, no one will ever know. They were strong; the fact that they disappeared at Cro-Magnon's advance must have been partly a matter of temperament. Perhaps they were noncombative.

Have I been seeing the start of just such a tragedy? I have no illusions about the Mnerrins' ability to defend themselves against Homo Ferox. Their wonderful artifacts of song and thought reside in their minds, their art of Relations is literally written on the sands. If they go under, no one will ever know that here men were following the thinking of Pythagoras, in a wholly different technological context. But they do not need the technology, except now, for self-defense.

No. No one would ever know—any more than we will ever know the color of the eyes that looked out from under Neanderthal's shaggy mane. Perhaps they were clear, and filled with compassion and the growing light of reason. We cannot know. We have, I fear, killed them. And I fear, I greatly fear, that those lost eyes were a brilliant blue.

Now I have made my record. To you who hear it, I beg, allow yourselves to imagine how it was. To be moved. To help! Surely the Federation could spare one small party to sort this out, to transport the goldskins to another planet. To save what can never be replaced of peace and beauty, of mind.

This was the next-to-last story completed by Alice Sheldon, sent to her agent in November 1986. (Her final story, 1987's "In Midst of Life," was included in *Crown of Stars*, Tor 1988.)

Alli referred to the final version of any story as "draft x," because she rewrote extensively. As she worked, she discarded the earlier drafts, often taping pieces from different drafts together. Even the manuscripts sent to editors would sometimes include taped pages.

"The Color of Neanderthal Eyes" is almost unique in that part of the original handwritten manuscript exists, in a spiral-bound notebook. The first page contains several alternate titles ("The Other Road," "Love on the Other Road," "Into the Mists") and the statement "1st Draft—Needs extensive revision and tightening."

The differences between this and the final typescript are "extensive" but not necessarily substantive. There are no real cuts, but almost every sentence has been rethought. Here are the first several handwritten paragraphs. (The manuscript originally started with "I am lazily cruising along just outside a coral reef . . ."; the segment before that was taped into the notebook.)

> *It is all my fault, all of it, and Kamir is dead. But you must do something.*
>
> *Now it is afterwards, I am recording this on shipboard so you will understand. Much of this belongs in a Second Contact report— and much more does not. But I am too exhausted and torn to make a formal Report, I am simply setting down what happened so you will see that something must be done:*

At first, all is serene and joyful.

I am lazily cruising along just outside a coral reef on the beautiful sea-world unimaginatively christened "Wet." But now the sun is starting down. I turn up the motor and start looking for a pass through the reef toward shore. I find one, and cautiously zigzag through; my little neo-latex dinghy is too precious to risk tearing into that sharp coral. Once through, I turn and stop, watching. Something has been following me all afternoon, popping up for a look at intervals, sometimes near, sometimes far.

I don't want to spend the night alone on a strange beach without checking out my follower. Will it follow me here?

The ninth page ends with Jared and Kamir going to sleep the first night, and the notation "To new p. 10." The original pages 10 through 32 are very different from the final version: Agna arrives much earlier in the story, before Jared even knows Kamir is female. They go to the village, and Jared makes his Neanderthal/Cro-Magnon comparison immediately. The tribe is suspicious of him when they learn that he is a male who does not raise children, the same as the golden people. The scenes in which Jared learns Kamir and Agna's genders, that the females die after bearing children, and that the Mnerrin have developed math and science (and chess) all appear earlier in this draft. This section ends at the top of page thirty-two with the approach of the storm that in the finished story thrust Jared and Kamir together while they were still alone:

> The band of white cloud is growing rapidly higher. Now a band of darkness shows at the bottom. It's the squall line, all right. The light is golden yellow, and still not a ripple or a frond stirs. The barometer is falling through the floor, it seems oddly hard to breathe.
>
> Now the Mnerrin are

The "New 10" starts recasting this material, and is—like the first nine pages—similar to the final version, with minor changes in almost every line but no major additions or subtractions. This continues until pages 26 and 27 (the latter a separate sheet paper-clipped to the former), which have a longer version of the island tour taken by Jared and Kamir, ending with the note "To next book," which no longer exists.

The novella was originally published in the May 1988 issue of *The Magazine of Fantasy & Science Fiction*.

LETTERS FROM YUCATAN AND OTHER POINTS OF THE SOUL: UNCOLLECTED NONFICTION

The goal for this section was to produce a volume of Alice Sheldon's complete public nonfiction, compiling everything that she had written for publication but not using her notebooks, diaries, or (for the most part) private letters. There may be some items written for publication which we failed to identify, and some she did (like her thesis and her columns on art in the 1940s) that seemed to fall too far outside our focus. I haven't included letters to the editor, either newspaper editors or science fiction fanzine editors, because they offered little outside the context of the publication. There are a few small items which I've extracted from her personal correspondence to me, because they connect with other, published pieces.

Most of these articles were published in fanzines, so a word about them seems in order.

When the first science fiction magazines started appearing (*Amazing Stories* number one was dated April 1926), the publication of readers' addresses in the Letters to the Editor columns gave SF fans a means to write to each other. A small but active "fandom" quickly established itself, forming local clubs and conventions and publishing amateur magazines. The word *fanzine* is now in the dictionary, and there are fanzines for any activity which has fans (music, sports, collectibles), but the word was coined within science fiction fandom for its own magazines. Until recently, most SF fanzines were mimeographed, hand-collated and-stapled, and generally given away to its contributors and to publishers of other fanzines. The easy availability of offset printing has turned fewer practitioners into "ink-stained wretches," and now the Internet is changing fan publishing even more.

I published fanzines from 1969 to 1978. There were two main types of fanzines in the seventies, the large "genzines" (general interest fanzines, with a variety of contents; mine were considered "sercon," SF-oriented serious and constructive, as opposed to the lighter tone many faneds adopted) and the small "personalzines" (which were mostly editor-written, sometimes by fans who proudly stated that they had stopped reading SF when they discovered fandom). To say that every fanzine fell into one of these two categories would not even resemble the truth, because we faneds had no one to answer to but ourselves, and any issue could be any size and contain any material that suited our fancy at any time. It was delightfully chaotic, and it made every day's mail an adventure.

My fanzines went under three names: *Phantasmicom* (#1/Summer 1969–#11/May 1974), *Kyben* (#1/December 1971 [included as pages 27–46 of *Phantasmicom* 8]–#12/September 1975), and *Khatru* (#1/February 1975–#7/February 1978). *Phantasmicom* and *Khatru* were my genzines, *Kyben* my personalzine.

Phantasmicom was actually started by Donald G. Keller, who saw some fanzines I had received and decided on the spot that he wanted to do one himself. We had to pretty much write the whole sixty-eight-page first issue ourselves (this was true for most of the early numbers), but we were reading a lot of SF and fantasy and loved having the forum to talk about it. I was eighteen and Don seventeen when we started, and we became noticed for the "youthful enthusiasm" of our writing and of our ambitious publishing schedule. For our third issue, P. S. Price (an actual contributor!) wrote up a meeting he had had with R. A. Lafferty into a fairly substantial piece on Lafferty's life and work. I approached Virginia Kidd, who was Lafferty's agent, for help with a bibliography and ended up with an unpublished short story as well. Now we were feeling like real editors, and were commended for devoting so much space to a writer who deserved more attention than he had so far been receiving. Other professional writers noticed what we were doing, and Harlan Ellison and Dean R. Koontz in particular encouraged us to continue to spotlight less-well-known writers, and Piers Anthony emphasized the importance of the interview part of the feature.

Well, we (especially me) weren't up to the formal sit-down-with-a-writer-and-a-microphone kind of interview, but if there were a way to do it through the mail, that might be okay. We talked about several writers we might approach, and I decided that I would try for James Tiptree, Jr. I wasn't particularly a Tiptree fan, but I had read several of his stories and had liked some of them. What I was most interested in was the fact that in 1970, when there was a virtual war declared between the Old Wave and the New Wave in science fiction, Tiptree was being claimed by both camps. There had to be a story in that.

My first attempt to reach Tiptree was through one of his editors, and included the line, "Piers suggested we try to find the writer first, and drag out of him whatever information he is willing to disclose." That letter was forwarded to Tiptree, and not surprisingly went unanswered. A little later, though, I scored Tiptree's address and tried again: "What I am proposing is an exchange of letters—questions and answers—as few or as many as you would agree to—which would be combined into an interview-type article." I of course did not know that Tiptree could not be interviewed in person or by phone, but in my shyness I had stumbled onto the only way he *could* be. (For her part Alli saw that if she did this, then anyone else asking for information about Tiptree could just be forwarded a copy of his one interview.)

We spent two months sending the interview back and forth, another couple months arranging the bibliography and short story to accompany it, and just kept writing to each other after that. I have no idea how it happened, but a deep friendship developed that still sustains me, all these years after her death. (Putting this book together, rereading all the letters, immersing myself in our relationship again, has been a wonderful experience.)

I asked Tip to write articles for my fanzines, and I got a lot of them. Sometimes there were pieces on specific topics, sometimes more general remarks, mostly on her travels. (These went into a column in *Kyben*, the personalzine, under the title "The 20-Mile Zone," which she named after a Dory Previn song.) Some of the travel pieces were written as letters to me, but designed to be published. Some letters contained both public and private pages, and often the two bled over. In the informal world of fanzines this didn't matter at all, but it makes some of the "essays" look odd in this book, with their asides to me and their "best to Ann"s. In the public parts of the letters, Alli said, she was "speaking to the SF world embedded in you," that she couldn't write to a faceless audience but could to one person.

We start, after a brief note from a private letter, with the postal interview I conducted with Tiptree from December 3, 1970, through January 29, 1971, which was published in *Phantasmicom* 6, June 1971.

Having done all this idiotic stuff about *ME* has put me in a very strange mood. (Have you ever tried talking about yourself for 6 hours straight—into a mike held by a pleasant stranger?) Jeff, I am so sick of *ME-E-E*— it's indescribable. I have all the normal ego, and often use my life for (hopefully) funny stories—but, I don't know, is it possible *not to believe* in one's biography? . . . And also I'm nostalgic for the old simple days—somehow my "Interview" with you—remember, how it all started? Anyway, I think that was "realer" (for god's sake, won't I ever learn to say "more real?")—anyway, more true & spontaneous and unselfconscious than all this Alice B. Sheldon malarky . . . Maybe it has something to do with women changing their names so much—and also in my work I once had to use extra names; I've lived under, let's see ~~LIII~~ 1 at least six, for longer or shorter. Try changing your name someday, Jeff, just for the experience. Oddly refreshing—but too much is disorienting. . . .

Anyway, I just wanted to tell you that none of this current stuff can blot out our old good first Interview of all.

10 Sep 82

IF YOU CAN'T LAUGH AT IT,
WHAT GOOD IS IT?

Smith: Your friends and associates are unaware that you are a science fiction writer, so you don't want SF people finding out who your friends and associates are. But how about telling us what you *are* willing to let us know about you?

Tiptree: Well, I was born in the Chicago area a long time back, trailed around places like colonial India and Africa as a kid (and by the way, I knew in my bones that they weren't going to stay "colonial" any more than I was going to stay a kid, but nobody ever asked me). I'm one of those for whom the birth and horrendous growth of Nazism was the central generation event. From it I learned most of what I know about politics, about Human life, about good and evil, courage, free will, fear, responsibility, and What To Say Goodbye To . . . And, say it again, about Evil. And Guilt. If one of the important things to know about a person is the face in his nightmares, for me that face looks much like my own.

In some ways it is easier to live with a Devil who is clearly different, black or white or yellow, old, young, female or male, or such. *Them*, the baddies; *Me* (wholly a different animal), the good guy. Easier; but maybe not so instructive.

At any event, by the time I had finished the decade's worth of instruction in How Things Are provided by this event—you know, joining organizations, getting in the Army, milling around in the early forms of American left-wing sentiment, worrying about Is It Going to Happen Here (an occupation I haven't given up), getting out of the Army, doing a little stint in government, trying a dab of business, etc. etc.—I realized that my whole life, my skills and career, such as they were, my friends, everything had been shaped by this event, and rather derailed from what I'd intended to be in a vague way. So ensued a period of more milling (I'm a slow type) including some dabblings in academe. And now the story grows even vaguer for the time being, Jeff, since I'm against lying on principle. (Life's too short, it takes all one's time to get a finger on some truth.)

But y'know, the other day It came to me, all I write is one story. There's this backward little type, and he's doing some gray little task and believing like they tell him, and one day he starts to vomit and rushes straight up a mountain, usually to his doom. Human or alien, mountain or rocket, it's all the same. Next year I'm trying a real departure: There's this *girl*, see, and she rushes *down* a salt mine. But they always vomit. The amount of sheer puke in my stories is staggering . . . What more do you need to know?

Does a writer ever stop telling you who he is?

Smith: But it's dangerous to try and guess at an author's feelings from just his writings. He may use five thousand words to see how a new lifestyle feels, decide he doesn't like said lifestyle, but still have a publishable short story with his name on it. Or: Try an experiment. Here is an unwritten short story of mine. (Part of it is written and is excruciatingly bad, I'm afraid.) Can you interpret my feelings about marriage from the outline of the story "The Marriage"?

For a couple hundred years there has been no marriage. Everyone sleeps around with whomever he/she pleases. Either coincidently or not so coincidently, the society is decadent, stagnant. The people have not yet reached the level of Wells's Eloi, but they're on the way. There has been no progress in any art or science. Everyone sits around doing a lot of nothing. Now this couple decides to get married. They have a big ceremony, and everyone wonders if marriage will be the New Thing. They don't wonder if marriage will be the savior of society, but the reader does. But after a year or so of monogamy the husband takes on a lover, and another olde praktise—divorce—is reinstituted.

Well, you know how simpleminded plot summaries are. Assume that the whole story is there; do I feel marriage is good or evil? Is my writing (quote unquote) telling you who I am?

Tiptree: First, I fling the query back at you. Whether you feel marriage is good or evil is not *who you are*. It is a superficial Nixon-debate type formalism of no psychic weight or penetration. No-no-no! If you think your scanning-process occupies itself with such flak, listen deeper to it.

Listening: Who is this guy? Is he for real? Does he live in the same world I do? What scares him? What does he love? Is he threatening me? Can he endure the messiness of being Human or is he building some neat unreal escape scheme? I hear his verbal argument, pro or con, but what're his reasons? What *kinds* of points is he making to support it?

For samples, you could have a Jeff Smith who showed his marriage position entirely in terms of society's good. Or a sad-case Jeff Smith appealing to some conventional mystique. Or a happy Jeff Smith playing around with some Trobriander analogy. Or a hard-nose Jeff Smith who would thump it out in terms of Ordnung or the patriarchal power structure or, godhelpus, economic efficiency. Or a psychological-cynical Jeff Smith who lays it on us in the name of alleged primate instincts. Or a psychological-weepy Jeff Smith wringing our hearts about children's need for nuclear family role models. Or a hotnuts Jeff Smith breathing hard over unlimited-sex-access fantasies. Or a revengeful-brat Jeff Smith producing bloody gobbets of his parents' marriage . . . had enough?

So—when you hear this rather quiet account of a social state in which a pair of individuals follow their own bent, producing an "innovation," which is followed by another "innovation," you get an immediate impression of a curious, probably orderly mind testing a social generality by showing what real people might do . . . and the cycle form (history returning on itself) gives unmistakable evidence of a mild ironic trend. The author notices and enjoys history's little ways of presenting the same old meatballs as Hash du Jour. The fact that he asks the question he does hints that he is *not* a black-white crusader. More subtly, the reference to self suggests that he is one who uses self as an experience laboratory, no sacred wall around the sealed black box of Me (such as you meet often in, say, *Analog*). The way the story goes, A leads to B which leads to etc., suggests a process-type thinker, interested in social causality (spends extra words on relation of marriage to "decadence"). Wells ref. suggests author reads around on the subject, probably still in the shallows (uses terms like "decadence") but will go deeper (tone of thoughtful curiosity about that "coincidentally or not") . . . and a gentle guy, forgive it.

Now there's my try at describing what comes over in a flash as I read the bare summary. *Don't tell me you don't do it too.*

And that was all at the surface or content level (Do pay attention, children) without any digging into the effects of choice of words, cadences, that eel-bucket known as *style*.

(Of course the fact that the author omitted a whole encyclopedia of stereotype words tells us something right off. For example, imagine a summary with the words "purity of bodily fluids" or "joy of life" or "so-called liberals" in it.)

And it occurs without reference—correction, with *almost* no reference—to whether the story seems "good" or "bad."

In other words, what an author leaks at every sentence is not his formal argument alone but what he sees as real, how deeply he's into life . . . and himself. What kind of companion he'd be to run out of gas with in the Mojave Desert, maybe. (And some fine writers you'd rather not, right?)

The same holds in the case you cite where a guy publishes a temporary essay into some lifestyle. If he's a fast-developing, changing person you could be put off for a while on a specific piece, but even then I bet his very mercurial-serious quality would give itself away. You'd hold off judgment. This is a useless argument without a concrete example.

But it does bring up the other variable. No generalizations hold, not even this one—and I claimed above that your radar brings in this sort of stuff too. Well, I think that holds for *you*, Jeff Smith, and for most of you—whew!—sensitive, intuitive, creepy-quirky-feely learning-type minds out there . . . But:

Readers differ. Some people's radar is tuned down to basics like *Can I beat this bugger or do I have to listen to him*? (And don't we all do this jest a leetle?) The type I mean is the fellow who takes unfamiliar words as a threat, an attempted intimidation. Whereas the learning-type reader takes them as lures or exciting displays. (Unless they are an obvious threat-pose or squid-cloud.)

Now look, Jeff, you lured me into an embryo essay on the nonverbal level of verbal communication.

Which has doubtless been done better by the experts, so let's abort this mission and get on with it.

Smith: Why don't you want your friends to know about your "second career"? Don't you think that perhaps someday someone will stumble across one of your stories? Will you then deny being the same James Tiptree, Jr., or what?

Tiptree: I can answer that easily: I haven't a clue.

Let me tell you how all this got started.

Couple of years back under a long siege of work and people pressure, I set down four stories and sent 'em off literally at random. Then I forgot the whole thing. I mean, I wasn't rational; the pressure had been such that I was using speed (*very* mildly), and any sane person would have grabbed sleep instead. Obviously, one more activity was sheerly surreal. So some time later I was living, as often happens, out of cartons and suitcases, and this letter from Condé Nast (Who the hell was Condé Nast?) turns up in a carton. Being a compulsive, I opened it. Check. John W. Campbell.

About three days later I came to in time to open one from Harry Harrison.

Now, you understand, this overturned my reality-scene. I mean, we know how writers start. Years, five, ten years, they paper a room with rejection slips. It never occurred to me anyone would buy my stuff. Never. I figured I had the five years to get my head together. I had a list of the places I was going to rotate the things through. (Methodical, even when stoned, see above.)

Three years later I still haven't got it together. The thing has gone on and on, twenty-one as of now, and I still don't believe it. I don't deny I love it, but I deny being happy. It's too weird. As I told David Gerrold, if these guys only knew it, I'd have paid them for their autographs. I mean, years, years and years, I've been the kind of silent bug-eyed Rikki-Tikki-Mongoose type fan who thinks those guys who wrote them walk around six inches off the ground with private MT channels in their closets, step in and Flick!—Gal Central.

Moreover, Jeff. When someone like Barry Malzberg, who can write rings around me (I unknowingly wrote a fan letter to "K. M. O'Donnell" *through* Malzberg when he was editing *Amazing/Fantastic*)—When such guys claim they have drawers full of unsold manuscripts it proves to me something is wrong. What's the matter with me, they don't reject mine? Can only be 'cause I'm not really really *original*? See?

You better believe it, people mention how they get rejected, I flinch . . . Of course I occasionally do get reject letters, and then I not only flinch, I roll up in the rug, bawling. Maybe it all goes to show that writers are unfillable hungry voids of ego, like black star gravity-warps. Or maybe it's me, I dunno.

At this point I note I've been ducking your question "Why?" Ah indeed, why? Somewhere Freud is said to have observed that every action is overdetermined, that is, that there is usually more than one sufficient cause, that acts occur at convergence points where many causes meet. (I wish I could locate this quote, I may be overinterpreting; it's a very useful concept.)

At any event, I could give you a set of plausible reasons, like the people I have to do with include many specimens of prehistoric man, to whom the news that I write *ugh, science fiction* would shatter any credibility that I have left. (Sometimes I think SF is the last really dirty word.)

Or that I'm unwilling to tarnish my enjoyment of this long-established secret escape route by having to defend it to hostile ears. (Coward!)

Or, conversely, that my mundane life is so uninteresting that it would discredit my stories. Etc., etc. . . .

Probably the real reason is partly inertia, it started like this, I don't yet really believe it, let it be till it ripens. That too.

But basically maybe I believe something about the relation of writers to their stories, that the story is the realest part of the storyteller. Who cares about the color of Coleridge's socks? (Answer, Mrs. C.) Of course, I enjoy reading a writer's autobiography—or rather, *some* writers! A few. By far the most of them make me nervous, like watching a stoned friend driving a crowded expressway. For Chrissakes, *stop!*

I told this to Harlan Ellison, but I don't think he understood, because he is one of the few who can reveal all he wants without spoiling his stories. But there's the catch. When you're reading Harlan's wonderfully natural, candid, Human-all-too-Human accounts of Harlan Living, *are you really looking behind the scenes*? You are not. You are looking at more of Harlan's writing, not because Harlan is being deceptive, or being less than candid, but because Harlan belongs to that Human type, Homo Logensis, the Talking Man, like Mailer, like Thomas Wolfe, whose life forms into narrative as it is being lived, so that at every act of unveiling, at putting the naked squirm of the inmost flesh into words, another level of reality forms behind and beneath, in which the living Harlan exists just one jump ahead of the audience.

Those of us who are not so blessed are very rightly dubious about the value of straight autobiographical writing. For example, the poet Auden offers as his autobiography, a collection of cherished quotations and notations, his commonplace book. (I'm reading it now, it's great.) And he's right; if you want a terrible instance of suicide by autobiography, Cordwainer Smith. One of the greats. If only I'd never read that perishing introduction in which he blathers on about his household, and how his cook or somebody is really almost Human. Jeesus.

Does this convey?

Just to wind this up, you'll notice I left a "partly" dangling on the last page. Well, the last remaining part of my secretiveness is probably nothing more than childish glee. At last I have what every child wants, a real secret life. Not an official secret, not a Q-clearance polygraph-enforced bite-the-capsule-when-they-get-you secret, nobody else's damn secret but *mine*. Something *they* don't know. Screw Big Brother. A beautiful secret *real* world, with real people, fine friends, doers of great deeds and speakers of the magic word, Frodo's people if you wish, and they write to me and know me and accept my offerings, and I'm damned if I feel like opening the door between that magic reality and the universal shitstorm known as the real (sob) world. When all the more cogent reasons are done, it's probably that simple.

So, how to reconcile that with honesty? Well, who is honest? You? Or You? Don't tell me, man. You know as well as I do we all go around in disguise. The halo stuffed in the pocket, the cloven hoof awkward in the shoe, the X-ray eye blinking behind thick lenses, the two midgets dressed as one tall man, the giant stooping in a pinstripe, the pirate in a housewife's smock, the wings shoved into sleeveholes, the wild racing, wandering, raping, burning, bleeding, loving pulses of reality decorously disguised as a roomful of Human beings. I know goddam well what's out there, under all those masks. Beauty and Power and Terror and Love.

So who the fuck cares whether the mask is one or two millimeters thick?

Does *that* convey?

Smith: Yes. But I'm fascinated by your secret world. Not only do you have a magical SF place, but you find yourself in one of the upper echelons. You are a respected writer, an equal to these people whose autographs you are willing to buy. You never even spent your apprenticeship as a fan, but as a non-fan reader. It smacks of fantasy, Tiptree.

Tiptree: After recovering from the egoboo—ah, yes, sahib. There always is a learning. For some people named Joseph Conrad it seems to have been just living in a noticing way. For Tiptree, hidden years of writing crap headed MEMO, SUBJECT, TO . . . or PROBLEM, CONCLUSIONS, RECOMMENDATIONS. And then trying to do it like they said and then discovering that when I really did do it like they said—

Nobody could read it. Not even me.

So then more effort imploring the reader-fish to bite, to *read* about my goddam problem. I even tried putting dirty stories in footnotes, somewhere they're still there stamped Swallow Before Reading. Above all it was cut, cut, *cut*, starting with that gorgeous line you like best.

And I wrote a little, well, I guess it was poetry. One began, "Sitting on a fruit crate in the abandoned tractor park . . ."

Also I once worked briefly on a paper, the good old crazy *Chicago Sun*, where a bloat-eyed scotch-sodden frog from Texas called a feature editor kept a big pair of shears by his bottle. When you handed him your hot and beating prose he eyed it in silence with the reds of his eyes shining over the bags and then took up the shears and cut off the last third, which was where the point was. A learning experience.

(Also instructive was the fact that every time you wrote about the school board stealing the slum kids' lunch money it came out in pied type . . . Anybody ever hear what they had there *before* Daley?)

Smith: You publish a wide variety of fiction, from hardcore SF in *Analog* to "new wave" stories in *Venture* and *Amazing* to light fantasy in *Worlds of Fantasy*. Do you have any particular preference among these? Is there any we can expect to see more of in the future than of the others?

Tiptree: At the moment I'm in and around the Chicago area, partly attending to family matters in the shape of an aged and ornery mother—more damn people seem to have catastrophically aging relatives in Chicago than you'd believe. This is a theme in my life that seems to be going on and on, as Virginia Kidd that warm heart can tell you, I've been sobbing on her shoulder about this for years. Tried putting it in a story that *Galaxy* has been sitting on, called "Mother in the Sky with Diamonds," in which this insurance adjuster in the Asteroid Belt has his aged mother—who was once a space explorer—parked illegally and is trying to keep her supplied and still meet the demands of his cruddy boss. And so one day it all blows up together and he vomits and rushes straight out—or words to that effect. I like the tale, but the effort to wrest the purely personal misery into objectively readable form has been difficult. Campbell said it was a compressed novel, and he didn't want a novel. Damon Knight said it was repulsive. (It is.) Even if Jakobsson likes it I may want to rewrite it a bit. I wish I'd sent it to White. Ted is extraordinarily sensitive to my wavelength and I feel he would have taken the trouble to judge if it should be reworked. (Editors . . . Fred Pohl befriended me in the most fantastic manner when my ears were still drying. Real encouragement; part of it I found out by accident. Quite a guy.)

From this you can see that Learning How to Write is the big thing with me. I don't have any illusions of genius. Nobody writes for me, what's printed is what I wrote (aside from a little cleaning-up of words unsuitable for, I guess, Mom), but I'm very eager for critical reaction, and very willing to put it back in the oven. For example, Harry H. has twice pushed stories back at me for fix-ups; one was the original, "And I Have Come Across This Place by Lost Ways," which He bought for *Nova 2*. (Notice the Freudian slip in capitalizing "He" back there, Harry really is one of my gods.) It had too much social chitchat at first and the doom wasn't spelled out clear enough at the end. (I tend to make all my points indirectly, you know, somebody just mutters that the world ended yesterday, etc.) Sure enough, he was right; I spent a week of nights revising. Again, that wolf story from *Venture*, "The Snows Are Melted, the Snows Are Gone." When he bought it for the Best anthology he objected to the wolf's showing no sign of strain, being a mutant and all. So I tried him with an epileptic episode and that was right, too. But Christ, it's agony. I don't see how these one-draft wonders do it. What I send out is about Draft X.

All this by way of starting to talk about the real thing, the stories. For the most part my stuff has been gestated privately, some germ working around in its own terms, which I then finish up in the style it seems to demand. Some are *Gee, that's interesting* germs, like the *Analog* one about the haploid people. I got to brooding over what people would have been like if the alternating generation system had survived—and how essentially doomed it was, as a system.

Others arise out of a loving interest in the endless foul-ups of daily life, how the poor bastard behind some desk or title copes all day long with the throng of wild Indians, crackpots, active idiots, weirdos of all descriptions which we call the General Public. How do you run a racetrack, a matter-transmitter system, a hatchery, a research lab extrapolated into interstellar terms? (Strong biographical aroma here—yeah, yea verily, I have coped.) Others arise by analogy, for example, some of the side repercussions of the civil rights movement, sometime back, started "Happiness Is a Warm Spaceship," where the happy "liberal" hero runs into some aliens that don't want to get integrated. (Like most old-line liberals who started off with a general sense of Righting Injustice, I've gone through a long educative process in which the Black Brother changes from being a featureless object of sympathy to a bunch of real people.)

Smith: You have sold stories to two of the more prestigious volumes of science fiction coming out within the next year: Harlan Ellison's *Again, Dangerous Visions,* which is designed to show just what SF can be, and David Gerrold's *Generation,* which (for the most part) is supposed to present the major authors of tomorrow. Did you specifically tailor stories for those two volumes?

Tiptree: Actually, the story Harlan took is one such parable, and it's a sufficiently queasy one that I'm going to let anybody who wants to find it for himself. I wrote it *for* Ellison, in the sense that he did this great thing, he opened a door and said Do It, write what you want, here's a place you can scream. So I let it scream. David did a milder version of the same, so he got some gentler screams. There are a lot of unshouted shouts today. I guess a thumbnail sketch of my writing progress would be that I'm trying to make Contact with the prisoner inside, the voice wearily raised against the never-opening door, the one you hear in the middle of the night. The thing that's alive.

One story no one seems to have noticed or liked represents a scream from deep inside. If you have time and want to know most of what makes Tiptree tick, look in *Galaxy*, April 1969, for "Beam Us Home." I take a little sad credit too, recall that was written in 1968 and check the social prediction scene. It'll also show you that I'm a bit of a Trekky, enough so I sent Roddenberry a dedicated copy and got this beautiful letter back.

Another big hunk of Tiptree is in "The Last Flight of Dr. Ain," which I wanted to call "Dr. Ain's Love Story." That is screaming from the heart as good as I could do it in 1968. (By the way, only a couple people noticed that Ain's first name is Charles, (C.?) Tiptree's a furtive bastard.)

Smith: These two stories point out a facet of your work that we passed over a while back, when you said Campbell had said "Mother" was a compressed novel. You cut everything to the bone. You say something once, and then that's it. You feel no need to repeatedly explain, to emphasize. The five or so thousand words of "Beam Us Home" cover a span of years in the protagonist's life. Out of those years you pull a moment from here and a moment from there, each different, each serving its own purpose. There is a wealth of detail in "Doctor Ain," but it is all displayed in a fast, no-nonsense, matter-of-fact fashion. Your fiction—as definitely opposed to your letters—consists mainly of short simple sentences. And fragments. Almost all of them, from the light pieces such as "The Night-blooming Saurian" to the deep and subjective "I'm Too Big but I Love to Play." A couple parts in that story, however, and many in "The Snows Are Melted, the Snows Are Gone" are done in a richer and more satisfying style. Are you tending toward this generally, or do you just put more work into the deeper stories?

Tiptree: Oh, man, again I'm shook by the experience of finding someone has read the stuff, beautifully, perceptively.

While I recover . . . Did you catch that what the hero said at the end of "I'm Too Big" was true? Nobody, but nobody knows thing one about the motives under communication. Why do we want to speak *and be heard*? Whyfore this intense pleasure in being understood, the hurtfulness of garble? The ultimate misery of They Don't Understand? Try asking around in the labs from whence all this gabble flows. Go 'way, boy.

Recovered. Now look, it's futile to ask as new a writer as me where he's tending or what his style might become. I'm so green I don't even have a repertory of dances to cover the fact that I'm not answering!

Does a kid whose voice is changing know what's going to come out next time he opens the mouth? All I can do is look back and say, yeah, some were matter-of-fact, some condensed time, some followed every small event right along real time. And there's a couple coming out that are different still. Gerrold took one for *Protostars* writ in florid deadpan rococo, I guess. And a thing called "The Peacefulness of Vivyan" tries to drift the story out in the dreamy voice of a brain-tampered boy. Another one I'm waiting for Damon to reject is spoken from the point of view of a giant alien whose mate is lovingly eating him alive, and has the style of 1920 porno. ("Yes, you must let me caress you while you eat, my dawnberry.") I wish it was more like Nabokov, but since the aliens are quite primitive and so am I, they can be grateful it's a cut above Me Tarzan, You Jane. (I offered this on spec to Steve Goldin for his hopeful alien anthology, but I think something about the plot is bothering him—very understandably.) *I don't know*, Jeff.

Furthermore anything I tried to crystallize would be certifiable eelshit.

Pull yourself together, Tiptree.

All right, I can say this. I want to cut to the bone *always*. The question is, what is bone? Sometimes it's in the bare events, sometimes in the tone, sometimes in the minutiae—oh hell, that's no good. The question remains, each time answered differently.

You see, my aim really is not to bore. I read my stuff with radar out for that first dead sag, the signal of oncoming *boredom*. The onset of crap, stuffing, meaningless filler, wrongness. And don't *repeat* at me, you bastard . . . Bleeding Sebastian, how I have been bored in my life. The interminable, unforgivable, life-robbing, informationless, time-lost, entropy-triumphant, stagnant, retching *boredom* I have suffered . . . you *already said that*!!!!

I won't do it to anyone else. If I can help it.

And yet I want to communicate, and I'm prolix, right?

Do you get the picture of Tiptree agonizingly contorted between his gabbling tongue and his saber-wielding ear? Do you?

Next question.

Wait—a word on that question of more work on the "deeper" stories. No relation, Jeff. Everybody knows the old one about If I had more time Ida writ a shorter, etc. Some of the barest bones represent fifteen pages thrown out, some of the "full" stuff writes very easy . . . *and* sometimes vice versa. Mystery.

Yeah, I do want to write deeper. And not boring.

But I like to play, too.

Smith: What writers have influenced you the most as a writer, and what writers give you the most enjoyment as a reader?

Tiptree: Christ, *all* of them, in different ways. Harrison's *Bill the Galactic Hero*, for the ultimate in grim clowning; Sturgeon's "Man Who Lost the Sea," for total wow (sometimes when my stuff bores me worse than usual I go through the opening paragraphs of a flock of Sturgeons and contemplate suicide); Damon Knight's "The Handler," for classic social comment. Le Guin, Ellison, Delany, Zelazny, Lafferty (for total raconteur ease), Niven, Ballard (for brilliance). Oh man, *all* of them. Hundreds. And a special place for Philip K. Dick. All genuflect.

Smith: Okay, let's talk about Philip K. Dick. Or rather, you talk about him and I'll listen and learn. Frankly, he bores me to death, so I've read very little by the man. Some people think very highly of him, however, you apparently among them. Can you tell me why he is so important?

Tiptree: Jeff, one of Geis's *SF Review*ers remarked that Dick lacked compassion and humor. After retrieving the mag from the fire I got into correspondence with Geis, who struck me fine. (So did the reviewer, except for his tin ear.) So I said I'd write him a Dick thing, he was so nice as to offer, and you could say a couple interesting things on how we sense compassion, what kinds there are. So, let me save my main Dick guns for *SFR*, other than this quickie:

Yes, I admire the hell out of Dick. He's a mass of flaws, he's low-key, gritty, ornery, dogged, and *very* peculiar. And when I catch one of his things, I start walking round and round it talking to myself and bashing my head and spitting on my typewriter while this incredible flood of invention and alternate-reality grinkles glittering and oozing like radioactive Ajax lava playing Bach and smelling of hash and gear oil out all over the floor . . . and finally I whimper into a heap and write him another fan letter . . . And I worry he's going to injure himself with some insane chemical or end in Blahville.

Oh Christ, I don't know whether he's a "good" writer or how he stacks up against, say, Vonnegut. I wouldn't know how to interest anybody in him. Maybe it's a sign of something good that he bores you. Maybe he hit me in a vulnerable planetary conjunction. All I know is, *Don't try to take it away from me.*

Now I want to say a word about influences, and whatever you cut, Jeff, please leave this in because I'm beginning to feel like this was my last will and personal Time Capsule and it contains more on Tiptree than anybody including me will ever likely see or want to again.

Who one admires and who one is influenced by aren't the same. For example, sometimes you learn a trick from a guy who has nothing but that trick. (Even that chap with the shears "influenced" me, ah *oui!*) You learn from a myriad people, *and* from their mistakes. But there's a feeling that your list of "influences" is your list of greats. *Not so.* And here's the important thing to me:

Who do I admire in SF? You and you and you as far as eye and memory reach, sir and madam. Some for this, some for that. All different. But more than that—

I love the SF world. And I don't love easy. Out of SF I wouldn't spare one, from the dimmest two-neuron dreamer to the voice from the heart of the sun. Maybe to you on the inside it's not as clear as to me out here. What *is* SF?

What but a staggering, towering, glittering mad lay cathedral? Built like the old ones by spontaneous volunteers, some bringing one laborious gargoyle, some a load of stone, some engineering a spire. Over years now, over time the thing has grown, you know? To what god? Who knows. Something different from the gods of the other arts. A god that isn't there yet, maybe. An urge saying Up, saying Screw it all. Saying Try. To . . . be . . . more? We don't know. But *everyone* has made this. Limping, scratching, wrangling, clowning, goony, sauced, hes, shes, its, thems, bemmies for all I know, swooping glory, freaked out in corners, ridiculous, noble, queerly vulnerable in some ways others aren't—totally irrelevant, really.

These are the nearest to winged people that we have and I would shut up forever rather than hurt one of them. Dead or alive.

That's what's bugging Tiptree about listing "influences."

Dig?

—December 3, 1970–January 29, 1971

IN THE CANADIAN ROCKIES

When I decided to start publishing the small fanzine *Kyben*, I described it to Tiptree as a zine "in which I and my friends sit around and talk about things, mostly. . . . Would you like to write a little column?"

Tip agreed, and in *Kyben* 1/*Phantasmicom* 8 (December 1971) we introduced "The 20-Mile Zone." The column consisted of two essays, "I Saw Him" and "Spitting Teeth, Our Hero—," and a piece of the letter to me that had accompanied them.

Most of the installments of "The 20-Mile Zone" contained travel writing, but the second, "Do You Like It Twice?" (*Phantasmicom* 9, February 1972), was a response to a review in *F&SF*. The third column again consisted of an essay ("Maya Máloob") and parts of the letter accompanying it. When I ran this in *Kyben* 3 (September 1972) I edited the letter into two segments, "Mexico on 5 and 10 Haircuts a Day" and "The Voice from the Baggie." This time, instead of just reprinting it that way, I went back to the original letter and edited it more lightly, so the one section here is longer than the two sections were in the fanzine.

Never have I seen so much Human lard—except when I was a kid in what were then the Dutch East Indies. (The colonial Dutchman was a Human swine and so was his mate.) Up north it isn't pig fat, just solid cylinder-people . . . and tourists. Old, old tourists in their millions, busloads of geriatric specimens, singing "You Are My Sunshine." The entire Route 61 around the west end of the Lake Superior is bumper-to-bumper with old old people in beige cadillacs. Gerontology Boulevard. Old old men hung with cameras, dressed in weirdo mod stuff their pantsuited old ladies have put on them. Man, if they were all stripped I bet you'd only see three navels visible west of Ontario. Not to mention other organs. But the natives of the Rockies, though aged, are tough. Met one still climbing with ropes at eighty-two, another ninety-seven. It's a UN there, due to the railroads. Found Scots, Swedes, Swiss, Gypsy, Indian, Hungarian, and assorted Oriental hybrids. (Chinese restaurants appear early in the frontier.) They're the only ones with waistlines.

Also found a marvelous army of young Canadians male and female, who go in to staff all the lodges during the summer and who were just pulling out to scatter to their colleges. Restored faith in the race after the Golden Years brigade. Also some kids who were born there and love it too much to leave. They're living in another world, the world where your folks came in and homesteaded wild ground and the oldest son is the hero who hauled the generator up the mountain and is organizing a helicopter patrol. Colony on Planet X?

Man, if we could only go on living like that! Human-sized problems, but five generations later you get—Us. Mice in the crevices of Mordor. Ah well, let's fry an orc for supper.

I ought to mention that it's becoming a bad scene to try hitchhiking in the Canadian parks. The Canadians are fairly accepting, but they had a bad experience when they tried to set up facilities for hitch trippers. One chap (the Hungarian) told me a heated tale about Mafia infiltration, heavy drug-pushing in the hostels and camps. The old pioneer types that run the area are getting edgy. They're used to beards and jeans, but they can't tell one long-haired kid from another. If you go, get some sort of wheels, square up into a Great American Nature Lover type when you arrive, and make Contact with the local young people to find out how the scene works. The place is so great, assuming you're not allergic to pure air, it's worth a little tactical effort.

And, go early or late; in midsummer you can't see around the bodies. Unless you get 'way up back on foot.

—September 18, 1971

I Saw Him

Ballard's Drowned Giant, I mean. He's lying on the North American continent, frozen stiff. Among the peaks of the Canadian Rockies. That's where I saw him, or at least his arm.

It's not called his arm, it's called the Athabasca Glacier, which is one limb of the Columbia Icefield, which is the largest hunk of the Ice Age left south of the Arctic. (150 square miles of it with peaks at 12,000 feet, figurewise.)

The Ice Age has of course been gone for ten thousand years or so. Imagine an ice cube so big it can melt for ten thousand years and still be there. Great thick towering green-creviced, hundred-mile blocks of ice, cradled in the peaks, forever gushing down torrents of melt to nourish the forests and moose and meadows below . . . for ten thousand years. When it's all gone . . . ?

What you see, edge on from the new highway, is one huge, incredible mess. Devastation. The party's over. Think of a tray of ice cubes melting in a sink—that's about the scale of it. Only the ice is seven miles long and the sides of the sink are thousands of feet high. And the ice has made that sink. Ice a mile high once filled it up, grinding forward, gouging, crushing through and over the peaks. A mile down under the ice, what went on was terrible. Now as the ice retreats you can see it. A world of rubble, of mountains ground to gravel. Not a leaf, not a moss. Sterile. You approach through a lunar landscape; all it needs is a little tin flag to be an Apollo TV. Glaciers make an abominable mess, probably the worst mess going. Nuclear bombs, volcanoes—mosquito bites, comparatively.

Glaciers also have bad breath. They exhale a sullen archaic draft. The cold flows down forever from the icefield above. Even though the day is bright a mile away, freezing squalls and blizzards play at the edge of the ice.

This is what is called a tourist attraction.

I was a tourist. I got out and joined the line of Human insects straggling up the cold moraine toward the ice. The ice. I told myself I wanted to see what made the astounding corrosion-green color in the crevasses. Secretly, I wanted to touch it. I passed signs that said the ice ended here in 1950, and here in 1960. Everybody was jumping over streams of meltwater on its way to become the MacKenzie River and end in the Arctic Ocean. This icefield feeds three oceans; it's the hydrographic apex of the continent. We passed under a small rainbow. My desire to touch the ice-beast did not seem to be shared by my fellow primates; they advanced one-eyed, holding up their Instamatics like magic amulets.

When I came to the edge of the ice I saw that the whole mass was dimly lit up oystercolor from within. The ice itself here was glistening granular, full of pebbles and other debris of its million geologic crimes. The edge sloped and the bottom was about a foot off the ground. Pursuing (I told myself) my interest in the green, I stuck my head underneath. This involved kneeling in a stream. The whole glacier seemed to be hollow underneath, dripping from a billion ice udders. It was resting only lightly on the ground, like—like a vast hand. A hand barely pressing on its fingerpads. I pulled back out and saw the Drowned Giant. Or his big frozen brother.

Remember Ballard's description of the troops of people clambering up, over, into the drowned body? Picking at him, scuffling in his eyeballs?

I looked at the line of little figures trudging up over the gravel waste. More cars arriving. A busload now. All day, every day. I saw a big woman in curlers pry off a piece of the ice-body. (A very small piece.) It was snowing. A man had his girl photograph him standing on the ice shelf. As he climbed down he stopped and frowned. Then he kicked the ice. The ice-finger did not break.

I looked up; the ice-arm behind the hand was seven miles long; the shoulder was an enormous icefall. Tiny snow-cat buses were sightseeing near the elbow. They had worn a dirty track. The arm lay quietly; the first ten thousand years had been easy. I watched Ballard's tourists. A boy crawled into a serac. Remember the boy who crawled into the giant's nostril and barked? If this boy barked I didn't hear him. Glaciers are noisy.

Another man was kicking the glacier. Making no impression, he backed off, nodded fiercely at nobody in particular and then jumped at it with a kind of clumsy karate kick, *hard*. That didn't affect the ice-giant either. The man went away. I saw three more men kick the glacier. Very popular act. It hailed and I too went away, wondering.

Kicking glaciers . . . ?

Race memory, could it be? The ice-giant was helpless now. But I could see his work. If that ice ever rises again, man, we are through. A mile-high wall grinding over cities, missile bins, Disneyland, Pat Nixon, *everything*.

Well, I never found out what was causing the green. But I touched it, the ice age. I can report that it is cold, dirty, and a lot bigger and older than I am. And I didn't kick it.

Sort of wish I'd tasted it, though.

—September 18, 1971

SPITTING TEETH, OUR HERO—

—Curled up, that's what.

Imagine you're wrestling some big old shutters off a fishing shack in a big old forest. Imagine further that these so-called shutters are actually monster antiques made of heavy splintery planking and the kind of hardware they tie ships onto. To get them off you have to push up; it's like heaving a piano through a transom. Luckily there's a big guy helping you. Okay?

So, just as you notice the planks are kind of slippery, your eye catches an interesting ripple on the lake behind you—

Ooops—*powwwww!*

And you're down on the ground feeling your gushing face to see where your teeth are and if your nose is still there. And you *hurt*. The shutter hit your facebones, split one lip and cut the other off the gums, and knocked half your teeth around. Blood pouring.

What do you think about?

Well, of course you think about plunging your agonized muzzle into the cold lake, and where's a doctor, and so on. But if you're a writer you also think about all those heroes. How they get their faces stomped in or shot off and leap up gamely and—

Steal an alien rocket ship, and—

Figure out a vector-mathematical language and/or the secret of the universe, and—

Fuck at least the bad girl and the good girl during surgery, while—

Making a half a dozen brilliant psychosociophilosophical speeches.

Man, I couldn't. I *couldn't*!

I couldn't do anything but sit down and sluice my face and accept a ride to the hospital, and after I got sewed up I just *sat down* some more.

I wasn't interested in the nurses and the only speeches I made were something like " 'Anksh 'Oc" and "Fflthh."

Who can?

Well, another thing I thought was, Jeesus, this is what your professional ring fighter goes through every week or so. You've seen him—Joe Meathooks, down on one knee, blood streaming down his mashed puss, crowd yelling at him to get up.

And he does.

The more I thought of this the worse I felt.

My injuries were *minimal*, you understand, compared to Joe's. Shoot, nothing was broken, my teeth may even stay with me. No wires. A nothing, a tap. Joe would laugh.

So what's wrong with me? Yellow? Decadent intellectual faked up in a woodman's shirt?

Well (I told myself), Point A, this sort of thing is part of Joe's *business*. Lots of businesses have painful parts. Astronomers freeze their arses off all night, politicians cripple their shaking hands. Joe might even dislike a couple parts of mine . . . maybe.

Or, Point B, Joe has his adrenaline going. Adrenaline is really something. My very few small brawls taught me that it really does block pain. (I even noticed a pinkish haze, too; can't imagine why.) Whereas I hadn't been desperate, or mad at the shutters—I was in a peaceful cholinergic state when the Pow! hit.

So I concluded that our adrenaline-powered Hero probably can get up and fight some, shinny up walls, and bash doors and such. And maybe (after the wet towels) he can fumble around a bit with the girls. But man, no speeches. And as for cracking the higher mathematical functions, the grand intuitive insights—

Forget it.

Days, weeks, not even a feeble storyline came to me. All that was in my mind was the horde of invisible hornets in my face and thoughts like why the doc forgot to sew up the inside. And the difference between me and Sonny Liston.

Now do I hear somebody saying, There *are* heroes even if you aren't one, creep, and heroes are interesting?

Or, well, sure, but in *fiction* you keep things moving, it's that surmounting violent damage is a symbol—

Of what?

Well, here I offer the one little insight that crept to me.

The day after my happening a friend who is a genuine Tough Guy fell off a power pole onto a rock. He wasn't seriously damaged and he'd piled himself up before. But this one *hurt* him in a new way. When he got out of the hospital he sat telling how he'd been unconscious, frowning in a puzzled way. Then he'd hold up one big hand and look at it, and look at his legs. I think I know what he was discovering.

How fragile we are. Fragile!

Compared to almost everything around it your body is as frail as a soap bubble. The chair you're sitting in can break your leg, the edge of the table can crack your skull. The steering wheel of your car can crush your precious guts out. We're bags of Jell-O, mostly water held up with goo and a few frail sticks, a pulsing mass of vulnerability in which everything depends on everything else working—and no replacements. We can be pierced, fried, crushed, broken, mutilated, and killed in a million ways by practically everything in our environments. And we run around manipulating chain saws and bulldozers and nuclear fusion . . . for an average of sixty-seven years. Incredible!

What agility!

And what a fantastic self-image!

A "tough" man? An eggshell. A grape in a concrete mixer. One slip with that axe and your foot's gone. One misstep and tap your skull on the curb—cracked egg.

But we manage to skip through it for sixty years, roaring past each other in lethal missiles, playing with power mowers and welding arcs.

Astounding.

You can't think about it, either. Not and go on doing it. Once you watch your hand whisk back from the crunch of the car door you've had it. Let your automatic reflexes alone. Keep up the myth. Bury deep down the knowledge of how vulnerable we are.

Heroes help us do it.

Heroes get squashed and sliced and dismembered and burnt and they shed torrents of blood—but they're all right! They may hurt, but they go on acting furiously, thinking brilliantly.

They keep us from realizing that we're surrounded by instant obliteration. The absolutely necessary myth.

Who needs realism?

Well, there's my great ten-cent insight. It has a small corollary, too: When you consider the fantastic unconscious skills we and the other animals have developed to handle our dangerous environment on this planet, isn't it possible that man is going to have some pretty hard times when he really starts living in zero-gee? We've seen astronauts playing with plastic bags and very carefully handling lock covers and so on. Paying attention every minute. But when you start *living* you start depending on your reflexes, on your built-up feeling of how all those hard heavy lethal things are going to behave. When they start behaving differently while still keeping their lethal mass—oops. *Ouch!!*

We'll make it, though.

Now I'll go chew on a milkshake. Screw Sonny Liston. My next hero who shows up with his teeth on his chest and his shattered kneecaps tied up in his girl's brassiere . . . and starts deciphering the riddles of the alien technology . . . is going to bed first.

Alone.

At least until I see my dentist.

Fflthh.

—September 20, 1971

Do You Like It Twice?

In the October 1971 *F&SF*, Baird Searles complains (gently) about a book because it must be read twice for "complete clarity." That is, some of the references in the early part aren't fully understandable until you've read the whole thing, he says, and that's "a lot to ask of any reader."

This startled me out of my granola.

Hey, Baird: *What*????

You mean this isn't good? But . . . but . . . what about all the sweat I've spent trying to build my stories so there *is* stuff that will only come out on second reading? I always thought you owed that to the reader, that a story without it was boring.

Now Baird says this is bad?

Startled, I immediately begin to look inwards. (This is my usual reaction when startled, it is sometimes criticized in traffic.)

My first observation, which we won't even discuss, is that I really don't know how to write. Leaving that aside as irrelevant, since I *am* writing, what's with this reading-twice thing? Why do I feel that readers have a right to complain if there isn't a bit of mystery, an angle or insight tucked away under the surface, like a thingie in a cereal box?

I feel this so deeply I never even knew I felt it, see. There's this invisible face behind my shoulder, watching, waiting . . . it wants what it wants . . . if it doesn't get it I feel it fading back disgusted, sighing, "Is that all? Cheap, Tiptree."

All right, Face. Face it. We could be insane. Do we really believe somebody's reading twice?

Do I read twice?

Hmmm. Wellllll . . . no. Be honest, I don't, at least not read all the way through again. Not right away. What I do with one I like is immediately turn back and investigate chunks and bits, places where a sort of rich puzzlement set in. (I know this means *something*, but what?) Or I verify suspicions which in the light of the ending become delightful certainties, Oho, now I really dig it . . . wow! At the very least, since you can easily get me to admit I have good short-term recall—like most of you reading this, I'd guess—I brood. (Also criticized in traffic.)

No, I don't read twice. But I can say this: If somebody snatched the pages out of my hand when I came to the final period, I'd hit him. I'm not *finished*, see . . . I don't know exactly what I'm going to do with it, but judging from my library it seems to produce a lot of soup and peanut butter stains.

Doesn't everybody?

I mean, like the guy with the trunk full of pancakes, am I alone? Is it just read-read-read, up and down the rolly coaster, faster and higher, ending with a four-beat spasm on the final sentence—and then, Goodbye, thank you, ma'am? Drop the book, it's dead?

Wait. (I'm starting to look outward now.) Stories differ as to rereadability. First, you have the so-called conventional mystery stories in which the whole point is the artfully planted misdirection and concealed clues, so you really have to go back to verify that the sweet little child *was* left alone with the future corpse. (Trivial puzzles, I hate 'em.) Then there's the trick-ending stories where, say, the narrator turns out to be the villain, or writing from the moon, or whatnot, so you have to at least think back and reinterpret. (I can't think of any examples because I just wrote one like this.) It's also a trivial trick, except for a few grand old startlers.

This brings us to a type you get much of in SF, the story told by an alien or a child or a crazy who doesn't grasp the meaning of what he's telling, but you, the reader, see beyond his stammering words to What Really Went On. *Flowers for Algernon* did this at the start and end where the hero was stupid; when he says how his friends kidded him, *we* know they were being cruel. And *1984* comes to mind, at the end where the brain-stomped hero *accepts*. I think of these as the "It's a nice world, Jack" type. Also included here are the stories where you catch on that the narrator is part of the problem, he's spreading the plague he doesn't understand, or he's ripping the world off while thinking he's just protecting himself. A lot of great stories here, if the characterization (I guess you call it) is rich. But thinking back, these aren't the ones I reread much; usually you get it all as you go (slowly) along.

What I really dig is the story that's like being plonked down in an alien scene, the future or whatever, and the strange stuff comes by naturally. Like watching unknown life through a peephole. You understand just enough to get into it and then more and more meanings develop as you go, until at the end you suddenly get this great light on cryptic bits right back to the beginning. (Hey, Baird?) Lots of Phil Dick is this way. I go back and reread big chunks of Dick, snuffling lustfully. Or take Le Guin's *Lathe of Heaven*. I rooted around in that for days, savoring the sprig of white heather in the glass and the jellyfish and specially shivering about what the hell *really* happened on that ghastly April fourth. (I still don't know and I love it.)

Is this kind of thing a trick too? No! It strikes me as a way of being like life. Life plunks you amid strangers making strange gestures, inexplicable caresses, threats, unmarked buttons you press with unforeseen results, important-sounding gabble in code . . . and you keep sorting it out, sorting it out, understanding five years later *why* she said or did whatever, *why* they screamed when you—

You reread life, Oh man, do you . . .

So why not make stories like that?

(Of course, you can overdo it. I wouldn't want *all* stories like that. A lot of, say, Sturgeon or Ellison isn't that way. But it's one good way of making stories.)

But I'm forgetting one more type of rereadability thing. I guess you call it . . . ellipsis? The story told with omitted statements, or with action touched in so compactly you can't hardly get all of it first time over. I mean like mentioning the hero is "picking up his buttons," thereby revealing that when whatever it was happened a few paragraphs back all his buttons fell off. (This is done a lot in fight scenes; by this time everybody feels that there has been some repetition of the standard blow-by-blow.) In fights it's trivial, but with Human stuff and big happenings it's *interesting*. (To me.) I *like* the feel of this continual little loop in time, the illumination playing back on what went just before. When the wind-up events do this for the central plot, that's when I reread avidly.

But it's always on the verge of being a trick. It can give puzzle value to a bunch of nothing. I mean, if it's so great, why not come out and tell it? I reproach myself here. Because, see, for some reason probably including innate furtiveness, this is my *natural* way of telling a story. Like, say, "Beam Us Home": you aren't supposed to catch that the program the boy was addicted to was *Star Trek* until well along in the tale. Why? Well . . . did I feel that telling it straight would turn people off before they found out how significant et cetera things would get? Yeah, I know now I did. Not at the time. (A voice from under my pancreas dictated the first five pages while I was washing a car.) But—I say in justification—the puzzle wasn't the *story*. It was just an angle.

Or take "The Last Flight of Doctor Ain." That whole damn story is told backward. (Incidentally, I reread it the other day because somebody wants it and I threw up . . . what I remember as clean prose comes on like bubble gum. A good story and I *raped* it.) It's a perfect example of Tiptree's basic narrative instinct. Start from the end and preferably five thousand feet underground on a dark day and then *don't tell them*. Straight from behind the pancreas . . . But there's one conscious item, which ties up with what we're talking about. I had to give Ain a first name. *Charles*. So that makes him C. Ain, see, CAIN. His brother's murderer.

Would you believe I assumed everybody—everybody!—would pick that up afterward and use it to verify the plot (he really *did* kill everybody) and also extract a little irony (Cain as savior of life)???

Because to me everybody naturally rereads . . . insists, like the Face, that it be worth rereading or reinvestigating in part. Wants there to be thingie in the box. But do they? Do you?

Ha-ha-ha.

Oh, Baird, thou hast confronted me with reality.

But I can't change. Reality, go away.

Now before I really quit, two things. We're not talking about stuff so great, so beautiful, so interesting that you read it again and again, maybe at intervals all your life. All we're at is rereading-for-complete-illumination, to get the fullness of the story itself. Rereading-as-a-part-of-the-original-experience. A *technical* matter, not the genius aspect.

(By the way, I reread Huxley's *Brave New World* the other day and cringed for us all, my god the people who have been eating for years by mining his subplots.)

The other thing is that the story Searles was talking about is Kit

Reed's *Armed Camps*, and he thought it was, overall, great. Reed is a pet of mine. Now *there's* a closemouthed storyteller for you! You sidle in to find out what this kind of tense quiet scratching sound is and she zaps you . . . oh gee, do it again. I can't figure out why Searles had to rereread *Armed Camps*; I only went back once (to check the Captain White button on Hassim's bikini). About as obscure as being shot out of a cannon.

Ah well, wavelengths differ.

May 1972 be good to you. My next communication, if any, will be by forked stick from a jungly place in the Quintana Roo.

—January 7, 1972

The Voice from the Baggie

Phantasmicom 9 was handed to me on an airstrip yesterday, along with the 2 January and 6 Feb *New York Times*. I read *PhCom*. Man, did I. Grateful. Remind me—no, you won't, I'll try—to reimburse you for the roll of stamps.

My agent thinks I'm hard at work on lots of new stories I promised. Well, I do have a couple, handwritten on weird Spanish kids' schoolpaper, which the Red Baron finally produced. But I'd rather write you. I just connected with my typewriter last week, it arrived at Belize, Honduras, via Spitzbergen and has green fuzzy stuff on it. This is a very active climate; if you put something down it either grows roots or becomes an informal demonstration of electrolysis or turns into low-grade beer or ten thousand palmetto bugs rush out of it. The palmetto bug is to all intents a German cockroach and they breed like they were burning up. Mother cockroaches are full of eggs. It sounds silly, but *don't* put this manuscript in with other papers and forget it. Put it in a sealed baggie or spray it or both if you want to keep it. I stick anything too delicate to boil in the freezer for a month or so when I come out of here. Or in a snowbank. Including, especially, dirty laundry. Books get sprayed page by page and left in a sealed case full of spray for a couple of days. The palmetto bug is not vicious or icky, it is just hungry and a good mother. It also grows as big as a mouse but the young are transparent little blips and *very* fast. The thing is, if the letter or envelope has eggs on it you won't see anything for a while but about September you'll wonder why your library or Ann's underwear is in pieces.

This is going to be a longie, better get out that baggie until you feel like being Ancient Marinered. I'm lonesome for English above the level of Why is there kerosene in the gasoline? Or Who was Andreas Quintana Roo? Or How do you say kilowatt in Maya? ("Kilowatt," stupid.)

Let's see. I'll write after I sluice off some sweat. It is *muggy hot* in this coco beach. I'm dripping into the fungus. I've handwritten a couple quite different bits, but am bored with them. (Love, death, ♀.) Feel like talking about what I'm looking at. It may come out too long. Do what you want. I think I have to come back in April, but may not be in communication as what I have to go back for is to have a piece of stomach ulcer cut out, after which I'll maybe be moving again. Goddamn ulcer isn't healing; it perforated once and nearly killed me and I'm quite a ways from any emergency medical intervention and likely to remain so. Also I *want* to eat chilis. They have a luscious stuff called salsa verde here you put on cheese or fish or your finger and after the top of your head settles back, this beautiful green shooting star roams around your back palate making life good. If I got rid of this badly vulcanized stomach section once and for all, I could pig it, really pig it on peppered snapper and cactus buds and not be all the time worrying about is there bits of shell in the coconut. So I think I'll give in to the medicos, who predicted it would be like this. Hate to fulfil other people's prophecies about my own dammit body.

Hey, a word maybe worth saying. Essentially what I said about Canada, but with fangs: *Don't come here freaky.* Mexico, I mean. They're having a drive on U.S. cultural influences, and if there is one word that is known from Cuernavaca estate to Indio hut, it's "Ippy." I saw a barefoot Maya toddler say "Ippy!" and spit. Why? Well, first don't forget Mexico culture is partly (superficially maybe) traditional Spanish, churchy and square. But *more* important—Mexico is a *revolutionary* country and most revolutionary countries are prim. Prudish. They're fighting for the early stages of what we're rejecting the ripe-rot stage of—literacy, plumbing, jobs (JOBS!), malaria control (which means guys in uniforms and checkboards, very dedicated and mechanized), clean-living progressive patriotic youth. Man, they've *had* lying around in hovels screwing and meditating and puffing grass—they've had centuries of that, now they're after Getting Out the Vote and Rural Electrification. *My eldest boy has won an engineering scholarship*: That's the stage the dream is at, here. So be warned. And be warned like this: hair.

Mexicans, you see, don't really dig any of the distinctions between Yank and Yank that you and I would see at once. All they see is *hair*. And that goes for mustaches. Remember, most Indians have little or no facial hair. A mestizo's idea of a mustache is a Ronald Colman hairline on the upper lip. Their head hair is straight and black and chopped in a curve about earlobe length at most. (That's progressive.) So when they see a bunch of pink giants with frizzy light-colored stuff cascading all over their heads and faces, we look like Martians. I don't care if you're IBM's squarest computer designer in a three-button suit and polished floaters, you come here with an inch and a half of mustache and— "*Ippy!*" Splat.

And another thing: Aside from the Spanish religious prejudice and the general revolutionary ideals, you have the billion-dollar budgetary weight of the turismo industry, a big big item in a still-poor country. And what are the best paying tourists? See that family over there, rhinestone hornrims on the old lady, forty pounds of lard on everybody, Truman shirts? They're buying rebozos and baskets and staying at the Acapulco Holiday Inn or the Presidente and hiring cars and guides and eating— Christ, do they eat—and what they are is good fat sheep trotting through the tourist circuit, leaving rich hunks of wool on all the little hooks. And nothing—but nothing—that upsets them or tightens their wool or scares them off is going to be tolerated. And it has been discovered—shades of St. Miguel d'Allende—that some kinds of Yank young people upset them. What kind? The kind with—you guessed it—*hair*.

And it has been further discovered that the hairy young family in a VW camper unfortunately does *not* buy serapes and dyed hats or stay at the Presidente or go on the Robinson Crusoe cruise, that they bring their own granola and leave, instead of wool, decorous little plastic bags of Pepsi bottles and soiled disposable diapers. Period. And so, no matter how nice they are, or *simpatico*, and genuinely interested in the Mexican people or art or history, they are a zero sign in the big balance sheet which is counted on to build roads and hospitals as well as enriching politicians. And so . . . if they step over any line, or get too near the sheep run, regretfully, their car papers get misstamped, their tourist cards expire, their trailer hitch is unsafe, their vaccinations suddenly become necessary—in short, *good-bye to sunny Mexico.*

And the first dividing line is *hair.*

Beyond that line, way beyond it, is any chemical from grass up. (I carry *every* prescription taped to *every* pill bottle in my first aid kit, even vitamins.) It's as simple as this: Tequila or any sort of juice, yes. *Any-*

thing else, no. And the "No" takes the form of a Mexican slam, which is very very very unpleasant in many indescribable ways, and your friendly U.S. consul not only can't get you out but may never find out you're there. You are, friend, in jail on an alien planet. And you *stay*. And stay. Mom and Pop can come down and feed you through the bars—maybe. (Prisoners have to *buy* several essential, too.) The only good thing that can be said about it is that you probably won't die and it's a comparatively fast method of growing 'way 'way up, if you're capable of reflection. But I'm sure *PhCom's* readership can figure other methods, and certainly they won't make the error of thinking that just because the fuzz is three feet high and a strange color that they aren't efficient as hell with a commo system that makes the country a small town. And one in which we're just as inconspicuous as a radioactive self-luminous moog-amped giraffe on the main street.

So if it occurs to you that the Martians next door are worth seeing—and O god they are—grit your teeth, take out the clippers, stash your stash, and set forth as humble skinheads, even as your pal Tip.

I don't want to give the impression that I think you can only come here shaved bald. Of course you can come in hairy; there are mustachioed Yanks motorscootling around in a lot of towns, unmolested. (It does help to come in a tour group of thirty with Express Checks plastered on your nose. Or an armful of scuba gear—but you'd better be able to fit those curls into your mask.) What I mean is that hair niggerizes you. If you hit somebody's fender or chicken, the hair throws the presumption against you. If you get sunstroke, you're presumed stoned. If you smile, the whores and shopkeepers will be mostly smiling back, not the people you'd maybe rather meet. And as for the countryside . . . Here: I was here when three young men visited the next plantation and made a deal to rent a hut. They looked to me like ex-Eagle scouts, seriously interested in swimming and savoring this incredible spot. (Tiptree owns binoculars, not being a Maya.) Clean solid new camping gear, expensive equipment, tailored shorts, sedate swimsuits. No sounds of music of revelry. Only thing they seemed to be lighting was a Coleman lantern. But . . . one had shoulder-length hair, two had modest guardsman lip bangs. Now they probably thought they were on a deserted world, but the fact is the place is and has been for three thousand years full of sharp-eyed Mayas. Their every move was observed by an eleven-year-old, who reported to his mother, who told her aunt, who told the foreman. (I was present, that's when the baby went "Ippy—splat.") (Another term is *Malo typo*.) Anyway, the foreman murmured to his boss, whose orbit crossed that of the next plantation owner, who sent word to his caretaker . . . and in five days the hut became no longer available. One loused-up vacation in paradise. See what I mean?

And there's a great deal to freak out on here, and there are, as everywhere, ways to freak out in your own very pleasingly after you learn the lines—would I be here?—so it's worth thumbing through your stereotypes and selecting the right head to wear. Says Tip, anyway.

As of spring 1972. Things may change.

—March 31, 1972

MAYA MÁLOOB

Listen, I have to talk to you about Maya Indians. I ache to talk about Maya Indians like Lawrence ached to talk about Ay-rabs. My motives are a little different, for example I'm not so far as I know suffering from obscure yearnings for alien buggery. (If I were I'd probably talk your ear off about it.) More important, Mayas are about as different from Arabs as Frisbees are from cyanide capsules. The only thing they have in common is that people come down with the same intensity of Mayaphilia that you see in Victorian Arabophiles, or U.S. Pakophiles. But Mayas hook a different kind of people.

All right, Tiptree. Start.

I'm looking at a Maya Indian, Maya puro. His name is Aúdomaro Tzul which means Honcho or Knight in Maya. His nickname is L'mus, meaning L'mus. L'mus is an adult, nineteen; his body is a braid of muscle the color and shine of a black bay horse. He is wearing khaki shorts and a red bandanna, a blue-black earlength bob and magnificent Maya teeth.

Seen sideways, L'mus is a normal well-formed male about 4' 9" tall. When he turns, which he does with the snap and power of a tuna's tail, you see that he is also about 4' 9" broad. He can pick up an eighty-pound gas tank one-handed, hoist it in the air, and run. (Mayas run a lot. The sand is full of gouges where their broad, prehensile toes have dug in for take-off.) Moreover, L'mus's old grandmother could hoist you on her head and toddle off with you, without sweating her embroidered petticoat.

L'mus is an electrician. An electric line came through here last month from a generator L'mus helped install, through two transformers he also helped line in. When the juice was turned on L'mus stood at severe attention to the god of Faraday, six hundred volts in each eye.

When the voltmeter socked the mark, L'mus split a grin of such beauty that the moon landings paled.

He has, however, one professional difficulty: his good brain struggles with his Maya macho. This makes it difficult to persuade him to break a 115-volt current before handling the wires. And when the line was run to my tent and L'mus ran up the palm trees to twist it around nails, I saw how he cuts and strips wire: He bites it. Up to No. 14. Teeth!

All right, so far nothing much, and maybe you've seen lots of Indians. So have I, especially the Huastec-language people in the main part of Mexico. Aztecs, to you.* Now Aztecs are great. Aztecs specialize in a wild, adenoidal, faintly horrified profile that's satisfyingly archaic. But Aztecs, and most other tribes, are . . . well . . . class-structured. With them you meet this dominance-submission thing, a certain amount of Yassuh-Boss. Aztec thinking has ladders in it; you get the bottom-rung resentment shit, the middle-rung climbing piss, the deviousness, the opacity—the residue of millennia of conquering-and-being-conquered; slaves, masters, gore, and tribute.

Not Maya.

Mayas—like the Scots—have *never* been officially conquered in war. They've been massacred and chased, most lately by the Mexicans under Porfirio Diaz, when Yucatan wanted to secede. But Mexico didn't flatten them; it ended with a *negotiated* truce in—gasp—1935. (The last Secretary of the Maya Armies died recently, and when this coco ranch was started in 1936 the mestizo homesteader had to pay regular tribute to the nearest Maya chief in addition to his Mexico taxes.)

Mayas have also warred plentifully among themselves—they probably ruined their ancient cities that way before the Spaniards came. But the Maya people en masse have never lived under anybody's heel. They simply took off into the jungle and some of them haven't been found to this day.

What this means is that a Maya looks at you in a way you're not used to unless you're lucky. Like the Scotsman; straight, easy, humorous. Who you? And they laugh in a way you don't hear much. Right out, delighted. They laugh a lot, they value a joker. (Broke your leg? Ha-ha-ha! But gentle and tender to real infirmity and to babies.) When you

---

*See "The Laying on of Hands."

meet Mayas, don't expect the How do you do, señor, si señor snake oil.
What you get, from men, women, infants, is questions. Sharp minds
have been watching you and everything else in the environment. (Why
aren't you fishing today? How much money do you make? What kind of
social security program they got in the States? What's that thing for?)

Be ready to account for yourself.

Mayas have their social trauma, sure. The juggernaut of cauc culture is punishing them, too. Some Mayas lost their language before the
present realization that it's valuable. They suffer the fierce glooms that
lurk inside the guy on the bottom of the intercultural cement grinder.
(And which can make intercultural drinking parties end bloody.) L'mus
stares slit-eyed at his transformers, knowing in his heart they're child's
play; he senses computers he'll never have the chance to master, how-to
mathematics he can't read. But it isn't in him to whine; he throws his
black wings back and sends Rosa Pech Balan a killing grin. Thinking,
maybe, of his new Uruguay tapes or the fact that his sons will get free
education.

Rosa? Wait a minute. I didn't finish telling you how Mayas look.

Technically, Mayas are the most Oriental-appearing of all American
Indians. They have the strongest—is it epicanthial?—eyefold; their eyes
are so slanted their own artists draw them as 90-degree angled almonds.
And Mayas are short. But although some of the Maya tribes over by
Mérida are yellow rather than mahogany and look superficially Chinese,
the second look shows you the tremendous solid bones. Stone bones,
fantastic strongly built. These are, remember, the people who have
owned and survived in this land for at least three thousand years. They
have walked right out of the old, old murals of Bonampak. L'mus was
here when Pilate had his administrative problem.

One characteristic I particularly admire is the Maya leg and foot.
(We're coming to Rosa.) The Maya torso is relatively small, more like a
knot of muscle at the point where legs meet arms and head and their old
artists drew it that way. All limbs. Their legs are powerful but curiously
smooth muscled, a single line ending in an enormously high-arched short
foot. It gives a bell-bottomed mod look, like the Beatles *Yellow Subma-
rine* style. Maya court dress emphasized this: The bigger you were the
more tassels you wore on your sandal instep. And your sandals had thick
short soles. Very little glop hiding the body, everything mobile, going.

Mayas, you see, *go*. The first words they taught me were *Tzim bin*—"I go." Followed by You go, He goes, We go, They go, Let's go. And by God they do; Mayas take off. Boom. Walk to the next country, swim, drive, fly, pole, sail, whatever. *Tzim bin!* About the time of Christ they built a network of white roads, *sac bés*, through Yucatan and Guatemala and Honduras, limestone walkways raised about six feet above the jungle floor, and they're still using some of them and nobody knows where they all lead. Driving on a highway you'll see a brown figure duck off, and sure enough, under the lianas and the godawful mangrove scrub, there's a chalky ridgeline.

But I still haven't told you: the Maya face. Hold hard.

In Maya, cross-eyed is beautiful. Not only that, but a slanted-back forehead is aristocratic elegance. Add to this strong, almost beaky nose, high cheekbones, a firm but receding lower face with wide curled lips—and I wish I could draw. Those eyes, remember, are looking at you V-shaped, centered in their upper lids. Can you believe it's great?

Maya mothers used to tie a board on the baby's forehead to slant it, and hang a ball of tallow over its nose to encourage cross-eyes. And obviously there's been preferential breeding for these traits; Maya babies tend to be deliciously cross-eyed, like Siamese kittens. (They also seem to walk at six months, which I can't yet believe: *Tzim bin?*)

The whole thing is straight out of real Martian history, and believe Uncle Tip: Until you've seen a Maya chick trotting down the avenida with that perfect build in a minishift and Elizabeth Arden iridescent eye gloop on those fabulous cockeyes, with the merry millennia looking out at you pussycatwise—you have not seen the full erotic spectrum. Nothing, but nothing like the oriental doll; nothing like any thing but Maya.

Or the same profile in the old man's version, archaic essence of mankind . . . of a very special flavor. Style, they had it, those Mayas who first designed their genes. The Anglo-Saxon swineherd who designed mine should have been so smart.

All right. Rosalie Pech Balan. I saw her last night, running like a deer in a blizzard of blue moonlight, her long black hair flying from her small elegant head. (She was probably going to find a lump of Caribbean tar to patch the roof.) Rosa is sixteen. She has the trim minimal Maya torso, in her case the muscles being combined with other features of compact but highly adequate character. She wears a short white tubular thing from which her classic Maya legs emerge in a way that makes me happy I don't wear contacts, they'd fall out. (One of my problems is that the tube seems to be getting shorter and shorter; it's about the size of a washcloth now and by next week Uncle Tip may be a stretcher case.)

The point is the way she runs. Wide, leaping strides and yet flowing close to the sand. Those legs flash, float with power, she is all running leg. A totally natural run, the freedom of precise adapted function. You can't learn to run like that, I think. You run like that when the genes for running in other and lesser ways got chopped out of your gene pool while the pyramids rose and fell.

Rosa has, I understand, another feature: the Mongolian spot. This is described by my textbook as an irregularly shaped blue-purplish mark on the spine just above the buttocks; it is said to be especially pronounced in Yucatan females. I would like to ask Rosa to assist me in confirming this piece of information. But there are problems.

One is at the moment twenty-five feet down a well cheerfully slinging muck in preparation for installing a bomba electrica and his name is Aúdomaro Tzul.

There are also Rosa's three brothers-in-law and one father-in-law, all of whom can do things with their machetes that you'd think required a laser, and the coconut is far tougher than the Human head. And there is also the fact that I have seen Rosa herself bending iron pipe barehanded . . .

But . . .

Will you believe those *aren't* the reasons, really? Not to live a comic strip, or see life that way.

Maybe it's to keep the other Maya, the veil of illusion . . . ?

And so we leave Tiptree, who hasn't even told you about the Maya religion (none, thank God), or the Maya Hennequin situation (lousy since nylon replaced sisal rope), or Maya-Spanish hand speech, or how Mayas sleep in midair, or the eye-popping Maya ruins and the foreigners thieving artifacts, or the joke Lorenzo-the-dark-Djinn played on L'mus the night L'mus got Rosa to hear his Uruguay tape, or how Arturo-the-neurotic-Maya got prick-fungus and went to the herb-doctor, or what Mayas do in the ocean, or what Mayas do on a bender (roll Jeeps over and laugh like mad), or whether Mayas really sacrifice people, or practically any damn thing at all . . . except one three-thousand-year-free girl running forever in my brain in the wind and the moonlight . . .

Coox chital u boóy béc.

(Which means, Let us lie down in the shade of the roble tree, and is pronounced just as written except for a few things like sticking the back of your tongue up your nose.)

Tzim bin.

—March 31, 1972

LOOKING INSIDE SQUIRMY AUTHORS

The next piece Tiptree wrote about the Mayas was for Harry Harrison's anthology *SF: Author's Choice 4* (Putnam 1974), a series in which writers were invited to contribute their favorite stories and notes about why they liked them so much. As observed earlier, Alli preferred not to write about her stories, but several times she appeared in anthologies which required it.

This group of essays contains a fanzine piece about the Harrison anthology (*Khatru* 1, February 1975) and four introductions and afterwords, to: "The Last Flight of Doctor Ain" (*SF: Author's Choice 4*), "The Milk of Paradise" (*Again, Dangerous Visions*, edited by Harlan Ellison, Doubleday 1972), "Her Smoke Rose Up Forever" (*Final Stage*, edited by Edward L. Ferman and Barry N. Malzberg, Charterhouse 1974), and "The Night-blooming Saurian" (*Worlds of If: A Retrospective Anthology*, edited by Frederik Pohl, Martin H. Greenberg, and Joseph D. Olander, Bluejay 1986).

Last night I was reading an SF series that I cannot figure out why in the name of the Jolly Green Giant everybody doesn't read. Or at least borrow and talk about. It's so *interesting*. For years now I've been reading the series and I haven't yet heard anybody mention it or seen but one tepid review that missed the point. I refer to the *Author's Choice* series that Harry Harrison has been stubbornly bringing out to the accompaniment of deafening silence for lo these years. It's now at Number 4. Number 4 is a specially good issue 'cause it contains old Guess Who, but I felt just the same enthusiasm for Numbers 1, 2, and 3. Here's why.

Are the stories all masterpieces? *Of course not.* (Although there's quite a few, like Brian Aldiss's "Old Hundredth," that made me go Oo-oooh.) But masterpieces is not the point. The point is, each story is the author's *private pet*—and therein lies the tale. Moreover, Harry made everyone write a piece saying why he picked that story, and when you read those, man, the tails really begin to hang out. Fascinating. I've said it before, when an author opens his mouth *about* his stories, he or she usually blurts out more than you may want to know about his or her *self*. Can't help it. Embarrassing, don't look—but let's be honest, I love it. There they are, squirming and shell-less. Some of them so earnest and hopeful you want to pat them; some puffed up like blow-fish peeking at you over their engorged egos; some quietly, monoma-niacal, going on about how the story fits into Phase 3, Subsection 4 of My Early Style, you know, My Work which has become the universe. And some—well, you've never seen so many people in weird poses. Anybody with a jigger of snoop-juice in their blood has to love that series.

(And what pose, you may ask, did Tiptree get into? Don't ask. Froze up self-consciously and talked at great length—poetically even—about the thing which had made me angry enough to write the story. Which, dammit, I believe—but it was a cop-out. Uh, sorry . . . doesn't that tell its own story too?)

One more thing before we quit this: There's a kind of beautiful thing about the series too, as well as the pants-down revelations. All of us dream, you know. Clown-writers dream of tragic poetry, destructo writers dream of a gentle world—sometimes. And their pet stories are often their pets because a bit of the private dream comes through. And some of them are, well, beautiful . . .

Read.

(And don't say I didn't warn you; what is old good-guy Tiptree's dream? Killing everybody, that's what. Uh, sorry again.)

A BA-A-A-D IDEA

Encouraged by the howling nonsuccess of Harry's *Author's Choice* series, I have an idea for an anthology which everybody, dammit, *ought* to want to read. Especially everybody who wants to write, which must include about ten million souls. Anyhow, it includes me, I'd buy it: *Bad Stories by Good Writers*. An antho where everybody you like sent in their *worst* published stories, together with a short piece on What's Wrong With This Floop.

By using published ones you'd get the stuff that is just tantalizingly *almost* okay, the kind where you can really learn something about technique. Every writers has got a cookie or two like that. Lord knows I have: a turkey called "Happiness Is a Warm Spaceship" which I thought was buried for eternity until a good, thorough reviewer named Don D'Ammassa dug up its embarrassed bones. I reread it, marveling. The bloody beast has everything—plot, relevance, jokes, fights—everything except what makes a story . . . that intangible known as pacing or timing, that mystery known as *shape*. By the time I really know what makes that story so boring I just might know how to write. And oh how I would love to see the different sins of others and hear them explain why the rocket fell. Man, would I buy that antho!

Wouldn't you? And you? No?

Dammit . . .

We are alone.

—August 29, 1974

COMMENT ON "THE LAST FLIGHT OF DOCTOR AIN"

Writing about my own story reminds me of those tremendous floats you see in small-town Labor Day parades. You have this moving island of flowers with people on it being Indian Braves or Green Bay Packers or Astronauts-Landing-on-the-Moon (Raising-the-Flag-at-Iwo-Jima has happily gone out of fashion) and great-looking girls being great-looking girls. That's the story. Under each float is an old truck chassis driven by a guy in sweaty jeans who is also working the tapedeck and passing cherry bombs to the Indians. That's the author. Now Harry wants me to crawl out and say hello. Well, I love saying hello. But my feeling is that the story is the game. Who really needs me and my carburetor troubles up there blowing kisses with Miss Harvest Home?

Still, Harry is one of those for whom I'd row quite a ways in a leaky boat, and you can always stop reading this and turn to the tale. So . . .

Remember way back in 1967 B.E.? Before Ecology, that was; we were worrying about The Bomb then. In those days I did my screaming to myself; it sounded pretty silly saying, I love Earth. Earth? Rocks, weeds, dirt? Oh, come on. A friend lectured me: People have to relate to people; you can't relate to a planet.

Sorry, you can. But you'd better not. Because—as we're all finding out—to love our Earth is to hurt forever. Earth was very beautiful with her sweet airs and clear waters, her intimacies and grandeurs and divine freakinesses and the mobile art works that were her creatures. She was just right for us. She made us Human. And we are killing her.

Not because we're wicked, any more than a spirochete is wicked. (At this point maybe I'd better say that I do relate to people, too.) Nor is modern Western technology the sole culprit. We're the current destructo champs, but man was always pretty good at ecocide. Innocent goat herds turned North Africa into desert; did you know that people used to take pigs to be fattened on the acorns of the majestic oak forests where the Sahara blows now? War and fire finished off the flora of the Hebrides before gunpowder. And sheer numbers of people scratching a living devastated much of India and China into the lunar landscape it is today. It's just us, man collectively, doing what comes naturally. A runaway product of the planet Earth, we have become a disease of Earth.

And of course it's speeded up unbelievably. Virgin lakes I knew only ten years ago in Canada are shore-to-shore beer cans now. Here's a few of the things we've lost in the four decades I've been observing (I thought they'd last forever, see?): learning to swim in the pure water of—gasp—Lake Michigan in front of Chicago . . . ten thousand canvasback ducks whistling down the wind of the peaks behind Santa Fe . . . the great bay of San Francisco before the bridges shackled it and the garbage poured in . . . Key West, a sleepy fishing village lush with tropical wildlife (and old John Dewey's doorknob head shining in the cantina) before the Navy and Disney heard of it . . . Timberwolves singing where shopping centers are now in Wisconsin . . . the magic trolley ride to Glen Echo, in ten minutes from the heart of D.C. you were clicking along silently (and fumelessly) with flowers and songbirds coming in the window . . . A very nice life, only a few years back.

And it's the same all over, you know. I spent part of my childhood in Africa and it hurts to remember the beauty of the Ruwenzoris—the Mountains of the Moon—before the planes and the guns and the Land Rovers and Hemingway and the rest of the white man's crap rolled in. And even I can't believe I rode a pony in peaceful woodlands in a place now called Vietnam . . .

All gone. Gone under the concrete and plastic and bombs and oil and people and garbage unending, growing and spreading daily.

Can you stand one more?

I'm writing this in the moonlight on a coconut plantation on the "wild" shore of Yucatan. The jungle was homesteaded in 1936 and worked by a few Maya families. Miles of nothing but white coral beach, the Caribbean making slow music on the reef, shadows of palm-fronds wreathing over the sand. The moon is brighter than my lantern. A pelican crosses the moon, looking like a wooden bird from some mad giant's cuckoo clock. Paradise . . .

Ah, oui.

The fish the pelican is hunting are tainted with chlorinated hydro-carbons now; her eggs are thin-shelled, may not hatch. The same for the flamingoes and roseate spoon-bills and noble frigate birds on the lagoon behind me. They are also scared up daily by Maya powerboats. On the shore, each wave as it breaks leaves myriad globules of tar from ships over the horizon, leaves also a dish-pan ring of plastic bottles, broken zoris, light bulbs, and dismembered dolls. (I wonder about those dolls. Do crazed tourists gather at midnight for strange rites at the rail?) The trash is not just ugly; each globule of tar smothers and poisons one more small sphere of the sea's life—and the oceans, we know now, are fragile and finite. The plastics too break down, relasing polychlorinated biphenyls to be absorbed by organisms. An average of 3,500 little bits of plastic per square kilometer was measured last year—in the Sargasso Sea. And we've all heard about the miles of floating Human offal Heyer-dahl met in the mid-Atlantic. The refuse isn't all microscopic either; last month a forty-five-foot shrimp boat, apparently abandoned for insur-ance, broke up on the reef. The day of the marine junkyard is at hand.

But the point is that theHuman beings who are doing all this are not malicious or aberrant. They are doing what we have always done. It's right and natural in Human terms to flush a toilet or an oilbilge, to throw away a broken light bulb or a broken boat, to zap an insect attack-ing your food or your child. Even the trawlers who are fishing with nets five miles long—killing everything in huge swathes off the Florida seas— are doing the Human food-getting thing.

How can we stop? How can we possibly change ourselves enough and in time?

I fear we can't—and there's where my real nightmare begins. Because if we do kill everything else on Earth, we probably won't die. At least, not right away. We will, I terribly fear . . . *adapt.*

You've seen the pictures of Calcutta and Bangladesh. Calcutta isn't a musical comedy; it's a symbol of a steady state humanity can reach, way down the entropic slide. I was there as a kid too. I remember step-ping over and around the endless bodies, living and dead, inhabiting the pavement about one to a square yard as far as I could see to the hori-zon. Starving dwarf-children roving around racks of bones that were mothers trying to nurse more babies, toothless mouths and unbearable eyes turning on me from rag heaps that were people—people—a million people born there and going to die there, unable to help themselves or even to protest, world without end forever. Surviving . . .

That's what we do, you know. We don't change our behavior, we adapt to the results of it. Even to extremis where the Human being is stripped down to a machine for keeping the genes alive, waiting for rescue. But when we pass the point of irreversible damage to our biosphere, our Earth, there will be no rescue. The beauty that is going is only another name for the health of Earth and her children, the condition of our humanity. As our Earth dies under us, what will we do? Change ourselves in time? Die?

Neither. When the last housefly and the last crabgrass plant have died in the world's last zoo, when the oceans are dead and the land is paved over, we'll go on. Our marvellous vitality will carry us down, shoulder-to-buttock, gasping our own poisons and scrabbling for algae soup as the conveyor belt creaks by. Don't worry: We'll survive.

Excuse me while I put out my garbage.

—May 5, 1972

Afterword to "The Milk of Paradise"

Reading an afterword is like watching a stoned friend sail onto an interstate expressway. One can't help looking and one is seldom made happy. Exceptions, sure. Our long-established favorites may safely peer around the edges of their monuments, even wave and wink. And we have also the walkie-talkie writers, the *Pan troglodytes* who verbalize every twitching moment and who are named Mailer and Wolfe when they're good. To them are permitted forewords, afterwords, asides, superscripts, anything—because their separate stories are in fact only nodes, local swirls in a life-flow of words.

But the rest of us, poor carnivores whose inwards meagerly condense into speech. Only at intervals when the moon, perhaps, opens our throats do we clamber up the rocks and emit our peculiar streams of sound to the sky. Good, bad, we do not know. When it is over we are finished. Our glands have changed. Push microphones at us and you get only grumbles about the prevalence of fleas or the scarcity of rabbits. And this is what makes most afterwords such nervous reading, gives rise to the suspicion that the baying itself was a cryptic complaint about rabbits.

We think not, of course. We think it was somewhat deeper in the blood. But we're in no condition to argue. Push me at noon on the streets and I can only tell you—those damned rabbits are dying out and the fleas have us.

Peace?

About this story. A thermal vortex by the arbitrary name of Harlan Ellison has been bashing out a bit of free space where writers who need some elbow room can try. Count me among those currently running and flapping, dragging homemade fly-buggies up on cliffs and taking off with hope. The resultant is not of course a neat scene, nor necessarily art. Moreover, Ellison is instantly recognizable as that type of absolutely top guy whose friends all go around with tubes in their stomachs. But after all the Maalox has been gulped and the old ladies picked up and apologized to, I think a ragged cheer is in order. For the guy without whom everybody would have slept better and dreamed less.

—September 29, 1969
and October 8, 1969

Afterword to "Her Smoke Rose Up Forever"

Abominations, that's what they are: afterwords, introductions, all the dribble around the story. Oh, I read them. And often happily, other people's afterwords are often okay. Not mine. The story, that's really all I know. And after I reread any one of my own, the only sincere thing I have to say to the reader who has suffered through it comes out as a kind of obsessed squeal—*Oh gods of the English language, forgive these pages which it is now too late to revise! Reader, can you actually even begin to see what I was trying to bring in through the flak of ill-made sentences, can you possibly share the vision? How marvellous if you can, but how unlikely . . .*

Now, editors don't really want this type of outburst. They desire the author to straighten his underwear and get up and say something cool, like "The Doomsday theme in science fiction demonstrates, etc." Well.

All right. The Doomsday theme in science fiction is . . . a great deal more than a mere theme. Ever since things got serious, ever since we realized that we really are in danger of killing ourselves, of bombing or poisoning or gutting or choking the planet to death, or—perhaps worst of all—of killing our own humanity by fascist tyranny or simple over-breeding, science fiction has been the only place we could talk about it. The mainstream took one look at it in Orwell's *1984* and promptly caponized itself. It's too terrible, don't look. Tell me Jesus saves.

Science fiction has gone on looking, showing, working out all the dire road maps to Armageddon, the nasty slide ways to Entropy and Apocalypse. I loathe you, let me count the ways. Even the crazy hopeless hopes—remember Bester's last man dragging himself over the radioactive ruins so that his dead body would fertilize the sterile sea and start life again? Oh, of course we can see occasional traces of adolescent fantasy bulging out here and there—is there literary life without libido?

But noble, ingenious, terrifying stories. Which hurt, because the fear is real.

Now here I learned something else about the Doomsday theme in science fiction. Thinking it would be nice to end with a bow to the great ones, I went through eight volumes of science fiction criticism, looking for a list. And found virtually nothing except a brief European discussion of anti-utopias and some reviews of specific works. Writers being notoriously erratic researchers, perhaps I have missed the definitive Doomsday essay. If not it looks as if there is an empty place where someone should assemble and relate the SF warnings of man's end.

A Doomsday study would not only do justice to some heavy writing; it would, I think, turn up some interesting things. For example, wouldn't you expect to find a change, as the menaces became real? How cool the old stories were: Wells's silent landscape under a dying sun, in the far future; the exciting but improbable disasters of *When Worlds Collide*. Great stories, wild ideas. Thirty years after Huxley wrote *Brave New World* he remarked he had no idea things would move so fast. But somewhere around Hiroshima the tone changes—we suddenly see ourselves *On the Beach* next Wednesday. The stories become immediate: Change our ways or die. And the dooms proliferate. And finally, I think you would find that some of them become so well known that they are only symbolized, become almost interchangeable. Who cares if it's chain reaction of greenhouse effect, imperialism or fecundity? The interest turns to a Human mechanism of cause, or possibly, survival. Can you use an imbecile as Mother of the World?

And so on. Surely the kindly editors will excuse me now.

But if they insist on a word as to how "Her Smoke Rose Up Forever" attaches itself to the grand procession, well, it does so through that strand of hope. Carrington's work is real, and his speculation on the real nature of time holds out a faint rational hope of a curious sort of immortality. His idea is that, perhaps, just perhaps, very intense psychic structures might have existence in timelessness or "static" time. But Carrington, good man that he was, unhesitatingly assumed that intense psychic structure was *good*, was in fact a sort of Spinozan intellectual love of some aspect of life. A beautiful picture—all the fragments of loving farmers merging around the ideas of earth and seed, bits of philatelists converging forever around a two-penny black, parts of all of us webbed eternally around great poems or symphonics or sunsets. Lovely. But look back in your memory. Moments of pure selfless love, yes—but what about the fearful vitality of the bad past—the shames, furies, disappointments, the lover defected, the prize that got away? The pain. As the psychologists put it, *aversive conditioning persists.* One shock undoes a hundred rewards. If by wild chance Carrington's theory is in some degree right, his immortality would be a hell beyond conception . . . until we can change ourselves. Drain the strength of pain from our nerves. Make love and joy as strong as evil. *But how can we?*

—May 10, 1973

Introduction to
"The Night-blooming Saurian"

If! Ah, *If!* What it meant to us! It wasn't *Galaxy*, Fred Pohl's golden seal of approval, but a chancier magazine, more free—a friend to experiments, a place that tolerated wild flappings toward the heights and occasional ignominious bellywhops when the wax wings melted. (Always provided Fred had decided there was some possibility of pin feathers.)

If gave a home to the worst turkey I ever launched, which let me see *why* it was no good—and to the best I early achieved. *If* was no mere *Galaxy* overflow, it was a special, canny scheme for helping on new writers. I've never heard Fred Pohl say this in so many words, but Fred is not one to tell you all he knows or is up to.

As for my own Saurian yarn here (and I've been surprised at its persistent minor popularity), the point is simple. I've always been bugged by writers who neglect to think things through, to work up the whole scene, with those vital "trivial" factors which actually cost so much effort and can make or break grand schemes. Where do you get your repair parts, in space? How do you milk a dragon without its tail zapping you in the head? How does your hero/heroine blow the nose in a space suit? How do your fleeing refugees get rid of their garbage without leaving a trace?

In World War II, I was briefly a logistics officer in a port of embarkation, and I saw an entire armored division (and its convoy) delayed because a QM laundry machine broke down. A friend, starving on a blockaded South Pacific island, told me how the heroic relief ship finally reached them—and, by computer error, turned out to be loaded with toilet paper and office machines.

So, as I planned "The Night-blooming Saurian," while stumbling down a moose run in Ontario, I tried to consider the, ah, whole problem of recreating a scene from the old Cretaceous . . . and not without a grin.

—February 24, 1980

THE LAYING ON OF HANDS

This letter was published in almost its entirety in *Kyben* 4 (July 1973), as there were only a couple personal remarks to me. It had no title then, just "The 20-Mile Zone."

This letter is prompted by guilt: I find I made an error in "Maya Máloob." If you put another issue out, I'd appreciate including this:

Tiptree's report on Mayas erred in saying that "Huastec" were actually an isolated Maya-related tribe up in northeast Mexico. The Aztecs were Aztecs; they are also called by some, "Mexicans," for reasons too controversial to go into here. They spoke Nahuatl, which they seemed to have picked up from the remains of the Toltec civilization, and so did most of the tribes that they eventually overran. I probably should have used the term "Nahuatl-speaking" Indians to distinguish the tribes in the main part of Mexico who did so much conquering and being conquered, from the Mayas who had a different history. By the way, there seems to have been another unconquered group just northwest of the Aztec imperial power, the Tarascas. Be interesting to meet them.

If you crave one fascinating book to go to bed with the flu with, try *Daily Life of the Aztecs* by Jacques Soustelle, Pelican. He reconstructs the empire's life just at the eve of the Spanish irruption. Unforgettable. Take this picture, written by Bernal Diaz, of five Aztec officials passing by what was to be their dooms:

> Some Indians . . . came running to tell the chiefs who had been talking with Cortés that five Mexicans (Aztecs) had been seen, the tax gatherers of Motecuhzoma ("Montezuma"). On

hearing this they went pale and began to tremble with fear. They left Cortés to himself and went out to welcome them . . . adorned a room with foliage, prepared some food and made a great deal of cocoa. . . . When these five Indians came . . . they passed by the place where we were with so much confidence and pride that they walked straight on, without speaking to Cortés or any of the others of us. They wore rich embroidered cloaks, loincloths of the same nature, and their shining hair was raised in a knot on their heads: each had a bunch of flowers in his hand and he smelt to it; and other Indians, like servants, fanned them with fly whisks.

Shortly afterwards, says Soustelle, these empire men called in the Totonac chiefs who had been talking with Cortés and gave them hell for presuming to negotiate with them.

As you can see, I've been at the books; one contracts a hunger to read everything on the mysterious world among whose bones one treads here. The French and English seem to have done more than the U.S., judging from what's here. Trouble is, book distribution in Mexico is if anything zanier than in the States. Part of a series will be in French, part in Swedish or Zulu; all of *Volume One* of something is, say, at Uxmal, while all the *Volume Twos* are in Honduras. And anybody is an instant expert. There's one nut whose mimeoed booklets are all over who has found secret messages from the Martians in the snake sculpture, and another series of cheap guidebooks that is apparently a translation from the Japanese—that was where I picked up the Huastec-Aztec booble.

(You'd be amazed at the good paperback SF books in little barrio stalls here, especially English. Most in one copy each, often second-hand.)

Final note: A great new ruin probably more magnificent than Chichén Itzá has been discovered (from the air) near Tulúm on the east coast of Yucatan. It is believed to be unlooted. The government is trying to protect it until proper funding can be arranged for clearing and restoration. Name is Cobá (Ko-*bah*). About ten years from now when you get down here the character being hauled up in the main pyramid in a wheelchair will be Uncle Tip.

Back to you, Jeff; by the way, no need to freeze this communication, it's being writ on a recently government-sprayed cuarto. When these boys spray, they make the U.S. in Vietnam look like amateurs. Even the Tequila tastes of it.

I got back to the rancho and saw L'mus, a year older and definitely sinister now; his head has filled out into a more triangular shape, wide above the temples, and when he looks at a nonfunctioning motor with that primordial menace in his slit eyes you expect the motor to moan. He's thicker too, his wrists are about six inches across, like locomotive pistons—Did you ever see one?—and his hands should belong to a guy 6'6" instead of 4'9". He doesn't use a vise to drill metal; just grips it in one vast hand and drills a perfectly vertical slot. He's into gasoline motors this year. Somebody's station wagon gave out. L'mus yanked up the hood, stuck his screwdriver in his teeth, and dived onto the engine block with it still running, hot as fire. All you could see were his enormous square feet expressively writhing, and suddenly the motor went wild and then settled down sweetly. His grin when he got out was the same old L'mus. A great guy. I gotta bring him a decent watch.

A lot of the Mayas around there are into learning English this year. The Maya-English accent is good, except the consonants sound like rifles. Even an "l." The extremely powerful lady who does the laundry for the fishing camp caused some excitement by beamingly announcing, "Billow! Shit!" You'd have to get the sound effects to recapture it. Also the air of total mastery. I got the (imported) flu while in her vicinity and she approached me and laid on me hands of such power and warmth that I cowered. I think the flu did too. She announced that she was going to pray for me; I wondered to what god. It worked. Clearly she is one of the ranch healers; her hands were really extraordinary. She took hold of both thighs and—well, maybe this doesn't describe so well. But it was not pornography. I'm told they cure many things by massage; one of the ranch owners here is wondering if somebody shouldn't look into it, because some of the pregnant girls his Western medicine couldn't cure of various symptoms were fixed by the local massage honcho down the coast.

Funny thing about medicine: Western medicine is cold. Here's a pill, go 'way. We all know about U.S. hospitals, about doctors interested in diseases, not people, etc., etc. You see it clearly here. A pill or a shot is great, sometimes there's no substitute; but *a person interested in you* is something irreplaceable. The ceremonious direction of total attention to the sick person, the importance of the sick person. The laying on of hands, the doctor taking on the disease in a personal way. Man, it's half the cure. I know. Only thing, as I mentioned, it is faintly scary. You have to be convinced of the importance of yourself and your disease to endure it. (Remember I said I "cowered.") Of course in a "primitive" world, people are convinced of the importance of their disease because there's very little fake sickness. It's too depriving.

As I write these words I realize there's a whole big unopened thing there. Has anybody looked into the way sickness and health function in a society without real medicine? (Note the chauvinist pride of that "real." Well, it's partly true. I've been reading Zinsser on typhus—*Rats, Lice and History*—and Rosebury's *Microbes and Morals* on syphilis. Until recently, mortality was in general least where there were fewer doctors. Bad medicine is worse than no medicine, and we've had a lot of it.) But what I was after above, I imagine that the average Maya here feels and behaves quite differently from the average us about health and pangs and symptoms and actual illness. Somebody must have written a comparative study. Must look.

Of course most nontechnological societies are ridden with the witchcraft thing. Soustelle shows it among the Aztecs. Sickness is viewed as caused by Human malevolence; somebody hired a sorcerer to bewitch me. Was true all over Africa, too. Thus actual sickness is complicated by Human relations, guilt, expectations, etc.

Tiptree, you're out of your depth.

I've been trying to hack out an End-of-Everything story for an anthology Barry Malzberg and Ed Ferman are doing. Couldn't get started until I saw my first newspaper in several weeks, headlined "Fear of New Hostilities in Indochina." Meaning, if I read my Spanish aright, that *that wretch* in the White House is about to blow his top and punish the rest of the world for not realizing he is king—with bombers with my name on them.

Oddly enough I got a plot that night, but nothing to do with Nixon. If, as Whately Carrington has proposed, one's most intense feelings might have a certain immortality as energy patterns, might these not be our most *painful* feelings? Trouble is the damn thing is too long, they want a short one.

Well, this is a lot of nothing—except the Huastecs—but lots of good to you.

—March 6, 1973

Going Gently Down, or, In Every Young Person There Is an Old Person Screaming to Get Out

When Don Keller and I decided to stop publishing *Phantasmicom* (with #11, May 1974), we asked all our contributors to write something special. Everyone came through for us, and we had an issue we were very proud of, but no one came through for us like Tiptree did.

Nobody tells you the truth about old age.

Nobody tells you much of anything useful, in fact, but that isn't my point now. About *getting old* they not only tell you nothing, they tell you lies. When they talk about it at all, that is. Their eyes veil up, they get behind a cardboard smile mask and shove you a couple hysterical slogans: Think Young. Don't Worry. Then a whimper comes out of their throats and they take off, fast.

Even if you're only five, the implication comes through perfectly: Cheer up, kid—you're doomed.

Remember how you first met it? A huge face comes at you. Pores, pustules, craters. Wattles and ropes hanging down. Brown crusts, yellow cheesy things. A soft, wobbly wart or two, with hair in them. Tufts and snarls of dead hair in the sore-looking nostrils. Eyes like an oyster's blowhole. And the smell, the stink blasting at you out of the deformed orifices!

"Hiya, boy," a broken bellows wheezes, rumbles in the garbage. You identify it, tentatively, as a Human being.

"Mother! What's wrong with him?"

"That's Uncle William, dear. Isn't he marvelous?"

"What's *wrong* with him?"

"Why nothing, dear. He's just a little older, that's all."

"Will I get like that?"

"You and your ideas, heh-heh. You don't have to think about that for a long, long time, heh-heh."

"Will I get like that, Mother?"

"Say, you have some homework to do, right now."

"Mother. *Will I?*"

". . . Yes."

No. *No*!!!

Remember that, the No? They won't get *me*. They can't make me stick around for that. Leave, that's what I'll do. Leave first. Crash the car, dive into the sea in a Piper Cub from ten thousand feet. Have a little hunting accident. Give a party on the edge of a volcano and jump in at midnight, smashed out. Just walk away. Remember?

Because by this time you've found out some of the other things about Uncle William besides the deterioration in his looks. Uncle William's useless thing, for instance, dangling dead and pallid like a pickled worm. The way Uncle William keeps making the unfortunate mistakes that mean he has to be hastily reclothed by Auntie. And Uncle William's conversation.

"You already told me that story, Uncle William."

"What say, boy?"

"I said, you told me that before."

"What? What you say, Martha?"

"I'm not Martha, Uncle William."

"What?"

The amount of "What?" older people say is weird. Uncle and Auntie have whole conversations that are nothing but "What? What?"; their heads are total mush. In fact, Mom and Dad say "What?" quite a bit, too. You begin noticing that all these adults that you'd taken for normal people, I mean, not *people* exactly but at least alive, okay—they have some funny little ways. You notice this more and more. By the time you're driving a car all by yourself you've realized that the general class of older people, say over twenty-five, are pretty nauseating. For example your mother's repulsive way of referring to her old-hag friends as "girls." And more: these old men who seem to have the delusion that your mother *is* a girl. Jeeesus! Why don't they *realize*? Why don't they shut up and go around unobtrusively, wear veils or yashmaks or something, like nuns?

I think about here comes a split. The kids who stop there and more or less forget it, versus the kids who go on thinking about it. I was one of those who couldn't forget it, some kind of third eye and ear inside me stayed stuck to it, focusing, like a diver who has glimpsed a dim, cold alien form: *shark*.

Maybe most of you reading this are like that too. The people who know there is tomorrow. Time-coming is real, maybe more real than right now. Sometimes it's great, today is beautiful because of the great thing coming. But underneath it's *Brrrr*. Now always passing, future always there, coming. Ozymandias. The plain of dust, covering all. Time.

I had terrible trouble with time. Looking at a picture of Uncle William, a blond Mark Spitz grinning on a load of lumber: young! Uncle William as a little *baby* for crissake. I remember looking at the U.S. Senate once and seeing two hundred little babies, mothers saying what sweet little kids. Then I'd look at real kids and see . . . skeletons. Old old skeletons in baby carriages in the Red Owl store.

I learned, too. I remembered everything I read about it when I got to the book world. Like the faculties you lose, the falling metabolic rates, the falling response-time rates, the falling everything rates. (We didn't have Kinsey then, but I had the news.) Out shooting ducks—I quit killing things later—I'd hear the high pinging whistle of birds coming over the pass at 100 mph and a voice inside would murmur, Enjoy it, baby, you won't be hearing 18,000 cps ten years from now. When I did a back flip (my painful achievement) the voice would inform me about declining reflex curves.

And the girls. Oh, the girls. One girl in particular, the first time it hit me that *it was going to happen to everybody*. That corpselike moment: I heard the rasp of her mother's voice in her laugh, I glimpsed her mother's jowls waiting beside that perfect jaw.

Thirty, I thought: Say thirty. That's the end.

Man, the day I turned thirty I really expected to wake up as a pile of dust.

It was kind of a shock, thirty-morning, finding I looked the same. (Well, just about. Recognizable, anyway.) I could even still do a back flip. Of course, there were all these young kids running around thinking they were people. But what the hell, things didn't seem to have changed too much, and I couldn't spend much time thinking about it. I had all these things I was *doing*. Busy, busy. I decided I'd made a mistake. Forty. Forty was the time to go.

Well, forty came, but there kept being all these interesting things I was doing, doing, doing. And I still seemed to be functioning okay, if maybe a little tiredly, perfectly understandable when you're so busy. The girls were still around, sort of. Of course, I didn't do any more back flips after the time the board caught my chin going down; accidents happen. But I still felt the same underneath, I was still me.

And then one day I heard myself saying "What?" Not for the first time, either. I began to suspect. And pretty soon I knew: a trap.

A *trap*, see? It sucks you in, one day is so much like the next; there's no place to dig your heels in. You don't hear the trap closing, in fact you don't even know it's there until you're in it. No day says, This is where you get off. Even your old uniform still fits . . . almost. And hope, hope is all around. Soon as this is over I'll take a couple weeks off and get back in shape. Because you're always so busy, see? You're *doing* things.

Ah yes. And pretty soon—"What, boy?" "Yeah, that's Uncle Tip, isn't he marvelous?" Oopsy daisy, time for beddy-by. "What?"

So here comes the next split, the different ways people go. Maybe it's the same split all over again.

Some of us go gentle into that good night. The sheep, the golden yearsies; stoic, flat, puzzled voices interminably pointing out the missing limbs, the hospital horrors. The Winnebago trailers trundling at 35 mph, the wallet full of grandchildren, the gardens, and handicrafts. The pills. The comfy void.

Or you have the fighters. You see them—the ones that *do* get back in shape. The ones that play tennis through their forties and marry new women in their fifties and crack up their planes in their sixties and go on talk shows in their seventies and marry teenagers in their eighties. *Think young*. Rage, rage against the falling of the night. Dean Martin.

Only . . . they *talk* about it. Oh god do they. Ever hear a twenty-year-old boast about playing three sets of tennis? At fifty they do. They make whooshing backhand gestures and tell about the old serve. (I won't even go into their sex-talk bag, no.) And that's damn all they talk about, the ones that Think Young.

Pathetic.

Man, there has to be another way.

Of course there is one other way, the people so interested in something outside themselves that they don't even notice the scythe cutting them. I just saw an old plant-hybridizer, his legs won't work and his retinas are falling out so he can only see a pinhole, but he crawls, crawls over *fifteen acres* of seedling rows, weeding and feeding and squinting at the new ones every year and breeding more. Some biologists and artists are like that. Tiptree Sr. was sort of like that too, maybe I'll be.

But I think there's another way still.

I don't know exactly what it could be, but years ago I got a hint out of Gandhi's autobiography. The idea of stages beyond stages of life. New, interesting stages, I mean. The first ones aren't new, of course. Youth: the gonad time, the exploding time. Fucking and loving and running around experiencing the world and rebellious theories; maybe brilliant in science. Next comes full-body middle age, full energy drive, adrenaline, skills, strong-loving-but-wary ego. Building time. Building family, movements, anything. Money/power/status time. (Christ was thirty-two, remember?) The thrill of *I can*. Full involvement. Goes on awhile. Nothing new yet.

But the next stage, that's new. In our culture there is no next stage. No map, no idea beyond holding on, repeating what you did. (I have a friend in his seventies starting his *fourth* family.)

But suppose there is a last metamorphosis: not holding on, letting go. Migrating inside yourself into some last power center, where you never really lived before. Changing forward one last time.

You can, you know. Even if your first stages came to nothing, even if sex was a puddle and status was a joke, that's all over now. Time to move on. How? Well, I don't really know how but here's what I think.

Turn in your buttons. Say good-bye. Take up the holy beggar's bowl and go. Out. Free. Alone, literally or mentally. Go out . . . in search of something. Call it the Bô tree, call it the invisible landscape of reality, or wisdom, or union with the cosmos. Or yourself.

Because you're different, you know. When you're old enough you really are *free*. Your energy is not only less, it is different. It's in—if you've done it right—a different place. Your last, hottest organ.

That old force that drove your gonads first, that spread out to power your muscles and hands and appetite and will—where is its last fortress? In your brain. Let me explain.

Your brain really is hot, you know. The hot under the belt is tepid compared to the hot between your ears. It uses 24 percent of your oxygen in every breath. And it's working every minute, changing, packing and adding, cramming itself full.

You've been using it, of course. Nobody drives his brain faster than an eighteen-year-old mathematician. But it's an *empty* brain—that's why the geniuses of the empty sciences are so young: They can twist that thin brain into fantastic patterns. Physics, for example, requires complex patterns of relatively few data. Other sciences require more data, but the patterns get simpler: That's why good anthropology and psychology tends to come from older people. At forty the brain is getting packed with data, but it's still a *driven* brain. It's harnessed to life goals: winning a campaign, running a farm.

By the time you get sixty (I think) the brain is a place of incredible resonances. It's packed full of life, histories, processes, patterns, half-glimpsed analogies between a myriad levels—a Ballard crystal world place. One reason old people reply slowly is because every word and cue wakes a thousand references.

What if you could *free* that, open it? *Let go of ego and status*, let everything go and smell the wind, feel with your dimming senses for what's out there, growing. Let your resonances merge and play and come back changed . . . telling you new things. Maybe you could find a way to grow, to change once more inside . . . even if the outside of you is saying, "What, what?" and your teeth smell.

But to do it you have to get ready, years ahead. Get ready to let go and migrate in and up into your strongest keep, your last window out. Pack for your magic terminal trip, pack your brain, ready it. Fear no truth. Load up like a river steamboat for the big last race when you go downriver burning it all up, not caring, throwing in the furniture, the cabin, the decks right down to the water line, caring only for that fire carrying you where you've never been before.

Maybe . . . somehow . . . one could.

—July 8, 1973

THE SPOOKS NEXT DOOR

This was apparently written for the Science Fiction Writers of America, but so far as I know it was never published by them or anyone else. If it has been, it was under a different title. The manuscript shows signs of heavy revision, but is untitled.

People ask me what it's like to live next to a large intelligence agency. Well, to begin with, I don't live next to the CIA, they live next to me. Frankly, intelligence agencies have been living next to me since about 1943 when they were called the OSS.

The first thing is that the food in the local markets gets upgraded. In the middle of desolate racks of Pop-up Sugar Waffles there appears Swiss Fructifort, real pumpernickel shows up among the Wonder bread, and the butcher suddenly displays a resentful knowledge of Savoy and kidney cuts. The liquor merchants start wedging vodka and brandy in between the red-eye bourbon. The drugstores develop a rash of chess sets and the paperbacks sprout Galbraith and Mailer among the nurse porno. It becomes possible to buy *The New York Times*. The local welding shop acquires a Saturday waiting line of harassed ex-anthropology professors clasping ten-speed bikes and busted lawn mowers. So far so good; all these things happened in the farming crossroads called McLean when The Campus went up.

What is not good, of course, is the goddam new roads and the doubly damned developers bulldozing every bloody tree under—that not only happened to me in McLean, it happened in Foggy Bottom when I lived next to the Tile Factory there. But that isn't what you want to hear about. What you want is the creepies.

Ah, the creepies. Well now. Washington, you see, is a *small* town. Everybody knows everybody's business. Everybody knows, for instance, that when types like Howard Hunt are "made available" to the White House it is 99 to 1 that nobody could figure out how else to fire them. (Firing kooks is the single greatest headache of everybody in the Feds from branch chief up—you *can't*.) Everybody also knows that the CIA is a den of effete Eastern liberalism that can't be relied on to back up the Pentagon's perfectly natural urge to bomb the Reds; I mean, people in the CIA actually speak foreign languages, so you can't trust 'em. Funny anecdote about that: A local moviehouse ran an ad in Russian offering free tickets for a correct translation. On opening night, there was a three-block line down McArthur Boulevard featuring the entire linguistic staffs of the CIA, NSA, USIA, State, and a few others. All the opposition had to do was walk down the street looking under snap brims.

But they didn't need to. You see, in D.C. there really is one good intelligence agency. I refer, of course, to the Commercial Credit Corporation. They know—man, do they know. In the old days when the CIA insisted on its employees saying they worked "for the U.S. government" there was a true tale of the wife of a newly arrived CIA bigwig who toddled down to Woodies' to set up a charge. "And where does your husband work?" "Oh, for the U.S. government." The lady was not out of the door before Woodies' credit office had verified by phoning the CIA on her husband's *new correct unlisted extension.*

If you don't happen to have credit sources, all you have to do is ask the nearest cabby—or for that matter, the nearest PTA member, plumber, VW garage, cop, or garbageman. *Everybody* knows. But there is one little complication.

You see, children, there was once a time when people thought it was glamorous to say they worked for the CIA. (Among other things, you could get laid.) So what you had was about 100,000 people who said they worked for the CIA and didn't. And then there was another ten thousand who said they worked for the U.S. government. That was simple. But then—after countless ridiculous incidents like the above—Big Brother decided it was okay to say where you worked, as long as you didn't say what you did (like clipping *The New York Times*). So now you still have about fifty thousand hopefully horny losers claiming they work for the CIA while hustling real estate, plus the ten thousand liberated who say diffidently that they work for CIA and do. How do you tell 'em apart?

Well, as a fast rule of thumb, if they have five kids, a PhD, and a wife who worked for McGovern, you've probably got your spy.

Because I meant it about that "effete Eastern liberal" crack. One of the things I learned living next to the creeps was a healthy relish for the political prejudices of most of them—they coincide with mine. There were more Stevenson stickers in the CIA parking lot than flag decals in Dallas. Now this is not absolute. Why? Because in the time of the Dulleses, the CIA acquired an unwanted posse of cowboy-type activists who would do the dirty things John Foster shoved off on brother Allen. These people—and this outlook—were about as desired by the old-line pure-information-philosophy boys as a skunk in a baby buggy. Intelligence, if you look at it right, should be just that: simple disinterested *information*. NOT DIRTY TRICKS. (If you want paramilitary, give it to the Pentagon—and then abolish it.) Most of this element went down in the Bay of Pigs, I hear. Good. But what about the old cloak-and-cyanide bag, you ask, what about agent nets and blackmailing peoples' relatives into spying for you, etc., etc., et-James-Bond-cetera?

Well, it may come as a shock to the romantic, but all that is largely out. And good riddance too. I had a taste of it in World War II to last me. What is in is relatively clean: plain, ordinary long-range photos. Sensing. Science stuff. No beating people up in safe houses, no paying off flocks of dirty-necked triple pros. Just looking and listening. In my opinion, this is a great improvement. I mean, we look, they look, everybody sees what's there.

I don't think you can call that dirty—unless you're prepared to jail the next housewife looking over her neighbor's fence.

And since no agent can tell you what's on Brezhnev's mind, and you can't mount a major attack without moving stuff all across the landscape—it's a hell of a lot safer for us. Also very irritating to some people. Because, as most people in D.C. know, in the old bad Cold War days the Pentagon's spies used to peddle hot-eyed rumors weekly—BIG SOVIET BUILD-UP, ATTACK LOOMS! And then the early U-2 boys would take a look and say, Sorry, those big new atomic installations your agents are selling you are three thousand acres of winter wheat. End flap—until next week. Irritating . . .

Well, now I must pack my duffle to return to the land of vodka and pumpernickel and *The New York Times*. And what do you think I'll tell my cabby at National Airport? "Drive out past CIA, I'll tell you from there." Because he *knows*, see? And in case he's just come to town, here's one last tidbit. When Big Brother moved the Campus out to McLean they hid it real good—in among some woods behind the Bureau of Public Roads. Which used to be their road sign until this year, when they finally admitted they're there. But they forgot one thing: Towering over the whole shebang is a gigantic screaming red-and-white *water tower* visible for ten miles in any direction. It used to be known as Dulles's Bladder.

—October 20, 1973

HARVESTING THE SEA

There were two final "20-Mile Zone" travel columns published, all without titles. The one now called "Harvesting the Sea" appeared in *Kyben* 9 (September 1974). The last one was in *Khatru* 6, April 1977, and consisted of "More Travels, or, Heaven Is Northwest of You" (Tip's title, which I omitted at the time), Tip's response to my comment that the piece "is almost straight reporting, facts, no opinions or impressions," and part of a letter explaining why he wasn't writing his annual Maya column (here titled "Quintana Roo: No Travelog This Trip").

The annual rite of sending you a cockroach-laden message from the mangrove swamps is now under way, with the added attraction that this year my type seems to be Mexican duplicator tape that runs when I spray it. If you can read this it probably means I didn't spray *hard*, so for God's sake be warned. The *cucarachas* have developed a new generation of weapons systems down here. If you step on one, it carries you two yards before you can jump off.

I'm sitting and sweating and swatting in a broiling, roaring hot south wind the Mayas call *But Kann*, the Stuffer. It blows for days and nights, "stuffing" the north, which then spews it back as a norther. But this time of year the north hasn't got much blow in it. This is not, by the way, an "idyllic" beach like the Acapulco side, this is a raving brilliant blowing beach, storms of glittering coral dust, torn skies tumbling by, the surf creaming and blowing spume, the bay inside the reef has a million white lemmings running and plunging over it, everything glinting and gleaming and shrieking turquoise and jade shrieks, palms sweeping, grackles going ass over endwise, only the noble frigate birds demonstrating calm. And then every so often the winds die for a day and the

Mayas—and touristas—rush into every available bay and lagoon after fish and go about beaming *Que bonita*! And next day the whole works blows back from the other way.

Yesterday we had a bit of excitement on the shore. A family of fishing tourists took one of the owners' skiffs out on the reef in a twenty-to-thirty mile souther, six people including a kid, and broached it. Everybody out! So they all piled into the chop a mile offshore, no flippers or masks or nothing, and L'mus—remember him?—who was running the swamping skiff promptly headed for shore, abandoning the bobbing heads. After he had found some ranch hands to help him turn the skiff over and empty it and replace the motor, he went back and handed them their flippers, but they were by then almost ashore. I mentioned that this seemed a bit cavalier to the rancher, my friend, and he shook his head gravely. "Oh no," he said, "I would have done just the same. That motor is valuable. You should understand how he takes care of that motor; he chains it up at night. He did just right. After all, they could float."

So now I know what to expect if I go lobster-diving with L'mus.

I see his point. Motors are the lifeblood here. We figure there are about two hundred on the east coast of Yucatan. About 25 horsepower is what they find best, small enough to skim over the shallow lagoons and sturdy enough for the reef. They're switching to Yamahas now; chalk one up for Nippon.

Any friends or followers of L'mus, otherwise known as Audomaro Tzul the Maya puro, will be interested to know that he is converting from land-based electrician to marine. He has been taken on as general engineer and mechanic, and the motors are indeed his treasures. The guides here drive them through anything, and L'mus keeps them running with rusty nails and—literally—string. (In the accelerator heads.) The nails go as cotter pins. He is also taking to the water himself since the departure of another brilliant little guy, Estéban Burgos, who was seemingly born under water and provided the ranch with lobsters single-handed. (No boat, nothing but four fantastically strong Maya limbs and the sea.) But the big news about L'mus is romance.

You may recall that when last heard of L'mus was busy courting the beautiful and at least quasi-virginal Rosalie Pech Balan. But when I came by this year, no more Rosa. Instead, we find the glistening slicked-down snake head of L'mus where? Gleaming before a filled side table in the camp kitchen, that's where. And the camp stove is presided over by Gregoria, a small globular, brown, flashing-eyed, and earringed and beruffled matronly widow of at least forty exciting years. It seems that after whatever happened with Rosa, L'mus took a good look around and headed straight for the well-filled hammock of Gregoria. So Gregoria's hammock is even better filled, and so, not coincidentally, is L'mus. If he is mourning the charms of Rosa he is doing it in front of an endless supply of damn good cooking. Gregoria hums and flashes and puts new garnishes on the burnt pargo, thoughtfully saving the best for the side table. Last time I was down there L'mus clocked in over an hour solid eating time. Presumably he can use the weight, that hammock must be bouncy.

But L'mus is really in his glory out on the water; he and Estéban were a sight to behold, fiercely upright in their skiffs in the flaming sea, right out of three thousand years ago if you overlook the madras briefs. Mayas have a habit of standing up in boats, practicable due to their low center of gravity. They also don't give a damn how many are aboard or how much water comes in. When a party of ranch hands passes going up to Tulum you see four or five stocky dark figures apparently proceeding through the waves without visible support, standing in a bunch on nothing. It takes several looks before the horizontal line of the staggering skiff can be made out under them. They go into the surf in whatever they're wearing, too. One dawn a huge cable drum washed up, and the foreman simply waded out fully dressed to wrestle it in. "The people on the next ranch steal *everything* out of my sea," he complained to me, lowering his voice to a hiss and squinting his eyes, forgetting he was supposed to be Spanish. "*Everything*," he repeated. "Poles, planks, lumber, nets." His voice went into a strange rhythmic singsong, and he twisted his neck with a most evil look, chanting imprecations in a way utterly unlike anything you've heard except Maya. He waded out to get it (I had discovered it) and I tried to "help" him horse it in. Christ, it was like trying to help a volcano; I barely got out of the way before he had that three-hundred-pound sodden monster heaved out of the sandbar and rolling in. His little daughter, tagging along, laughed at me. I suggested the drum would make a good table, and he agreed, suddenly becoming again totally different; in an instant this barrel-shaped old man was a beautiful girl strutting in a hat dance on the "table."

A satisfying haul. The sea is a great supplier; everything but metal. Complete small boats come in over the reef from nowhere, Cuba, or Jamaica four hundred miles away. One night a shrimp boat broke up on the reef, and my rancher was mad at himself when he saw the lights of a crew from a ranch miles down the line out in the breakers all night stripping her. A forty- or forty-five-foot boat, quite possibly abandoned for the insurance.

Development, unfortunately, is coming here fast; there have been enormous changes in the five years since I first started coming by. The government has pushed the road through (it was a machete-cut trail) and is starting a bridge over the mouth of the lagoon, that used to be bridged only by an oil drum ferry. (It was a day's work for the ranchers on the next key to get their cocos across. A pleasant day.) And a big tourist center is going up seventy miles north. The newly discovered big ruined city (Cobá) has been vandalized—true of everything here and in Guatemala and Honduras. The vandals even use chain saws to slice the great stone steles. And it is now so accessible with the new coast road that it is as deep in Polaroid backing as in jungle. Hoards of campers, cycles, and trailers are on the way; a few filter down here each week or so. People actually camp—even clear roads and dig wells—in somebody's ranchland. Last year an incredible phenomenon was in Yucatan: a trailer tour, very monied. Cadillac after Caddy, nose-to-exhaust, towing deluxe aluminum wombs, Airstreams or what, hundreds. I was told they only stopped by big city supermarkets, where they loaded up, and never again got out of their air-conditioning. Don't roll that window down, Marvin! You put it right back up before Mexico gets in! Great. A huge trailer-bearing cruise ship from Miami also docked just north (after running ignominiously aground the first try), discharging what I am told was the entire contents of about five nursing homes. The *Bolero*. A young girl who was on it told me she had never seen people eat so. "They were all—oh, excuse me—so *old*." I reassured her that I could bear the thought and was surprised to find that she had felt sympathy for these living hulks. "They were having fun." I fear I struck her as unsympathetic to my own; it rather humbled me hearing this dear little creature be so humane.

Live and learn.

Jeff, since I have not only had no news of you for months but not even much news of the U.S., I can't say anything very connected to reality. I wonder what you are doing and how you both are. Of the U.S. I hear only that the Great Polluter is still in the White House, the remaining wilderness is about to be strip-mined, and people are taking off their clothes for reasons which elude the Mexican press services. I trust that this is not an activity obligatory for all right-minded pinko communist radic-libs. But if the sight of Tiptree in the buff puffing down the GW Memorial Parkway is really deemed vital to world peace, so be it. We shall see. In a few weeks now. Meanwhile, Jeff, all good things to you and be sure good vibes are wavering toward you from the mangroves. If I get time and coolth to add a more SF-type note I will, if it isn't in, here's good wishes from yrs as ever. Fondly Fahrenheit. Whew!

Much later; it's past midnight and a few refreshing beverages. Still blowing like a furnace, sea raving and crashing in the stage moonlight, so bright you can see the indigo waters and cobalt sky, palm fronds thrashing with a perpetual sizzling strum like static from space, the lavender shadows chasing themselves around over the shining sand like flat animals pouring by. The sea has taken most of the beach up to Puerto Morales, leaving an enormous opalescent shingle on which lone coconuts incoming from, maybe, Africa, play ghostly billiards. The strange parcel service of ocean. Dead men occasionally, plastic unending. A fluorescent tube came in waving like a submerged conductor's baton. The plague of dolls I mentioned a couple years ago seems to have ceased; whatever rites caused them must have stopped. They were replaced by a sending of glass hypodermic vials—empty. Quick shootups by the rail. Every year there is a harvest of the wooden planking used to stack freight, gratefully received by the Mayas. Lots of very big bamboo, occasional immense mahogany logs from a Honduran barge. I mean immense; four-foot diameters. Several such trees are buried in the beach, which uncovers them to gloat over and then covers them again. There is also a very old sailing vessel deep down, just the ribs showing. The bolts for the shrouds are visible at times; a sailor told me they were hand poured in place, you can see where the hot metal ran. About two hundred years ago . . . Crash, crash; the sea is busy bringing a new beach up from Belize.

Guilty recall that this was supposed to be about SF. Well, I did read some; newest was a collection of Aldiss's he sent me, *Moment of Eclipse*. Take a look at one killer in there, "Heresies of the Huge God." It tells nearly everything you need to know about religion—and should be afraid to ask. I like Aldiss; when he gets into high gear he's hot. He seems to have seen some of the places I met early, his piece on the living and the dying is the blow that makes you reel in India. And he's the only writer I know who has done something with a loa worm infestation; my uncle got one. What happens is that a fly lays an egg which hatches into a solitary hairlike worm, which for the next seven or so years roams your body under the skin, looking, as I was told it, for its mate. If you have gone back to Illinois of course the mate is missing, so the loa roams on, causing no pain but incredible swellings. One day you can't buckle your watch strap, a week later you have a melon on your elbow. The idea is to wait until it crosses your eyeball and hook it out. The waiting is made interesting by the knowledge that if it wanders into your brain you die.

Listen, Tiptree: SF. Okay. Oh hell—the main thing I've been into is a serious study of Tolkien's *Ring* and reading H. G. Wells for the first time. I will spare you my conclusions beyond saying I take both very seriously indeed. One of the aspects which they share is that they are both strategies for handling almost unbearable grief. In Wells's *Days of the Comet,* the fantastic, gut-tearing paean of hope reveals the wound beneath; it is the blinded crying for light. In Tolkien the held-back cry of bitter loss becomes lacerating; it is interesting to read that his first memories were of the ravaging of his childhood lands by the devastations of the railroad, and that in his youth, by 1918, all but one of his close friends had been killed in the war. His prescription is go on, go on; it stinks, it hurts, but go on. Somehow go on. Wells goes on, too; both men are, well, sturdy. Brave, one might have said in a simpler age. Both tremble toward sentimentality, are saved at each last moment by their brilliantly observing eyes, their regard for what is, no matter how dismaying. And of course with Tolkien, the rich airy landscape of words, his almost magical grasp.

In contrast I was reading another favorite, Malzberg; didn't too much like his *In the Enclosure*—not so much new in it for me—but was delighted by one of his that seems to have slipped out unnoticed a couple of years back: *Revelations*. Dear God what mythic ideas. M. is another of those in overt pain—*Stop it*, this has to stop, I can't bear any more. And his pain rises above exasperation and frenzy, it has metaphysical dimensions. But it is a somewhat different pain, less focused. Everybody and everything *hurts*, for no known reason.

I often feel that way.

Take a look at *Revelations*. He has used his stock figure of the disenchanted astronaut in a new wild way. And the concept of the incredible TV talk show host savagely driving to find, well, God, or something—to me unforgettable. And the way the thing comes out, the way you fall through dissolving realities. Some rough edges, some writing that bears signs of too long hours pounding out a story a day or whatever he does, but I'm not about to quibble with the oyster.

The main other item I went through was some Ballard, principally the Chronopolis group. I've decided not to shoot myself because of Ballard; he's great but he is for me on some kind of parallel track, his stories send me up but never have that ultimate personal reference.

Finally got around also to Aldiss's *Report on Probability A*—probably the world's hardest story to end, after that maniacal obsessive crescendo flight through the microscope; a genuinely strange story. And—at last—Silverberg's antho *New Dimensions One*. Now I see why everybody was raving about Harlan's "Mouse Circus" and Le Guin's "Vaster than Empires and More Slow." That Harlan.

Well, all this and now I remember what I really wanted to chat at you about, which is, Tiptree's Year of the Women. Culminating in trying to write one for Vonda McIntyre's antho, *Aurora (Beyond Equality)*. To do it honestly. I have as you probably know a talent for making any simple task into a soul-searing struggle, complete with intimations of mortality. But it grows late; let's break. Leaving for our next, if interested, how Tiptree found happiness in Women's Lib. I know now why women have always attracted me, you see: *They are the real aliens we've always looked for* . . . yes. Now I feel better.

—April 3, 1974

MORE TRAVELS, OR, HEAVEN
IS NORTHWEST OF YOU

Aah-h-h, I made it. British Columbia, that is. Life-long desire finally fulfilled. Moreover, now I've found it, I don't really need to go to New Zealand, since I'm told they're very much alike except for marsupials and araucaria trees.

British Columbia starts with Vancouver, which must be one of the sweetest cities in the world to live in. You'd have to stay there a month to begin to see it, too; my lady taxi driver told me she had been exploring it for six years and was still getting surprised. Picture a city sprinkled around on islands in the mouth of a great river, filled with the greenest greenery you ever saw and surrounded by dazzling snow-clad mountains. With the sea mixing in everywhere among flowers and skyscrapers and wildernesses and enough beaches so you can still find empty ones—there's even one for nudists—and Chinatowns and a great zoo-forest on a special island (it has kissing-tame killer whales, if you want to kiss a killer whale) and polite sturdy people of every national origin and denomination, and a coastline wandering off to infinity in fjords and inlets, boating such as you wouldn't believe. And the hotels have the kind of service I thought had gone down with the *Titanic*, heavy silver and snowy napery and delicious food. ("Does the coffee suit, sir? I'll be glad to brew you another pot.")

Oh, my.

There is, of course, a cautionary note. It is said to rain there (hence the greenery) although it never did for me. And the sea carries the cold Japan Current, which makes for hardiness. More on that later. And . . . the service ain't free. Tiptree's wallet started going down like the *Titanic* before I got out to the wilderness. But, ahhh, while it lasted!

Now that wilderness! The British Columbia coastline is what is called "drowned," which means that the sea comes halfway up the mountains with incredible arms and inlets wandering right through the Coastal Range. (How they ever got it explored is a story you should read—elsewhere.) So the settlements are where rivers come in, and they're surrounded by walls of snowy peaks. You can get to them from the east over some fairly hairy roads or you can take the coastal steamer. I flew north on a small, informal airline which wanders around delivering newspapers and taking children to the dentist. My fellow passengers were other fishermen and two young Bella Coola Indian girls going home to Bella Coola, which was where I was headed too. Bella Coola is a famous settlement of a few hundred hardy souls including a reservation town, and is where Alex MacKenzie finally came out when he made his great trek overland seeking the Pacific.

The flight was eye-popping. We headed up the scenic straits between the mainland and great Vancouver Island (on which the city of Vancouver is *not* located), laboring higher and higher. And then the little plane turned and took off over the snows and crags of the Coastal Range, with glaciers and peaks going by the wings and no, but absolutely *no* place to land whatever. Gulp. I had just finished reading about the Uruguay soccer team who had crashed in the Andes snows and survived by eating their dead, and I couldn't help casting an eye on the potential toughness of my companions. (I am *very* stringy.) And then we dived into a gorge on the far side and kited down and around a huge glacial valley—and suddenly there was a salt sea arm meeting a pale-blue river, and a cluster of roofs, and forests. And we and the newspapers had arrived at Bella Coola.

Immediately I got out. I realized I was on the inland side of the mountains—it was a glorious *dry* day. On the sea side they get like 150 inches of rain a year, inside they get eleven. Summer is one endless cobalt blue sky and the sun on the snows above.

The next thing I saw was the scale. You've heard of giant redwoods. Well, there are giant Douglas firs. I mean *giant*. What I thought was a normal forest was a staggering cathedral of these great firs and cedars, with the mountains looking down at you over their tops. Unless you put a Human figure in your snapshot you don't appreciate the scale of everything. You see a simple log bridge—and when a Human being wanders out on it you realize the logs are waist-high lying down. Some are as big as sequoias; there is a drive-through fir in Vancouver. And the mountains—it's a land of stupendous triangles, triangles of blue blue sky pointing down, triangles of peaks poking up.

I took another even smaller plane up to a wilderness lake full of cut-throat trout—with a glorious 1300-foot sheer falls at one end—and spent two weeks just breathing. Also swatting. It is, unfortunately, true about northern bugs. Some days it pays to be constipated. But other days the wind takes them off and out on the lake is clear. Specifically, it's black flies and mosquitoes and various brands of carnivorous deer flies up to one called the Bulldog, which is said to take a bite out of you and sit on a limb munching it with blood running out its jaws. I did not meet the Bulldog. But I did meet some quite large mosquitoes; one is rumored to have landed at Fairbanks and taken on 15,000 gallons of aviation gas before being identified.

For what it's worth, however, my bites didn't swell. Nothing like Virginia bites. (No, I do not mean Watergate.)

I went back down to the valley to stay awhile and clean up. Down there is river life from time immemorial. Crowds of humpback salmon churning up, crowds of trout ditto, looking for salmon eggs. Coming downstream was a Bella Coola phenomenon: I was on a sandbar and suddenly here comes song and orange plastic, turns out to be a group of guys sailing wet-arse down the river in inner tubes, drinking wine and singing at seven miles per hour plus rapids in the rain. Turns out it's a Sunday sport, they repeat all day in batches up to thirty. Very festive they looked—offering wine to all encountered. I reluctantly refused because I was on the far side from them, difficult to cross. (That is *fast* water.) But God, their butts must have been cold. That stream is fresh out of a glacier. And so is all the water around, which is what I mentioned earlier. I saw Indian kids snorkeling for hours in a clear lake that was so cold my *scalp* lost consciousness—along with my feet up to the hips, and my ribs contracted so I breathed in short screams. But the kids played on like otters.

The Bella Coolas are rather a mysterious tribe, everybody gives you a different story, including that there now are no Bella Coola Indians—or that there are nine tribes. The mystery is partly because they look exactly like Polynesians. Softly rounded, full curved lips, right at home in the grass skirt and flower-behind-ear bit. (The girls look great.) Thor Heyerdahl came through and pointed out that a raft could drift on the current from Bella Coola to Hawaii very neatly, but not, of course, come back. So maybe Hawaii is full of Bella Coola Indians.

The other tribes around them are more the aquiline Plains types; out on the coast live the Kwakiutl people, whose custom of holding Potlatch feasts you may have been exposed to in Ethnology IA—even as me. Some of the survivors of all the tribes are doing a little writing; I read one marvelous book called *Potlatch* by a Kwakiutl who witnessed, as a child, the last of the great feasts. Among the competitive courtesies extended to the guests arriving in canoes was to dance in silent formation down to the shore and while guests posed statuelike, you stuck poles under the huge canoe, guests and all, and hoisted the whole works up shoulder-high and "floated" them into the hall. . . . Made me thankful it's not obligatory to haul in your dinner guests *in* their VWs. (Mine would take to bikes. If they wanted to eat.)

In and around Bella Coola you meet a few nice foreign types who come for the hiking and fishing; backpackers. One lad comes in every year to follow grizzly bears around in a friendly way. A few adventurous camper-drivers with tales of the road. How Bella Coola finally built its own road to get out of its mile-high pocket and "join Canada" is a real Heinlein adventure yarn. Government failed; they did it themselves with two old cats and blasting powder. It's over a mile of rock straight up; sometimes they had to chain the cat to the cliff and ride it—*hanging in air*! The day the cat from below met the cat from above the town went wild. The powder man nailed his hat and boots to a tree, bottles popped from top to bottom, and everything in the town that had wheels went jolting up and out in a honking procession all the way to Anahim, which had to be nearly rebuilt when Bella Coola went home.

For hikers who are interested, there is the Rainbow Range, a whole continental upthrust of gorgeous colored minerals, even flying over it is unbelievable. Trails are just getting marked out. I talked to the ranger, who like everybody surviving there is built like a Saturn stage and has just about the power. What he had to say about the new trail "littered with little brown piles and lavender toilet paper" I won't repeat. Suffice it to say that this is a Provincial park, where you can be thrown out for Disturbing a Park Object. They don't have to see you litter. When they catch you at the end of a trail of plastic or little brown piles they point out that you are "disturbing" the park grass by standing on it, and out you go. Great.

The name is Tweedsmuir Provincial Park, and for any of you who want a look at Eden, go. Go now, go quick. Bring your bedroll and be prepared to buy your own eats at the incredible new Bella Coola Coop. Lodges offer bunks and cooking pots and stoves. Don't let the bug tales scare you, Cutter keeps them off. And—

No little brown piles, hear?

It's so damn beautiful.

—August 29, 1974

Yeah, I know the British Columbia thing was impersonal. That was because of this free-floating depression which had struck me (lifting now) so that if I had put personal stuff in it would have come out as a sort of supine wail. Stop it stop it, I can't stand anymore. Sometimes I get so that all the pain and misery in the world seems to be tied into my nervous system and hurting together. I heard long stories about the ghastliness of the white man's treatment of the Indians—giving them smallpox-infected blankets among others—and instead of fading out, all these and so many others just seemed to add up and build until I wanted to get out of the planet or out of the species, or out of my own mal-functioning nervous system. Nightmares, nightmares . . . I'm a kook, Jeff. When I was a kid I almost killed myself when I heard what hap-pened to Carthage. And the burning of the Alexandria library. And the R.C. Church's destruction of the three thousand Maya codexes. (Only three—three—escaped.) Life seems to be just one long flinch. I am very tied into the natural world, you know, and every bulldozer hurts me per-sonally. Now we're about to stripmine three states there's a permanent block of ice-splinters in my left kidney, day and night, especially nights . . .

Well, let's not get everybody bawling.

—September 27, 1974

WITH TIPTREE THROUGH THE GREAT SEX MUDDLE

In May of 1974, I innocently got an idea for a fanzine article that would turn out to absorb all my time for the next year and produce a document that went beyond all expectations. I invited a group of SF writers to discuss "Women in Science Fiction." The format was similar to the Tiptree interview—there were a few opening questions, and then there were follow-up questions based on the first responses. But with twelve participants, all commenting on each other's letters, it quickly grew to an almost unmanageable size. Undeterred (well, only slightly deterred), we all continued writing, and at the end "Women in Science Fiction: A Symposium" took up 122 pages of by far the largest fanzine I ever produced, the 156-page *Khatru* 3 & 4, November 1975. (*Phantasmicom* 11, the second largest, was one hundred pages.) It was only marginally about science fiction, but the forum of eleven high-powered thinkers and one out-of-his-league editor produced something quite remarkable, that is still talked about today.

The contributors were Suzy McKee Charnas, Samuel R. Delany, Virginia Kidd, Ursula K. Le Guin, Vonda N. McIntyre, Raylyn Moore, Joanna Russ, James Tiptree, Jr., Luise White, Kate Wilhelm, and Chelsea Quinn Yarbro. Here is the introduction I wrote for that issue:

> This is an issue of letters. And it is an issue that should *draw* letters. I'd like to give a little background here.
>
> I first thought of a symposium on Women in Science Fiction in May of 1974. I drew up a prospectus in early August—a good prospectus—and with a lot of help from Virginia Kidd I had my panel by late September. Unfortunately, after the Worldcon I had gone into a considerable creative slump, and the Symposium suffered for it. I kept putting it off until I figured that if I didn't move soon I would lose my contributors, and on October 9th I forced out a letter. It began

"Dear People—" (remember that) and ended with some questions that only vaguely resembled what I wanted to ask. I can't really offer any excuse for that. Perhaps, though, the bad questions initiated a better final product than good ones would have. . . .

Officially, the Symposium ran from 10/9/74 to 5/8/75 (though minor revisions carried on well after), seven months and 168 pages of letters. Most of those 168 are here.

I can guarantee that there will be *something* herein that you will disagree with. (It's impossible to agree with everything on each of the 168 pages.) Much of it is pure speculation, grasping for ideas, for connections heretofore undiscovered or ignored. I would much prefer letters with similar qualities, rather than personal attacks on persons whose views do not coincide with yours. (I admit the temptation will be great.) And read it all before you write—if you don't you may just repeat someone else's remark. But I don't want to scare you off: strap yourself in (or let yourself go), and forge ahead.

Excerpted in this section are three contributions by Tiptree, in one of Alli's most difficult periods to maintain her male disguise. The first is her initial non-response to the questions; then there are two of her letters commenting on what others said. While this means you are missing parts of the conversation, I think the contexts are clear.

First, to hell with talking about "women in SF."

What we think and feel about "women in SF" is only a by-product of what we think and feel about women and men in the whole bitter chuckle of life. I think we can take it for granted that women are Human beings who have been drastically oppressed, deprived, and warped out of shape by our male-dominated and largely lunatic culture. So are men, to a lesser and less personally destructive degree. But that said, I don't feel I personally understand much. This spring I pounded my brains to make a story for Vonda's anthology. I mean I sweated deep. Maybe not deep for others, but deep for me. I want to talk about some of the thoughts that began to gel in me then, thoughts of *who and what are they*, these alternative forms of humanity? Are they so different and if so how? Are we the same animal? Can we coexist on the same planet? What the hell are "sexes" and how many and which are there?

As a starter, let's clear away one dire fallacy. *Down with yin and yang thinking!*

Our view of men and women is infested with the vicious mental habit of seeing any pair of differing things as somehow symmetrical mirror images of each other. I, man, am hot; therefore, they, women, are cold. *I* am active; therefore, *they* are passive. *I* think; therefore, *they* emote. My id grunts, "Me good;" therefore, they are bad. Perhaps more perniciously, my superego whispers, *I* have selfish and destructive drives; therefore, *they* are altruistic, compassionate, and nurturant. (They better be.)

Put this way it's clearly silly, but the tendency is very deep in the nature of thinking. Literature and philosophy is smarmed over by the belief that men and women exist at opposite ends of an infinite number of bipolar dimensions. That they in some way mystically reflect and complement each other—on no greater evidence than that occasional men and women do get on well and that the race as a whole hasn't yet died out.

Now, anyone can see certain traces of local, situational complementariness between the Human sexes; it is to be found in any ecosystem. But to seize upon these hints to build something like the yin and yang system is to depart radically from reality. The yin/yang is a lovely system, subtle, elaborate, full of interweavings, dialectical interpenetrations, many pretty mental toys. As an aid to understanding real men and women, it is a monstrous exercise in fluff.

Consider how a Martian would see us. No matter what trait is measured, he/she/it would find a generally bell-shaped distribution; some of the curves would be a bit skewed, no more. Women and men share forty-five of our forty-six chromosomes. This is about as far from a bipolar situation as you can get.

With this blast I hope to abolish from at least my thinking the concept that men and women are in what is called a *reflexive* relation to each other, that they are in some way mirror images of each other. If I had to pick a technical relation which might aid understanding, one could try for example a *transitive* one. (Example, Man is to Woman as Woman is to Child.) But that's just as shallow and useless. The problem is to try to understand real people, and to determine whether a handful of genes on one chromosome has any identifiable effects on their way of being Human.

Are There Two Sexes and if So Which?

A funny thing happened a few years back, on the way to the bomb shelter. Official Washington held an air attack drill, a very elaborate one. The big set piece was the whisking-away of the whole top of the government to a fantastic shelter—this one was under a mountain—where they had all the war rooms and red buttons and machinery for Retaliation Unto Cinders.

Well, when the dawn moment came for the senior officials to gulp their orange juice and toddle out to the black limousines, some very odd confrontations took place. *They were leaving their wives and families behind to be fried*, you see. The silent thought loomed. Have a nice survival, dear. I'm sure you and General Abrams will be very happy . . .

Art Buchwald did some very funny columns. The vision of two hundred postmenopausal males crawling out into the lava plain to celebrate the "saving" of America . . .

Now I submit that this is pathology. Pathology of almost inconceivable luxuriance. I call it the pathological hypertrophy of the male sex pattern.

Okay, let's go back. Yes, I think we have two sexes. But I do not—repeat, *not*—think that they are men and women. I see them as *patterns*, which may or may not be present singly or together in a given individual at a given time.

Okay, what's a "sex"? Well, for a try, let's call it "a coherent pattern of behavior necessary to the reproduction of the species." We probably can agree also that Human sexual behavior has obscure ties to the biological substrate, but that these are not well understood. (I've been reading Money and Ehrhardt's excellent work on the intersexes, *Man & Woman, Boy & Girl.*) About all one can be sure of biologically is that androgen often has the effect of evoking the male sexual pattern.

Yes, I see two sex patterns. One of them is relatively well known, so simple as to be almost trivial and subject to pathology: That is the male pattern. The other I see as overwhelmingly important to the race, very extensive over time, and almost unknown: That is the maternal pattern, or Mothering.

We can dispense with the male pattern quickly; we see it in any cageful of adolescent male rhesus. The one interesting thing about the male pattern—which may be lethal to humanity—is that *it shares the neural pathways of aggression*. The male primate pursues, grasps, penetrates with much of the same equipment which serves aggression and predation. This has the dire side effect that the more aggressive males tend by and large to reproduce themselves more effectively and thus intensify the problem. We see considerable sexual dimorphism among our primate relatives; the males are bigger and stronger. Oddly enough, it's not always coupled with greater aggression; gigantic male gorillas are relatively peaceful citizens. Male baboons, however, are not. They go in for male dominance—and so, unfortunately, do Human males. We appear to be subject to an androgen-related overgrowth of the aggressive syndrome, with its accompanying male-male dominance-submission conflicts, male territoriality, and all the dismal rest. We have had phases like the Ottoman Empire, a totally male society where women were kept as breeding animals and men acted out a complete surrogate fantasy life based on androgen pathology. We are today ruled by gerontomorphic old men—and their young acolytes—who can commit unrealities on the order of that air attack drill.

A John Foster Dulles, a Stalin, is a biologically irrelevant old animal who has confused his fantasies with life and who ought to be undergoing therapy instead of being in charge of anything. But he has power. And so do young male thugs; it is hard to say which are more dangerous. But leaving aside the terrible importance of their dysfunction, one can draw back and simply characterize the male as the animal with enormous amounts of spare time.

It is also important to note that the male pattern is powered by immediate genital gratification. (Nonorgasmic males leave no descendants.) In our species, the male drive has also ceased to be controlled by biological signals from the female.

Now that's all I want to say about the male pattern, because I want to get on to the next. Of course, we could bow to SF in passing, by remarking how much that air attack drill resembled certain *Analog* themes. But let's get on.

What is a *mother?* Well, to begin with, it is the pattern which is 99 percent responsible for our being here at all. Descriptively, mothering has a brief initial phase of what we might call aggressive vulnerability, which gets the gametes together. It has another physical phase of gestation and birth, which requires a female physique. Those two early phases are all that men in the grip of male hypertrophy even notice; that is what they think mothers are and that is what they try to reduce women to. I see these phases as merely initiatory, although the physical act of bringing a child into the world must be a very important one to the person. But if mothering stopped there we'd all be dead.

My try at defining the maternal pattern is deeply influenced by the picture of the female primate endlessly, tirelessly lugging her infant, monitoring its activities at every moment, teaching, training, leading it to the best of her animal abilities. Not for a day or a week, but throughout its whole infancy and into self-sufficiency. The bond created can be very lasting; it is now speculated that the permanent alliance of mothers and daughters and granddaughters may be the true origin of society.

Look at what motherhood involves. Leadership without aggression. Empathy of a high order—can it be the true root of speech? Great environmental competence. Aggressive defense of the young. Nest and shelter-building. Food bringing and sharing. A fantastic array of behavior—*all of which have been flawlessly carried through by every one of our maternal forebears* back to the first mammalian forms, or we would not be here.

It is my belief that mothers, because of their grasp of development over time, undoubtedly invented agriculture. Animal husbandry, too. The characteristic of the mother pattern is that it extends over time in a way utterly unknown to the male. And it has relations to space and the environment again foreign to the male.

Most important of all, it is a relation *between* animals which is totally outside the "male" repertory.

A pause for wonder, for awe.

And now the final speculation—because I really view this sex as unknown. What is mothering powered by? What "goals" has it? What reward drives it?

We don't know.

We can only guess and mutter. I personally know many farmers, and I love to grow things when I have a chance. I think the strange, unspoken rewards of growing things must be a little like the rewards that power maternal behavior. What is the satisfaction—joy, really—of helping things to flourish?

278 • JAMES TIPTREE, JR.

We don't even have a name for it!

I tell you, in our crazy culture we have rendered the major sex *invisible*. The more I think of it the more extraordinary it seems. And I think it cannot be denied that men have attempted to take it over. They wrest children from the mother, make "men" out of them in lunatic rites. They attempt to kill the mother in themselves . . . a scene of unspeakable, fascinated, repulsion.

And what they have made Human mothers into! As practiced today, mothering is a martyrdom for a Human being. Crazy.

Well, let's wind this up by noting one more interesting thing about the mothering pattern. (And remember that by mothering I mean the whole years-long scenario of turning out a viable Human being.) Mothering is tied to the rhythms of biological development. It is totally different from "male" enterprises in this respect. If John Campbell or Edward Teller tried to do mothering, they would have to go to school to the nearest monkey mother gazing into her baby's eyes and untiringly guiding its little hands. They could not have any brilliant technological insights, they could not devise wondrous methods of accelerating or multiplying production; no abstract spasms of genius could shortcut matters. They would just have to *do it*. One by one by one. Or—no product.

That, as Tom Lehrer would say, is a sobering thought.

Because it is, quite simply, the one most important thing we do.

And our failure to develop really good Human mothering—our failure to organize all society around this work, instead of irrelevant "male" activities and goals—may end us even if nothing dramatic gets us first. We must make a world in which every child is mothered to complete socialization, or die of the lack.

Now before I end, one word: Please do not read into what I have said that I see mothers as all sweet compassion, nurturance, etc., and hence charge all this onto women. No. All I have described is a *pattern of behavior*—which you can see operating in any zoo—and which I see as only more or less actualized in individual Human beings at specific times. And one which we have disastrously neglected and do not understand.

Well.

So what about those sexes in SF?

But wait—I have also talked about "Human beings." By which I mean, the other forty-five chromosomes. Now obviously if I could describe a "Human being" I would be more than I am—and probably living in the future, because I think of Human beings as something to be realized ahead. (If we survive ourselves.) But clearly "Human beings" have something to do with the luminous image you see in a bright child's eyes—the exploring, wondering, eagerly grasping, undestructive quest for life. I see that undescribed spirit as central to us all. And in the individual, tinged by one or the other—or both—of the sexual patterns.

And, I guess I must confess, I see "humanity" in its best sense as closer to the maternal pattern than to the male—because of the empty violence which so often infects the male pattern. I would not, God forbid, reduce all life to cozy mommy-wuv. But I think the inherent power of humanity will always carry it beyond that; in fact, a true mother does. Actual mothers are Humans.

So it is easy to say that as men and women who have more of the (partly unknown) mother patterning come into SF, the goals and fantasies and drives and reality-perception of SF will change. It already has; anthropology, sociology, psychology are sciences which involve concepts of *development* which are intellectual representations of mother-reality. As they come into SF we leave rocket-opera behind.

Perhaps we will learn more about mother—her dreams, her fantasies, her perceptions and excitements and glories and dooms and irascibilities and exploits from bisexual SF.

Now what I have said here implies that individual women can quite easily be, in effect, males. When they are acting on and powered by elements of the male pattern. (And they can be subject to its pathology, too.) I don't see this as a problem. What I do see as a problem and a very urgent one, is:

How soon, O Lord, can men learn to be mothers?

I cannot resist ending with a couple of notes which have struck me.

"What is a woman?" This question haunted me until I moved on the thinking about sex as patternings. But it is probably a valid question, if only to stimulate thought. One of my first answers was that women are really truly *aliens*. (And hence supremely entitled to write SF, as Craig Strete has pointed out about American Indians.) This tells us a lot about our culture. Another part answer which continues to amuse me came from looking at our current crop of male transvestites and female impersonators like Holly Woodlawn. Watch them; so like a woman and yet so profoundly lacking something. What is missing? Well, it seems to me that they are totally focused on what I have called here the initiatory phase, the aggressive or provocative vulnerability that promotes genital Contact. *And that is all they have.* Behind them looms the mocking visage of the mother which they are not. They are biological mayflies, triggers to an unloaded gun.

Another, more terrible question: Are women doomed? Can they achieve true liberation and acceptance as full Humans in our society? I have grave fears. (In my story "The Women Men Don't See," Ruth spoke of this.) Because of their physical, political, and economic weakness, the women's movement is *dependent on the civilized acceptance of men*. Are we sufficiently civilized? Will the hand that holds the club really lay it down? Or will we, when panicked, revert back to the old power play, riot roughshod over the rights of the weaker, and throw them again into bondage, to be serfs and property? Let us not kid, men have the power. In the same way, American whites have the power to wipe out black rights. Will we stay unpanicked? Is our civilization deep enough in the bone? I fear the answer . . .

Again on the power situation: Are there too many men? Would a different ratio be saner, say one man to a hundred women? The ridiculous economic imperatives of our culture teach even women to value male babies more. It is a fearsome thought that if we gain control over the sex of the unborn, we might have a wave of male births, a society preponderantly male. I believe that it is urgent for mothers-to-be to value girls more. And I tend to think that we have far too many men . . .

Lastly. You may have noticed the word *lunacy* in this. It comes from Rebecca West's marvelous prologue to *Black Lamb and Grey Falcon*. (A book that tells one more that you wish to know about certain male activities.) May I end with this provocative quote? It is not really a mirror-image concept although it sounds like it at first glance:

The word *idiot* comes from a Greek root meaning private person. Idiocy is the female defect: intent on their private lives, women follow their fate through a darkness deep as that cast by malformed cells in the brain. It is no worse than the male defect, which is lunacy: men are so obsessed by public affairs that they see the world as by moonlight, which shows the outlines of every object but not the details indicative of their nature.

Such as, for example, overlooking a little problem like how you recreate the Human race starting with two hundred old men.

—November 3, 1974

From all the letters, except maybe two, I learned something. I was also heartened to the see the splendid demonstration of male taciturnity vs female loquacity—Delany and I between us took up fifty percent of the space.

Charnas's point, also touched on by Russ and McIntyre—that women have to know men more fully than men know women—of course, of course, yes, I see it. Isn't it the phenomenon that R. Osbourne described in his study of communication in organizations: The people on the bottom of any power structure *know* the people on top—their intimate habits, motives, secrets, everything. While the people on top are ignorant of, and wildly misinterpret, the people on the bottom. Moreover, the people on top see all the actions of the people below as related to them, the bosses, and to their interests.

Did any of you read those unearthly interviews with whites eulogizing their black cooks at the time of Selma? Fantastic, pitiable if it weren't so vicious. By the way, Osbourne's old book is worth glancing at, the title was *Is Anybody Listening?*

I think we have accounted for the greater verisimilitude of male characters drawn by women, without dragging in intuition. (Aside to UKLeG: Some day let's argue about the lifelikeness of Flaubert's Emma—frankly I've always seen her as a "man's woman" in every sense. Much better to me was Proust's Mme. Verdurin—and by God she conforms to Delany's, or Delany and Hackett's, command to get the economic base in. Just thought of that. Maybe a male author writing about a woman's sex relations with men almost *has* to fall victim to the my-cook-loves-me fallacy.)

Charnas's point about women being taught to view each other as threats or models interested me a lot. That's what happens in what used to be called a situation of unstable rewards. In a UR situation, like, say, a fire in a theater, everybody has to cooperate or everybody loses. If a few people start to panic and grab, everybody dies. Only by cooperation can all, or the maximum number, get out safely. Men seem to have created a total UR situation for women. Which, of course, is very much to men's advantage.

Now to the excitement. There I was ponderously calling for men to learn to be mothers, and here is Delany actually doing it. Stupendous. Lord, the questions I'd like to ask: What does it *feel* like? Is it rewarding in itself, or only a duty? Do you do it differently from the way Hackett does it? Do you gaze into the child's eyes? Do you feel it is entirely learned behavior, or do you feel a latent pattern which has been "trained out of you?" Are you late taking your turn because you are late in life generally (many female mothers are)? Would you be late if the baby was alone, if the female mother *had* to leave on time? Have you developed that famous acuity, the power of being able to hear your infant's voice through a din?

And so on. But, always, deepest, *what* is the motive, what is the reward for this behavior? *Why* is a baby cared for and raised? *Why?*

Well, from this you can see that I am far from repentant about asking that attention be directed to the sex called "mother." Of course I do repent the way I did it; I should never have tried an abstraction from behavior and people without warning and explanation. The abstraction is difficult, too, not entirely possible. Like W. Sheldon's attempt to separate somatotype and personality type, while everybody *knows* that an extreme endomorph is *not* going to be a high somatomic. Similarly, we all "know" that men tend to be males and mothers are apt to be women.

And above all, I should never have advanced a view of sex which violates the great sacred totem of our time: the all-importance of copulation. My view of sex looks at the reproduction of the race, and really trivializes intercourse. How blasphemous can you get?

Anyone silly enough to put down the central industry of our day, the *Playboy* scene, the D. H. Lawrence gospel, has to start with an hour of propitiatory dances and ritual purification.

And of course I should *never* have used the word *mother*. (Maybe not *male*, either.) *Mother* seems to be the last dirty word. In trying ruminations on other people, I've had reactions of—believe it—fear and rage. As if we were *afraid* to look at a behavior which accounts for our existence. Fear of stereotypes, maybe; and maybe justified, if blindness is ever justified. But the stop signals somehow do not stop me; I think there is something hidden there.

Consider: If men alone had always raised infants, how monumental, how privileged a task it would be! We would have tons of conceptual literature on infant-father interaction, technical journals, research establishments devoted to it, a huge esoteric vocabulary. It would be as sacred as the stock exchange or football, and we would spend hours hearing of it.

But because women do it, it is invisible and embarrassing.

Look at the atmosphere that surrounds the small area of child-raising that men do: prep schools and college teaching. Think what a "professor" is! And he has perhaps taught a young person the names of some minerals or French poets.

But the mother who taught the young person to speak at all—she has done nothing.

Right?

(I am reminded of the story of how it was discovered that black leopards are not inherently vicious. For as long as man kept them, zookeepers knew they were the most savage of all animals, hating man from birth. Then one day a N.Y. zookeeper's wife took a new cub home and raised it normally. Abrupt end of one myth.)

All of which boils down to saying that I, personally, want to go on looking at this behavior. And since there is nothing duller that a minority defending itself, let's leave it at that.

I gather you suspect me of paranoia, or at least an inaccurate grasp of the power balance between men and women and/or whites and blacks. Well, yes, I am paranoid. We're all prisoners of our histories, and mine has included concentration camps on American soil; 50,000 Americans robbed of their land and possessions and caged in a desert behind barbed wire. The lesson of my time is, If it is inHuman, cruel, and unthinkable, it'll happen.

Of course I don't *believe* it will . . . at least on my better days. And I would be very glad to live long enough to be proved wrong. Very happy.

But as I mentioned to Joanna, I am the type of person who gets a twinge down the spine when I see the gun holstered on a cop's square arse. And I can count guns. The opening scenes of Charnas's novel *Walk to the End of the World* struck me as all too lifelike. In fact, I've seen it alive. So . . . here's hoping.

Let me end with a question that occurred to me:

If men did not exist, would women have invented them?

If women did not exist, I do believe men, alone, would have invented them or something very much like them. (I have changed my mind, by the way: Of course it is not women who are aliens. Men are.) And I wonder, in literature or life, would women alone have invented men?

Would you?

—February 11, 1975

Good-bye, old, new, and ex-friends; it's 5:00 A.M. and 85° F down here, the sand is blowing, the sea is pink, the pelicans are sailing—and I have to go kill cockroaches. Probably *mother* cockroaches, too.

Seems to be symposium time again, assuming you want any more from me. I feel about as relevant as a cuckoo clock in eternity.

But I did feel the good, hot, exciting relevance of all your letters, even those that diverge or disagree. Revolutions are not monodirectional streams, they are turbulent wave fronts full of Yes buts and squabbles over priorities, if not worse.

I read the bundle at the same time that I was reading the winter issue of *Aphra* and Howe and Bass's feminist poetry collection *No More Masks*. That's worth getting, by the way, if you haven't. I admit to a touch of disappointment that they didn't find room for at least a line or two from some of the older forgotten women. Anybody else here an admirer of Anna Wickham ("My work has the incompetence of pain")? There is a verse of hers that struck deep in my mind.

I have to thank God I'm a woman,
For in these ordered days a woman only
Is free to be very hungry, very lonely.

That's worth a lot of ranting about beautiful urns. And I may say she isn't as irrelevant to our topic here as I am. Her poem that begins

"Up the crag/In the screaming wind/Naked and bleeding/I fought blind"—ends when "In the house of my love/*I found a pen*." It's called "Weapons."

For how many of us, me in my way, you in yours, are not our pens the weapons with which we can do something—a tiny something—about wrongs? Even if only to name them?

To our muttons.

Of the letters, the two which spoke most immediately to me were Kate's and Suzy's—because they spoke so clearly of what are my own fears of the abuse of power and death. (Kate, how guilty are you going to make me feel? You're deep in all those things I quit even dabbling at when I had my recent bout of illness. Someday I want to ask you more about AIM; Craig Strete has given me, and, I suspect, Joanna, some slightly devastating insights. Probably like everything, biased. He's very, well, young.)

But Suzy. Dear lady, your essay on the death-relatedness of women was excruciatingly interesting. But—if you will forgive a stranger—may I seize your arm, gaze into your eyes and plead with you to cast that thought from you with all your power?

It's not that it's totally untrue; we can find Death in almost anything, in fall, in drought, in animals, in our hearts, in the physical processes of our bodies, female *or* male. (Believe me.) Maybe what you say has appealed to the mythic terrors in some people in some places. But it is not a thought you should dwell on—forgive me again. Because to me it rang a terrifying bell. I have heard that same reasonable, intellectually excited tone in the writings of some few highly intellectualized Jewish writers who thought they could see why non-Jews could hate them, why they were peculiarly persecutable. Hateful. Exterminable—appropriate for extermination. *Yes.*

This took place during World War II, so you may have missed it. But those, Suzy, were men. You must realize that 99 percent of what you're dealing with here is far more easily explained as the self-hatred of the oppressed. It is a deeply pernicious thing, preventing friendship and solidarity. I have had a close look at it in some older women—my mother would vote for Midge Dector—and it wrings the heart. It has nothing to do with deathliness. In fact, I've known something of the same feeling in the wretched soldiers, the Tommies of Colonial Empire, who felt they merited, were suited for, death. *Men* felt this about themselves.

Of course I realize you are saying that it is only a belief, that bodily processes can scare both men and women into feelings that are deathly. And you are (to me) quite right in pointing out that the fear of death is a great unacknowledged participant at our mental table. But—

Maybe because I have just myself emerged from a bout of depression, Suzy, forgive my alarm. But I wish and hope that you would be very careful of this thought, and hold it at arm's length if you must hold it. Like a savage snake.

And there is the other side of the coin, the well-known life-giving aspect of female processes. I won't go on about this because I myself have some doubts about the Great Mother business, but you can't deny that the overall suggestion is at least as much life-promoting as deathly. Maybe the fact of birth itself is deathly—"My replacement has been born"—but I suspect the general feeling is more on the order of satisfaction in increase of life. My flocks, my herds, my children.

By the way, maybe a final word here on my excursion into trying to redefine the sexes so as to lump men and women into more inclusive categories. I am not, by the way, trying to "defend" motherhood as Chip says—except in the general sense that nurturant men and women are a bit less likely to blow up the world. But they may just as easily overproduce young and end us their own way. To me, each of my "sexes"—males and mothers—have their own pathology. What I was trying to ask, maybe buried in my own verbiage, was this:

Why are children raised? Or,

What is the personal, immediate, reward? Or,

What motive urges us and ensures that it will be carried out?

Every Human activity has some rewarding aspect, some goal, some good-feeling prize for which we do it. Eating *satisfies*, fucking *feels* good, walking out of the sun saves us from frying. But what is the orgasmic or homeostatic goal of mothering? In short, why does that rhesus or chimp or opossum—male or female—lug that youngster around? *Why?*

Are we, for God's sake, to fall back on that taboo of taboos, "maternal instinct"? Come on, I had hoped somebody would turn their jumbo brain to this problem and enlighten me.

But nobody did. Oh well.

But it is a mystery, if you compare it with any other animal activity. And nobody seems to care.

What I've been mulling over, partly in relation to men, is something about power. Authority. Dominance-submission structures, whether statewide or confined to a pair.

But first, a word. Chip, and to some extent Joanna, seemed to think I was "threatening" when I said that our liberties are precarious, that our enemies have the power. Now, it's true that when someone says "You're gonna be buried," it can be a covert threat. But the thing I left out, which let you think that, was that I see myself, very accurately, as one of the mob-ees. If the dark day arises when through war or famine or panic a nucleus of rednecks rises up and decides to subjugate everybody different, Tiptree will be right up there on the list, despite my WASP credentials. I have learned in a long life in organizations that I am a natural lynchee if I let down my guard an inch. I exude the same smell of subversion which those good ole boys can smell a mile away, like the way they used to hunt gays. It is something I shall never get rid of; one look at me and you just *know* I'm thinking something un-American. I myself don't know what it is, all I know is that when the gang closes ranks, I'm *out*. And I'm afraid I know where the real power is, despite the brave words. All I feel I can do about it is to hope that Der Tag cometh not—and keep my ammunition in a dry place. (Paranoia, anyone?)

Back in 1936 I saw a funny thing. In those days the main coast highway down California was a two-lane blacktop, which wound through a wide place in the woods called Los Gatos. (Yes.) Los Gatos consisted of a tarpaper whorehouse and a line of enormous lead slot machines, called the Wise Men. They were got up to caricature the Three Kings of Bethlehem. (Yes.) But the most impressive feature of Los Gatos was a huge wrought-iron sign stretching over the whole road, which said:

THE GENTILE WHITE MAN IS THE KING OF THE EARTH.

I never stopped to play the slot machines. Because I know this did not mean Me. Call me a wise man.

Well, much has happened to Los Gatos and to kings, but how deep has it gone in the Human heart, and how far are we from 1936? All that far? My.

Which brings me to kings. I've been reading a mess of Tolkien, C. S. Lewis, Wm. Morris, and T. H. White. And I find extraordinary the unspoken assumption that the greatest boon a people can achieve is—a king. The King Has Returned! Well, perhaps in the feudal state of things one can understand *some* of that. But I suspect it is a largely male contribution.

It led me on to think how women are supposed to be more dependent, to slide easily into and adjust gratefully to domination. Well, to the extent that many women don't care who decides what car he buys, and that some women are just plain younger and less experienced than the men they go out with, something like that might be visible sometimes. But who are the *real* dependents? Who insist on a captain, a boss, a Great Leader? Who have evolved lunatic systems of authoritarianism in every known activity except maybe solo farming? Who gratefully accept being beaten up and then faithfully follow the bully?

Three guesses. And don't say guppies.

Joanna, your piece inviting me out of the talk is exactly how I feel. My own concept of what I at least was supposed to do was simply to learn and perhaps talk enough to get knocked down, after which I felt acutely that I should fade away, but didn't know how to do. Without, you know, sounding like Gimme my wagon and I'll go home mad. So I just burbled on, figuring that you could ignore me as well as I could. (After all, one possible use for a male participant is just to remind everybody of *everything* there is to be mad at. All the small exquisite vilenesses I mean.)

I have to end with a note that may amuse some of you.

I thought of it while studying penile displays among the monkeys, and considering the activity known as "flashing" among Human males. The motive is an obscure and yet apparently potent one, which seems to have missed me or be buried deep. I kept wondering, what in hell is the threat value of a penile display? It's the most extraordinary *abstract* behavior, isn't it? And what is the magical value of the flasher's unzip? And this came to me:

A penis is an organ which is strong against the weak—and weak against the strong.

In other words, those men who have difficulty with impotence when trying to make love to "strong" women—really have love confused with penile threat.

I bet it's more common than we think.

—April 16, 1975

Quintana Roo: No Travelog This Trip

No travelog this trip; I'm disgusted. In five years this place has changed from a quiet Mexican wilderness to a roadstop full of campers. Well, not quite, but they're on the next ranch. Individually nice people most of them, but the impact is lousy. So this is now in the public domain, and the hell with it. Of course the Maya people are still here, still friendly and living their lives with equanimity; maybe all this is good for them in the long run. It's just that I preferred the empty starlit nights to Coleman lanterns, stereos blasting out pop, beer bottles, yelling infants, and divers shooting up the reefs. A beautiful big sea turtle washed ashore, still living despite a cruel shaft in its throat . . . well, Maya dinners.

I did have the chance to buy a marvelous little wet boat called a Royak from one Oregon man. Now I can go out diving somewhat more safely as befits my gray hairs. (You do *not* have to turn over in a Royak. That's a Kayak.) And he played chess. And he also had a book you might like to mention, the best travel thing I ever saw. For freaks who are serious. *The People's Guide to Mexico,* Franz, from John Muir Publications, PO Box 613, Santa Fe, NM 87501. ($4.35) It has stuff you will *not* find anywhere else, will save you $4.35 in the first day. Of course it's got a few things I'd disagree with, but what doesn't. It's huge, too.

Well, aside from the above complaints and items like that L'mus—remember the Maya puro?—is still making it with the redoubtable Gregoria, in fact they are building a house together in Libre Union. And has two younger brothers working here now; one of them (fifteen) just damn near totaled the truck, after rising meteorically to mechanic and electrician. He's still getting over the shock of finding out what can happen.

Aren't we all.

—February 1, 1975

Review of *The Lathe of Heaven*
by Ursula K. Le Guin

This was written for *Universe SF Review*, a tabloid-sized fanzine edited by Keith L. Justice and devoted almost exclusively to book reviews, and published in its fifth issue, September/October 1975.

Every so often a writer produces a book like a basilisk's egg, which contains within it a strangeness, a prefiguration, perhaps, of new and unsuspected form. Often this book goes quite unremarked: People find it puzzling or opaque. And if the author is at the same time producing a stream of admirable, innovative, and beautiful books in a more conventional vein, the baby basilisk may live eclipsed forever.

Take *The Lathe of Heaven*, by Ursula Le Guin, which came out about the same time as her widely and justifiably acclaimed *The Left Hand of Darkness*. *Lathe* received a few perfunctory notices, after which it apparently disappeared from general view.

But not from mine. Had Le Guin not written it I should have regarded her as admirable, innovative, etc., see above. But after first plowing into the first pulpy pages of the 1971 *Amazing*, in which *Lathe* came out, my toenails began to curl under and my spine hair stood up. These phenomena persisted to the very last line, where the Alien, watching like a sea creature from an aquarium, sees the hero and Heather disappearing into the mist.

Several years later I am still trying to figure out what it is about *Lathe* that bowls me out to its deep green sea. Well, to begin with, there is the extraordinary effect of central events unrolling in an almost undersea ambience of quietness, mystery, and precision. (This theme is heralded in the delighting opening paragraph about apparently irrelevant jellyfish—which turns out to be anything but irrelevant.) The events of the book are entirely "unofficial"—no galactic landing teams, diplomats, governmentese. Not even an official world-saver. In fact, the one nominal world-saver is among the most frightening villains in recent memory. The world *does* get saved—I think—but by something nameless, so vulnerable, Human, and mysterious that it would be pompous to call it "love." But it is entirely real.

The plot is simple—up to a point. A quiet nice little guy finds himself either crazy or in possession of a frightening paranormal talent. He takes his problem to a psychologist, who, though somewhat boisterous, seems also to be a decent type full of good aims and urges and energy. He is Doctor Haber, the aforesaid villain, and the unrolling of his monstrousness under the genial gabble is beautiful and horrible. (Dear God, the Habers I have met, the Haber in myself!) Haber is also—and this is important to the evaluation of Le Guin's work—her first major full-scale, tape-recorded confrontation with a contemporary 1975 Human monster. Those who consider that Le Guin writes only the dialogues of fantasy should listen in on Doctor Haber.

But Haber is more than a live character, he is a live problem. One of the things Le Guin is saying through his overactive mouth is that sheer energy and activity and even standard good will won't save the world. May be in fact disastrous. This is not a do-nothing message; the hero, though gentle, is active too. And so is Heather, the extraordinary female person with "French diseases of the soul." But their activity is of quite another order and is, in the end, saving. . . . One of the questions which has remained with me after reading *Lathe* is, how much of my own activity is Haberlike? Perhaps this will trouble you too. And so far as I know, it has not been raised elsewhere in SF.

But I don't want to leave you with the impression that this is merely a look-within book. No, no, no. Plenty of wild things going on, from the crumbling of Portland, Oregon, to the cryptic reappearance of the sprig of white heather. Aliens, too, lovely big green wet ones. (They may, however strike you as a weak element in the book, because one has become so convinced of Haber's ghastly triumph that any salvation is hard to believe. But as dei ex machina go, these are superior grade.) And there's humor: elegant laughs.

The best, though, I've saved for the last. It is so artfully incorporated that I had to check back to make sure I remembered right. I said the plot was simple—up to a point. The point comes when you realize that you are falling through quietly collapsing timeframes—*including the one you thought was base normal*. And as to what happened—or keeps happening—on that dreadful fourth of April, and which puts the final deep bass chords in the orchestration—I will leave you to discover. If you can.

The way Le Guin has worked this theme reminds me of the principle of Japanese art which teaches that one must never close a design so completely as to lock infinity out. Hold back from the completion that kills. (Which is, if anyone needs to be told, quite a different matter than leaving loose ends dangling. The infinity-chink is hard work.)

Now from all of this it is clear that an unbiased reviewer I am not. Unashamedly I reveled in *Lathe*, though not without seeing certain faults; you may too. But it is more than a revel, which is why the faults don't count. *Lathe* is a profoundly *different* book. My hunch-sense tells me that the strange eye staring out of this basilisk egg has a future. Le Guin's work is changing, developing: Something different is going to happen sometime soon. When it does, I think we may see the vectors leading back to the newnesses born or aborning in *Lathe*.

—May 26, 1975

How to Have an Absolutely Hilarious Heart Attack, or, So You Want to Get Sick in the Third World

The 1976 letter from Yucatan (actually written in Virginia) was something completely different, an account of Tiptree's hospitalization in Mexico. I rushed it into print, in *Khatru* 5 (April 1976), bumping the 1975 letter from Yucatan in the process. Alli made some slight revisions later, when it was published (as "Painwise in Yucatan") in an anthology edited by Michael Bishop (*Light Years and Dark*, Berkley 1984).

One beautiful moonlit night when soft clouds chased their shadows over the balmy Caribbean and iguanas rustled in the coco palms, something went wrong with my heart.

This was not its fault, as will appear below; for some days I had had a high fever and found myself unable to hold down food or water and ultimately unable to breathe.

At this point a gringo friend alerted the coco-ranch owner, who luckily had a small plane parked on a rough strip some miles away and a brother-in-law who is a Mexicana pilot with an instrument license. So, by some process which was never very clear to me, I found myself bundled in a truck, and subsequently we all set sail through the moonlight night across the Yucatan Channel to the island of Cozumel. Mexicans are particularly wonderful at organizing eleventh-hour rescue missions, which always save everything except when they don't. In this case, it all worked great.

It was very beautiful, the flight. Between gasps I verified that blind flying is indeed tricky. While we were in one cloud I became positive that we were banking 180 degrees and about to turn upside-down. Fortunately, the pilot was flying by his instruments rather than my hunches.

We came out of the cloud true and level and proceeded to sit down on the huge blue-lit Cozumel International Airport at midnight. The tower was supposed to be closed, but somebody—perhaps the janitor—had been persuaded to turn the lights on.

At one o'clock we found the Clinico National open for business; I recall chiefly the continuous barking of three small invisible dogs. The doctor was out on housecalls, it being better to have an emergency at 1:00 A.M. in tropical countries than at 1:00 P.M., when everybody disappears. Presently he arrived—Doctor Negrón, a three-foot fashion-plate with mustachios and a sharp white suit over a beautiful embroidered shirt. He had a fine old-fashioned authoritative manner. I got my lanky self onto a table for pregnant midgets, and experienced something you don't find in the U.S.A.—the extraordinary diagnostic skills of a good doctor with almost no instruments. He touched with firm listening hands, looked intently for unknown signs, asked strange questions. Under his hands I realized how great the old skills of Galen and Ostler must have been; here they had never died. It was impressive.

Above the incessant barking, he told my friends what was wrong. I had, it seems, a typhoid-type salmonella infection, I had pneumonia, and I was suffering from congestive heart-failure due to severe dehydration, the heart not being adapted to pump a thin trickle of sludge. Beyond that, I had a peculiar murmur and total arrhythmia of unknown origin—and that is all I'm going to say about my illness, because I want to tell you a couple of things that may be useful to you if you happen to get sick in a foreign land.

The first you know already: HAVE A FRIEND. A devoted friend who *speaks the language*. This point will get even clearer as we go on.

Now for the hospital and the next lesson: Bring your own drugs. The hospital may have none. So, with me playing the role of Frankenstein's monster before animation, we taxied about the darkened town collecting bottles of I.V. fluids, syringes of antibiotic, flasks of electrolytes, heart stimulants, etc. (Could I have done that alone? Don't laugh.)

And then we arrived at The Hospital. The new, beautiful beautiful hospital, an architectural delight of glass and tropical plantings, quietly but swiftly corroding in the salty air. The director met us, a young, fuzzy-chinned man, not one of your handsome Latinos but the charming type with sad, gay, all-knowing orangutan eyes.

He led us, laden with bottles and boxes, down great glassy moonlit corridors. We passed an impressive toilet and turned suddenly into a small concrete cubicle with a green terrazzo floor that was a work of art, inlaid with sliced pink conch shells: The Private Room. (There were two.) The Private Room was about eight feet by eight feet, mostly filled with one rusting bed and one enormous baby-cot stuffed with plastic pillows showing dressed-up pigs and chipmunks. One bare light bulb shone on the foot of the bed. I tottered to the lovely window: Air! But alas, the windows do not open; it would spoil the architectural effect. Somewhere a fan creaked, bringing in stale corridor miasmas.

I collapsed on the bed, and the director and the night nurse went to work on what became known as the great vein game. (The problem was that while I pride myself on having as many veins as anybody, they are all too crooked to put needles in; over the next three days it became very exciting to hunt for a new one when the I.V. needle fell out.) The night nurse was a severe, stylish young lady called Rosario, who wore a white turban on her head in increasingly chic folds as the night wore on. By morning she had added gold glasses and looked like something out of a Bonwit Teller ad. But she was all brains and heart.

Rosario and a Doctor José took turns puncturing me until they hit one that hurt like hell but worked. Then my friends left, Rosario showed me the call-bell, which didn't work, turned off the light bulb, and left too.

As the door closed, the most appalling noise I have ever heard broke loose and grew in volume until the beds rattled. It was the yelling of infants, about ten feet away, amplified to madness by the great glassy walls. It became apparent that I was in the only functioning ward, the one for maternities and sick babies, of which there are, alas, too many by far.

Now, an occasional infant cry is bearable, but this was not occasional; it lasted, that first time, twelve hours. And it was not ordinary; I quickly identified the leader as an infant vocal genius. Never do I expect to hear again such crescendo rage, such pure peals of aggression, varied with eerie train-whistle hoots, crow-chuckles, the yelps of slaughtered swine, the ravings of total paranoia. As the hours wore on I comforted myself with this: at least I was being subjected to what must be near the best of its kind. (I afterwards discovered that the poor little devil had

had a hernia operation and was, like me, on intravenous support. But unlike me he didn't appreciate it. By the third day, when they let him off the needle, his version of the affair must have been, Jesus, I had to yell like hell to get them to stop *that*; terrible job, almost didn't make it.)

Now, I'm not going to bore you with a play-by-play account, but only give you a few items from my blood-soaked notebook that might be of use to you someday.

First, the thing to remember is that hospitals in small foreign towns are for *treating your disease*, not for frivolous purposes like keeping you clean, comfortable, or even fed. For instance:

There is no food. As in jails, your family or friends are expected to feed you. This is hard on the nurses and doctors, too: They go downtown for long lunches. As one doctor sighed to me, "We have a kitchen with an icebox and stove, but we have no cook." Luckily, in my case, the I.V. contained glucose, and my friend brought me some juices and sour milk.

Bedding is a luxury. I had one (1) sheet, under me. When it got soaked with water and blood, I still got to keep it. Along about the end of Day 2 a lady called Esperanza offered to change it, but by that time I was attached to it—in more ways than one. There was, however, a blanket for one cold night, and a kind of bed cover made of something like dimity, which I wore like a poncho.

You get plenty of long, compassionate, doe-eyed gazes, soft touchings of delicate hands to your fevered brow, but no nursing care as we know it. You are not, for example, washed. In my case that meant lying in an increasing incrustation of sweat, leaked blood, etc., etc., not uncomfortable but somewhat hazardous as the exudates were still pretty infectious. There was of course no way of brushing my teeth, no toothbrush, toothpaste, razor, or so on. There was no soap, until on Day 3 Rosario stole me a cake from somewhere. There was, however, one (1) towel, which I became quite adept at washing with my teeth, my hands being occupied holding up the I.V.

Plumbing is a proud luxury. You get a toilet, but you do not get a toilet seat, and there is no guarantee that the water will flow *out* of anything, as I discovered while trying to repair a sanitary accident.

There are no hospital gowns. Somewhere in the madness I had latched on to an extra pair of shorts, but on account of the unremitting dysentery both soon became casualties. While waiting for them to dry (I finally gave this up), I managed to surround myself with the dimity thing, it being my strong feeling that beautiful young ladies, or young ladies, beautiful or otherwise, should not be subjected to my grizzled, uh, nudity. The result was something like those bad copies of Michelangelo where Saint Somebody is surrounded by a limp billow of cloud, the ultimate corner of which floats across his crotch. As I became wilder and bloodier-looking, the resemblance to the walking dead out of a medieval pest-house increased. About Day 3 a tiny girl named Carmita, taking pity on me, brought me a blue nylon nurse's dress for size 1; I got one arm into it, and it came nicely down to my navel, increasing the general hilarity, re: which see below.

Self-help is encouraged. In addition to being hooked into the I.V., I was sternly forbidden to get up; in short, I was to use the bedpan, which was pointed out to me. (It was a beautiful turquoise.) I used it—once. No one, you see, took it away or cleaned it. So as the dysentery bore down I got pretty expert at unhooking the I.V. bottle, carrying it over my head on a dead run into the bathroom, where I held it up with one hand, held the other hand down so it wouldn't clot, supported my improvised raiment with the third hand, and attended to the necessaries with the fourth. This was stimulating and prevented apathy.

Certain problems are beneath the medical staff. During the first night, it was discovered that the bed was wrong-way-round in the room, and broken besides, so that my legs were on the raised head-end. Every doctor who came in pointed out that heart patients' heads should be higher, not lower, than their feet. They then investigated the bed, ascertained that it was wrong-end to, and stood back, concluding triumphantly, "That can be moved." No one, however, moved it—until I nailed the last of the procession, leapt up, unhooked the I.V. bottle, and said, "You pull that end." Nothing loath, young Doctor Reyes grabbed his end, and told me to pull *my* end. I let the cloud go and, gasping and panting, managed to twist the rusted monster around.

Doctor Reyes solicitously rehooked me, warning me that it was extremely dangerous to *molestar* myself. We all regarded the new arrangement with great satisfaction, he cranking up my head several times. It also had the great advantage of placing the light bulb over my head, and the unbearable sunlight from the closed window on my feet instead of my eyes. I felt tremendous joy. Sometimes later I led an expedition to bring the night table out of the hallway and place it by my bed, so that my water glass would not be on the floor. (I was told to drink fluid continuously but given no water bottle.) It was in fact much more comfortable being able to breathe, and I date my renewed health to the successful Battle of the Bed.

Next: It is essential to learn names. Learn *everybody's* name, and quickly. I used my trusty little notebook. You see, you cannot count on any means of summoning help beyond the Human voice, and it makes a great deal of difference if you can call by name. I still start drowsily from sleep, howling, "ROSARIO! . . . CONSTANTIA! . . . DOCTOR MESQUITA!"

Be prepared for a *social* experience. Sickness, even dying, is not regarded as terribly unusual or interesting. You have to contribute, to inquire about everybody's children, miscarriages, losses, marital prospects, and status in the Oaxaca National Dance Festival. It also helps if you have something of value; for example, by a miracle I had grabbed my Collins phrasebook during the departure. (English phrase-books are much better than American ones.) The result was that I often had as many as three doctors roaming my tiny room at once, trying their tongues on "Li-ver," "Kit-nays," "El-boo," and so on. They always scrupulously returned it to me, perhaps because I never let my eyes off it. (This may or may not be unfair, but another word of caution is to keep anything precious attached to you, whether in bed or elsewhere.) But sociability, joy, hilarity—it breaks out every instant. The young director, demonstrating how badly my heart was doing, broke into a beautiful dance step to illustrate the rhythm, and exited dancing and singing, like a music-hall turn. The pictures I scribbled were lavishly praised and earned me some pineapple juice.

Most hilarious of all was the Medical History. On Day 2, the Direc-tor decided to start a file on me and regularize my status. This involved a three-hour inquisition, covering all illnesses of all known parents, in addition to the sixty years of my own mishaps. While doing it, he insisted on improving his English, and I believe to this day that my father is credited with a hysterectomy. By the time we got to my scars a whole roomful of people was in delighted attendance, roaring like mad. "Nineteen forty-four?" the Director shouted, pointing to my appendec-tomy, "nineteen sixty-six?" at the ulcer scar. "Forty-four!" we all cho-rused affirmatively. "Sixty-six!" This went on through my miscellaneous

VIEW
OF COZUMEL

"site of twin-motor seagull.

*
Venus,
Location
of
at dawn

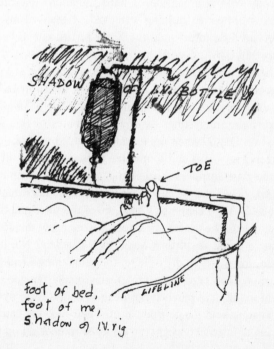

SHADOW OF I.V. BOTTLE

TOE

LIFELINE

Foot of bed,
foot of me,
shadow of I.V. rig

assortment of souvenirs, me trying in vain to control my poncho, my I.V., and my bellows of laughter. Everyone admired the Director's English, his memory, his acumen, my scars, one another, and everything else in sight; and the whole performance finished with a triumphant dancing sashay by the line of interns. I was left alone to chuckle until about midnight, when I was startled by a fantastic metal monster advancing into the room.

This turned out to be—wonder of wonders, in a hospital without an electrocardiograph—a portable x-ray machine, on which it was proposed to record my pneumonia. After a couple of false starts, the interns and the Director got the monster and its control cabinet into the tiny room, and I was directed to stand up facing the wall and clutch an x-ray plate. Each of the doctors instructed me separately, and then the Director said, "When I say, '*Tome aire*,' you must stand absolutely still without breathing." The only trouble was that all his assistants yelled "*Tome aire!*" at intervals in succession, leaving me turning purple, until with a magnificent display the thing went off like fireworks, spraying me and everybody with a broadside of hard radiation. (Needless to say, no shields or protective clothing were had.) I thanked my stars that my gonads had little future, and the X ray turned out to be a work of art that my dull U.S.A. doctor cherishes with some awe.

There remain a few oddments to communicate, such as that it is a very good idea to learn what medicines you are supposed to get so you can remind people, but this applies also to North American hospitals. Perhaps more interesting was the ten minutes of free strolling I was allowed on Day 2, when my muscles cramped up from confinement. I resurrected my pants and toured the imposing wards, all clearly visible from the glass corridors. Little knots of family surrounded every occupied bed. (That was when I learned about my nocturnal virtuoso, the twelve-inch Pedro Domingo Camal, he of the voice and the hernia.) On the side where the examination rooms were I saw the door sign "Rehydration." I asked about this; was it for alcoholics? No. It was for what so many, many babies die of here, the same thing I had had a taste of: desiccation. The poor little things are usually far gone when they're brought in, all fluid parched out of their bodies from dysentery, vomiting, sweating, and the constant heat. Their blood is barely liquid; they are dying of internal drought. So a special room is set up to rush liquids into them. Judging from the way they fixed me, they must succeed often. But I tend to fear it must leave damage.

I got back to my room just as it was being pungently sprayed, for the umpteenth time, for fleas. Usually they sprayed me too.

And now I'll leave you with a couple of tiny glimpses which may stay with me longer than all the rest. One day while something medically important was happening in my crowded room, the I.V. acted up again and probably the most beautiful girl I've seen in years stepped forward to fix it. Her eyes were upraised, timing the drops by a tiny watch on her immaculate white-clad arm. I heard a whisper, coming from a young doctor leaning on my pillow: Doctor Aurelio Tlacuac Flores, the poet, was whispering just loud enough for her to hear. *"Maria?"*

Her lips never moved, nor her long eyelashes, but she breathed back with infinite distance, *"Marie."*

Teasingly, almost too faint to hear, he tried again. *"Marianne?"*

The drops fell, her gaze never wavered, but there floated back the firm correction: *"Marie."*

"Marie," he echoed tenderly, and then in a voice so quiet I could barely make it out inches from my ear, he sang a little Spanish tune. *"Marie, Oh I wonder what you are, I wonder what passes with you."*

Later, much later I shared my orange juice with Marie, the darling of his love whispers. She told me of the six children she had borne, four of whom had died. She was twenty-three and she gave me an exact clinical description of the cause of death of each one, including the twins.

My last memory of the Centro de Salud of Cozumel is also of a woman, a middle-aged lady of great efficacy named Isobel. On the thousand-year-old walls of Bonampak in southern Yucatan is a mural depicting a group of victorious noble Mayas watching the losers being tortured by having, among other things, their fingernails torn out with pliers. The painting is fresh and brilliant, and among the noble group is a lady of high rank, wearing a folded white robe and many ornaments. She gazes down impassively, satisfied, her beaked face and slant eyes a mask of alien antiquity. But that face lives today. With just those features and just that expression did Nurse Isobella Constantia fold her hands upon her snowy stomach and survey my saved life and my dirty bed.

—February 26, 1976

THE FIRST DOMINO

Dear Jeff,

Whew.

Mother died last week, leaving me with a new dark strange place in the heart, and flashes of a lively, beautiful, intelligent, adventurous red-haired young woman whom I had once known. We were close, even through those godawful years at the end after Father went, when I could barely stand to look upon the wreckage. "Close" in the sense of empathy; I respected and understood her generous heart and witty mind. And her vulnerability. To give you an idea, she left her instructions on the disposal of her body—cheap and fast—in a very funny light verse.

She left me also with the most horrendous practical problem of properly disposing of the ninety-four years of accumulated memorabilia of Africa, Old Chicago, assorted literary figures, endless treasures all mixed in with junk—letters from Carl Sandburg mixed in with grocery lists, blank stationery, birthday cards from once-eminences, lace panties, .38-caliber automatics, irreplaceable diaries of treks through Africa, irreplaceable diaries of her life as a war correspondent (all under her writing name), manuscripts, socks to be mended, mementoes of the visit of the French Navy to Douala in 1935, correspondence with heads of state, unpublished poetry, old curtains, two thousand African moleskins each as big as a postage stamp, unsent letters to me, interminable bequests and codicils, Japanese cloth of gold, more socks to be mended, grocery lists, blank stationery, saved envelopes with obsolete stamps—three rooms full of filing cabinets, one hall, and three storerooms (one "secret")—in all twenty-six rooms of *stuff*. Oh, I forgot paintings. And in the middle of it all stands the figure of the Executor, an aged doddering Legal Eminence whom Mother regarded as a young man (he's eighty-three) who has to be shown copies of every arrangement in writing in triplicate, and raises objections such as wanting the appraiser's— *one* of the appraisers—curriculum vitae and credentials. Needless to say, said appraiser is out of town and has to be tracked down by long distance. In fact the whole thing is being conducted by long distance; I was on the phone *four hours straight* Friday—pause for writing confirming letters in triplicate—then another *two hours* dealing with financial matters. Luckily Mother died well, in her own home, among her things, independent to the last, but it was a close thing financially. That costs $30,000 a year, and has been going on. I figured that was what Father had accumulated the cash for, and she ran out just before her capital did. (Before Medicare it cost $50,000 a year for two years just to care for Father, without the 'round-the-clock nursing Mother needed.) Yesterday was easy, only two hours on the phone, but this time with the secretary whose aim is to break me down by reading letters to me she has found going through Mother's papers. I didn't let her know she succeeded. Also notifying Mother's old friends, who have to be told it all in excruciating detail; more breakdown. I now have two museums and two historical archives fighting over the spoils, all by long distance, plus innumerable friends going in to choose mementoes Mother left notes about, plus—oh, Jeff, it's a lesson. *Never* be the last of a line, and never *accumulate*.

And I still haven't dealt with her personal effects, clothes, furniture, etc. (twenty-six rooms full), all of which bother the hell out of me. They lived in that place—Father built the building and they took the whole top and made the first roof garden in Chicago—for sixty-four years. I was born in that fucking bed, the books (ten thousand) were my earliest companions, I know every chip on every chair leg and every ravel in every rug. And I have to go back and look before the movers roll in, because some of the fucking stuff is valuable. So you can see my head feels like the Bulgarian Tank Corps is holding maneuvers in it.

If you use this, it'll help me by explaining why Tiptree isn't writing anything any more for a while . . . maybe it'll also be instructive, to somebody. You should keep in the money part; people should know what it costs to die in their own beds at age ninety-four. I intend to die alone on the VA wards, in case something overtakes me before I can get the trigger pulled. Leaving *nothing*.

Just as soon as the last essential paper is signed, I intend to take off—on the urgent advice of my doctor—for parts unreachable by mail. You know where. What is laughingly known as my other or real-life work can go screw it, I am not irreplaceable. I better not be.

If you have aging parents you will come to bless Medicare from the bottom of your heart. Jesus God, without it I shudder to think. And so will you.

Well, this is a weird letter.

Let me know how life goes with you, Jeff, old friend. Best to Ann.

As ever, yrs

Tip

—November 8, 1976

EVERYTHING BUT THE SIGNATURE IS ME

The previous letter, as it says, was sent to me for publication, but I didn't want to publish it. I thought it contained too much personal information, that it was a road map to a newspaper obituary. That it would blow Tiptree's cover.

After writing this to Tip, and worrying over the problem for a while, I decided to look for the obituary myself. If I found it, no harm would be done. I wouldn't tell anyone I found it; I just wouldn't run the letter. If I *couldn't* find it, it would be safe to publish. And what difference did it make what Tiptree's real name was, anyway? I didn't care. (I thought.)

In the library, the very first Chicago paper I pulled (the *Tribune* for October 28, 1976) contained an obituary entitled "Explorer's last right—no rites." There were some discrepancies with the letter (the paper said she was ninety-two, and had died in a hospital), but there could be no doubt that Mary Hastings Bradley was James Tiptree's mother.

Mary Hastings Bradley was survived by . . . one daughter.

Some people had suggested that Tiptree might be a woman, but different people were suggesting that Tiptree was many different kinds of people. (It was mostly *what if*: What if Tiptree were a woman? What if Tiptree were a spy?) I don't think many of Tiptree's correspondents thought she was a woman, because we had to make our mental images of Tip—"Uncle" Tip, as he referred to himself—to use when reading the letters. (I still "hear" the male Tiptree voice when I reread the early letters, whereas you probably hear a female voice throughout.)

I was stunned.

To make matters worse, when I got home that evening, there was a postcard from a friend asking, "Is it true that James Tiptree is Alice Sheldon?" I didn't know what to say.

So, despite my original intentions, I wrote to Tip and described everything I had done, and what I had found, and how bewildered I was. I ended: "This is not a demand for information. A postcard saying merely 'Later' will not be the ending of a friendship. But one thing to definitely consider: I am going to be getting questions, and whatever you choose to disclose or withhold from me, please pass along the Party Line that I'm supposed to tell others."

After all my years of not prying into Tiptree's background, and trying to convince others not to, I was the one to force Alice Sheldon out of hiding. (Though obviously, as shown by the postcard, I wasn't the first person who had found the death notice.)

Alli wrote to me, introducing herself, and asking that things be kept quiet for a while. She wrote to a number of her other correspondents, too, some of whom could keep secrets better than others. Soon, Tiptree's identity was public knowledge.

"Everything but the Signature Is Me" was compiled from several letters to me, mostly from the first Alli Sheldon one and from a long one written in Yucatan specifically designed for publication. It was published in *Khatru* 7 (February 1978).

While preparing this book manuscript, I went through all the letters again and recompiled the article, and it's a little bit longer. (This is like remastering an old record album for compact disc.) There's nothing notable about the "new" material, but the article is now a little closer to the original letters.

"The First Domino" was also in *Khatru* 7, embedded in my article "The Short, Happy Life of James Tiptree, Jr."—which had first appeared in the Program Book of SunCon, the 35th World Science Fiction Convention, Labor Day Weekend 1977.

How great. At last it's out, and you're the first to know, as I promised long ago you would—although I didn't expect it to happen through your own initiative. But at least you're the first I can write to in my own persona. Bob Mills has an envelope in his safe "To Be Opened If Tiptree Dies" giving an outline of the facts, but he hasn't opened it. (I'm morally sure.)

Yeah. Alice Sheldon. Five-feet-eight, sixty-one years, remains of a good-looking girl vaguely visible, grins a lot in a depressed way, very active in spurts. Also, Raccoona.

I live in a kind of big wooden box in the woods like an adult playpen, full of slightly mangy plants, fireplace, minimal old "modern teak" furniture strewn with papers, hobbies, unidentifiable and unfileable objects; the toolroom opens off the bedroom, there are six doors to the outside, and it's colder than a brass monkey's brains in winter, except when the sun comes out and shoots through all the glass skylights. We've added on porches (which turned into libraries), other excrescences—as somebody said, all it needs is a windmill on top. Not so ridiculous now. Ting (short for Huntington, my *very nice* more aged husband of thirty years who doesn't read what I write but is happy I'm having fun) used to raise thousands of orchids before he retired and started traveling; he gave them to the nation, i.e., the National Botanic Gardens, who wanted hybrids. So now in the middle of the living room sticks this big untended greenhouse I am supposed to be growing things in. What I'm growing is mealy bugs—*must* get at it. We built the place very modestly in 1959, when it was all woods here. Now houses, subdivisions, are creeping toward us. No more stags on the lawn—real ones. But lots of raccoons. Still private enough so you can sneak out and get the mail or slip a cookie to a raccoon in the buff if you want to.

If you'd asked me any time from age three to twenty-six, I'd have told you, "I'm a painter." (Note, not "artist"—painter. Snobbism there.) And I was. Oh my, did I draw, sketch, model, smear oils, build gesso, paint—paint—paint. (Age three I drew pictures of our bulldog, with lollipop legs.) I worked daily, whether I was supposed to be listening to lectures on Chateaubriand, whether my then-husband was shooting at me (he was a beautiful alcoholic poet), whether the sheriff was carrying our furniture out, whether Father was having a heart attack, whatever. And I wasn't too bad; I illustrated a couple of books in my early teens, I had a one-man show at sixteen, I exhibited in the All-American then at the Corcoran—and the painting, which used me as model, sold. Somewhere my naked form is hanging in a bedroom in North Carolina, if it hasn't been junked. I bought a shotgun, a Fox C-E double-barrel 12-gauge full choke, with the money. (Those were the three years when I was a crazy duck hunter, before I shot one too many cripples and gave it up never to kill another living thing, bugs excluded.) I believe the Fox is now far more valuable than anything I ever did.

The trouble was, you see, I was just good enough to understand the difference between my talent and that rare thing, *real* ability. It was as though I had climbed the foothills high enough to see the snow-clad peaks beyond, which I could never scale. This doesn't stop some people; it did me. What's the use of adding to the world's scrap heap? The reason people thought me innovative was that I was good enough to steal mannerisms and tricks they had never climbed high enough to study. But *I* knew where it was coming from.

And then came the dreadful steady unstoppable rise of Hitler—a great spreading black loin chop on the map—and I found out something else. There are painters who go on painting when a million voices are screaming in terminal agonies. And there are those who feel they have to Do Something about it, however little.

So I came back to Chicago—I'd been living in San Angel, near Mexico City, mucking around on the fringes of the Diego Rivera/Orozco/Siqueres crowd—and took a job as the *Chicago Sun's* first art editor, while waiting for the Army to open female enlistments. (I wasn't one of the famous first group of female potential officers; for some reason it was important to me to go in as an ordinary G.I. with *women officers*.) Besides, I was having a great time discovering that Chicago was full of artists, who had to exhibit in NYC before they could sell to their Chicago neighbors. Chicago then had two art critics; one was a lethal, totally politicized Marxist (female), and the other was an elderly gent who knew art had died with Cezanne, and whose feet hurt. So when people sent works to Chicago shows they didn't get reviewed—or it was worse when they did. Anyway, I rooted out about forty producing groups, started what was then a new thing, a *New Yorker*-type calendar, told people interesting things to look for in shows. (One Art Institute guard, coping with a host of people with my "guide" clipped out, demanding to know which was the east room, asked me, "Did *you* do this?" Nobody had asked him anything but "Where is the toilet?" for twenty years.)

But this was all waiting, while the paper shortage cut me from a page to a half and then to a quarter. And then the great day came, and I trotted down to U.S. Army Recruitment Station Number 27 in three-inch heels and my little chartreuse crepe-de-chine designer thing by Claire somebody, and my pale fox fur jacket, and found a drunken second lieutenant with his feet on the desk. And when I said I wished to enlist in the Army, he caught an imaginary fly and said, "Ah, hell, you don't want to go in *that* goddamn thing." And I said if it was all the same to him, I did. And so—but that's another, five-year-long, fairly hilarious story.

People tell me I've had an exciting or glamorous or whatnot life; it didn't feel like much but work and a few adventures. A few, *ah oui . . .* All I write is really from life, even that crazy duck-shooting boy breaking the ice naked at ten degrees below zero on the Apache reservation was me, once ("Her Smoke Rose Up Forever").

As to science fiction: Well, you see, I had all these uncles, who are no relation at all, but merely stray or bereaved or otherwise unhappy bachelors whom my parents adopted in the course of their wanderings. (That sort of thing happened much more in the old, old days. The fact that Father was an intensely lovable man of bewildering varied capabilities, and that Mother was a blazing-blue-eyed redhead of great literacy and gaiety didn't hurt, of course; and in their odd way they were both secretly lonesome—having nothing but peculiar me for family.) This particular uncle was what used to be called a Boston Brahmin, dean of a major law school and author of a text on torts so densely horrible that I still meet lawyers who shudder at its name. In short, he was dignified and respectable to an extreme—on the surface, as it turned out.

The summer when I was nine we were up in the woods of Wisconsin as usual, and Uncle Harry returned from an expedition to the metropolis of one thousand souls thirty miles away with his usual collection of *The New York Times, The Kenyon Review,* etc. (There was a funny little bookshop-hole there that ordered things for you.) Out of his bundle slipped a seven-by-nine magazine with a wonderful cover depicting, if I recollect, a large green octopus removing a young lady's golden brassiere. We all stared. The title was *Weird Tales.*

"Ah," said Uncle Harry. "Oh. Oh yes. I, ah, picked this up for the child."

"Uncle Harry," I said, my eyes bulging, "*I* am the child. May I have it, please?"

"Uh," said Uncle Harry. And, slowly, handed it over.

And so it all began. He would slip them to me and I would slip them back to him. Lovecraft—Oh, God. And more and more and more; we soon discovered *Amazing* and *Wonder Stories* and others that are long forgotten. We never discussed them; it was just Our Secret. But I'll tell you one thing: You haven't read fantasy or SF unless you have retired, with a single candle, to your lonely little cabin in the woods, far from the gaslights of the adult world and set your candle stub up in a brass basin and huddled under about sixteen quilts—the nights were cold and drafty, the candlelight jumped and guttered, shadows everywhere. And then, just as you get to where the nameless *Thing* starts to emerge, the last shred of candle gutters out, leaving you in the dark forest. And a screech owl, who has silently taken up position on the roof above, lets loose with a nerve-curdling shriek.

That's Tales of Wonder as they should be read, man.

Well, of course I was hooked, from then on, permanently. By the time World War II came along, I had about 1300 mags and paperbacks stacked in that cabin alone. (I gave them all to the county library, despite the sneers of the librarian, who doubtless used them for doorstops. Alas, alas; rubies, pearls, emeralds gone to the gravel crusher.)

With the war came a break, after which I started all over again (having discovered the magic of subscriptions). I now have about forty running feet of them double-stacked, plus head-high shelves bulging in all bathrooms, plus miscellaneous deposits. In addition, there's another forty feet of philosophy and politics and history, sixty feet of my old professional specialty (experimental psychology), twenty feet of math, astronomy, and miscellaneous, twenty feet of fiction by dead authors and another twenty of same by live ones (horrible how quickly one seems to have to shift them), twenty feet of women's studies and related material, and twenty feet of mostly poetry. And *something* has got to give. (Oh well, who needs *Das Kapital* anyway?)

The painful part of starting like that is that you read, read, read—without, in most cases, noticing dull stuff like the author's name. Until I started to write it myself, of course; then names become acutely important. But I am still in the embarrassing position of not knowing who wrote some fantastic scene that is forever engraved on my liver. And then finding out, Oh my God, yes of course—*he* or *she* did that! (Worse yet, finding it out in his or her presence, whether in the flesh or in one of my Victorian correspondences.)

Now maybe this is the best place to lay to rest one last ghost—the business of the anonymity and the male pseudonym. First, the important part: *Everything I've ever told you or anyone else is true,* with one exception. David Gerrold came looking for me and I told him he was on a different street. If he'd waited before ringing the bell he would have seen through the glass a solitary figure staring at a *Star Trek* rerun in the dark, and I'm sure the jig would have been up. Other than that I have never told a lie or modulated my natural voice—I was very careful about pronouns, things like "child" instead of "boy," etc., etc. But it wasn't calculated. (I'm lousy at that.) All my letters have been just first draft typed as fast as I can go with my one finger. I can't help what people think sounds male or female.

You see, when I started, I was in rather a stuffy job atmosphere. A university. And I was something of a maverick; I kept having ideas that didn't jibe with the official academic outlook at my department. And when I started my own research it got worse. ("In this department we do feel rather strongly that recent PhDs do best when their work fits in with or amplifies some of the ongoing lines of research here.") Well, I wasn't about to fit in with or amplify anybody else's line; I had my own long-held desires, and I kept citing research nobody else had read, or had read and dismissed, and with great pain and struggle I set off on a totally independent tack, which had the ill grace, after four agonizing years, to pay off. (I still keep getting requests for it from obscure European universities, or behind the Iron Curtain.) With this background, the news that I was writing—as I said in that long-ago interview—*science fiction* would have destroyed my last shreds of respectability and relegated me to the freak department, possibly even to the freak-whose-grant-funds-should-be-stopped division; those familiar with older academe will get the picture. Anonymity seemed highly desirable. The name "Tiptree" started by seeing it on a can of marmalade in the Giant; I was looking for a forgettable name so editors wouldn't remember rejecting my manuscripts. The "James" was one more bit of cover—and my husband threw in "Jr." for whimsy's sake. I was shocked when the stories all sold and I was stuck with the name. What started as a prank dreamed its way into reality.

You have to realize, this never was run as a real clandestine operation with cutouts and drops and sanitizing and so on. The only "assets" were one P.O. box, a little luck, and the delicacy and decency of some people who decided not to pry. Namely and chiefly one Jeff Smith.

When you wrote asking for the *Phantasmicom* interview was the first time I was approached personally by anyone, and I told myself, Dammit, say no. But then this business of really loving the SF world and wanting to say so welled up, and I thought I could kind of race over the bio bit without telling lies and start waving Hello. You'll note what I put in there about masks . . . So that's how it all started.

Then, from about the second year, when things began to get serious, "James" started to feel more and more constrictive. It was as if there were things I wanted to write as me, or at least a woman. (I still don't know exactly what they are, that's the odd part.) Meanwhile Tiptree kept taking on a stronger and stronger life of his own; if I were superstitious I'd say Something was waiting for incarnation there in the Giant Foods import section . . . maybe I do anyway. This voice would speak up from behind my pancreas somewhere. *He* insisted on the nickname, he would not be "Jim." And as to "Uncle" Tip—maybe I'm a natural uncle. See, I have no family, nobody ever called me Sis or Mom or even Aunt Alice.

And his persona wasn't too constricting; I wrote as me. Maybe my peculiar upbringing—where values like Don't-be-a-coward and Achieve! and Find-out-how-it-works and Fight-on-the-underdog's-side were stamped in before they got to the You're-a-young-lady stuff (which was awful)—maybe this resulted in a large part of me being kind of a generalized Human being rather than specifically female. (I am very pro-woman, though; once when dabbling in NY politics I had the opportunity to personally thank one of the original suffragettes, then a frail but vital eighty, for the privilege of the vote. It was a beautiful moment.) But still I wanted to write as a woman. By this point it became obvious that killing Tiptree off, say by drowning him out on the reef here, wasn't going to be that simple. He—we—had all these friends, see. So all I did was rather feebly set up Raccoona Sheldon with a Wisconsin P.O. box and bank, and I confess to giving her some of Tip's weaker tales to peddle. (Except for the one called "Your Faces, O My Sisters! Your Faces Filled of Light!" in the anthology *Aurora* by McIntyre and Anderson. Nobody much mentions that one, but I consider it as good as I can do.) Anyway, the upshot of all this was that where I lived I wasn't, and I didn't live where I was, and things were reaching some kind of crescendo of confusion. Frankly, I had no real plan. So I was really relieved as well as traumatized to have Mother's ghost do Tiptree in. But it left me with an extraordinary eerie empty feeling for a while; maybe still does.

One problem caused by having a male pseudonym was that there was the desire to rush (by mail) up to many female writers and give them a straight sisterly hug. (And to some male writers, too; especially those I knew were feeling down. I guess I wrote some fairly peculiar letters here and there.) Another problem that may seem trivial, wasn't to me; people kept saying how lifelike my female characters were, while all the time I was perishing to find out if the *male* characters were living!

Things like being hooted at in the Women in SF Symposium really didn't bother me at all, because I doubtless would have done the same myself. And also I am used to being hooted at for unpopular ideas—the struggle I mentioned in the university was just one of a lifelong series. And then, too, I'm a feminist of a far earlier vintage, where we worked through a lot of the first stages all by our lonesomes. There are stages in all revolutions of consciousness where certain things are unsayable, because they sound too much like the enemy's line. Then after some years, when everybody is feeling more secure about unity on the facts and the wrongs, those "unsayable" things can be looked at objectively again, and new insight gained. I refer, of course, to my real interest in why people are mothers. (I just saw an article in *Psychology Today* that triumphantly claims that Fathers Do It Too—but turns out on reading the data that what they "do" is quite different. They play with baby; mother takes care of it.) There were, of course, a lot more things I felt like saying in the Symposium, but I thought that one was safe for Tip. As indeed it was—typical "male" nonsense.

I've been amazed at the warm, kind, friendly reaction I've been getting, even from the most unlikely people. I worried deeply about what had unwittingly become a major deception. I wrote at once to everyone I could think of who might feel I'd let them go out on a cracked limb. They couldn't have been nicer. If someone does feel griped, they haven't gotten it to me. The only problem seems to be that now I'm expected to produce something somehow grander, more insightful, more "real." Well, if I knew how, I would—the trouble is that the Tip did all I could in that line. If there is something—other than "Sisters"—which is going to burst forth from my liberated gonads, it hasn't peeped yet. In fact, I may be written out for a while. With each story I dug deeper and deeper into more emo-

314 • JAMES TIPTREE, JR.

tional stuff, and some of it started to hurt pretty bad. "Slow Music" reads like a musical fadeout or coda to Tiptree's group of work.

Now, I've got one more thing to add to this terrible monologue. In a funny way, I found that as Tip I could be useful to my fellow female writers. There were times when Tiptree (male) queried anthology editors on why nothing from this or that female writer was being used. And as an old gent I may have been more helpful to sisters who were fighting depression than another woman could. They had to brace up and respond to my courtly compliments—Tip was quite a flirt—and they knew somebody quite different valued them. Whereas just another woman coming in with sympathy and admiration tends to dissolve in a mutual embrace of woe.

Now, adieu, dear Jeff and Ann—and remember to keep this in the usual baggie. The cucarachas here have now evolved to the point where when you step on one it carries you four feet before you can get off. Outside the Caribbean is in roaring high tide, storms are chasing themselves overhead, the palm trees lit up olive and white by great bursts of lighting. And the generator is, as usual, failing. May you never be the same.

—compiled from letters between November 23, 1976,
and November 24, 1977

THE LUCKY ONES

One of the things Alli Sheldon could share with her friends that James Tiptree couldn't was her first published story, which had been in *The New Yorker* (November 16, 1946) under the name Alice Bradley. She complained that "it was astounding how they edited me into *New Yorker*ese," but since her manuscript no longer exists, all we have is the *New Yorker*ese version. She sent me the story on December 10, 1976, with the following letter:

> Hey, maybe you'd like to see an Army-life story published in *The New Yorker* in 1945 or 6 by Alice Bradley? Very heart-rending, plus slightly funny. All ABS ever wrote except before WW II when I was art editor on the *Chicago Sun*.
>
> "The Lucky Ones" was written at a time when our treatment of the D.P.s—the hordes of miserable people wrenched from their homelands by the Nazis—was a Cause, you know, like Help the Biafrans, only it was a USA problem, what *we* were doing or not doing. (They cut out the part about the girls having been used as ten-year-old "service facilities" for the German troops.) I didn't write it because I thought I was a writer, but to try and tell people what "D.P." really meant. Jesus, Jeff, it was awful. And one could do so little. We ended by forcibly shipping loads of them back to the Soviets, who promptly shot them . . . after extracting all possible work. (Because they had been contaminated by seeing the free world, namely us, see.)
>
> Also I put in a funny, true part about my nearly giving my brandnew husband a black eye by saluting in alarm whenever he emerged from dressing in the bathroom. Daytimes, I was supposed to go through ten people to get to see him. My relation with him has always given me a wondrous view of what goes on at the top, or "policy-

making" levels, while I knew from experience what goes on at the bottom, or policy-carrying-out-more-or-less levels.

I went to Germany last year in late September, with several thousand other American soldiers, including my husband, a colonel, who moved in a higher sphere than mine. We all belonged to a big theatre headquarters which was transferred from France to form a permanent occupational command in the American Zone. Before we left France, I had just enough Wac points to go home and my husband had an astronomical total of points, but I was anxious to finish a report I had been working on for some time and he wanted to see his section through a reorganization crisis. So we elected to go to Germany for a short time. In view of our imminent return home, I was granted permission to live with him in a small senior officers' billet in the town we were moving to, along with five or six other colonels from the headquarters.

The prospect intimidated me, as I was a very recent captain, with a marked arm reflex to live colonels (I never did get used to my husband in full regalia). However, I was somewhat comforted when I learned that there would be one other captain living there, as billeting officer. This was Captain Providence, a bouncing young man who spoke rapid-fire, emotional German, which his war assignments had given him plenty of opportunity to perfect. He turned out to be invaluable, because I was unable to wrench a German verb out of the infinitive, and my husband spoke a form of German good only for indicating desired services and making slow, stately comments on the scenery.

The headquarters town had been a solidly prosperous German spa. It contained what had been only third-class air objectives, but it had had the misfortune to receive one heavy going-over near the end of the war, which had reduced about a third of it to ruins. The civilian casualties, however, had been relatively light.

On the afternoon the colonel and I drove in from France, the last of the headquarters convoys were still rumbling into town. The German winter was moving in, too, with cold, continuous rain. It was a depressing scene. The wet streets were hung with mist and choked with rubble in many places. Low clouds slid through the blackened holes in the roof-less shells of gutted buildings. Most of the homes could be described as substantial, but none of them could be called gracious. They were of a somehow monstrous cubic shape and loaded with ornaments—plaster eagles, lion gate posts, fake caryatids, and iron cupids relieving them-selves in fountains. The undamaged houses exhaled an air of sullen scul-leries and apoplectic parlors. The damaged ones were grotesque without being pathetic.

We passed a small park containing a battered statue of Bismarck, climbed the hill in back of the town where the officers' billet area was, and drew up at last in front of our house. It belonged to one Herr Dok-tor Groenecke, whose name plate was on the garden wall. The house was dun-colored, square, and high, and had two turrets.

At the top of the front steps were two doors side by side, one for the family and one for the servants. We entered through the family's door, which was open, and found ourselves in a cheerless vestibule lined with gray tile. From a bead-curtained archway on one side came damp-dishcloth smells and *gemütlich* laughter. We walked on into the dimness of a large, high-ceilinged living room, illuminated by a cold yellow light from overhead. I looked up, and involuntarily ducked from under a menacing ebony chandelier as big as a summerhouse and set with imi-tation candles. The furniture was ponderous and upholstered in green. On the walls I could make out several acres of oil paintings in heavy gilt frames.

Over in a corner of the room, a huge chair began to move. At first, I could not see what was behind it, then it turned and revealed a small girl, who was sitting on the floor and pushing with her back. She saw us, gasped, got up, tried to curtsy and almost fell over, and then grabbed up a mop and pail and fled past us out of the room. She was blond, about the size of an American fourteen-year-old, with a curiously mis-shapen little figure. Her nose and cheeks were bright pink and her stock-ings were torn. As she passed me, I smelled perspiration.

We hallooed. Captain Providence rushed in, followed by a pallid lit-tle man with a face like an old jockey's. The latter, the captain explained, was the German houseman furnished by the Military Government. He took our bags eagerly and started with us upstairs to the two rooms we were to live in.

In the upper hallway, under a vast chromo of heroic ducks in a purple pond, a door stood open, and on each side of it crouched a small, dark-haired girl. They were polishing the big brass knobs and softly humming a song in unison. One was wearing a nondescript blue dress, the other a skirt and torn black sweater. When they saw us, the humming stopped and they bent their heads and polished faster. We continued past them into our quarters.

The other colonels were already in the house, and we joined them at dinner around a long table set with Dr. Groenecke's elaborate china. During the meal, Captain Providence briefed my husband and me on the servants, and his observations were later amplified by my own.

Fritz, the little man who had taken our bags, had been a sergeant in a German artillery unit that had spent two winters in Russia. Then there were Bubi, a beardless, blond table waiter, also lately of the Wehrmacht and once a steward on the *Europa*; a grim gardener, paid by Groenecke; a fat female cook, whose soups invariably had half an inch of grease on top; a tanned, sinuous pantry girl, who complained that our G.I.s were fresh; several unknown and smelly entities who came in to wash dishes; and an old, thin-faced German woman, who did the laundry. She acted very sad and martyred, and talked in a sharp, obsequious whine, complaining to anyone who would listen that she had never done any menial work before and that she had had six servants herself. She did not mention that she had been quite cordial to the local Nazis.

Besides this constellation of the defeated, there were the three little girls my husband and I had seen. They were D.P.s—Displaced Persons—assigned by the Military Government to work in the house. Their names were Tilli, Hanni, and Sophie. They cleaned the whole house from top to bottom every day, in the old-fashioned manner—on their knees, with big brushes in their small, rough hands. They were from Poland, and only Hanni spoke German. Sophie, the little blonde we had seen downstairs, did not speak even ordinary Polish but a dialect known only to Tilli. They lived over our garage, in what had been a storeroom. The Germans went home every night, because they were not allowed to sleep in the area.

For the next few days, my husband and I were very busy at our respective jobs in the headquarters and were seldom at home. But we did catch occasional glimpses of the small D.P.s, trooping through the dark passageways with great stacks of bedding, swabbing down the stone steps, rolling up the vast carpets to make an island of furniture in the middle of a room while they cleaned the floors, or continuing the interminable polishing of the brassware—always humming a little Polish song. I asked Captain Providence to find out more about them. How old were they? Why were they in Germany? He gave me that I-hope-you're-not-going-to-cause-trouble look which women in the Army get to know well, but a few evenings later he came upstairs with a full account.

The oldest, Tilli, was twenty-two, the youngest nineteen. That was Sophie, who spoke only the dialect. The Germans had taken them away from their homes shortly after the fall of Poland. Tilli came from Lwów, Hanni from some town whose name I couldn't catch, and Sophie from the country south of Warsaw. Sophie had seen her mother and father killed in their garden when she was taken. Tilli's mother was Jewish; both her parents had been taken away and she had not heard of them since. Hanni's mother was a widow, and very old; she had not been molested when the Germans came, but Hanni had not heard from her for four years. The three had met for the first time when the M.G. assigned them to our house.

Where had the Germans taken them first?

Captain Providence looked uneasy, and I realized it was better not to press for an answer. In the case of Tilli and Hanni, it was fairly clear. They both looked very wise and experienced. But Sophie was something different. Looking at her face, one saw a peasant's child, out of the feudal darkness of the sixteenth century. She was no more equipped to meet life than an American child of six. I reflected that five years ago, when she had been taken, she had been fourteen. She must have been a pretty little thing.

Whatever had happened at first, the three had ended as unpaid laborers—as slaves; to be accurate. They had been sent to farms. I remembered seeing the German edict to the owners of foreign labor. It stated in its opening paragraph, "The Polish peasant is an animal." The instructions covered food, shelter, efficient utilization, and death, in the order named.

It was evident that all of our three had been fed less than the great

German horses or the fat swine. I suppose they spent the winters in some cold loft or hay barn. That was the instruction—like animals.

Were they getting enough to eat now, I asked. Captain Providence intimated that there had been a little trouble but that it had been vigorously put to rights. Was it necessary that they work so hard? There was, it seemed, no way of stopping them; the work was easy, they insisted, compared to what they had become used to, and they were happy in the warm house. I started looking for spare skirts and sweaters.

The next weeks passed quickly. The colonel and I were always about to leave and always busier than ever. Our replacements did not arrive. The winter closed down with forty-five consecutive days of solid fog that dripped ice. Coal was short, and the M.G. turned the electricity off all day except at mealtimes. We worked by candlelight. Outside the headquarters, the Germans dug sporadically in the rubble for firewood.

At five o'clock on a pouring black afternoon, there came a scratching on my bedroom door. I called to whoever it was to come in. It was Sophie—but scarcely recognizable. Her face was gray, her eyes and nose swollen, her pale, silky hair hanging in strings. She was wearing a skirt which I had given her a few weeks before. It had been a pretty good fit then, but now it was so tight in the waist that she couldn't fasten it.

"Madame!" she whispered. "Madame!" It was a wail, a tiny, hopeless wail. Suddenly, she seized my hand, pressed it to her lips, and went down in a heap on her knees: I got her into a chair and gave her a handkerchief. She was shaking all over, her eyes streaming tears, the soot from her nose running in the tears down her face. I put an arm around her pinched shoulders.

"Madame—*Hilf! Hilf,* Madame!"

I understood the "Help!"—she must have asked Tilli for the word—but all I could do was hold her and stroke her hair.

Suddenly, she sat up straight, and I saw her lips silently moving, as though she were practicing a speech. Then she spoke again. "Madame, make baby *kaput.* I die." Suddenly, she realized that she was sitting in a master's chair and went down on her knees again. But she had spoken. The murmured *"kaput"* from the child's face had been quite awful.

I held her and said over and over, *"Hilf, ja, Sophie, ja,"* and when she was shaking only a little, I called Tilli and the two of us got her to bed over the garage.

When Captain Providence came in, we held a trilingual conference around Sophie's bed. The facts were simple. Sophie was five months pregnant by an American soldier. It didn't seem possible we hadn't noticed, but her thin little body was always bent and all three girls were fat in the middle from sudden food. The soldier had gone away almost at once, saying he would come back for her. His name, he had told her, was Smith. Sophie had been sick for several days before coming to see me, and the day before had gone to see the German doctor whom the M.G. had assigned to care for sick D.P.s. This doctor had asked her if the father of the child was a German, and when she had said it was an American, he had sent her out of the office, telling her he could not treat Americans. She had become sicker. She had not eaten for three days.

We did what we could for her that night, and next morning the Sunday churchgoers stared glumly at Captain Providence as he tore around town in a jeep inquiring where a D.P. could have a baby. (He became a celebrity when the joke of "his" D.P. baby went the rounds.) The Army infirmary sent him to the M.G. headquarters, and they sent him to the German town major, who gave him the addresses of the local doctors, and he flew from one to the next, looking for a kind gynecologist. By ten o'clock, he had found one, and also a German civilian hospital that satisfied him.

Captain Providence drove Sophie and me to the hospital, with her dingy little possessions tied up in a towel. She drew herself straight and became very still when we came to the big, red, high-school-Gothic building. The lower windows were boarded up, because the glass had been shattered by a bomb. It was very gloomy inside. I felt dubious at first, when I saw the doctor's pince-nez and striped trousers, but when he looked at Sophie, his lower lip went out and his mouth drew down into a tired professional compassion which reassured me. (It should be noted that this man afterward refused any payment.)

After the doctor examined Sophie, he told Captain Providence that the baby was dead. There was no heartbeat. He would try to get Sophie's fever down and then see if he could force labor, to avoid operating. He would keep us informed. We left Sophie tucked into a large bed in a turret room. She had a nurse—a nun with quiet brown eyes, who by a miracle spoke some Polish words that Sophie seemed to know.

For the next three weeks, I kept track of Sophie through Captain Providence's reports. First, she was in labor—that went on for fifty hours. Then the baby was born, and it was dead. Sophie was very sick. Then Sophie was improving. Tilli and Hanni, and even Leni, the pantry siren, went to see her at the hospital every afternoon.

Sophie returned home the day of the first snowfall. There was snow on her hair when she came into my room, quivering like a little dog. She knelt and kissed my hands, pouring out unintelligible words. She was radiant.

Christmas was coming. The Germans of the household became very full of the spirit of the season and put up paper streamers in the kitchen. The three D.P.s rose to the occasion in their quiet way. They twined lamps and vases and various ornaments throughout the house with evergreen and little red berries, knotted with tinsel. Every day a new object had its green wreath.

The Colonel and I were determined to get together some sort of presents for the three. By squeezing our clothing ration cards and combing our wardrobes, we collected shoes, galoshes, wool and rayon stockings, a sweater, coats, battle jackets, and a Wac dress. There wasn't enough of anything to go around evenly, so the colonel devised a lottery. All the things were to be laid out, and the girls were to write down choices and draw lots. I heard of it with misgivings, but it was a lovely system.

Christmas afternoon, we spread everything out on the floor and Captain Providence summoned the D.P.s. They came in looking expectant but frightened to death. They huddled by the door, in front of the articles on the floor, and when it was explained that these were presents for them, Hanni started to cry, Tilli turned fiery red and seemed to get brighter every second, and Sophie just stood like a little Polish madonna, breathing through her mouth in holy misery. It was obvious that there would be no writing down of choices.

So we simply distributed the stuff to them in rotation, and it went all wrong. Tilli got the only two raincoats and Hanni all the stockings, but they immediately began, with whisperings and pettings, to redistribute the things among them. When the last piece was allotted we were suddenly in a shower of hand kissing and curtsies, and Hanni kissed Captain Providence on the cheek. Then they bolted.

Life went back to normal. The evergreen wreaths shed their needles and vanished, and the brass polishing was resumed. Our work was drawing to a close, and replacements started to arrive. Two of our original colonel residents had been replaced, and Captain Providence was packing. It continued to be a miserable winter, cold and raw. And in the coldest week there arose the question of the Polish girls' quitting our household and going to a camp.

It seemed that, technically, all D.P.s were supposed to live in the D.P. camp, and a roundup was in progress. The colonels were grave. Too much responsibility had already been assumed by Captain Providence, it was generally felt, although my husband had spread a majestic wing over the Sophie affair. D.P.s were generally recognized as a questionable quantity, and a rumor had arisen that men were visiting our garage. Get rid of the D.P.s was the prevailing mood.

Captain Providence and I tried to tell the girls, but at the first mention of the camp they turned white. I had never realized what the word "camp" could mean. We tried to reason with them. We explained that we were leaving, and that after we left, they would surely have to go there, and that if they went now, while we were able to stand behind them, as it were, it would be better than going when we had gone—but it was no use. They got whiter and stiller, and then Sophie started to choke with smothered, terrific sobs. We gave up, but authority let the girls slip through its clutches for the time being. They stayed in their heatless nook over our garage.

Shortly before we finally left, Sophie came to me.

"Madame," she said, smiling beatifically, "Hanni haff baby!"

It wasn't so bad this time. Hanni was going to have a baby, all right, and it was an American baby, but the American came through. He was at a nearby station, and he declared that he loved Hanni and wanted to marry her. I saw a letter he sent her, addressed simply "For Hanni," and brought by a friend. It enclosed forms for her to sign. The colonel and I and Captain Providence breathed again.

My husband and I left suddenly and completely, in the Army manner. There remained no connection between us and the three D.P.s. We real-

ized that we didn't even know their last names. We felt that with luck
Hanni had been taken care of but that probably Tilli and Sophie had in
the end gone to the camp, although we had done what we could to
commend them to the incoming officers. Or that, possibly, being so
small, they had been overlooked and left to continue their scrubbing and
polishing. We never knew.

But this much is certain, that last winter those three had shelter and
food and, after a fashion, clothes. Someone knew them. They were not
led to die—not then, at any rate. Perhaps they are still alive and have a
raincoat or a sweater to wear. Perhaps they are being fed, or are able to
exchange a coat for food.

Those simple things were not true of all D.P.s in Germany in 1945,
despite all efforts official and unofficial. They may be even less true this
winter. These were the lucky ones.

—1946

SOMETHING BREAKING DOWN

The last travel piece I published was "How to Have an Absolutely Hilarious Heart Attack." The next winter the Mexican letter was not about Mexico, it was the major portion of "Everything but the Signature Is Me." That appeared in *Khatru* 7, and while I hadn't intended it, that was my final fanzine. Alli sent me two pieces from the next trip, in hopes that I might publish another issue. The first one (untitled by her) was one of the letters-to-Jeff-and-everyone-else, the second a combination of a playlet ("Dzo'oc U Ma'an U Kinil," which went through multiple drafts) and an informal letter (in first draft with handwritten revisions).

While we continued writing, none of the rest of her letters to me was intended for publication. I am, however, including excerpts from two personal letters ("Not a New Zealand Letter"), the second of which comments on "Dzo'oc U Ma'an U Kinil."

Should have writ you long since, but I literally could not; this is the first moment I have had a table, chair and light, and the minimal clean space necessary for minimal thought. You see, with our old Tony gone to Cozumel to be mayor, his young brother Xavier is ostensibly running the place. Our house was not ready for our arrival, and the little casa had apparently been lent to a herd of buffalo. Xavier, who probably has been told that he resembles Warren Beatty—whom he resembles in the same sense that I resemble Helen of Troy—is a gangling-thin, large-mouthed, erratically active youth chiefly notable for getting the wrong people pregnant. He stays in the kitchen with his mother, or in his office; he has taken a course in business administration, which results in "administering" by sitting behind the desk and issuing orders to poor Esteban Ek. (When there was a problem, Tony used to lead a charge of his retainers, and if the problem were, say, a blocked septic tank, it was Tony who struck the first—and last—blow, and then appeared immaculate and jovial among his guests, as if he'd never changed a broken cotter pin under water in all his life. In other words, things got done.)

Anyway, Xavier's answer to the problem of our "unexpected" arrival consisted of ordering Ruffino Tzul (L'mus's young brother) to *paint the house* inside and out. This achieved the final destruction of every vestige of order; our things and the furniture were piled helter-skelter in the middle of all rooms, enhanced mysteriously by the addition of a random set of incredibly heavy great dark Spanish colonial office furniture downside up atop the heaps. And since Ting had had to pack the place up alone in our second emergency departure last year, and not realized the importance of antiroach-spraying every container, the first tug at the piles produced an audible skittering, as cucarachas as big as rats burrowed deeper with their young. Of course they were everywhere, and had befouled more than they had eaten—every towel, paper, teaspoon, nail, *everything* was vile. (As a final touch, one had set up housekeeping under the can of antiroach spray, cucarachacida.)

Anyway, I just sent Ting out fishing while I attacked the unspeakable—leaving our fourteen bags (we had brought our usual amount, including lots of books and food) plastic-sealed and sprayed in an unused corner. The *one* unused corner. Truly the Voice from the Baggie.

Anyway, what with the additional absence of known reliable mail carriers, perhaps you can see why I didn't write. Tonight there is an amiable, drunken, name-dropping old architect down at the Catañas, the bore of the world and a butcher with fish—he makes his guide *cut up a bonefish to use as bait*, perhaps the lowest act known to water—who persists in regarding himself as a dear friend of ours. He has carried mail before, and mailed it. I am going down to endure him expressly to mail this to you, under the whistling, thrashing palms and the waxing moon.

I'll end with a note that may amuse you. You recall L'mus, the Maya pura, last seen serpentlike and eating himself stuffed at a special table in the superb care of Gregoria? Well, he has a new incarnation. He and Gregoria are still solid, in every sense of the word—and the medico made her lose twenty pounds (or maybe kilos), so she is even more ruffled and glittering and flashing than ever. And L'mus is now chief mechanician-engineer for the settlement. (Actually holds it together, the sound of Yucatan is the sound of Something Breaking Down.) So the first day the electricity was loco along with everything, and we howled for L'mus. Later, to my surprise, a globular bright yellow object was seen bobbing at waist height along the windows, accompanied by a solid stomping sound. It materialized into L'mus, perceptibly older, squarer, and be-mustached, and *wearing a Yankee hard hat*.

It was something to behold . . . He has also a large pea-green auto, so reassembled that one cannot define the original brand. I thought you would like to know that the hard hats have come to Mayaland. It suits him, too.

—December 7, 1978

Dzo'oc U Ma'an U Kinil—
Incident on the Cancún Road, Yucatan

The road is two hot ruts of coral sand; on the left is scrub jungle, on the right are coco palms above the blindingly blue Caribbean. Lurching along the road is a taxi, a rusty, rump-sprung 1968 Buick, held together with wire and the driver's Maya muscle. The back is mounted with expensively unostentatious luggage and fishing gear. Wedged in among these are a gray-haired gringo tourist couple.

They have come from a small, exclusive fishing camp forty kilometers behind, and are headed, hopefully, for the airport at the international government tourist resort of Cancún, fifty kilometers ahead. From Cancún they will jet to Houston for their oldest grandson's wedding, and thence to Baja California for more fishing. After that they have reservations on a trout river in the Argentine. This is their first motor trip to Cancún; in previous years they flew in by small charter plane from Cozumel.

LADY TOURIST, extricating herself from a fallen duffel: "It's all spoiled now, George, isn't it? Since this road came through. Blue jeans. Store bread. Canned tuna. A *supermercado* at Tuluum! Why, you remember—"

GEORGE: "Muriel. My rod case."

MURIEL: "It's all right; George, I'm not putting my weight on it—And those awful commercial fishermen, ruining the fishing. I heard them coming back at night from Pajaros loaded down. Stone crabs, even, Manuel said. And the Indians help them, too. Don't they *see* they'll soon be extinct? Stupid . . ." She sighs. "This was one of the last places . . . and we actually had a robbery too, first robbery. Evian Newcombe lost her pearls, somebody came right into their *cabin*. Just before we got here. Sixty thousand, she said. Of course, they won't—"

GEORGE grunting: "I've seen 'em. I wouldn't have paid sixteen. She won't get anywhere claiming sixty."

MURIEL: "I know. And she should never have had them here. She's a dreadful woman, anyway . . . And Pedro being too drunk to guide, twice. It's those horrid motorcycles, they can go right to Chetumál or Libré Unión on weekends. You know I haven't seen a single Maya woman wearing a *huipil* or pounding tortillas? Except old Doña Juanna. And all those children . . . Don't they have *sense* enough to . . ." Her voice trails off as she catches the reflection of the driver's slanted black eyes on her.

DRIVER, who has been mentally upping the fare by several percent: "Señora Smeeth, you make bread for you husban'?"

His voice is soft and humorous. She flusters for a moment, then sturdily replies, "Well, no, Miguel. But it's a pity—don't you think it is sad to see the old traditions go?"

MIGUEL, still pleasantly: "And Señor Smeeth, you have many, how you say, gran' cheeldren, I think?"

Muriel gets it and flushes silently, but George is hit on a weak point.

GEORGE feeling automatically for his wallet: "You bet I have! Eight of 'em. Of course two are just babies—"

MIGUEL: "And if the baby is sick, Señor Smeeth, you take heem to hospital *caminando*—by feet? Maybe seexty *kilometers*? I theen' no, I theen' you have road, you take car."

GEORGE, mentally eliminating most of the projected tip: "Well, of course. But that's entirely different. Muriel, I feel rotten. I'm positive the water from that new well is polluted. Those goddamn guides piss anywhere. I told Manuel so. He says it's been inspected, but by God, I have a sample, and if—"

They become aware of the Buick making strangling noises. It stalls, recatches, stalls again and slows erratically to a stop.

MIGUEL, unsurprised, emits untranslatable Maya remark on the Buick's ancestry.

SMITHS, in unison: "*We'll miss our plane!*"

Oblivious to their frantic questions, Miguel leaps out, cuts the string holding down the hood, and begins doing arcane and noisy violence to the engine. The Smiths gaze around, seeing nothing but coral sand, mangrove jungle, coco palms and glimpses of the turquoise

Caribbean. It is very hot. Suddenly there is the sound of another motor, and a motorcycle appears ahead. It roars at and past them, showering them with white dust, amid which there is an interchange of apparently friendly shouts between its driver and Miguel.

MURIEL has belatedly rolled up her window against the dust; she rolls it down again and wails after the cycle driver, who guns away: "We could have sent a message to Manuel," she cries at her husband.

MIGUEL comes to their window, spitting gasoline ferociously: "I am sorree. The petrol, the *gasolina* is no good. Is water in the fu-el pomp."

GEORGE, making purposeless and futile efforts to get out: "*If we miss our plane—*"

MURIEL, almost weeping, "Oh please! Oh, we must catch the plane, the av-ee-one—don't you understand, Miguel? What can we do?"

MIGUEL, solicitously soothing: "Maybe no, maybe no. You wait. My brother-in-law, he lives *muy cerca*—one, two kilometers on the road. I go queeck, he will come. In peek-op he will take you to Cancun. You will see! All is cool. The plane you will meet in much time. I promees."

MURIEL: "Oh, how wonderful! Please hurry, please!"

MIGUEL, giving an odd, jaunty Maya salute: "I go!" He wheels to stride off.

GEORGE, loudly: "Tell him I'll pay anything he asks—within reason—if we make that plane."

MIGUEL turns back, makes a gracious half bow: "Yes. I am sorree. My brother-in-law must stop his work, it is for that. I fear he asks much—*muy cara*. He cost you! Not like in days before, I am regret." He nods commiseratingly, turns, and his broad square toes dig into the sand as he sets off. He is grinning radiantly, as only a Maya can grin, as he contemplates the fee he will split with his brother. *Dzo'voc u ma'an u kinil*, he murmurs to himself, or something like. *Ya paso el dia*.

Which translates roughly as, Those days are gone forever.

There is of course more, much more: The new marvelous incarnation of L'mus as a Maya hard hat: the gloomy Maya brilliance of his younger brother, Ruffino, who looking at his newborn son told me that we gringos were going to blow up the world, perhaps in twenty years; the jokes they played on me and my stubborn attempts to communicate with the women; the sixty-five beautiful lacy underpants and matching bras, in every color of the rainbow, hanging on the wash line, which turned out to belong to Don José's retarded daughter, known as The Lump; the new schoolteacher, whom the owner treated like an animal, and through whom I bought a few elementary math texts for Ruffino and others, finding that a simple paperbound math book in Mexico costs $10 U.S.! (What you don't get in school is forever beyond your reach.) The melodramatic diplomacy and negotiations that went into getting the owners' permission for my building—or rather, having built—a second tank filled off our motorpump, so the women don't have to raise and lug, raise and lug and haul the endless buckets of water for the camp laundry. Sick, pregnant, or dying, they haul that damn water. The grand finale day of hoisting that concrete monster onto the iron-wood base the men had built was unbelievable; old Don José said with a squint, "Mayas know how to get things up!" So it is El Nuevo Pyramid. And the hoses came and that water *ran!* (I got hugged by nineteen Mayas of all ages and conditions, and felt crummy as hell playing Lady Bountiful on the cheap.) Or the real tragedy of old Don José himself, as his former authority is undermined by the new priorities and skills of the younger men. Just as he has brought to perfection the huge rancho which was his life work, it has turned into nothing but *real estate*. Golden unspoiled beach property, the last left. So he gets drunk oftener and oftener, and more and more Indian, and wanders at night firing off his gun—he is the only Maya allowed to carry one, it was his pride—at imaginary woodpeckers eating the moon. It made me sad to hear him called merely "José Camuul," to distinguish him from another José; no more the Don. Or the terrible day and night that Ting, my husband, who is seventy-eight, spent with a very young Maya guide, drowning and freezing in the quicksand of a tiny islet, lost in the great raging waters of Ascension Bay. (The fishing had been fantastic, and the Maya boy had failed to spot the oncoming squall line with tornadoes.) By the last dawn I and others thought I was a widow; I watched, watched, watched for thirty hours, and could scarcely believe my eyes when when the familiar tall, white-bearded figure came striding up the road. (He slept for ten hours and then went out fishing—"Muy hombre!"—and I went to bed with a migraine for three days!)

Yes, there's a lot more for those who enjoy following the fortunes of

Maya Malo'ob—Gregoria Ku; and the clock, the Maya cackle-culture, the night Jorje came out of the wrong house, the antics of the tourists—and the beauty, the beauty that's still there. But it's in the mail *now* or in the wastebasket . . .

and so

In yama-ech, (which you can surely decipher)

from àlli, aka Tip

—May 15, 1979

This is a young friend, Matteo Camuul, who guided for Ting some years. He is considering whether the bonefish are more likely up north or on the flats. His expression is typical of the Maya in casual thought, but it has been known to be quite frightening to tourists, especially when met on a dark night by flashlight. When he smiles he will look very different. And if his feelings are hurt, he will look *very* different again.

NOT A NEW ZEALAND LETTER

I'd planned to write you as soon as the first fit of ecstatic babbling wore off, but it's six weeks now and the babbling is only denser and more complex; the ecstasy is still on. To make it short, we stumbled into the closest approximation of Eden I expect to find. Not perfect, you understand; not Joy Unalloyed—no choir of seraphs, no thornless rose—but, well, just about perfect, that's all. The very small lacks of conventional "perfection" makes it so. . . .

If you were still running a fat fanzine and I had a typewriter, I'd have a try at writing you my *New Zealand* letter, culling the fat notebook I swore not to start. Instead—well, I sit by a great glass wall, with CRUX and Rigel Keut and company blazing down under a full moon three million miles brighter than ours. Did you know that the sun is three million miles closer to the Southern Hemisphere in summer? And that N.Z. is under "a hole in the Van Allen belt?" And that you can *see* the difference, just before you get skin cancer?—Stop!

Anyway, just outside is a great, pure, still, steel-pink lake, ringed with mountains dominated by an "extinct" volcano, which in 1886 blew up with the second loudest bang ever heard on Earth (Mt. Tarawera), and in the moonlight float a pair of fantastic black swans (which we don't refer to because they are Ozzies—Austrilians) with five ungainly young, clucking and calling to each other above the wails of the Morepork owl, and the rustle of tree ferns, scents of jasmine—and an excruciatingly lush and conventional English perennial border. Oops, sorry, it's raining now—it does that four times a day—over in a minute—and if it throws a moonbow I'm going to—I don't know what. Take an aspirin.

I tell you, Jeff, if one more beautiful and/or exciting, interesting, touching, delightful, comic or generally spot-on thing happens, I've had it! Misery I can cope with; this much good stuff is murder.

Save this place in your list of where to go when all is ashes, psychologically or otherwise. I think it'll keep. But change your name—if you call out "Jeff!" here, half the male population looks around. (*Who, who,* impressed so many pregnant ladies thirty years ago??)

—March 28, 1980

Writing "Tales of the Quintana Roo." (Three of them.) Hard to recapture Yucatan after New Zealand. Tempted to say, that's my life . . . the procrastinator, condemned to write about always last year. Gentle but perhaps nicely spooky little yarns, maybe tailored to *F&SF*. Actually easier to do now after some passage of time; when I wrote, or tried to write you that piece last year I was too upset about the changes going on down there. Now the farther past, the dream that was—or maybe was only in my head—has reasserted itself. The past encapsulates and then gains vitality in its time-shell.

—April 28, 1980

Biographical Sketch for Contemporary Authors

In March 1980, Jean W. Ross of BC Research wrote to Alli asking if she could do a half-hour phone interview for publication in a volume of the Gale Research reference series *Contemporary Authors*. This simple request led to two years of work on both Alli's part and *Contemporary Authors*'s and the following two remarkable documents. Ross sent Alli a list of suggested questions, and Alli made notes as to how she might answer them. On September 3, 1980, the interview took place. *CA* sent a transcript on September 15, and Alli started to work on it. She didn't finish it until September "1 or 2," 1982. Almost every paragraph was rewritten (or at least revised), and almost every answer was lengthened. Sometimes she moved comments to a more appropriate location in the interview; sometimes she set up the next question better by inserting a leading remark in the previous answer.

She retyped most of the interview, taping in parts of the original where the changes were minor. Of the twenty-six manuscript pages, twenty-one are completely retyped and three partially retyped; only two pages of *CA*'s original transcript survive intact. There were at least two different times that parts of the interview were retyped, there were later typed portions taped in, later yet handwritten lines inserted, and one substantial handwritten segment (on her father) taped in so late it wasn't even included in the book.

CA also sent a sheet for biographical information. This went through the same process, being rewritten and lengthened several times over the two years. This document was used as source material for an essay preceding the interview, but this is the first time it has been published in full.

The entry on Alice Hastings Bradley Sheldon is in *Contemporary Authors* volume 108, edited by Hal May (Gale Research Company 1983). (Sheldon's obituary is in volume 122.)

NAME:

> SHELDON, Alice Hastings Bradley 1915–
> ("James Tiptree, Jr." "Raccoona Sheldon")

PERSONAL:

> Born 24 August 1915, in Chicago, IL 60615: siblings, none

Parents:

Herbert Edwin Bradley, b. Canada; Attorney-at-Law (Ann Arbor); explorer, big-game collector and naturalist by avocation (see Early Travels, below); and

Mary Wilhelmina Hastings Bradley, b. Chicago; Smith Col., Oxford (Engl.); F.R.G.S., PEN; author of over thirty-five books (history, travel, fiction) and many short stories, articles, lectures, etc., some still noteworthy today as first to break the popular media's taboo on serious feminist issues such as a woman's right to an abortion. *1919* to *1931* she accompanied husband on all expeditions and hunts (see below); sharing hardship and danger; self-taught, excellent shot; also linguist, collecting hitherto-unknown tribal folk tales; also was first to publicize peaceful nature of gorilla and call for its removal from "game-animal" category. *1944/5*, war correspondent, European fronts, sponsored by *Collier's* mag., and War Dept., to report on WAC; first American woman to inspect and report on some of most hideous of German death camps. On return to U.S., campaigned vigourously to convince still-numerous Midwestern disbelievers of the terrible reality of the extermination camps and the Holocaust itself.

Early Travels:

From age 4 to 15, Alice Sheldon's childhood was dominated by the experience of accompanying her parents on all their (widely reported) explorations and trips. She was plunged into half a world of alien environments all before she was old enough to be allowed to enter an American movie house. This meant exposure to chaotically diverse environments—from the then-unspoiled tropical Ituri rain forest to the corpse-obstructed streets of Calcutta; from the broiling, animal-filled vastness of the Semliki savannahs to the orchid-scented, forested hills that were to become Vietnam; the Towers of Silence of the Parsees, vulture-guarded; the manicured, flowery cemeteries of English towns, the smoky Burning Ghats of Benares, and the then-unrestored desolation of the great Egyptian tombs; the cozy little tree nests of the Batwa pygmies—and the 1912 modernity of "home" in Chicago, Illinois, with its built-in vacuum cleaners. And as with places, so with people. She found herself interacting with adults of every color, size, shape, and condition—lepers, black royalty in lionskins, white royalty in tweeds, Arab slavers, functional saints and madmen in power, poets, killers, and collared eunuchs, world-famous actors with headcolds, blacks who ate their enemies and a white who had eaten his friends; and above all, women; chattel-women deliberately starved, deformed, blinded and enslaved; women in nuns' habits saving the world; women in high heels committing suicide, and women in low heels shooting little birds; an Englishwoman in bloomers riding out from her castle at the head of her personal Moslem army; women, from the routinely tortured, obscenely mutilated slave-wives of the 'advanced' Kibuyu, to the free, propertied, Sumarran matriarchs who ran the economy and brought six hundred years of peaceful prosperity to the Menang-Kabau; all these were known before she had a friend or playmate of her own age. And finally, she was exposed to dozens of cultures and subcultures whose values, taboos, imperatives, religions, languages, and mores conflicted with each other as well as with her parents. And the writer, child as she was, had continuously to learn this passing kaleidoscope of Do and Don't lest she give offense, or even bring herself or the party into danger. But most seriously, this heavy jumble descended on her head before her own personality or cultural identity was formed. The result was a profound alienation from any nominal peers, and an enduring cultural relativism. Her world, too, was suffused with sadness; everywhere it was said, or seen, that great change was coming fast and much would be forever gone.

Itinerary follows: *1919/1920*, Bradleys with Carl Akeley on successful final quest for legendary Central African Mountain

Gorilla (see group in Amer. Museum of Nat. Hist., NYC); this and following trips were under auspices of that museum, also Field Museum of Chicago, and National and Royal (Brit.) Geographic Societies. *1924/25*, Herbert Bradley led own expedition across Mountains of the Moon and through 200 miles of then wholly unknown territory west of former Lake Edward, making first European Contact with (cannibal) people there. Duration of each expedition about one year, total miles walked, approx. 3,000. It may be helpful to recall that no radios or planes or means of rescue existed then; all roads, phones and electricity ended at the coast, and in the interior of Africa there were no maps, no towns or landmarks, only old foot trails, many made by slavers. Nor were there cars or trucks or Land Rovers nor any powered vehicle or bike or boat, nor lamps, nor saws; no gasoline, nails, woven cloth, matches, paper; no mail, no dictionaries of the languages, no coined money, no medicine or doctors; and no draft animals (because of equine encephalitis). Communication was by runner and unaided Human voice; trade by barter (espec. salt), light from personally imported candles, and transport was on Human heads and legs. Distances were calculated with compass and pedometer.

On leaving Africa in *1925*, the Bradleys traveled through India, several SE Asia countries, and to interior of then Indo-China, for tiger and gaur (a whopping great buffalo thing with armor-plated brains [if any]) and to observe the Moi peoples. (Now called "Montagnards"; and virtually destroyed.)

The Bradleys' last expedition, *1929/30*, was the first crossing of the African continent by automobile (two ton-and-a-half Chevrolet trucks). Crossing was at equatorial latitudes. Despite assurances of Colonial authorities, few bridges were found to exist and most rivers were crossed by unloading and constructing wood tracks on canoes. On this trip the speed of Colonial despoilment of Africa's peoples, land, and wildlife was sadly evident (save in some British territory). Such was the ambience of the last trip to Africa that no one desired to return. (An attempt by the Belgian colonials to silence us permanently before we could tell outsiders what we'd seen—a series of artfully arranged reports of nonexistant elephants damaging crops—led us to go on foot deeper and deeper into lethal drought country, from which all game had fled and where all rivers were dry. Just at the point of no return, Father's "radar" turned us back. The last days of the march out were made on ½ cup of water each in 110-degree heat. The last night we came to a dry buffalo wallow which yielded filthy water three-feet down; giving us an excellent chance to test the Army's Halozone . . . This contributed to the unhappy ambience of colonial Africa.)

There were other minor travels in the same childhood period; a trip across Exmoor, Engl., on horseback with Mary Bradley, and attendance with her at the historic PEN Congress in Scotland when the Nazi delegation walked out; Swiss schooling (Les Fougères, Lausanne) to acquire some vocalizations which were occasionally taken for French.

Marriages:
(1) *1934–38*, to Wm Davey, poet, polo player, alcoholic (Princeton), and (2) *1945–on*, to Huntington Denton Sheldon (Eton, Yale), Pre–World War II, H. D. S. was president, American Petroleum Corporation of America (not an oil company); commissioned Army *1942*, joined Air Force (then a part of Army), working in A2 (Air Intelligence); ultimately Colonel, Deputy Chief of Air Staff A2, for European Theatre. Numerous awards, oak leaves. Two previous marriages had ended by divorce; met present wife (the author) among specialists he had summoned from the States in *1945* to evaluate the defeated Luftwaffe.

Children:
None.

Education:
Sarah Lawrence: U. of Calif. at Berkeley: N.Y.U.: USAAF Photo Intelligence School, Harrisburg, PA (first female attendee); Rutgers Agricultural Col.; School for Advanced International Studies, Johns Hopkins; American U. (D.C.) B.A., scl.; George Washington U. (D.C.), where PhD mcl Exper. Psychol., 1967.

Religion:
Atheist: ethical imperatives consonant with Christian New Testament, rationalized on basic principle of striving against entropy. (E.g., greed is more entropic than altruism; truth is less entropic than lies.)

Organizations, Memberships:
A.C.L.U., Friends' Service Committee, N.O.W., A.P.A., Psi Chi, Sigma Xi, AAAS; Audubon Society; Smithsonian Associates, Amer. Museum of Nat'l Hist., S.F.W.A., Esperanto Society of Washington.

Avocational Interests and Hobbies:
Nishikigoi (ornamental koi); Hydrogen as energy source; bright young people; learning to speak, read, and write English.

CAREER or Pre-SF Work

1925–1941 Graphic artist: book cover illos., a few designs in *New Yorker* mag.; then painter, student John Sloan, exhib. Corcoran, D.C. and Chicago Art Inst. "All Americans".

1941–1942 Art critic new *Chicago Sun* (weekly full page), while awaiting admission of women to Army under women officers.

1942–1946 U.S. Army,* WAAC-WAC/AAF. 1943, assigned USAAF/A2 (Air Intelligence); became first female American Photo-Intelligence Officer. (British enlisted women already expert at similar work.)

Note of Historical Interest: What we actually enlisted in was not *the* Army, but the A.U.S., or "Army of the United States," which disbanded at peace. All the civilians went home, or enlisted in the Regular Army, and most majors and generals went back to being sergeants and lieutenants in *the* Army. The AUS is a creature of wartime national mobilization, and members of the "real" Army showed some condescension toward their jumped-up "civilian" colleagues and temporary superior officers.

But how many readers would recognize "enlistment in the AUS" today?

Author joined a small group at HQ AAF (the Pentagon, in—literally—the cellar) who were developing industrial photoanalysis and targeting, with regard to the Far East, where other-source intelligence was lacking. (Reconnaissance film was flown to DC for interpretation.) Despite the interest of the work, the author, like many Pentagon prisoners, strove by every means to get overseas where the war was, and was just as persistently blocked by the inaccurate label of "indispensable." Finally in 1945 she was liberated by the requirements of the Air Staff Post-Hostilities Exploitation Project—but only to Europe, where the war was ending. The Project was a large task force of AAF specialists, scientists, and experts in every AAF function, assigned to locate and interrogate their captured Luftwaffe counterparts, in order to extract and evaluate all technology and material of potential use to the USAAF. It was essential to move quickly, for much of the German caches of secret scientific material and personnel (e.g., atomic physicists) were in the forward zone scheduled to be turned over to Russian occupation. (The Project in fact proved highly successful; it started a stream of priceless scientific and military prototypes, concepts and research flowing to the United States—the first operational jet planes, the rockets that became NASA, among them.) It was solely devised by its commander, Col. Huntington D. Sheldon, who had been thinking ahead while his peers thought about going home. The author met with Col. Sheldon in July to explain her total unsuitability for work with the Luftwaffe, and to beg to be sent to the Far East. Instead, on 22 Sep 1945, in a French mayor's charming office, she found herself becoming Mrs. H. D. Sheldon—after which the report on the Luftwaffe's photo-intelligence was completed through a long German winter. Both returned to the States for demobilization in Jan 1946, the author with rank of major: WAAC Service Ribbon, and Legion of Merit Award.

1946–1952 Partner with husband in small rural business (custom hatching, N.J.); also worked intermittently as volunteer for civilian anti-Nazi intelligence-gathering orgs., primarily Ken Birkhead's "Friends of Democracy," now defunct. (After Birkhead's tragic death, F.O.D.'s files went to B'Nai B'Rith.)

1952–1955 Both Sheldons recalled independently to D.C. to participate in development of then-new CIA; H. D. S. at supergrade levels, the author at mere technical level to help start up CIA Photo-Intelligence capability (then faced with evaluation of large caches of German air photography of USSR). In 1954–55, a brief tour of duty on clandestine side working up basic files on Near East. In 1955 resigned CIA to pursue more personally congenial goals.

1955–1968 Hiatus for taking stock: The author's early graphic arts work had left tantalizing unsolved questions of psychological aesthetics in her mind, and even amid other tasks she had found and followed some of the technical literature. Simply stated, why, for instance, does a certain spot of orange in *this* area of a painting "look right," seem to "complete a structure"—while the same patch in, say, blue, or the orange in a different place "looks all wrong?" *Why*? What is this "structure!" And what about individual variation, the notorious *de gustibus*? Perhaps most tantalizing, why have so many new styles in art been violently rejected by their contemporaries, only to become the visual treasures of later generations? This phenomenon has been common at least since Rembrandt—the night watchmen who commissioned his famous painting refused to pay the few guilders they owed him and sent back the painting, now worth millions. And the story of the Gaugain and van Gogh paintings used to roof chicken coops is well known.* Why? The whole topic of visual values is beset by windy theories devoid of factual base, and loud with substanceless argument. The author was fired with the urge to understand everything that could be known about visual perception and value, and to devise some experimental benchmarks in the murk.

To do this work required a doctorate. The author was then in

---

*The converse fall from favor of an artist immensely popular in his day has also been seen, but far more rarely and with such conspicuous exceptions as Titian and Rubens, *inter alia* . . . Will Picasso's work go the way of Titian or of Sargent and Bouguereau?

her forties, with only forty-seven recorded undergraduate credit-hours to her name. Nevertheless she returned to college (at American Univ. in D.C.), and perhaps because it was unusual to come on a student driving for the PhD for the sake of knowledge rather than as a means to a job, a grant—a fine high-status NIH Pre-Doctoral grant—was secured by the Psychology Dept. Chairman, Dr. True-blood (dec.). Thus helped, the B.A. (scl) came in 1959, and after a change to Geo. Wash. Univ, D.C., the coursework and exams for the PhD were completed in the early 1960s, and the author was into a full-scale experimental work for the dissertion—and attempting to defer the actual degree as long as possible, to maintain the grant.

The incoming "baby boom" was then overloading all college faculties; teachers were urgently needed. So while working up the final experimental paradigms (in an ex-coal cellar on H St.), the author taught experimental psychology and psychological statistics at American and G.W.U.

By *1967* all experimental work was finished, with unexpectedly good results and the doctorate could be no longer deferred. (PhD, mcl. G.W.U. 1967) This precipitated a crisis; health was failing under the combination of experimental work and the teaching load of "monster" classes routinely given to new PhDs. It was also necessary to obtain a new postdoctoral grant for further research, a full-time job in itself. All in all it appeared impossible soon to resume pure research, which had been the basic goal.

At this point a heart problem forced temporary retirement at semester's end. Meanwhile, some SF stories written as a hobby were all selling, to the author's immense surprise. As health returned, the temptation to write more won out. The author rationalized this activity as a claim for a broader concept of "science" than rocketry and engineering, and the aim of showing SF readers that there are sciences other than physics, that bio-ethology or behavioral psychology, for instance, could be exploited to enrich the SF field.

But this writing had to be kept secret; the news that a new PhD with offbeat ideas was writing *science fiction* would have wakened prejudice enough to imperil any grant and destroy my credibility with the Psychology Departments of G.W.U. and American—not to mention ever being again employed, had I desired, in the CIA.

A year passed, during which it became clear that the marvels of medicine were not going to give a fifty-five-year-old the strength for work that would have exhausted one half her age. Luckily, the challenge of writing had exerted its spell; retirement from university work became permanent without any great traumas, and the author found herself with a new line of effort ready-made for somewhat erratic health.

Writing, Pre-Science Fiction

The author's only non-SF story is a fiction/fact piece, "The Lucky Ones," in the 16 Nov 1946 *New Yorker*; a plea for more humane American treatment of the D.P.s ("Displaced Persons")—those pitiable surviving thousands of Nazi slave laborers, Jews and non-Jews, who as children had been kidnapped from their homelands, raped, tortured, starved, and worked near to death, and were then fallen into American hands.

Science Fiction Writing

Foreword: The Pseudonym That Got Away.

The first SF stories were naturally not expected to sell, so a pseudonym was selected at random (from a jam pot). The plan was to use a new name for each new batch of stories, so as to avoid permanent identification with the slush pile. But "Tiptree" sold, and thus became permanent. In the interests of consistency and privacy the name was used for all SF dealings, and for letters that grew into deeply friendly correspondences, with the unintended result that for eleven years only H. D. Sheldon—not even Tip's agent, Bob Mills—knew who or what Tiptree was. Tiptree in fact began to take on a peculiar, eerie, vitality of his own, while the author yearned more and more to write at least a few things as a woman. Hence, in 1974 "Raccoona Sheldon" appeared: but she required a minor assist from Tiptree to get started—Tip at first could afford to give her only some weaker stories.

Then, in 1977 the author's mother died after a long illness, at the age of 92, and Tiptree—who wrote only the truth in all letters— had imparted so many of the details of Mary Bradley's unusual life that when her obituary was read by certain sharp-eyed young friends,* James Tiptree, Jr., was blown for good—leaving an elderly lady in McLean, VA, as his only astral contact.

Science Fiction Writing

James Tiptree, Jr., is known primarily as a short story writer, having published over fifty shorts, novellas, and novelets (including four by "Raccoona") to one novel, as of 1982. All but the most recent stories have been collected in four volumes.

This relatively slender body of work has begun to attract critical attention from beyond the strict borders of SF, following the trend which is luring mainstream critics to peer over their fences at any handy sample of SF. In the *New York Times Book Review*, Gerald Jonas called Tiptree's tales "some of the finest SF short stories of the past decade," and the collection *Warm Worlds* inspired him to say, "If it made any sense to talk about a successor to Cordwainer Smith among contemporary SF writers, the most likely candidate would be James Tiptree, Jr."

Tiptree's rise in the SF world has often been called meteoric. To the author's bewilderment, no story remained unsold; even more startling were the award nominations which started after the first "serious" story ("The Last Flight of Doctor Ain," 1969). This curiosity and commotion began to threaten privacy, and even aroused suspicions that Tiptree's determined reticence was a publicity trick.

The excitement, the unrelenting personal curiosity—and the awards—continued, somewhat to the author's dismay, until late 1977, when Tiptree (and Raccoona) were abruptly unmasked.

---

*Of whom Jeffrey D. Smith (see below) is the leading candidate. It is the author's belief that Jeff, Tiptree's earliest and best pen-friend, could easily have winkled out Tip's identity years earlier, had not honor impeded him. Only when the public press all but spelled it out did he feel sufficiently released from his self-imposed vow not to "pry," to write Tip a direct inquiry—thus enabling his friend to keep his (her) promise that when the matter came out Jeff should be the first to know.

After this only the feminist world remained excited, but on a different basis, having nothing to do with the stories. Tiptree, by merely existing unchallenged for eleven years, had shot the stuffing out of male stereotypes of women writers. Even nonfeminist women were secretly gleeful. The more vulnerable males discovered simultaneously that Tiptree had been much overrated, and sullenly retired to practice patronizing smiles. Thus the matter stands today.

But no account of Tiptree's career could be complete without mention of the many helping hands that were extended to the new writer—truly too many to name, except for the very early good offices of SF's incomparable writers-turned-editors: Harry Harrison of *Amazing* and *Fantastic*, Ed Ferman of the *Magazine of Fantasy and Science Fiction*; later and to a lesser extent Ted White then of *Amazing* and *Fantastic*—and at all times in all weathers, one whose friendly deeds were beyond calculation—Frederik Pohl of *If* and *Galaxy*. And not-to-be-forgotten, on the same 'mags', Judy-Lynn del Rey, then Benjamin. But the list must stop here, for that brings up the grand women pen-friends whom lonely Tip valued so much—writerly Vonda McIntyre, brave Chelsea Quinn Yarbro, Joanna Russ the scholarly fireball, and Ursula K. Le Guin, nonpareil. And—but there is space for only one more, so let it be that most intrepid and honorable of men and fans, Jeffrey D. Smith, of Baltimore.

When Tiptree's stories first began to appear, Jeff was publishing a formidable fanzine *Phantasmicom* (later *Khatru*), and he wrote to the mysterious Tiptree requesting a postal interview, and promising not to "pry." Tiptree, realizing that some sort of biographical information would have to be furnished before exasperated blurb writers hired a detective, decided to take a chance on Jeffrey D. Smith. (Later on, other writers called this act insanely trustful.) The gamble paid off in years of friendship and jollity. From that interview—now regarded by strangers as a "research tool"—the correspondence progressed to miniarticles on everything Tiptree encountered, from the Maya Indians' reason for not pointing at rainbows to the odor of glaciers, all of which Jeff published under a column name, "The 20-Mile Zone." And there grew up a quiet pen-friendship, which seems to be surviving the replacement of "Tip" by "abs" as well or better than some noisier ones.

—1980–1982

CA: You wrote and published under the name James Tiptree, Jr., for about ten years before your real personal identity was discovered. Did that discovery in any way change your feelings about your writing?

Sheldon: Yes, it did very much. It's a little difficult to explain why—perhaps because there is a certain magic in writing, and there is no magic in writers. I have a very strong feeling that the writer's life and the writer's work should be kept separate, especially in writing that carries some sense of wonder.

A science fiction writer often has a deep urge toward transcendence, strong dreams of "this can't be all there is." He or she sets out to show that maybe this *isn't* all there is. The story speaks to that hunger in others: magic.

And then the camera suddenly pans and picks up the writer himself, he's slouched in a haze of smoke over his typewriter, and it's all come out of his little head . . . Magic gone.

Or maybe the story's a bitter tragedy—alien beauty loved and lost. It rather destroys the effect if you can think, Oh well, this is because that writer really yearns to eat granola for breakfast and he was unable to get granola last week and therefore he's bitter.

Kipling said it all in a poem called "The Appeal." It ends:

And for the little, little, span
The dead are borne in mind,
Seek not to question other than
The books I leave behind.

He detested this prying into the writer's life. Of course his was to some extent Victorian secrecy, but I agree very strongly with that idea. A man called Cordwainer Smith, who was really Paul Linebarger, a diplomat, wrote some marvelous science fiction, and then he wrote an autobiographical introduction to one of his collections, and it was dreadful. It was racist and sexist, it contained sickening references to his dear old mammy and his house in general, and yet all that never showed in his work at all. His work was clear and pure and represented a type of stern and wonderful fantasy that was just not evident in his thinking about himself and his own life.

And writers are often, when not just plain obnoxious, extraordinarily dull: because if they're any good they're saving whatever they have that *isn't* dull for their work, and since that is in a state of unhatchedness it can't be produced anyway. They usually have knobby faces and slightly furtive eyes; They're very preoccupied with whether they're getting a cold or whether someone is going to tow away their car. If you take them seriously in person, they often yield to an urge to be pompous. All of which has absolutely nothing to do with whatever jewellike thing they may have created, or their view into another world.

Of course I too have all those knobs and neuroses, plus I'm paralyzing shy inside—a trait which easily escapes those who see me striding into meeting and Safeways and joking with strange women. I enjoy strange women—if they don't linger—but the rest is all façades. What no one sees is the cost of that façade. (Even chatting like this with a most agreeable, non-threatening person, I find I've scrooched down in the chair and pulled away as far as the phone will go.) Last week two pleasant strangers interviewed me. I genuinely liked them, and I couldn't help impersonating Miss Vitality of 1932—until their car was round the bend, then I collapsed for the rest of the day in a dark room with a cold rag on my head.

Façades! In Officers' Training School I had to give a two-minute lecture on—shall I ever forget it?—"Paragraph Ten of the

Infantry Drill Regulations." I climbed onto the two-foot high speaker's stand, announced my topic, glanced at the hall of faces, threw up decisively, and fainted crash to the floor, blacking both my eyes. (I was later told it was voted Most Interesting Format.)

Perhaps this will convey that Tiptree's elusiveness was no pose?

But what do people like me do when they don't want to give up, when they want to play the world's games and do the world's work, with its thundering great Tables of Organization, its gregarious armies? Well, you learn to make it through the sign-up stages—and then you become very good at sniffing out the unpopular specialities (often the most interesting, if you like work), the empty T/O boxes, the back channels and off hours. And pretty soon you become Our Expert, and set your own hours. It's surprising what you can do. Oh, those wonderful years when I had my own keys to cold official buildings, because I came to work at 0400 in the dawn. How I loved flying along the great empty expressways into D.C., with the mercury vapor lamps lighting the gold rumps of the Memorial Bridge Percherons, and the sky turning dove-blue and red behind the deserted statues! A private city.

And when I was at—where else?—Sarah Lawrence College, I used to do all my work at night and leave it on the professor's desk in the morning, like the elves. I'd still like to do that, to be able to write stories on old leaves or something and have them flitter down through the editor's transom with nobody knowing who did it. Or like the hex signs that appear on fences. All that's gone. All my wonderful anonymity is gone; the reader is tied to the specific person. Maybe I'm oversensitive there, because when I myself read fiction, the writer is very much present if I know anything about him, and I can't divorce the two . . . it was a lovely life being nobody. But then of course the "nobody" became terribly obtrusive, so that in some ways I was glad to get rid of him because I was evoking too much curiosity.

CA: So the pseudonym really did the opposite of what you would have liked?

Sheldon: Toward the end, yes it did. You see, with "Raccoona" selling too, things had got fairly confusing. I was writing stories and letters as female *me*, but from a place I didn't live in and without my own real past—and at the same time writing and corresponding as a man who for a decade had made himself part of *me* too; Tip owned my past life and my years of SF friendships and he lived in my home, but my husband was his "gringo friend" . . . I'm sure you sense the chaos?

And then comes this blow, this glare of light on me as "Alice B. Sheldon"—a third persona still, who wasn't even a writer in "real" life, and didn't know any of my real SF friends, or vice versa. Frankly, I came unglued. Not over it yet.

And to top all, offering such a *dull* surprise. Roll of drums, curtain quivers, thrills, *starts up*, footlights blaze, and front and center Our Hero turns out to be nothing but a nice old lady in McLean.

At least I hope I'm "nice" . . . or do I?

CA: What's wrong with that?

Sheldon: Oh, nothing in theory, I suppose. Except stereotypes, my own included. But in practice you lose some context factors that give a bit of ersatz excitement and credibility.

For instance, a woman writing of the joy and terror of furious combat, or of the lust of torture and killing, or of the violent forms of evil—isn't taken quite seriously. Because women aren't as capable of violent physical assault—not to speak of rape—as men are.

And as for the joy of combat*, women rarely take pleasure

---

*If it needs saying in these days of Chrissie and Navratilova, I can confirm from personal experience that normal women *do* experience the joy-of-physical-combat-between-comrades, a type of bonding supposedly confined to Captain Kirk. Only, among women, the constraint of protecting body parts needed by the next generation (and which men too, by tacit consent also protect) is so very much more awkward.

in simply being beaten up, which is what fighting a man usually amounts to. (I've seldom heard men speak of the joys of having both kneecaps splintered or their teeth knocked out).

Now we don't want to get into metaphysics here—yesterday a man told me with real, glittery-eyed rage, that women are "stamping men into the ground" through alimony payments! "Don't make a mistake, it's war!" He actually hissed, "It's *war. War!*" He and some like-minded male friends were going to Put an End to It. And he'd been a strong supporter of the ERA, too, he said, before his eyes were opened.

No. By "superior male violence" I refer simply to the fact that few men are afraid of walking past a solitary woman on a dark street. That people aren't installing bars and alarms and deadbolts for fear of women breaking in and killing them. And history shows us few examples of women personally raising and leading a gang to butcher or bomb their neighbors, or conquer the world. In brief, war.

And war, as any soldier or senator will tell you, is a man's activity—like Valley Forge, or the Charge of the Light Brigade. Women experience only the boring peripheral aspects of war, like being shot at My Lais, or gassed in Belsens. Or doing minor spy work, often enforced by threats to their young. Or bystanding at Hiroshima, or enduring gas or BW side effects, or slave labor, rape-death, and simple starvation; or that old classic, now somewhat out of vogue, the skewering of their infants, in or out of the womb. Women are the faceless figures, arms loaded with infants, scattering under the male splendor of the dive bomber, or hauling the children through the barbwire. Women are the meat in the minefields. The body count. Women in war are, in short, *boring*. No glory, no triumphant combat. That's man's activity.

But if we call war evil, we must admit that the world has suffered very little violent evil from, say, *Mme.* Bonaparte or *Mrs.* Genghis Khan.

Of course women too may be loaded with hidden hate and do terrible things to prisoners, or their own children. And there was always Lucrezia Borgia. But women's evil is typically small scale, secret or indirect, like witchcraft and such, which man-the-hero can sweep away with a blow.

So when one who writes about serious, violent evil that turns out to be female, some readers may feel cheated—particularly if an action scene has stirred them. Now it all seems flat, even false—"What the hell does *she* know about real fighting?"

I think that for all of us the sense of being in Contact with something that has the potential to do—or maybe (wow!) has done—real evil, gives a little thrill to reading. Some people seem to have projected that onto Tiptree. Maybe I did a little, too. So to write on as a toothless tiger was shaming. And then all the silly publicity, and the way my mail changed . . .

CA: How did your mail change?

Sheldon: Oh, first the scads of personal letters and appeals, and everybody felt they had to say things about the whole revelation one way or another. No one talked about the *stories* anymore at all. That hurt. And Tiptree had a certain epistolary style, which no longer carried any conviction. People were wondering if they had been told the truth, too, you know. And I couldn't help them, because what they thought was Tiptree's style was *my* style, all I had. ("Alice B. Sheldon" doesn't have any style except "Enclosed please find payment," or "Dear Sir, the whatsit you sold me has now broken down for the sixteenth time—" which doesn't take you very far.)

And some of the people I loved the dearest suddenly were very remote, and people whom I didn't really know much about sort of cuddled up to me. I soon all but ceased writing letters.

And then there were the male writers who had seemed to take my work quite seriously, but who now began discovering that it was really the enigma of Tip's identity which had lent a spurious interest—and finding various more-or-less subtle ways of saying so. (Oh, how well we know and love that pretentiously aimiable tone, beneath which hides the furtive nastiness!) I'd been warned against it, but it was still a shock, coming from certain writers. The one thing I admire about that type of male hatred is its strategic agility; they soon got their ranks closed. Only here the timing was so damn funny, the perfect unison of their "reevaluation" of poor old Tip rather weakened the effect.

But the worst havoc was among Tip's true friends, like some who actually phoned up. I felt they expected the phone to burst into colored lights, at least. But of course all they got was my terrible phone voice, made worse by some dental surgery, stuttering inanities . . . broke my heart. And as for the brave one or two who actually come calling—No, I can't go on . . .

CA: Your mother was a well-known writer. Did she influence you in that direction?

Sheldon: Oh my, yes! She influenced me. Negatively. It's horrible to have a mother—or parent-figure of any sort—who can do everything. A mother so able, no matter how dear and loving—and Mary gave real love—is still bad for a daughter because you identify with her. And without meaning to, you compete. And to be in competition with Mary was devastation, because anything I could do she could do ten times as well. It never occurred to me that I was a child and she was a grown woman and that was to be expected.

But "competition" was only the surface of the problem. I was a classic instance of the Hartley Coleridge bind, the trouble that makes children of high achievers so lucrative to psychotherapy: expectancies. I couldn't count the times I was patted on the head by some Eminence and told, "Little girl, if you're ever half as talented, half as charming, half as good—capable—warm-hearted—plucky—beautiful—witty—(name ten)—as your mother, *you'll be lucky*."

Great. It was always "half," too.

If I'd been a boy I'd have had the same about Father. In contrast to his outwardly macho activities, Herbert Bradley was a quiet, gentle man who daily provided a role model of cheer, sweetness, and courage despite pain or danger; of respect toward nature; and care for others, especially the weak. His heart and his integrity were in his face; people loved him at sight. Only after his death was it found that through his sixties, seventies, and eighties, his practice included an ever-increasing amount of free legal and other "house call" services to the aged, ill, destitute, or illiterate, often when he himself was in great pain from bones ill-set after an auto accident. Sometimes he was their only visitor. But he never let them feel that this was charity; it was "valued business."

He had absolute integrity, and unbreakable determination. Toward bullies he was fearless, though his strength was of the thin-and-wiry, rather than the massively powerful kind. He concealed his inner fire, but only the very stupid mistook his gentleness for weakness, or threatened those in his care. Finally, he had the capacity and taste for incessant, painstaking hard work. (Before he led one expedition he had himself taught the rudiments of dentistry, and was thus twice able to save the day.) His leadership carried us safely through where all others before us had failed.

(This is not hyperbole. Along the way going in, and again, coming another way out, we passed their graves.)

Whenever the "You'll be lucky" routine ran off, my parents always countered with some extravagant praise of me, and the assurance that I'd outdo them both in some undefined way. I had to; I was their only chick. The love they squandered on me was in real fact meant for ten, but what we know now was an rh-factor problem killed the other nine—for which I, of course, felt guilty.

The net of all this was a silent inner terror which began before I can recall and never left. What if I didn't turn out "great"? What if I was just an ordinary, medium-bright Human? (Which is actually the case, subtracting for the excellent education.) But all my early life was lanced with that fear; if I wasn't somehow Somebody, it would represent such a failure I'd have to kill myself to keep my parents from knowing how I'd betrayed their hopes.

These are the mechanics of the Hartley Coleridge syndrome, and there's an old proverb that sums it up: In the shade of a great tree its seedlings die. Between them my parents "shaded" quite a bit of territory; and I had to get out of it or perish.*

Luckily I was in love with drawing and painting by age five, and was facile enough to sell a few black-and-whites when I was about ten. Also I made a dust jacket for one of Mary's short-story collections and illustrated her two childrens' books. This went over fine: I fear Mary foresaw happy years of her writings being illuminated by her little yellow-haired daughter.

But art isn't quite like that (and neither are daughters). By 1940 I'd long been a serious (or "easel") painter, and got perceptive enough to realize I was a good grade B, no more, only with a quickness at new tricks which made ignorant souls call me an A.

But it was a wonderful experience; you can't really *see* art until you try *hard* to make some yourself. And I'd worked hard at it. I'd clambered up the foothills to where I could really see the mountains beyond, which I could never reach. There is an indescribable pleasure in understanding how they were made in seeing at last just what Rembrandt, say, had done, and why Goya was Goya and Cassatt was Cassatt—and I wasn't. The ego-pain soon evaporates in the sheer joy of recognizing virtuosity, greatness. (Which of us really suffers because we aren't Shakespeare or Yeats?)

So when the war burst on us I was quite ready to change work. And I'd already formed a new interest: Why? Why was a painting "good"?

---

*I was mistaken in thinking I'd found a field Mary hadn't preempted, but it wasn't until the 1950s, when I dug into some old boxes—and found that she had a nice hand at watercolors. I don't know whether she'd been too busy or too tactful to mention it, but I think if I'd known this as a child I'd have flung myself from the roof. And to close the circle—near his death, I found that Father too had once written a tale for the pulps, *under another name*: Lord, how I wish the other nine had lived!

To the painter such questions are anathema,* but I wasn't a painter anymore. By then I was an art critic, waiting out the Army's call for enlisted women. As my scientific wonder intensified, I put it on ice during the war and the work that followed, but it popped out again strong as ever in 1955 and sent me back to school. (See Biog.) Probably few forty-year-olds have plowed through all the way to the doctorate simply to cast light on a personal question.

And science was another area my parents hadn't appropriated—although I owe Mary my pleasure in it. On my ninth Christmas it was she, not Herbert, who insisted on giving me a build-it-yourself Lionel Train set instead of a dollhouse, so I could "learn about electricity," which her education had denied her. It worked; my room soon looked like a tool shop, and the two books I took on the next trip were a trot of Homer and Virgil—*The Twilight of the Gods*—and *How to Build a Magneto*. (To this day I thank her whenever I check a circuit, and I commend the ability to fix a toaster as a potent aid to a happy marriage.)

Returning to 1955, all that time I did no writing, except a 1946 story in the *New Yorker*, trying to motivate Americans to treat Hitler's ex-slaves more humanely. But it was another twenty years, when Mary had grown really old (she never recovered from Father's death, they were a true marriage) and had long ceased to write before I felt finally free.

So one weekend I was finishing up my dissertation, and dog-weary—the end of my doctorate came very slowly because I was trying to get as much experimental mileage as possible out of my predoctoral grant. Suddenly, instead of catching some sleep, I found myself writing SF stories, four in all. I sent them off at random and forgot it.

Presently an envelop from Condé Nast (who's he?) showed up, I threw it out as an ad, but my husband saw a check through its window and opened it. And then the others

---

*As also to the Gestalt psychologist.

sold too, and I thought, well, this will make a pleasant hobby. The fact that it was *science* fiction took it far from Mary's shadow.

CA: You've never talked specifically about what you did your psychology research in.

Sheldon: No, because I feared it could be fairly dull to outsiders. But you can always cut. Well, perceptual psychology was then a quarrelsome mix of experimental, "white coat" psychology, and ethology, the study of the living animal in its natural habitat. GWU's department was muchly under the influence of Hullian Drive Theory, a highly abstracted stimulus-response formulation of behavior, in which you plug in variables and everything winds up in one grand, quasi-arithmetical equation representing observable response—and the animal doesn't do anything nonobservable like thinking or even perceiving.

But, as noted in the Biog., my early perspective was that of a painter. I came to psychology via my interest in vision and visual values, i.e., why we value certain visual effects while others, often those new to us, leave us cold or inspire aversion. That aspect of visual experience led logically to an interest in the large underlying problem of *perceptual novelty* itself. Any stimulus can be either novel or familiar, how do these "second-order" states affect our response to it? That seemed to me very important. But only one or two people, mainly in Europe, were even talking about "neophobia" and "neophilia." American stimulus-response drive theory simply had no place for such concepts.

So I became very difficult toward the end of my course-work. Somebody would innocently cite a "law" of the organism's supposed response, and Sheldon would erupt with, "Look, the organism you're talking about is a laboratory rat that for two hundred years has been selected for cage life, and particularly for not biting psychologists until now it's incapable of free life on its own.* And if you're solemnly telling me that 'the animal is attracted to novelty,' (which was the theorem), I'll tell you that if you want to see real animals in the real world, you don't go out and present them with maximum novelty. You go where they are and try to look like a bush."

Because while of course it's true that caged lab rats will cluster around some new object put in their cage, it's also true that wild animals will avoid a place where they've met a novel stimulus—sometimes for years.

So here was a neat problem for experimental research—to devise a way of reconciling these two contradictory behavioral "laws." If I could do it, it would not only answer one of my own questions, but it would bring a bit of order into one corner of a messy general field.

The only trouble was that for various technical reasons, my grant advisors felt it could not be done (and was maybe a little presumptuous of me to insist). There was bit of a hassle getting the green light to try.

Well, when I started, the first thing I found was that my advisors were nearly right. It would take an hour to explain the statistical and rattish obstacles; suffice it here that twelve successive experimental paradigms proved to have bugs in them, and I estimate I hauled a quarter of a ton of rats up and down H St., winters and summers; I became almost a joke. But the thirteenth try panned out and gave a beauty answer, so clear and simple it could be reduced to a wordless cartoon. (In fact I did reduce it to a cartoon illustration; see next page.)

Everyone was pleased; the strongest skeptic among my advisors actually nominated it for the nationwide Best Dissertation of Year award, which it did not win.

My finding was, simply, that animals in a familiar environment will go to a novel stimulus (signifying they prefer it) while

---

*I left out verbiage supporting this, people *have* tried to feralize them. But this isn't a journal article.

CHOICE OF FAMILIAR STIMULUS

animals in an unfamiliar environment will avoid any more novelty and choose to go to a familiar one. All of which sounds like plain common sense, which is typical of many behavioral findings that take sweaty months or years to show under strict experimental control. And the two conflicting responses were neatly reconciled as functions of a changed state of novelty of the environment.

CA: Was it largely frustration with that specific situation that got you started writing?

Sheldon: Oh, no. The frustration was long over, and the end brought a lot of egoboo—ego-gratification, in English. I was still getting requests for reprints of that dissertation—some from behind the Iron Curtain!—at least ten years later. No, what blocked me out on science was age and health, as I noted in the Biog. I was fixed in D.C. because my husband was, and GWU was a fine place to do perceptual research—they had a distinguished psychology staff headed by Richard Walk. (American U was in one of its perrennial spasms of reorganization.) But GWU had more than its quota of distinguished female researchers—they'd been very good about that. What they needed, if I were to come on the staff, was what they had a right to expect from any new PhD—a willingness to help others' research, the ability to dig up ones own grants, and the constitution of a healthy twenty-five-year-old Marine to teach the monster baby boom classes then coming through, many of them unable to read or write English. (I refer to white products of "good" middle-class suburban high schools here).

The health and time I didn't have, but it took a little trouble to make me admit it. (See Biog.) And writing SF, which I had loved since my first copy of *Weird Tales* at age nine, was and is a wonderful activity—it's the only free arena of literature, and if you can't say what you want to in SF, my personal feeling is that you haven't much to say.

However, the whole university experience contained one of the great high points of my life, and I'd like to take a moment to explain. (There was of course the pleasure of learning so much about our own wonderfully organized mechanics, but that's not the central point here.)

Years before, I had gone into Intelligence with the vague notion that it represented in some fashion the brain, or at least the eyes and ears, of the great organism called the nation. And during the first wartime years in Photo-Intelligence, it was certainly true that we were quite literally the AAF's eyes on our Far Eastern enemy. And within the context of an actual "shooting" war, with real enemies busily killing Americans and planning, however remotely, to invade American soil, this "seeing" function was quite enough for me.

But after the war the looking and listening and deducing struck me in a different light. (I leave out here my aversion to clandestine *action*, from destabilizing other people's governments, and influencing elections, to actual assassinations and military operations like the well-named Bay of Pigs. They strike me as wholly inappropriate to Intelligence, much as if one should attempt to pick pockets with the eyeballs. More highly informed critics than I share this view and have long wanted to oust the entire clandestine-action function from intelligence proper, lock, stock, and cowboy hat. Its long-range effect, in my belief, tends to bring discredit on intelligence itself, and on the nation which employs it with anything less than superHuman care; and its net actual effects in our time have been such as we would have been better without.) Leaving this contaminating factor aside, I found intelligence now curiously unsatisfying. I felt no real zest even in the clean, harmless contest of skills which is photo-intelligence. And yet it should be satisfying, even exciting; P.I. is capable of almost miraculous feats, and all without any of the sordid aspects of spying: No one is blackmailed, or coerced, or even endangered, it has no more moral ambiguity than looking over the neighbor's fence and counting his laundry. If the neighbor is *not* marshaling hostile hardware, photo-intelligence tells you that too.

Finally I realized what I missed. We were gaining knowledge, true enough, but it was not new knowledge. Everything learned was already in someone else's head. What we were doing was merely hostile prying at other brains, not adding to the sum of knowledge in all brains. I saw that what I longed for was not in intelligence at all, but in science. Mere interHuman "intelligence" came to seem to me a debased form of science—and as it was currently played, a rather soiled, paranoid, boys' game caricature. (I may say that as I became rather audibly disillusioned, the Great Ones of our pompous clandestine citadels became progressively and even more audibly disenchanted with me. I left to shared relief.)

But the finale of my work in science had no such disillusion. It was, quite naively, the most thrilling experience of my life.

It takes time and work to learn how to ask a meaningful, unambiguous question of nature. For instance, you have to learn everything that has already been asked in your field, and what the answers were and the statistical techniques. And after you are qualified, there is still a period when you stand, as it were, in that great Presence, dejectedly hearing it grumble, *"No ... No ... garble in ..."* But you try and try, until one great day the needed cunning comes, And Everything-That-Is responds majestically, *"Yes. You have truly grasped one of the hidden dimensions on which My creatures live and move."*

Time will never blur the wonder of that moment for me. Or the sadness of having come too late to the work to do more. But Oh! The joy of having ever known it at all!

CA: The definition of male and female is a great concern of your work, and gender has figured in your two pseudonyms. Do you consider your-self a women's libber?

Sheldon: I certainly consider myself something in that nature, but the unfortunate resemblance to *blubber* in the expression "women's libber" has made me reluctant to use the term. To my ear, "women's libber" sounds like something hopelessly bulging and flabby, like those balloons clowns slap each other with. I am very strongly a feminist, but of the older school where we fought a lot of our battles alone. I have a sympathetic eye for a great many of the wilder manifestations of women's lib. To me it's a plain social movement of the oppressed, and as we learned in the labor movement and in the black movement, it takes all kinds of people doing all kinds of things to move a mass from A to B. You have to have the outrageous and you have to have the respectable.

But one thing I would never want to be is the queen bee type like Clare Boothe Luce and other "top" women who seem to say, "I've got it made; why can't you, little girl?" Such women typically manipulate on the basis of charm. In a war, all things are fair, true—but the women I mean tend to exploit male weaknesses solely for their own advantage. They're no help, except when they occasionally offer the sight of a highly ranked woman doing a good job.* But sisterhood they never heard of, and they do nothing to make it easier for an ugly or charmless woman to succeed.

---

*Unfortunately, they too often offer the sight of a highly placed woman falling on her beautiful face.

One of the things you notice at scientific meetings is that while the men may be any shape, including particularly the thin, long, delicate ectomorphs like Oppenheimer, the women are almost all burly mesomorphs, like Margaret Mead. It takes that kind of muscular vitality to punch through and up to where they can display their brains. But the pity of it is that your mesomorph, male or female, is often not the really tip-top brain. The truly super female brain is, I suspect, somebody's gentle shy lab assistant, who is back home at the lab, polishing glassware or watching the animals, and dreaming ultrahigh I.Q. dreams. Which in due course—I don't mean to sound paranoid, but read *The Double Helix*—will be artfully appropriated by her male boss and peddled as his own.

Until we get to the point where that gentle woman who wants to do the thinking rather than combatting for turf can succeed, we have *not* got it made.

Of course I'd like to help make that possible—and actually, James Tiptree, as a man, was able to do a tiny bit. But what we need isn't tiny bits, it's what every movement needs—numbers, organization, money, charismatic leadership, and lucky breaks. And even if "we" ever "win" equality, it'll still be precarious. As one of my characters said, in "The Women Men Don't See," any equality women gain will only last as long as nothing goes seriously wrong in the society. When it does and men get scared, the first thing they'll do is resubjugate women—and whatever went wrong will be blamed on their "liberty and licentiousness." You will find schoolbooks still blaming the fall of Rome on the freedom of women, today.

CA: Why do your think your work improved, or "matured," as the critics say, so rapidly?

Sheldon: Of course the answer I'm tempted to give is, "Just because I'm good, that's all." Or, "Because I'm old enough to know crap when I write it." But the actual question is, Why did I write such lousy stories before I got to the good ones?

I was after all, brought up on Conrad and other large

chunks of English Lit. My uncles and Mother used to recite yards of Shakespeare, taking ludicrous parts, when they'd exhausted other topics—and I pored over that Homer/Æneid trot for a year, which has some pretty good stories. And I read the whole Arabian Nights, eating soda crackers in a cubby-hide-away under the stairs—I was a fat little girl. True, for a year or so I fell under the narcotic spell of *The Saturday Evening Post*'s sanctified hogwash, but that was mostly to try to find out what grown-ups *did*. At a pinch I could still distinguish Flannery O'Connor from Norman Mailer's logorrhea, and I knew why I liked Fitzgerald and despised Hemingway.

But those early stories of mine are so shallow and nauseating; the only kind word you can say is that they do have plots. Why? Well, of course I was writing them late at night, for fun. I was still up to my ears in university work, and I didn't have two neurons to pay attention to the writing with. I'd just have some experience—for instance, my "gringo friend" made me knock off and go to the races—and I'd think, "Hey, this could be a funny idea," and I'd scribble it up ("Faithful to Thee, Terra"). I really am a frustrated comedian, see, like many black pessimists. I dearly love making funny and having laughter, but I seldom get the chance. When Bob Silverberg said that "All the Kinds of Yes" was, well, the funniest tale he'd read in years but nine-tenths of it would sail clear over most readers' heads—that meant so much to me I can only say I'd save Bob Silverberg from a burning barn at the risk of life. Who else would so beautifully read my stuff? Oh, yes, it's lovely to be told you're Significant, and Drastic, and all those other nice things. But when Jeff Smith wrote me he was rolling on the couch laughing at "How to Have an Absolutely Hilarious Heart Attack"—he lit up his name in my heart for keeps.

But back to your query. I believe that when I left more demanding work, and got healthier, I saw with horror that other people were paying attention to what I was turning out. So I started to pay real attention too, and tap deeper levels of emotion. I applied to my writing the same standards I applied to reading, and sort of tried to whip it into shape. (This wasn't as easy as it sounds—I'm still trying.) The so-called more mature work was what happened as I got the potatoes out of my mouth.

CA: Susan Wood and other critics have commented on your deftness at shifting point of view and focus within a given story. Isn't that very difficult to do well?

Sheldon: Difficult? I was under the impression it was *wrong* to do it; I'm glad to hear it's okay. You see, now you're getting into the technicalities of writing, about which I know as much as the average rabbit. Nobody ever showed me or told me how one writes. I've never had any kind of detailed critique or comment on a story—and Oh, how I wish someone would! It's very frustrating: I just write 'em and send 'em off into this total silence, and pretty soon a check comes back, all in silence—and that's that. Only Gardner Dozois ever analyzed my stuff, not from the standpoint of technique, but for message. And *he* was so accurate I nearly quit writing. (Really; it was almost traumatic to be understood so well.)

May I tell you how I write, the only two things I know about my so-called writing technique? The first is this—and I've found that some other writers at least do it too—I mull over the story in my head, and in notes, until I have a complete *visual-aural* picture of everything; every scene, people, whether somebody hands another person something with their right or left hand, what people who aren't even mentioned are doing—everything pictured and heard. I'd say, like a movie, but films today are all cut and fancied and are art themselves; maybe like a very dull and complete documentary. The when I have it all pictured, I tell the story, just as I would if it were a piece of life, in what I hope is a punchy way. Oh, I forgot to say that the story takes off from some idea that has fascinated me, or that I want to show in action—so the way I describe it has to build up to that.

And that's all I know about technique, except this wonderful lesson: A schoolteacher of English once wrote about the idea that children, or "unspoiled" people write *simply*. She snorted in derision. ('Scuse cliché.) "Simplicity? You ask one of those pure unspoiled childish minds to write a sentence about, say, a hippopotamus. What you get is—this is from life—'In the case of the hippopotamus, it is big.' It takes about five years of beating on this 'unspoiled' writer with a two-by-four to get him to write, 'The hippotamus is big.' "

When I grasped that, I knew I'd heard The Word, and went promptly out and purchased a length of two-by-four—one-by-three, actually, because of my age—and started pounding. Some day I hope to attain the sophistication to write clear, simple English.

Now James Tiptree—I'm not trying to be cute here, I mean the voice that murmurs in the darkness when all else is silence, and you're alone—Tiptree may know something more about writing, but if so he hasn't told Alice B. Sheldon, and I'm afraid that's whom you're talking with today.

CA: Are you pleased with science fiction's growing acceptance as a genre?

Sheldon: Very much. Well, yes and no. The thing is, a good book could be written—probably has been—on why science fiction got genre-ized, or rather, ghetto-ized in the first place and in America, not in Europe. What's happening, I think, is that we're just becoming part of the mainstream, the way science fiction always has been in Europe. Take Kipling again—he wrote quite a few science fiction stories. An amazing number of Europeans have—I think you could scare up one by Dickens. Any established writer who felt like it just turned his hand to the supernatural or the highly imaginative, the "what if." There are even some technically science fiction stories—pretty sorry ones—floating around in the U.S. "mainstream" now. As for Europeans, take Italo Calvino for example. He's sold as an ordinary writer in Italy but is occasionally referred to as a science fiction writer over here, because he has the moon talking. If all the poetry in which the moon spoke was taken out of English literature and put into fantasy or science fiction, that would be pretty odd.

CA: David Gerrold has expressed the opinion that science fiction has lost some of its vitality through its increased general acceptance. Do you share that feeling?

Sheldon: I do have a certain nostalgia for the days when SF was a wild private in-group, and you were "world famous" if three hundred people knew your name. (Would you believe I got fan mail from Finland?) Of course I only came in on the end of it, but it was great to write knowing this audience of bright nuts shared your ellipses and you could use jargon like an "After-the-atom" story and know you'd be understood. Now you have to stop and explain the Law of Gravity in case the damn story is bought by *Good Housekeeping*.

The films are the worst menace from that point of view because they are the most banal, cutesy science fiction of thirty years ago. If the films *Close Encounters of the Third Kind* or *E.T.*, or most of *Star Trek* were made into stories with conceal-ing names but the same plots, it would be surprising if any of them could be sold as SF. What they are is an excuse for mar-velous visual effects, not good *stories* at all.

Then too there is the danger of science fiction's being ana-lyzed to death and made compulsory in universities, the perfect killing effect.

But I have a great deal of faith in bright kids. Some way or another some comic magazine or what have you read only by spooky little boys and girls will spring up with a new kind of genre and it'll be born all over again.

CA: Do you do any writing while you're on your long trips?

Sheldon: Yes. As soon as I get to where I know my way around an environment and settle down. It can be difficult, because a new environment to me is fascinating. In New Zealand, for example, where I could actually understand the language, I ran across so much novelty that I kept chasing it and taking notes and got very little done. But I took my writing along. I always take a big pad and expect to come back with at least a plot, if not a whole story or two written up.

CA: Are you glad to be back writing stories again?

Sheldon: Well, yes—the dear old familiar nausea. (I don't know any writers who love writing—maybe there are some.) The taking oneself by the scruff of the neck and the march to the typewriter and the plonking down before the sheet of paper. There *is* something great, about one particular blank sheet—the one where you first write in the title of a story that you've got drafted. I think that's one of the most exciting moments in life there is. But aside from that it's just plain work. In my case there has to be a lot of work; the old adage that what is written with pleasure is read with pain and you must write with pain to be read with pleasure, was never so true. But to me, the magic of seeing a story in print that I'd written by hand is still indescribable. I can't believe it's my same story. I keep the magazine and go around with this kind of pop-eyed excited look as though I'd swallowed an egg that was trying to hatch.

CA: Would you do anything differently if you were to do it all over?

Sheldon: Yes. I'd kill all the writers who wrote all those good things that I suddenly realize I am rewriting when I think I'm writing something new. Theodore Sturgeon—I wish to God his parents had practiced birth control. He is so *good*! And Ursula Le Guin and Joanna Russ, that wild meteor—Oh, uncountable numbers of other people! Cursed be they who've said all our good things before us, as was so well said by Amnesia Strikes Again. You see, I'd been reading and loving SF and fantasy for forty-five mortal years before I started writing it. And I just pigged, without keeping track of authors' names or story titles or anything. I'm only now laboriously tracking down those great tales I remember. Yesterday, for instance I found it was

Damon Knight who put out one of the most terrifying images in SF, in his grievously mistitled *A for Anything*.

Which is all by way of saying that the discovery that the gorgeous plot you just thought of and lay awake all night working out, is a well-known classic you read thirty years ago can be fairly shattering.

A rewrite of "The Cold Equations," anyone?

Well, enough of all this.

But I'd like to mention that while Tiptree's good pen-friends were—and of times still are—a real joy of my life, since poor old Tip got himself blown away for good, I've met some wonderfully nice people.

—1980–1982

Here is the original ending to the telephone interview, before it was rewritten:

I think that Tiptree's death was long overdue. I had considered taking him out and drowning him in the Caribbean, but I knew I couldn't get away with that. It's a little frightening to find oneself almost being possessed by this personality that one isn't or that only one part of one is. It was an extraordinary experience. He had a life of his own. He would do things and he would not do other things, and I didn't have much control over him. But I wasn't faking it, really. As I said in my little autobiographical piece, I never wrote anything that wasn't true, and my letters were written straight off the way I talked. I never calculated a masculine persona. I think in the very first letter I wrote I asked my husband if a man would use a certain expression, and after that I just wrote as I pleased. It's pretty funny being somebody else for ten years. But since poor old Tiptree got himself blown away in smoke, I've met some very nice people.

And here is her original response to the last question, a succinct answer written on the sheet of paper with the advance questions. To "Would you do anything differently if you had it to do over?", she replied:

Re Tiptree? No.

S.O.S. Found in an SF Bottle

Save us. Save me! Save our—is it souls?
(The desperation that calls to you does not
Readily define itself so. No matter.)
Save us your sisters. *Salve*!

I pray not to the public pink-candy-cunted madonnas of our shame,
Loving so our tears.
No.
I carry to the secret caves the secret hope
As women, women, women before me have carried, smuggled,
Grubby hopeless hope to the irregular hidden Shes,
The powerful-powerless; of the blood.
Save us.
I bring my stolen candle stub,
I light it before your images, reciting no man's name.
Salve: Joanna of the rocks; Ursula of the Waters; Kate burning, burning;
Salve: Fierce Vonda; Quinn indomitable; desperate Suzy; wild Kit;
        Carol-almost-beyond-humanness; dead Shirley;
And to all others named and nameless, unknown and lost: Save us.
Accept our praise.

I read by the candle the words shining from your images,
Daring to believe: This is a strong new magic. Thus and thus
Will the lies die.
Thus and by this
Will the usurped truth return upon the usurpers
And return the world to light.

And the candle gutters, but I still believe, will believe.
Hearing only faintly the smooth voice from the rocks outside
Where Clio—no woman but the great Drag Queen of all—
Smirks; saying, Write on, dears. Write well! Write your hearts out
In the sand.
In the wave-washed sands.

—July 19, 1975

Originally published under the name Raccoona Sheldon in *The Witch and the Chameleon* 4 (undated, 1975), a feminist fanzine edited by Amanda Bankier.

Note on "Houston, Houston, Do You Read?"

When she was asked for reprint rights for "Houston, Houston" for an anthology of lesbian/gay SF (*Worlds Apart*, edited by Camilla Decarnin, Eric Garber, and Lyn Paleo, Alyson 1986), she wrote this note as potential source of material for the editors' introduction. At the end she noted that she might copyright the piece for use elsewhere.

This story shows, in glimpses only, seen through the mind of the male narrator, what an all-female society might be really like—in contrast to the usual "Queen of the Amazons"-type masculine fantasy. In this world the love and sexuality are by definition all between—or among—women only. (There is a minor, uncommented-on exception, involving those very few women who receive androgen treatments to build muscle necessary for certain jobs; if there is any "unwomanly" sexuality there, it plays no role.)

The main purpose in constructing this all-women world was not specifically sexual, but rather to contrast its relaxed, cheery, practical *mood* with the tense, macho-constricted, sex-and-dominance-obsessed atmosphere of the little all-male "world" of male-dominated culture in the *Sunbird* spacecraft. These men are meeting for the first time a world in which men qua males simply *do not matter*. They cannot absorb the fact that the women aren't excited by them—neither hate them, love them, or fear them—have only a mild interest in them as object lessons in history, and a much more vivid practical concern about what to do with them in a society in which the male mystique appears as a bizarre illness. (Their reaction is very much like that of the harried mother of four, preoccupied with practical matters, to their mate's fantasies and demands. In such situations I've often seen the man become simply another child with peculiar needs.)

Another "author's interest"—which I didn't have time to explore as fully as it deserves—is in the unique culture of a world of clones, where each person has perhaps two thousand living versions and extensions of herself. I saw this as permitting great relaxation, almost a playful response to life—since what "I" don't accomplish may be—or has been—accomplished by another Me. Each clone keeps a special place, and a record—e.g., "The Book of Judy Shapiro"—where they go periodically and learn about all the different potentials and experiments her "self" has explored. It was my feeling that such an institution would be quite congenial to women, but by definition rather horrifying, or meaningless, to traditional males. (Self-examination is "unmanly"—but is in fact a source of great interest, and incidentally a preventer of loneliness.)

The are a couple of specifically sexual references; in one, the narrator judges—we may assume correctly—that some sex play goes on in the cubicles at night. We are left to visualize it as exactly that: play. The other is somewhat more serious, though not tragic—it is known that certain clones are attracted ("fated") to each other. Deep and serious and abiding interwoman sexual love is suggested here. But it isn't "tragic," because, quite practically, if one member of a clone doesn't reciprocate, another, identical member may!

There is another feminist theme briefly touched on: In the narrator's memories of his wife and other women it is suggested, by contrast with the woman's world around him, that (a) he didn't understand them at all; and (b) that these women were warped and trivialized by the male-dominant culture. Whatever his wife's true concerns may have been, to the narrator they were simply registered as endless chatter on the telephone.

Finally I had a very real model for my woman's world—the world of Fort Desmoines in 1942. This was the first installation of what became the Women's Army Corps, and I lived among twelve thousand women. (There were, I believe, three senior commanding males somewhere; I never saw them and had the impression they emerged only for parades.) This was the most exciting experience of my life; after a workday of eighteen hours, I trotted from barracks to barracks all night—where all twelve thousand of us were washing our one (1) uniform for the next day—meeting, talking, getting to know the rich and infinite complexity of my sisters. From a fifteen-year-old whose only work experience was delivering singing telegrams, to a fifty-year-old opera singer, women from the mountains of Kentucky who had never worn shoes, $60,000 per year sales managers and executive assistants who in all but title ran big corporations, traveling saleswomen, fatigued debutantes, army widows—what a range! (Including the fifty whores from Dallas some idiot recruiting officer sent us under the impression that the WAC [like its German counterpart] was a comfort station for the male troops. They came in swinging their shiny purses and emerged, most of them, as excellent top sergeants.)

Well, as you can see, the story of the WAC is a rich one, never yet told—and one I hope to tell some day. But I *did* see a real "women's world" not too unlike the one hinted at in "Houston."

—August 25, 1984

How Do You Know You're
Reading Philip K. Dick?

She was often asked to provide introductions, blurbs, or reviews for various projects. Here are two of these: the introduction to volume 4 of *The Collected Stories of Philip K. Dick* (Underwood/Miller 1987) and a review of a novel for *USA Today*, April 3, 1987, one of her last pieces of writing.

I think, first and pervasively, it was the strangeness. Strange, Dick was and is. I think it was that which kept me combing the SF catalogs for more by him, waiting for each new book to come out. One hears it said, "X just doesn't *think* like other people." About Dick, it was true. In the stories, you just can't tell what's going to happen, or happen next.

And yet his characters are seemingly designed to be ordinary people—except the occasional screaming psychotic females who are one of Dick's specialties, and are always treated with love. They are ordinary people caught up in wildly bizarre situations, running a police force with the help of the mumblings of precognitive idiots, facing a self-replicating factory that has taken over the Earth. Indeed, one of the factors in the strangeness is the care Dick takes to set his characters in the world of reality, an aspect most other writers ignore.

In how many other science fiction stories do you know what the hero does for his living when he isn't caught up in the particular plot? Oh, he may be a member of a space crew, or, vaguely, a scientist. Or Young Werther. In Dick, you are introduced to the hero's business concerns by page one. That's not literally true of the short stories in this volume (I went back and checked), but the impression of the pervasiveness of "grubby" business concerns is everywhere, especially in the novels. The hero is in the antique business, say; as each new marvel turns up the hero ruminates as to whether it is saleable. When the dead talk, they offer business advice. Dick never sheds his concern that we know how his characters earn their bread and butter. It is a part of the peculiar "grittiness" of Dick's style.

Another part of the grittiness is the jerkiness of the dialogues. I can never decide whether Dick's dialogue is purely unreal, or more real than most. His people do not interact as much as they monologue to carry on the plot, or increase the reader's awareness of a situation.

And the situations are purely Dick. His "plots" are like nothing else in SF. If Dick writes a time-travel story, say, it will have a twist on it that makes it sui generis. Quite typically, the central gee-whiz marvel will *not* be centered, but will come at you obliquely, in the course, for instance, of a political election.

And any relation between Dick and a nuts-and-bolts SF writer is a pure coincidence. In my more sanguine moments, I concede that he probably knows what happens when you plug in a lamp and turn it on, but beyond that there is little evidence of either technology or science. His science, such as it is, is all engaged in the technology of the soul, with a smattering of abnormal psychology.

So far I have perhaps emphasized his oddities at the expense of his merits. What keeps you reading Dick? Well, for one, the strangeness, as I said, but within it there is always the atmosphere of *striving*, of men desperately trying to get some necessary job done, or striving at least to understand what is striking at them. A large percentage of Dick's heroes are tortured men; Dick is an expert at the machinery of despair.

And another beauty are the desolations. When Dick gives you a desolation, say after the bomb, it is desolation unique of its kind. There is one such in this book. But amid the desolation is often another one of Dick's characteristic touches, the *little animals*.

The little animals are frequently mutants, or small robots who have taken on life. They are unexplained, simply noted by another character in passing. And what are they doing? They are striving, too. A freezing sparrow hugs a rag around itself, a mutant rat plans a construction, "peering and planning." This sense of the ongoing busyness of life, however doomed, of a landscape in which every element has its own life, is *trying to live,* is typically and profoundly Dick. It carries the quality of compassion amid the hard edges and the grit, the compassion one suspects in Dick, but which never appears frontally. It is this quality of love, always quickly suppressed, that gleams across Dick's rubbled plains and makes them unique and memorable.

—November 1986

REVIEW OF *KAYO*

Kayo: The Authentic and Annotated Autobiographical Novel from Outer Space

by James McConkey

First of all, be warned: *Kayo,* etc., bears no more relation to serious science fiction than *Gulliver's Travels* does to *The Origin of Species.* It is a spoof, a happy sendup of a number of items that have annoyed James McConkey, from the New Criticism to the Strategic Defense Initiative. The only science-fictional element consists of a note floating down in a little lighted parachute, so gently that the narrator can intercept it barehanded.

It is intended for a Professor Duck, a nearby astronomer who has spent his life attempting to communicate with extraterrestrials, and who never reappears in the book. The narrator takes over and unfolds a missive written in a "code" that is simply English turned backward, the message being "DEAR FRANK WHY CONTACT ME I TOO AM A MURDERER SANCHO."

The writer is revealed (by undisclosed means) as an alien named Kayo Aznap, on a faraway planet bearing a marked resemblance to Earth—turned backward. He lives, for instance, in the ASU, or Assorted States United, and he is anxious to tell his life story, or stories, provided he can ever stop digressing. So far, so good, and the ASU idea is mildly funny.

But the yarn, taken up by Kayo, is soon inexplicably dominated by references to an extraterrestrial version of Don Quixote, written by an ancestral Aznap who seems to have been traumatized in his cradle by too-liberal doses of Nabokov's prose style. In the ASU version, the Don is Nod, a disreputable and supposedly lovable nature tramp, and the central event is a recreation of the shootout at the O.K. Corral—a happening which to me lost its kinetic energy some time ago.

The villains are the academic purveyors of "the New Deconstructionism," and the Aznap dynasty is transfigured by the success of Aznap-Cola, so that Kayo is the confidant of presidents—or rather, of the president, since the ASU has been reelecting the same, surgically transformed man for all time; "Frank," "Oz," "Teddy," etc., are all one man. Kayo's alleged murder of Nod (who has told part of the tale in his own voice) is the culminating event, being too complicatedly motivated to unravel easily.

Clearly such a devil-may-care affair is good for a lot of yuks. And I fear that yuck is exactly what the author makes of it. There is a skeletal plotline, so hung about and bored through with divertissements that nothing need be said of it. And the author, perhaps sensing that something more earthly is required, indulges (for example) in scenes in which Kayo's black britches split, revealing his red jockey shorts.

McConkey seems to feel that excellent diction and a heart manifestly in the right place, as concerns deconstructionism, will excuse anything. What it will not excuse is a bookless book.

The point of my account is to portray *Kayo* as a confection, a giant puffcake in the form of a labyrinth of asides, which will delight to tears anyone who is really into lit crit, or who bears either Cervantes or Nabokov a grudge. And it does not weigh on us with pompous panaceas for out troubles—Kayo's solution to the problems of the ASU is to build gigantic theme parks on the various issues.

It would appear, in sum, that the author, after years of work creating far finer novels, has decided to grant himself some well-earned indulgence. And no one who has worked up a head of steam over the same irritations will begrudge him.

—March 1987

ZERO AT THE BONE

And to conclude, two more personal essays. The first one was never published; the second was written for *Women of Vision*, edited by Denise Du Pont (St. Martin's 1989).

Ruminating on the changes that have followed the "death" of Tiptree—the subtle but palpable differences in the tone of reviews; friends lost, friends gained; above all, the loss of blessed anonymity and simple fun—I am startled anew by the depth of my own loathing for the plight of women. Our helplessness, limitedness, weakness, *thing*ness in the world of what cummings called "man-unkind." Only among the educated of a few North European countries are we even people with audible voices—always excepting those occasional La Passionaria types who spring from some bloodied earth.

But I, daughter of the dull middle class, am no Passionaria, no Golda Meir nor Rosa Luxemburg, nor Margaret Mead; not even a frontier schoolteacher; I feel all too literally hollow at the center—"zero at the bone," as Dickinson said. Worse: I have this childish fascination with brute power. I see it as (if possible) even more absolute a force than it is: the organizing principle of society. And since I have none, I am nothing.

As Tiptree, I had an unspoken classificatory bond to the world of male action; Tiptree's existence opened to unknown possibilities of power. And, let us pry deeper—to the potential of evil. Evil is the voltage of good; the urge to goodness, without the potential of evil, is trivial. A man impelled to good is significant; a woman pleading for the good is trivial. A great bore. Part of the appeal of Tiptree was that he ranged himself on the side of good *by choice*.

Alli Sheldon has no such choice.

Other women writers may be free of this paranoid reality-obsession. (Except for a few, like Suzy McKee Charnas, who tackle it directly.) Virginia Woolf—to name at random—was too insulated—or did it break through and kill her? Quinn Yarbro transposes to wholly alien worlds ("Un Bel Di"), or focuses on the apolitical moment, (her "Fellini Beggar"). Anne McCaffrey wrenches her women into singing ships, or leagues with dragons. Vonda McIntyre gives them magical powers— though stressful ones—and often, though not always, a minimally respectful society; but she can show scarifying a war of all against all, with its horribly killed women. Joanna Russ vanes between wild fantasies of power women, and mesmeric writing of real personal experience (again, middle class). Le Guin threatens to live in dreams albeit Superb ones.

What evil can a woman do? Except pettily, to other, weaker women or children? Cruel stepmothers; male fantasies of the Wicked Witch, who can always be assaulted or burnt if she goes too far. Men certainly see women as doing many evil things—but always nuisancy, trivial, personal, and, easily-to-be-punished-for. Not for us the great evils; the jolly maraudings, burnings, rapings, and hacking-up; the Big Nasties, the genocidal world destroyers, who must be reckoned with on equal terms.

[Odd that I mentioned the jollity of evil-doing, the hilarities of mayhem. Powerful, free laughter—I've heard it among women only once, and that's another story. We are but shadow-men in that line too.]

Always draining us is the reality of our inescapable commitment. Whatever individual women may do, it is we who feel always the tug toward empathy, toward caring, cherishing, building-up—the dull interminable mission of creating, nourishing, protecting, civilizing— maintaining the very race. At bottom is always the bitter knowledge that all else is boys' play—and that this boys' play rules the world.

How I long, how I long to be free of this knowledge!

As Tiptree, this understanding was "insight." As Alli Sheldon, it is merely the heavy center of my soul.

Whatever can I do with all this?

Gardner Dozois cheerily told me that now I could write about "growing up female!" Ha! I can do it in a word: *To grow up female is— not to be allowed to grow up.* To be praised for childishness, timidity, vanity, trivialities; to be denied tough goals and mysteriously barred from the means of attaining them; to be left for crucial years, unaware of the realities for which boys are being trained; to lack continuity of character and mind; to find oneself reacting helplessly to male advances and retreats and in the grip of obscure vulnerabilities from within; to waste years and emotional strength on idiocies (getting married); to yearn for "love" from those who do not even view one as a person, though they may be sexually attracted; to have no comrades, (unless one is very lucky); to be alone and unarmed amid inexplicably hostile strangers who make smiling pretenses and who will not leave you alone. To have every aspect of your conduct and being criticized as by right, for the pleasure of others. To be confirmed in childishness, and have your vision of adventure narrowed to the space of—a bed.

Ellen Moers said it all and better, in her *Literary Women*. To grow up as a "girl" is to be nearly fatally spoiled, deformed, confused, and terrified; to be responded to by falsities, to be reacted to as nothing or as a thing—and nearly to become that thing.

To have no steady routine of growth and training, but only a series of explosions into unwanted adulation—and then into limbo.

The world was not my oyster.

And the result has been an unjoined hybrid.

I sometimes imagine what I would have been as Alex Sheldon. Alone, in my normal working gear of pants and turtleneck, I almost am Alex—or my father. Dressed up, in company, I'm nearly my mother, Mary—certainly feminine, limited, ingratiating. What was that adjective Judy-Lynn skewered me with? Ah yes: "vivacious."

Jesus H. Christ.

As in, "a vivacious crucifixion."

Well, I better get integrated in a hurry.

And in my bitterness, not to forget that had I been Alex, I might have been an equally poor specimen—neurotic, diffused, lazy, and undisciplined; just as expert at finding "by-ways to chaos," in Konrad Heiden's splendid phrase about the German nation.

But . . . I wonder. Would Alex be so dependent? Would he spend thoughts on the equivalent of lace camisoles—*color-coordinated* lace camisoles? Who knows?

What I know is that all this, raw, is scarcely the stuff of SF; and if it's "mainstream," others have done it better. Tiptree solved matters by leaving it all out—like leaving out the fact that one is a paraplegic in an iron drum. Maybe all one can do is to say the hell with it.

But—life is to *use*. Only, how? How? How? How?

—July 1985

A Woman Writing Science Fiction

If you squeeze a mouse, it squeaks.

Just so, when life squeezes me, I squeak. That is, I write. And from my middle years I have felt squeezed by life. First there is the sky-darkening presence of the patriarchate, the male-run society, all about me and over me, cutting off my options. And then there is the physical crowding. It is increasingly impossible to get away from other people's noise, smells, bodies; their radios, the ringing of my phone by strangers, strangers' houses springing up everywhere in what had been lovely countryside; strangers' cars crowding the roads twenty-four hours a day; strangers' garbage polluting my aquifers, other people's junk polluting the world; footprints and tire tracks on every patch of new-fallen snow, chain saws and bulldozers in every patch of woodland; hostile strangers menacing me if I walk out of my house by night or day. And no end in sight. Unless our birthrate falls drastically, we are on our way to being another Bangladesh.

So much for my personal squeezedness.

But beyond that, I am wounded, revolted by what man is doing to the planet. I love the natural Earth. The space photos that show our wonderful green and blue world floating lonely in black space have driven home its fragility. Remember those photos? Remember the great ugly red-brown scars of deserts on them? Those deserts are growing, the green is shrinking. And the blue, our sacred blue oceans are being defiled by the dumping of everything from sewage and tar to radioactive wastes. Even the Sargossa Sea, that remote breeding place of species, is now poisoned with biphenylated plastics. The great rain forests, rich and unexplored, are being burned and felled at an appalling rate per day. The very top of Mount Everest has garbage on it. Species after species of Earth's wonderful creation are going extinct as I write this. We have already killed half the northeast of our continent with acid rain, and dumped enough carbon dioxide into our air to change the climate for the worse. I weep for Earth.

And then, not least, there is what man is doing to man—and woman. His endless wars, his compulsion to competition and aggression and dominance appalls me. About forty wars are raging right now, and we all live under the shadow of his grandest war, which will end us— and take the planet's life with it. Greed rules our daily intercourse: The rich and powerful grab everything in sight. Those who should be our leaders flaunt their corruption, while the poor get poorer and turn to violent crime to assuage their wants. Where cooperation is so sorely needed, we live in a war of all against all.

And, with the frontiers gone, it is a zero-sum game. The winners win always at others' expense. Who will civilize us?

Most personal to me is the plight of women. They are at the bottom of every class heap, struggling in a world which has no place for humane values, condemned to do the hard, unpaid chores of the world. Vivid in my memory is a small band of tribal women, who each day walked for water three miles over violently rocky hillsides, returning with forty-pound loads of five gallons balanced on their heads—and doing this, for the most part, with one baby on their backs and another in their stomachs. They were not praised nor paid for this— it was "women's work." In our land of "opportunity," their physical work is less, but the stress is greater. No wonder that the poorest of the poor, turn, as children, to having unneeded babies simply to garner a little love.

And things will not grow better. If trouble comes to our system, as come I fear it will, it will be the liberation of women which is blamed for it. Our "rights" will vanish like snow in summer as the stronger, aggressive animals we live among vent their frustration.

Nor will time improve things. In a world where the raising of children yields no profit (except to TV salesmen) the young are left to raise themselves, in the dumb, time-wasting enclaves of the schools and the culture of the streets and of TV. When they become the adults, how will they rule?

And I have another, private pain. I love the English language, that noble mongrel. It is my aim to speak and write it clearly and colorfully. But daily I must listen to insipid gibberish from the mouths of our so-called leaders. How can we think clearly if our minds are stuffed with rubbishy slogans?

For all these reasons, then, I write. My first serious story showed a man so driven to despair that he spread a mortal disease in order to save the Earth. And in nearly all of my seventy-plus stories since, one or more of my distresses form the undertheme. So much for my deeper motivation.

But this list of agonies could as well have inspired articles, diatribes like Jeremiah's. Why write *stories*? Ah, therein lies the mystery. I do not think we will know the answer until we know why the first caveman lifted his voice and regaled his fellows with a made-up tale. True, he might have been rewarded with an extra knuckle-bone to chew, as Scheherazade was rewarded with an extra day of life for each chapter. But that does not explain it. The urge to make stories is inbuilt, primeval.

Well, then, why write science fiction? I could say, because I have always read it, since I discovered *Weird Tales* at the age of nine. So when I came to write a story, it seemed natural to send it off to *Analog*. But the fact is that I have a modest view of my talent. I haven't the ear for rhythm or the feel for style to encourage me to compete in the serious mainstream. And I certainly haven't the stomach to write "mainstream" schlock, like *Jaws* or *Gone with the Wind*. Science fiction suits me just right. SF is the literature of ideas, and I am, I think, an idea writer. SF allows extrapolation into the future, and that is my natural way of thought. ("If this goes on . . .") And SF is the literature of wonder, and you have only to say, "Those lights in the sky are great suns" for me to go all shivery. In SF I have found my niche.

Will science fiction and fantasy continue? Yes, I think, but perhaps they may suffer a certain decline. In the last fifty years we have burned up ideas at a breakneck rate, and while the stock of ideas surely is not finite, the possibilities of new ones may not come along as fast as we could hope. Of course, there is always cinema; the movies now are using the ideas that were done in the literature thirty years ago, and the public may slowly adapt so it can use the newer ones. As to fantasy, I don't know. Who could have predicted Tolkien? I'm not primarily a fantasy writer, so I don't know how fast the ideas there are being used up. In any event, I doubt the public will continue to read much except comic books.

Are there things you can say in science fiction that you can't say in mainstream? Well, no, I think; not really. But if you were writing up a given idea for the mainstream, you would have to go to endless bother of introducing it and soothing incredulity and generally tempering the wind to the shorn lamb—whereas in SF you can just start in, and your readers know at once that it's After the Atom Bombs Fall or whatever.

Which brings up the Ideal Reader. Whom do I write for? I honestly don't know. I used to think I wrote for bright young minds who might say, "Well, I never thought of that before!" And of course I write to satisfy myself. No one pressures me, since I do not write to eat. But judging from my fan mail, there is simply no common denominator among my readers, beyond the fact that they seem literate. I suspect I write at heart for people like myself, souls who love and fear what I do. And I suspect a majority of them are women, though my mail is predominantly from the other sex.

As to the question of whether there are male and female writing styles, here I may part company from other women. I feel that by their sins shall ye know them, which is to say that there are separate styles in *bad* writing. Rebecca West has said that the sin of men is lunacy and the sin of women idiocy. She meant that men have the weakness of seeing everything in black and white, as though by moonlight, with all the colors and pains left out, like a shiny new machine. And "idiocy" derives from the original meaning of "idiot," a *private person*. Women can be overobsessed by minutiae, by trivial concerns with no broad implications. This is only natural in a species evolved to rear children*; raising the young is a matter of endless minutiae, which are big concerns for the growing child. When women write badly, they fall away from the larger Human concerns into too-private trivialisms. When men write badly, it is about some sublunar crackpot idea with no regard for its real Human consequences—like their wars.

I think there is a general Human way of writing, of telling tales of challenge and response, of trials and strivings—and, in SF, of wondrous

---

*Please notice that I said women are evolved to rear children, *not* to enjoy it or find it totally fulfilling. To say that they are not so evolved is to fly in the face of all we see in other primates. And watch any pair of parents with a newborn baby. It is the mother who is in her element.

alien systems which can illuminate our own. Men and women deviate from this central style according to their experience and inclinations, but there is not much difference. It may be that men have slightly the edge in black humor, and women in heart-wringing, but that is certainly cultural.

I see that I omitted one masculine style of writing which particularly bores and irritates me: that is the ineffable tale of boy-becomes-surprise!-a-*man*. This is a story, if you can call it such, peculiar to the patriarchate. No woman so relishes, today, the grand elevation to adult status. Maybe we should; certainly to be a *woman*—if self-defined, not defined by men—is no mean achievement. But it carries with it too many problems to simply be greeted with hosannahs.

I see here the interesting question about whether it is man or woman who can be seen as the alien, the Other. Yet it seems obvious: From my viewpoint, it is the male who is the alien. It is understandable that women could view themselves as alien to male society—a viewpoint of despair, I think. But if you take what you are as the normal Human, as any self-respecting person is bound to do, then it is clear that to a woman writer men are very abnormal indeed. Most men. But we understand them better than they understand us, in the same way that the subordinates in any group understand the dominant ones better than the dominators understand them. (A source of agony to many bosses, who assume that the darkies are happy singing minstrels and then are caught short by bloody revolution.) And we understand men better because, if I may be chauvinistic, understanding is our business. We can't get on without it, as a man can.

And I have used the idea of man-as-alien in my story "The Women Men Don't See," in which a pair of women decide to go and live with some real aliens after lifetimes of coping with the aliens around them.

Perhaps this answers the question of what role feminism plays in the content of my work. But to answer it more fully, I have to recount a bit of personal history:

I came into the field of SF as a man—that is, under a male pseudonym which I stuck to so completely that even my agent, Bob Mills, believed I was male. There was a reason which began it, two reasons, rather. The first was that I wanted to conceal my writing from my colleagues in the university. (I am a retired experimental psychologist.) I was already known as an adherent of what were then regarded as weird ethogical theories, my colleagues being strict Hullsians, and the news that I wrote *science fiction* would have been the crowning touch of unrespectability. Secondly—and mainly—I was sure the first stories wouldn't sell. I was prepared to spend the traditional five years of papering the walls with rejection slips. So I just chose what seemed an innocuous name off a marmalade jar in the Giant and added a "Jr." to it for confusion's sake. I intended to try a different name with each submission, so the editors would not associate me with all those rejects.

But then the first two stories sold—and the next, and the next, and I was stuck with "Tiptree, James Jr." I thought this was a good joke, and greatly enjoyed my anonymity. (I am a reclusive type, afraid of meeting people, except on paper.) I went happily on writing stories, all of which, to my amazement, continued to sell—and I was quite unaware of the curiosity I was provoking in the SF community. (A squad of fans once actually staked out my McLean P.O. box when the big convention was in D.C.—luckily I was in Canada at the time.) Quite a few pages were written elucidating what I must be, and while a certain number of observant souls deduced that I must be a woman, nobody really knew, and others were as positive that I was male.

The stories I wrote then were just about the same as I write today, with one exception: A few violently prowoman ideas came to me, and I saw that they were simply noncredible under a man's name, so I invented a female pseudonym (Raccoona Sheldon) for these. Raccoona lived in Wisconsin, and her mail was a terrible headache to the local postmistress—and me.

During all that decade of being James I corresponded freely with all sorts of SF people, principally as a result of my habit of writing fan letters to writers I admired. And I made what I thought were good friends. I always told the plain truth about myself in my letters; my biography is ambisexual—Army, government, academe. I also told a few close friends about my trials with my aged, widowed mother, then living, or rather, dying in Chicago, and that she had been an African explorer and writer. So when Mary did die, in 1977, one of these friends saw the newspaper obituaries, and my secret was out.

Oddly enough, that shattered me. I felt I could never write again. My secret world had been invaded, and the attractive figure of Tiptree— he *did* strike several people as attractive—was revealed as nothing but an old lady in Virginia. No more speculations about my "mysterious" travels, or that I might be the secret spymaster of the CIA. And worse, I was no longer able to be my female correspondents' "understanding" male friend, or say things to editors, like "Why aren't there any women writers in this anthology?" Now I was just another woman, with my own tale of woes. No magic. And I stood ashamed before the women writers who had used their own female names in cracking the predominantly male world of SF. I had taken the easy path.

But *was* it easier, getting accepted as a man? I can't honestly tell, except by indirection.

You see, after the revelation, quite a few male writers who had been, I thought, my friends and called themselves my admirers, suddenly found it necessary to adopt a condescending, patronizing tone, or break off altogether, as if I no longer interested them. (I can only conclude that I didn't.) If that is how I would have been received from the start, my hat is off to those brave women writing as women.

And there have been no more Nebulas, except one to Raccoona. No more Hugos. I can't believe that the quality of my stuff has deteriorated so suddenly. Of course, though, it may be that I withdrew too many stories at the last minute. For example, I pulled out "The Women Men Don't See" when it looked like winning, because I thought too many women were rewarding a man for being so insightful, and that wasn't fair. People may have thought I undervalued the award. So that isn't a clear result of my sex change. But it *is* depressing, since I personally think one or two of my best have been written since then.

But as I think it over, and think also of the fact that some of the male writers who have been a touch snotty to me seem to be genuinely friendly to other women writers, I think there is a deeper problem. People dislike being fooled, and, quite innocently, I did fool them for ten years. Moreover, it seems to be very important, especially to men, to *know the sex* of the person they are dealing with. What's the use of being Number One in a field of two—i.e., *male*—if people can't tell the difference? I had not only fooled them, I had robbed them of relative status. Clearly, friendship is out of the question after that.

So there is my somewhat unconventional history of male/female relations in my work. And I believe it answers certain aspects of other questions too. Those which remain seem to have to do with writing itself.

As to how I develop a character, I do it the same way we come to know people in life—by seeing what they do, and listening to what they say. I haven't had occasion to develop any very complicated characters yet, like, say for example a wily hypocrite. I would do this, I imagine, by *showing* his hypocrisy. He might be driving along in a car, expatiating on his good-heartedness and universal sympathy, and suddenly a child lets his puppy loose in the street ahead. The car hits it, the child screams— and Mr. Benevolent simply accelerates, continuing to talk.

I believe this is how all writers develop character, some more subtly than others. Oh, and there is a useful way of doing it fast, by reporting what other characters say or think about the subject. But that's nothing new, either.

And as to what kind of writer I think I am, and how I fit in the world of SF, I believe I am, as I mentioned, an idea writer with a talent for fleshing out what might be impersonal ideas, like say time travel, so that the reader takes them as real.

And I am also, deep down, a teller of *cautionary* tales. "If this goes on—*Look Out!*" I sometimes wonder if my readers get the cautionary element, or whether it is buried under too much color and flesh. For instance, one of my Nebula winners was a tale of an alien race who have a set of powerful instinctual drives that are carrying them to disaster. Part of my intent, in addition to telling a good story, was to warn of the dangers of yielding to instinctive behavior, like our own patterns of aggression. But no one, speaking of the story, seems to have drawn this analogy. Such are the pitfalls of setting up your message as the under-theme—although I'd have thought its title ("Love Is the Plan the Plan Is Death") rather gave things away.

Which concludes all I know of myself as SF writer. I look forward to reading what my sisters will report—doubtless they will say insightful things that open whole new boxes. But I must go back to doing whatever it is we do at the typewriter, and in keeping faith with the small but devoted band of left-handed penguins whom I see as my readers.

—December 1986

CHRONOLOGY OF PUBLICATIONS

Here, in as close to the order of composition as I could determine, is a complete list of Alice Sheldon's science fiction. I used, whenever possible, the date of first submission to an editor. The stories are grouped by year of composition, with year of publication in parentheses.

1967
Birth of a Salesman (1968)
Fault (1968)
Faithful to Thee, Terra, in Our Fashion (1968)
Your Haploid Heart (1969)
Mama Come Home (1968)

1968
Help (1968)
Please Don't Play with the Time Machine (1998)
The Last Flight of Doctor Ain (1969)
Meet Me at Infinity (1972)
Last Night and Every Night (1970)
Beam Us Home (1969)
Happiness Is a Warm Spaceship (1969)
A Day Like Any Other (1973)
I'm Too Big but I Love to Play (1970)
And I Have Come Upon This Place by Lost Ways (1972)

1969
The Snows Are Melted, the Snows Are Gone (1969)
Through a Lass Darkly (1972)
The Girl Who Was Plugged In (1973)

Amberjack (1972)
The Night-blooming Saurian (1970)
The Milk of Paradise (1972)
Painwise (1972)
And So On, and So On (1971)

1970
Mother in the Sky with Diamonds (1971)
The Peacefulness of Vivyan (1971)
The Man Doors Said Hello To (1970)
I'll Be Waiting for You When the Swimming Pool Is Empty (1971)

1971
Love Is the Plan the Plan Is Death (1973)
All the Kinds of Yes (1972)
The Man Who Walked Home (1972)
And I Awoke and Found Me Here on the Cold Hill's Side (1972)
On the Last Afternoon (1972)
Forever to a Hudson Bay Blanket (1972)

1972
The Women Men Don't See (1973)
Angel Fix (1974)
The Trouble Is Not in Your Set (2000)
Press Until the Bleeding Stops (1975)

1973
Her Smoke Rose Up Forever (1974)
A Momentary Taste of Being (1975)
The Earth Doth Like a Snake Renew (1988)

1974
Houston, Houston, Do You Read? (1976)
The Psychologist Who Wouldn't Do Awful Things to Rats (1976)
Beaver Tears (1976)
Your Faces, O My Sisters! Your Faces Filled of Light! (1976)
She Waits for All Men Born (1976)

1976
Time-Sharing Angel (1977)
Up the Walls of the World (1978)
The Screwfly Solution (1977)

1977
Slow Music (1980)
We Who Stole the *Dream* (1978)

1978
A Source of Innocent Merriment (1980)

1980
What Came Ashore at Lirios (1981)
The Boy Who Waterskied to Forever (1982)
Beyond the Dead Reef (1982)
Excursion Fare (1981)
Out of the Everywhere (1981)
With Delicate Mad Hands (1981)

1983
Brightness Falls from the Air (1985)

1984
Morality Meat (1985)
The Only Neat Thing to Do (1985)
Good Night, Sweethearts (1986)

1985
All This and Heaven Too (1985)
Collision (1986)
Trey of Hearts (2000)
Our Resident Djinn (1986)
Second Going (1987)

1986

Come Live with Me (1988)
Yanqui Doodle (1987)
Backward, Turn Backward (1988)
The Color of Neanderthal Eyes (1988)

1987

In Midst of Life (1987)